D0945267

The *Schlemiel* as Metaphor

Studies in Yiddish and American Jewish Fiction

Revised and Enlarged Edition

Sanford Pinsker

Southern Illinois University Press
Carbondale and Edwardsville

The Schlemiel *as Metaphor: Studies in Yiddish and American Jewish Fiction*
is a revised and enlarged edition of the text originally entitled *The*
Schlemiel *as Metaphor: Studies in the Yiddish and American Jewish Novel,*
by Sanford Pinsker, copyright © 1971 by Southern Illinois University
Press.

Edited by Mara Lou Hawse
Designed by Shannon M. McIntyre
Production supervised by Natalia Nadraga

   Library of Congress Cataloging-in-Publication Data

Pinsker, Sanford.
   The schlemiel as metaphor : studies in Yiddish and American
Jewish fiction/ Sanford Pinsker. — Rev. and enl. ed.
      p.   cm.
   Includes bibliographical references and index.
   1. Schlemiel in literature. 2. Yiddish literature — History and criti-
cism. 3. American literature — Jewish authors — History and criti-
cism. I. Title.
   PJ5124.P5   1991
      813.009'352 — dc20   90-9980
      ISBN 0-8093-1581-5   CIP

For *Matt* and *Beth*,
who required no revisions whatsoever

Contents

Preface to the Revised Edition   ix

Acknowledgments   xiii

1   The *Schlemiel*'s Family Tree   1

2   "If I Were a Rich Man": Mendele and Sholom Aleichem   17

3   The *Schlemiel* on Main Street   37

4   The Isolated *Schlemiels* of Isaac Bashevis Singer   48

5   The *Schlemiel* as Moral Bungler: Bernard Malamud's Ironic Heroes   77

6   Saul Bellow's Lovesick *Schlemiels*   111

7   Philip Roth: The *Schlemiel* as Fictional Autobiographer   145

8   Woody Allen's Lovably Anxious *Schlemiels*   163

9   Conclusion   176

Notes   183

Index   189

Preface to the Revised Edition

Rereading the first edition of *The Schlemiel as Metaphor* twenty years after I had written it, I am reminded of what Benjamin Franklin says about the errata one collects over a lifetime: "I should have no Objection [Franklin writes in the opening page of his *Autobiography*] to a Repetition of the same Life from its Beginning, only asking the Advantage Authors have in a second Edition to correct some Faults of the First."

This revised and expanded version affords me the opportunity not of repeating my "life" but of tempering an excess here, a misimpression there—and of bringing the saga of the *schlemiel* up-to-date. In considering sentences written so long ago and in what now seems entirely "another country," I was surprised to discover how many of them still please me, how many of them fasten around a topic I continue to regard as important. That I chose to concentrate my discussion of the *schlemiel* in American Jewish literature on the works of Isaac Bashevis Singer, Bernard Malamud, and Saul Bellow made sense at the time, and their subsequent careers have confirmed my hunches. In other cases, what I now see as "omissions— Philip Roth, Woody Allen—fall neatly into that part of me that insists on "more *schlemiels*!"

When I was working on the original version of this book, American Jewish literature was neither as established nor as respectable as it is now. And while it is true that there were senior professors who encouraged my pursuit of a comic figure that they much enjoyed, there were others who asked me privately and in whispers if a writer with the unlikely name of Mendele the Bookseller actually existed. For a graduate student to invent such a writer might be daring—even funny, in a way—but it simply would not do in a scholarly dissertation. The times, as they say, have very much changed.

Moreover, I have benefited from, and built upon, the work of other critics of American Jewish literature. Initially, the voice that mattered most belonged to Leslie Fiedler. Later, I added Irving Howe and Robert Alter, Ruth Wisse and Daniel Walden, Irving Malin, Sarah Blacher Cohen, Mark Shechner, and a supporting cast of dozens, if not hundreds. What started out as a handful of formative books has become a substantial part of my library. If this is to declare myself on the side of the autodidacts, so be it. Like the chronicle of the hapless *schlemiel*, learning about his how and why continues. And of course, so does teaching and writing about his ongoing comic disasters. What they knew full well in the mythical town of fools called Chelm we have come to discover in America, and inside our own skin:

Now with regard to the school teacher of Chelm, it goes without saying that he was in every respect a true Chelmite. How could it be otherwise? Isn't every genuine school teacher, no matter where he may live and labor, a Chelmite? The one of Chelm was particularly shrewd in matters economic and financial. "You know," he said to his wife one day, "if I were the Czar, I'd be richer than the Czar."

"How so?" she asked.

"Easy. I would do a little teaching on the side."

Stories such as the one above have long been the special inheritance of children fortunate to grow up in homes where "jokes" were as much a part of daily living as kosher food and religious observance. For Judaism, religious values and expression seem to be part of the same folk processes—with "stories" serving as a mutually acceptable cement. In biblical literature, in talmudic commentaries, and, of primary importance here, in the wealth of Yiddish and American Jewish fiction are stories aplenty. As one of the characters in Isaac Bashevis Singer's novel, *The Family Moskat* puts it, with a quip that deftly combines celebration with exasperation: "The things Jews write—there's no end to them!"

The issue is further complicated in our time not only by the *creative* works that Jews write but also by the criticism, the scholarship, the sheer weight of "commentary," that has grown up around Jewish stories. To add yet another volume to the stack—and a revision at that!—makes a word or two of apology more than just a bow to renaissance convention. Nothing *can* be duller than a joke explained. One of the great "explainers" of our age and its humor was Sigmund Freud, but for all his work in the psychodynamics of jokes, for all the obvious value of, say, *Jokes and Their Relation to the Unconscious,* I have yet to come across a photograph of the Viennese Master smiling, much less laughing. Apparently, humor—like everything else Freud thought deeply about—was a deadly serious business. He had a sharp eye for the hostile projections that lurked beneath the joke's "innocent" surface. Moreover, Freud was especially intrigued by Jewish humor, no doubt because it so neatly balanced the aggressive with the self-lacerating. As Saul Bellow once put it: "Oppressed peoples tend to be witty."

But that much said, it is also a commonplace that those who often do the best with the ironies of artifice often do the worst with the ironies in their own lives. And it is here that Yiddish humor provides a sorely needed correction, a way of pulling down the vanities we live by—including our hope that even humor can be domesticated through academic study.

In short, then, evidence seemed to be mounting for a book that might tiptoe around the thickets of comic theory and instead talk about the origins of the *schlemiel* and the ways contemporary Jewish American writers have used that durable figure in their novels. I suspect that, in one way or another, every cultural critique begins with the same question—namely, "How do we see ourselves?" and in my case, the answer has been, more often than not, "As *schlemiels!*" My associates were kind enough to add whole chapters from the continuing sagas of their own comic failures, and soon I began to feel that there may indeed be a community of interest here. After all, there was a time in our cultural history when Horatio Alger might have been a good pick if one were to isolate a lively emblem of the American sensibility. Today, Woody Allen's anxious, bespectacled *punim* (face) seems closer, and truer, to our quotidian experience.

But if *asking* the right questions is tough, answering them is even tougher. We tend to be a generation of ersatz anthology makers, compiling mental lists of our favorite stories or poems or whatever, and then insisting that all of them appear whenever a thick anthology is published. To write about the *schlemiel* is to build in a high potential for disappointment. For those unhappy because I left out some minor character who once slipped on a banana peel, I can only offer my apologies and point out that imaginary books tend to weigh, and to cost, a good deal less than actual ones.

I have tried as much as possible to orient my remarks about Yiddish literature to the nonspecialist. All the Yiddish expressions have been translated and, if necessary, explained; all the source material is available in English language versions. Furthermore, what I suggest about Old World humor is more likely to interest readers of the contemporary novel than scholars of Mendele Mocher Seforim.

Finally, there is a sense in which the author of a book about *schlemiels* must be something of a *schlemiel* himself. If (God forbid!) you leave out somebody's favorite joke, you are sure to be chastised. On the other hand, if the book is filled with representative jokes that people have already heard, you're also in trouble. It's an old story—as well as an old joke:

When you tell a joke to a Frenchman, he laughs three times: once when you tell it to him, the second time when you explain it to him, and the third time when he finally understands it—for Frenchmen love to laugh.

When you tell a joke to an Englishman, he laughs twice: once when you tell it to him and again when you explain it to him—but understand it he never can, for he's too stuffy.

When you tell a joke to a German, he laughs only once: when you tell it to him. First of all, he won't let you explain it to him because he's so arrogant. Second, even if he did ask you to explain the joke, he wouldn't understand it because he has no sense of humor.

When you tell a joke to a Jew—before you've had a chance to finish, he interrupts you. First of all, he's heard it before! Second, what business have you telling a joke when you obviously don't know how to do it? In the end, he decides to tell you the joke himself, but in a much better version than yours.

Acknowledgments

I wish to acknowledge the generous, and continuing help given to me by Franklin and Marshall College during the writing of this book.

Parts of this book have appeared in slightly altered form in the *Reconstructionist, Chicago Jewish Forum, Jewish Social Studies, Modern Language Quarterly, Midstream, Modern Fiction Studies, Review of Contemporary Fiction,* and the *Georgia Review.*

In addition to the sources given in the Notes, special acknowledgment is made to the following publishers for permission to quote from the works indicated: Vanguard Press, Inc. for quotations from the following books by Saul Bellow: *Dangling Man,* copyright 1944 by Vanguard Press, Inc., and *The Victim,* copyright 1947 by Saul Bellow; The Viking Press, Inc. for quotations from the following books by Saul Bellow: *Seize the Day,* copyright © 1956 by Saul Bellow, and *Herzog,* copyright © 1961, 1963, 1964 by Saul Bellow; A. S. Barnes & Company, Inc. to quote material from *Fishke the Lame* by Mendele Mocher Seforim, copyright 1960 by Sagamore Press, Inc.; G. P. Putman's Sons for use of material from Sholom Aleichme's *Old Country Tales,* copyright 1966 by The Children of Sholom Aleichem.

Appreciation is extended to Crown Publishers, Inc. for permission to use quotations taken from *Tevye's Daughters* by Sholom Aleichem, © 1949 by The Children of Sholom Aleichme, and from *The Old Country* by Sholom Aleichem, © 1946 by Crown Publishers, Inc.

Grateful acknowledgment is made to publishers Farrar, Straus & Giroux, Inc. for permission to reprint from the following titles by Bernard Malamud: *The Magic Barrel,* copyright © 1950, 1951, 1952, 1953, 1954, 1955, 1956, 1958 by Bernard Malamud; *The*

Assistant, copyright © 1957 by Bernard Malamud; *A New Life,* copyright © 1961 by Bernard Malamud; *The Fixer,* copyright © 1966 by Bernard Malamud. From the following works of Isaac Bashevis Singer: *In My Father's Court,* copyright © 1962, 1963, 1964, 1965, 1966 by Isaac Bashevis Singer; *The Magician of Lublin,* copyright © 1960 by Isaac Bashevis Singer; *Gimpel the Fool,* copyright © 1957 by Isaac Bashevis Singer. From *The Great Fair* by Sholom Aleichem, copyright © 1955 by the Noonday Press.

And finally, to my former teachers both at Washington and Jefferson College and the University of Washington; to students who looked suspicious and made me try harder; to those friends who laughed on cue and those who happily provided examples of *schlemiel*hood from their own lives; and to my wife, Ann, who refused to serve leftovers as I labored on this revision—heartfelt thanks.

The *Schlemiel* as Metaphor

1
The *Schlemiel*'s Family Tree

Isaac Bashevis Singer once published a children's story entitled "The First Schlemiel," making this comic figure a citizen of the mythical Chelm. The result may not be accurate historically, but then again, providing an exact history of this folk figure is rather like asking for the exact date of a story beginning "Once upon a time . . ." Questors after the elusive archetype have shown us that heroes were always with us (only the names were changed to protect the innocent), and I suspect that roughly the same thing is true for *schlemiels*—but with this important difference: when hunting for the Ur-*schlemiel*, be prepared for contradictions. As Ruth Wisse points out,

Since Jewry's attitudes toward its own frailty were complex and contradictory, the *schlemiel* was sometimes berated for his foolish weakness, and elsewhere exalted for his hard inner strength. For the reformers who sought ways of strengthening and improving Jewish life and laws, the *schlemiel* embodied those negative qualities of weakness that had to be ridiculed to be overcome. Conversely, to the degree that Jews looked upon their disabilities as external afflictions, sustained through no fault of their own, they used the *schlemiel* as the model of endurance, his innocence a shield against corruption, his absolute defenselessness the only guaranteed defense against the brutalizing potential of might.[1]

Wisse is surely correct when she argues that the very *Weltanschuung* of the *schlemiel* strikes us as particularly Jewish, but this is not to suggest that influences from other quarters—Russian peasant humor, for example—have no place in his development. In fact, ethnic humor has a nasty habit of isolating universals into a setting of this time and that place. Switch the dialects, alter

1

a few details, and most black jokes can become Jewish jokes or Irish jokes or whatever with a minimum of loss.

At the same time, however, Yiddish humor—as opposed to its Borscht Belt incarnations—is not as portable, primarily because its "jokes" are tied to a specific cultural framework and a distinctive set of attitudes. Moreover, as Saul Bellow points out, in Jewish stories "laughter and trembling are so curiously intermingled that it is not easy to determine the relations of the two. At times the laughter seems simply to restore the equilibrium of sanity; at times the figures of the story, or parable, appear to invite or encourage trembling with the secret aim of overcoming it by means of laughter."[2] One thinks, for example, of the story Bellow himself includes in *The Victim*. A character begins by asking "Who's going to wait for the Messiah?" and then proceeds to tell an illustrative story "about a little town in the old country. It was out of the way, in a valley, so the Jews were afraid the Messiah would come and miss them . . . [so] they built a high tower and hired one of the town beggars to sit in it all day long. A friend of his meets this beggar and he says, 'How do you like your job, Baruch?' So he says, 'It doesn't pay much, but I think it's steady work" (pp. 253–54). In the best of Yiddish humor the tension between piety (in this case, a deep-rooted belief in a Messianic era) and skepticism's sharper edges (waiting as "steady work") produces effects that terms such as "bittersweet" or "ironic faithfulness" try with limited success to capture.

With the *schlemiel*, the urge to define has been a large part of his comic dimension. He is usually linked with his equally unlucky cousin, the *schlimazl*, in anecdotes that make up in good cheer what they might lack in precision. Everyone has his or her favorite, ranging from those supplied in popularizing books such as Leo Rosten's *Joys of Yiddish*—"a *schlemiel* spills his soup on the *schlimazl*"—to my own contribution to this dubious enterprise: "When a *schlimazl's* bread-and-butter accidently falls on the floor it always lands butter-side down; with a *schlemiel* it's much the same—except that *he* butters his bread on both sides first."

The *Universal Jewish Encyclopedia* puts it this way: A *schlemiel* is one who "handles a situation in the worst possible manner or is dogged by an ill luck that is more or less due to his own ineptness."[3] Some scholars of the Hebrew Bible feel there is enough linguistic evidence to link the *schlemiel* with a character mentioned in Numbers (9:19)—Shelumiel ben Zurishaddai. In

Numbers per se (which is largely given over to a census or "numbering" of the Israelites), Shelumiel plays an insignificant role. However, talmudic commentaries identify him with the ill-fated Zimri whose story appears in the twenty-fifth chapter of Numbers:

> And Israel abode in Shittim, and the people began to commit harlotry with the daughters of Moab. And they called the people unto the sacrifice of their gods. . . . And Moses said unto the judges of Israel: "Slay ye every one his men that have joined themselves unto the Baal of Peor." And, behold, one of the children of Israel came and brought unto his brethren a Midianitish woman in the sight of Moses and in the sight of all the congregation of Israel, while they were weeping at the door of the tent of meeting. And when Phinehas, the son of Eleazar, the son of Aaron the priest, saw it, he rose from the midst of the congregation, and took a spear in his hand. And he went after the man of Israel into the chamber, and thrust both of them through, the man of Israel, and the woman through her belly.[4]

According to biblical text, the "man of Israel" who so aroused Phinehas's righteous indignation was "Zimri, the son of Salu, head of a father's house belonging to the Simeonites" (Num. 25:14). However, talmudic commentators point out that Shelumiel had one less than *five* names—one of which was Zimri. To be sure, there are mixed reactions about Shelumiel's credentials as the first *schlemiel*—Nathan Ausubel, editor of *A Treasury of Jewish Folklore*, feels that "there is nothing to associate him [i.e., Shelumiel] with the *schlemiel*,"[5] while the *Universal Jewish Encyclopedia* lists the biblical story as the strongest possibility of the figure's origin.

Richard Rubenstein sees the story of Zimri/Shelumiel as a tale of castration anxiety involving "unbridled sexuality and rebellion against authority figures."[6] The biblical story would hardly support such a Freudian reading; however, the rabbinic commentaries are rife with possibilities:

> As the rabbis retell the story, Cozbi is no longer merely the foreign paramour of Zimri. She is the daughter of Balak, the Midianite king, who, on the advice of Balaam, is prepared to prostitute his own daughter in order to bring about the downfall of Moses. Zimri demands that Cozbi surrender herself to him. She replies that her father commanded her to yield only to Moses, Israel's greatest man. Zimri thereupon seizes her hair and declares that he is greater than Moses. This introduces a

hint of sexual rivalry between the leader and a rebellious member of his flock.[7]

Granted, whoredom with the daughters of Moab was wide-spread, but it is Shelumiel who is unlucky enough to get caught. On these grounds alone one might argue that he should qualify as more the *schlimazl* than the *schlemiel*. However, rabbinic commentary about the story also makes it clear that Zimri/ Shelumiel had a hand in his misfortune, not only by rebelling against the authority of Moses, but also by his sexual excesses as well: "Rabbi Hahman said . . . that that wicked man [Zimri/ Shelumiel] cohabited four hundred and twenty-four times that day, and Phinehas waited for his strength to weaken."

The commentary about this minor incident in Numbers sug-gests the "rabbinic fantasies" that Rubenstein finds in many of the legends of the Talmud. Very often, sexual repressions, as well as deep-seated guilts, were submerged into the stories that comprise the section of the Talmud known as *agada*. A short-hand way of viewing the matter might be this: Talmudic discus-sions are divided into *halakha,* or law (the Freudian superego) and *agada,* or homiletic explanations (the id)—with the inte-grated reader emerging as ego. When the rabbis set about reconstructing biblical myth they often added dimensions that had little to do with the historical situation but that spoke, sotto voce, to their own circumstances. For example, in the story of Jacob and Leah, the rabbinical commentators found a lively emblem of their own fears about cuckoldry. As Rubenstein points out, "They pictured Leah as cuckolding the patriarchal Jacob while he studied Torah in the Yeshivah, the rabbinical academy, of Shem. This fantasy anachronistically assimilates the biblical tale to the preoccupation of the milieu of the rabbis. The Yeshivah did not exist in the days of the patriarchs" (p. 48).

In Theodor Reik's discussion of the *schlemiel* as a psychological phenomenon, he recounts a medieval story that picks up the themes of cuckoldry and social reaction—this time, however, making the identification between the protagonist and the fig-ure of the *schlemiel* very clear indeed: "This man, Shemuliel, returned home after a year of absence to find that his wife had given birth to a child. The rabbi decided that the child was legitimate while the neighbors were very dubious regarding the paternity. The man had to accept the rabbinical decision and became the prototype of the Schlemiel who is involving himself in difficult situations from which he cannot extricate himself."[8] Later, in discussions of I. B. Singer's "Gimpel the Fool" and Saul Bellow's *Herzog*, I shall have occasion to expand the connections between cuckoldry and the character of the *schlemiel*. Granted, the story Reik chooses as the essence of *schlemiel* hood can be found in the folk literature of many cultures. What makes it distinctive, however, is the interaction between the cuckold and the rabbi, and even more important, between the cuckold and his fellow townspeople. The rabbis put a premium on the virtues of study, but they were also aware—at least unconsciously—of its possible consequences. The comedy of Shemuliel's story revolves around the complicated procedures by which the rabbi will "prove" that his child is actually legitimate—resorting to talmudic example, to the literature of medieval *responsa* (correspondence that set legal precedents), and a tortured form of scholastic hairsplitting known as *pilpul*. The rabbi no doubt would justify his decision on humanitarian grounds, arguing that the future welfare of the child is more important than the present embarrassment of its "father." The townspeople, on the other hand, see the *schlemiel's* horns for what they are, and thus he becomes the object of their condescending laughter—although always with the implicit realization that his fate might well have been theirs.

With the poetry of Ibn Ezra (1092-1167), elements of insight and self-mockery were added to the *schlemiel's* characteristic postures. In the biblical story, judgment was both immediate and harsh, a matter of religious law. For Shemuliel, the slings and arrows were more figurative. Even the laughter that followed the rabbi's ruling tended toward the ambivalent, as is often the case with cuckoldry. By contrast, the persona in Ibn Ezra's beats his neighbors to the punch, making the self-lacerating assessments that had once been their sole province. For example, at one point Ibn Ezra's *schlemiel* says of himself:

> If I should undertake to sell candles,
> The sun would never set;
> If I should deal in shrouds,
> No one would ever die.

At first glance such epigrams look thoroughly masochistic, the sort of self-destructive fare more appropriate to psychoanalysis than to literary criticism. For Ibn Ezra, *schlemiel* hood was more than just a run of chronic bad luck. A *schlimazl* is usually defined as one born under a bad star—the word *schlim* being the German for "bad," while *mazl* is the Hebrew for "star." In short, a *schlemiel*'s star is always in the wrong astrological alignment. Thus he is the perennial victim of circumstance and gratuitous accident, none of them of his own his making. The *schlemiel*, on the other hand, has a hand in his destruction; the more he attempts, the greater seem his chances for comic failure.

The *schlemiels* of Ibn Ezra were well aware that their propensity to spoil things had a way of creating consequences on a larger scale. Again, as the standard joke would have it, the *schlimazl* is the one who gets soup spilt on him. He can count on it because he is, quite literally, ill-starred. It is the *schlemiel*, of course, whose "accident" spills the soup—and everything else—onto others.

Small wonder then that *schlemiels* and *schlimazls* dog each other's heels; where there is one, there is usually the other. And not surprisingly, this leads to a certain amount of overlap, as the folklorist, Nathan Ausubel explains: "The two types did have an affinity; they both had their origin in the same economic swamp of ghetto-stagnation. Also their end product was identical—failure" (p. 343). Nonetheless, it was Ibn Ezra's version of *schlemiel*hood that survived the Spanish Inquisition and reappeared several centuries later in the humor of *shtetl* (small village) poverty. In one well-known anecdote a luckless *schlemiel* tries to borrow some money from the richest man in town. When he is refused, the *schlemiel* says:

> "But you've just got to give me some money!"
> "Why?" demanded the rich man.
> "Because if you don't, I'll go into the hat business!"
> "So . . . ?"
> "What do you mean, 'So . . . ?' If a man with my luck goes into the hat business, everybody in this country from that day on will be born without a head!"

For both Ibn Ezra and his future imitators, the self-destructive characteristics of the joke may be less important than the paradoxical way in which such humor was self-sustaining. In a world that offered few possibilities of success, that had little power in any of the conventional ways the term is defined, a humor-of-failure takes on a special importance. After all, a character such as Chaucer's Troilus must die—transcending the follies both of love and war in a mystical seventh sphere—before he learns the wisdom of laughter that more humble *schlemiels* knew all along.

And yet, for all the influence of an Ibn Ezra—however elusive, however hard to pin down by scholarly carbon-dating—it was a non-Jew, the German writer, Adelbert von Chamisso, who first introduced the term *schlemiel* to Western literature. The date was 1813, and the work, *Peter Schlemihl.* Evidently, Chamisso was familiar with some of the Yiddish traditions of the character, but he borrowed little more than the name for his creation. In fact, *Peter Schlemihl* is a romanticized reworking of the Faust legend, with the protagonist selling his shadow to the devil for a magic purse that will always be filled with gold. Perhaps Chamisso linked the Yiddish *schlemiel* with the dark and potentially romantic figure one finds in stories about the legendary Wandering Jew. In any event, Willy Pogany feels there is enough biographical evidence to suggest connections between Chamisso's own flight to the safety of Germany and his notion that "every immigrant is a Schlemihl: he arrives with nothing: no, not even a shadow—but then sets immediately to work to acquire all he can. Some succeed admirably; but as Schlemihls they start all the same."[9] Whatever else Peter Schlemihl might be, he is the quintessential outsider. He is forced to live "in the shadows," a dark figure whose torments anticipate Freudian analysis. The eventual loss of his shadow is as much a fantasy of castration as it is a Faustian pact with the devil. He ends by wandering from country to country—Tibet, Africa, and the glaciers of Greenland—until a final "accident" stops him cold: "Misfortune would have it that I should have carelessly treaded on a traveler's heel: I must have hurt him, for I received a violent blow." He is taken to a hospital where he "was called No. 12, and by virtue of his long beard, passed off for a Jew."

Aside from popularizing the term, Chamisso's romance had little impact in the development of the *schlemiel.* Far from the dark character who wandered alone through a hostile world, the Yiddish *schlemiel* was a character of social context. His comic misfortunes may have been portrayed in terms of the grotesque or the exaggerated, but at bottom, ghetto Jewry shared his fate.

To the German poet Heinrich Heine (1797-1856), the *schlemiel* became a metaphor of the artistic quest itself. In his *Hebrew Melodies,*[10] he equated the term with the

> Fate of poets! star ill-omened
> that harasses with such deadly
> Grudge the offspring of Apollo
> And that spared not even the father,
>
> Who, sweet Daphane erst pursuing,
> When he clasped the nymph's white body,
> Found his arms about the laurel—
> He the heavenly Schlemihl!   (P. 264)

In a later section of the poem, Heine recounts the biblical story of Zimri-Shelumiel, incorporating some knowledge of the talmudic commentators, but changing the emphasis until Shelumiel becomes the innocent *schlemiel:*

> But a legend 'amongst the people
> Has been orally transmitted
> Which denies that it was Zimri
> Whom the spear of Phinehas slew.
>
> And maintains that, blind with passion,
> Phinehas slew not the transgressor,
> but another who was guiltless—
> Slew Schlemihl ben Zuri Schadday.   (P. 265)

In point of fact, the talmudic rabbis embellished the biblical story to make Phinehas more than justified in killing Zimri. However, Heine sees the absurd death of Shelumiel as a prophetic statement about the Jewish condition:

> This Schlemihl I. was founder
> of the race of Schlemihls:
> We are lineally descended
> From Schlemihl ben Zuri Schadday.   (P. 266)

And although the revenge-ridden Phinehas has been dead for centuries,

> yet his spear is with us,
> and the noblest hearts it pierces,
> Like Jehuda ben Halevy's
> And like Moses Iben Esra's.   (P. 266)

And presumably, Heinrich Heine's heart as well.

Heine's sentiments are consistent with his general view that Jewishness is a misfortune of both. But if Heine saw himself as a *schlemiel,* it was a very different sort from the one we recognize in Yiddish humor. For Heine, the *schlemiel* was a pathetic character. Stabbed by a spear meant for another, he had to bear the wounds nonetheless. In short, he was guiltless and there was no need for Heine to be other than angered by the way an unjust world had treated Schlemihl ben Zuri Schadday. Rather than comic adjustment, Heine postulated social solutions to remedy social injustice. In the process the very essence of the *schlemiel,* both as folk character and cultural emblem, becomes distorted.

A more traditionally based Jewish humor derives from the folk and their collective experiences. Jacob Richman may be straining when he calls Cain's sharp retort, "Am I my brother's keeper?" a "splendid repartee,"[11] but he is surely right in seeing the Jewish Bible's extraordinary range of human interactions as a source for Jewish humor. Give Cain's question the right inflection and it ends more as quip than as query. And what is Job if not the prototype of *schlimazls* to follow? Granted, the unconvincing fairy tale ending of Job's story is meant to compensate him for earlier, absurdist losses, but when his *tsoris* (trouble) is mounting, one carefully placed "*Oy vay!*" and the book's house of existentialist cards could topple over.

I prefer, however, to argue that what we recognize as distinctively Jewish humor probably began with the Destruction of the Temple in 70 C.E. and continued through the Diaspora. Zion is remembered daily in the official liturgy; pledges never to "forget thee, O Jerusalem" were made by the Babylonian captives and repeated on *Tishah b'Ab,* a day of lamentations that commemorate the Temple's destruction; and throughout the ages, Passover Seders have ended traditionally with the words *L'shana Ha-Ba'ah Birushalayim* (" Next year in Jerusalem!"). In short, the religious establishment reasserted the Chosenness of Israel, disasters notwithstanding. And though they were homeless, scattered to the corners of the earth, official Jewry thought of themselves as instruments of Divinity. Among the nations they alone had been chosen to bring a code of morality to the world—to be "a kingdom of priests and a holy people" and if necessary, to suffer in the fulfillment of that mission.

Such was the religious line with regard to adversity. Perhaps Jewish humor began when somebody wondered if maybe, just once, God might chose somebody else! Or perhaps Jewish humor was never really "humor" in the ordinary sense of the word, but, rather, a weapon in Jewry's endless struggle for survival. With no land or army of its own—indeed, with none of the rights and privileges normally accorded to first-class citizens—staying alive as a people was a decidedly open question. In this regard Ausubel claims that "as identifiable types, *schlemihls* and *schlimazls* sprang into being with the first dramatic economic discriminations against Jews by the Byzantine emperors beginning with Justinian (530–56 C.E.)" (p. 344). Although powerless by conventional standards, Jews simultaneously kept their faith with *The Ethics of the Fathers* and mastered the difficult arts of self-mockery. As Freud points out in *Jokes and Their Relation to the Unconscious:* "The occurence of self-criticism as a determinant may explain how it is that a number of the most apt jokes . . . have grown up in the soil of the Jewish popular life. They are stories created by Jews and directed against Jewish characteristics. . . . I do not know whether there are many other instances of a people making fun to such a degree of its own character."[12]

From these roots the *schlemiel* gradually became a stock figure of Jewish anecdote. In some stories he seems to be a citizen of Chelm, and like each of its citizens, a comic misrepresenter of reality. For example, the medieval story of Shemuliel is often retold as it it happened in Chelm—with the *schlemiel* getting the comic "explanation" he deserves:

A young scholar of Chelm, innocent in the way of earthly matters, was stunned one morning when his wife gave birth. Pell-mell he ran to the rabbi.

"Rabbi," he blurted out, "an extraordinary thing has happened! Please explain it to me. My wife has just given birth although we have been married only three months! How can this be? Everyone knows it takes nine months for a baby to be born!"

The rabbi, a world-renowned sage, put on his silver-rimmed spectacles and furrowed his brow reflectively.

"My son," he said, "I can see you haven't the slightest idea about such matters, nor can you make the simplest calculation. Let me ask you: Have you lived with your wife three months?"

"Yes."

"She has lived with you three months?"

"Yes."

"And together—have you lived three months?"

"Yes."

"What's the total then—three months plus three months plus three months?"

"Nine months, Rabbi!"

"*Nu* . . . so, what's the problem?"

More typical, however, are the stories that focus on collective foolishness. Chelmites are forever meeting to solve the great issues of the day—as the following story illustrates:

The people of Chelm were worriers. So they called a meeting to do something about the problem of worry. A motion was duly made and seconded to the effect that Yossel, the cobbler, be retained by the community as the offical town worrier, and that his fee for this work be one ruble per week.

The motion was about to carry, all speeches having been for the affirmative, when one sage confounded his colleagues by asking the following, fatal question: "If Yossel earns a ruble a week, what would he have to worry about?"

Chelm is a community of fools, and in its most representative stories, *narishkeit* (foolishness) spreads evenly throughout the citizenry. By contrast, the Motke Habad stories shrink the comic foibles of many into the defining characteristic of a single figure—the indefatigably foolish Motke Habad. Like the superhuman exploits of Paul Bunyan in an American frontier context, the machinations of Motke Habad became a barometer for the *shtetl*'s sensibility. As one collector of Jewish folklore puts it, Motke Habad is "the Jew who is forever trying to make ends meet, but always in vain. Good-natured, well-intentioned, and desperately eager to get ahead in the world, fate seems to be contentedly against him, and he fails no matter to what he turns. He is the archetypal *schlemiel* and the mock-pathetic hero of countless anecdotes."[13] Sometimes Motke Habad has an unconscious hand in the making of his various failures, as the following story suggests: "Motke became a teamster, but he found the horse consumed all the profits. He determined to wean the beast from the habit of eating, and began by depriving it of oats one day a week, then two days, then three. After a month the horse seemed well on its way to learning how to get along with almost no oats at all, when it suddenly collapsed and died. Motke was beside himself with grief. Standing over the beast, he groaned,

'Woe is me! Just when my troubles were almost over, you had to give up and die!' " (p. 627).

At other times, however, Motke is the overreacher, a man so engrossed with life's forests that he keeps bumping into its trees:

Motke Habad was once summoned by the local Polish landowner and told to go to the fair in a neighboring town to purchase a French poodle for the baroness.

"Certainly!" cried Motke, all eagerness. "And how much is your Excellency willing to spend for a first-class French poodle?"

"Up to twenty rubles."

"Out of the question," Motke snapped. "For a really first-class French poodle one must pay at least—at least—fifty rubles!"

The nobleman tried to dispute this, but Motke was so positive that he finally yielded. Handing over the fifty rubles, he told Motke to hurry off, whereupon the *schlemiel* became covered with confusion and stammered: "Yes, Your Excellency, I go, I go. B-But please, Your Excellency, what exactly is a French poodle?"   (P. 626)

To be sure, Motke's "overreaching" is not cut from the same cloth that covers a Faust or a Macbeth. The Motke Habads of Yiddish anecdote have decidedly smaller goals; moreover, their "failures" allow for measures of good cheer on the part of the reader and protagonist alike.

As I've suggested, comic failures come in a wide variety of sizes and shapes. At times the *schlemiel* is the cuckold (Shelumiel) or the bungling entrepreneur (Motke Habad). On other occasions he is the henpecked husband—a fate as much to be feared as cuckoldry and deeply entrenched in a sensibility that had strong leanings toward misogynism. In these stories the shrewish wife becomes a grotesque of all that the *shtetl*'s male population unconsciously feared. As always, the laughter that generated from such humor was likely to be uncomfortable, especially when the *schlemiel*'s fate looked to be only an exaggeration away from their own. Consider, for example, this domestic scenerio:

A man was married to a shrew who ordered him around all the livelong day. Once, when she had several women friends calling on her, she wanted to show off what absolute control she had over her husband.

"Schlemiel," she ordered, "get under the table!"

Without a word the man crawled under the table.

"Now, schlemiel, come out!" she commanded again.

"I won't I won't" he defied her angrily. "I'll show you I'm still master in this house!"

The official religion may have talked about the nobility of their suffering, the God-given character of their mission, but as Clement Greenberg suggests: "When religion began to lose its capacity, even among the devout, to impose dignity and trust on daily life, the Jew was driven back on his sense of humor."[14] Thus, Yiddish—rather than Hebrew—emerged in the lands of the Diaspora as the language of daily living. The result was a condition that Max Weinreich tellingly describes as "cultural bilingualism"—that is, the development in the Ashkenazic Jewish community of "two *living* languages, one that was immediate [Yiddish] and the second mediated [Hebrew]."[15] From roughly 1000 C.E., Yiddish (a combination of Hebrew, Laaz, and German) became the folk tongue of Ashkenazic Jewry, and a perfect vehicle for transmiting the panoply of cultural values they called *Yiddishkeit*.

If the Gentile world could boast of its armies and its political clout, *shtetl* Jewry could offer up sharp retorts by way of putting such "power" into perspective. Jewish humor, then, was a way of exacting victories from the raw material of irony and skepticism. In the face of the world's injustice—and at times, even God's—the *shtetl* Jew solidly maintained his innocence. As a people they often characterized themselves as luckless *schlimazls*. At the same time, however, they also saw the *schlemiel's* ineptitude as an extended metaphor of their socioeconomic plight.

Far from being a shorthand for the masochistic preoccupations of the Jewish psyche (as, say, Freud and Reik tend to view the phenomenon), the *schlemiel* was a point of reference for the community that surrounded him. As the acknowledged "fool," he was free to criticize in a way that those with vested interests in social realities could not. And because he was a character literally defined by his ineptitude, by the bumbling way he misrepresented reality, his comic victimhood helped to sustain those who were only partially *schlemiels*.

Jewish humor is often described as a "laughter through tears," and in both the recognition and definable distance between the *schlemiel* and the average *shtetl* dweller, there was plenty of room for each possibility. In some sense, every *shtetl* Jew was a *schlemiel*—at least to the extent that he could identify with those who have had a hand in their own undoing. Max Nordau's term *luftmentsh* (literally, "air-man") points toward an inclination to live on "air," to give oneself over to schemes that have no substance. Given the rude facts of *shtetl* life, it was no doubt a widespread condition. On the other hand, the *schlemiel* is usually portrayed as a character who is blissfully unaware of his folly and in this sense, he lives on even thinner air than his ghetto counterparts. "They" could—and did—laugh at *him*. After all, it is nobody's fault if a man is a *schlimazl*. *He* is genuinely deserving of pity. But a *schlemiel* . . . well, him you could laugh at.

Like all folk material, the jokes I've been discussing are notoriously difficult to date. As Jacob Richman concludes his pioneering study of Jewish humor, "It is hard to tell when the first collection of Jewish anecdotes appeared. A little pamphlet of ten pages, written in fluent, but ungrammatical, Hebrew, and bearing the title *Katoves L'Chanukah* (*Jokes for Chanukah*), is probably the first book of its kind, judging by its discolored, moth-eaten pages. But it bears no date of publication. . . . *Sichas-Chulin-shell Talmide Chachamim,* a Hebrew collection of rabbinic bon mots and anecdotes, the second edition of which appeared in Vilna in 1880, is probably next in priority" (p. xxiii).

The impact of Hassidism during the latter years of the eighteenth century had its effect both on Yiddish and the sort of folk humor best expressed in that language. In 1864, Mendele Mocher Seforim published his first Yiddish novel and suddenly a language that had received no serious attention for some nine centuries became the dominant mode of literary expression. During the 1880s, Mendele was joined by Sholom Aleichem and Y. L. Peretz, and soon the attributes of *Yiddishkeit* were crystallized into the mythos of fiction. What had been an oral tradition transmogrified itself into a national literature.

Unfortunately, American readers are more familiar with the Yiddish humor of the vaudeville stage and the Catskill mountains. To appreciate the enormous differences between "dialect" humor and its more authentic Yiddish counterpart, Jacob Richman compares two "fire stories"—one from the standard repertoire of dialect comedy and the other from the traditions of Yiddish humor:

Take the conventional fire story: A Jew meets a coreligionist on the street. "Hello, Abe," he says, "I hear you had a fire last Tuesday."

"Shhh . . . it's *next* Tuesday!" informs the other.

. . . .

The following story, however, is decidedly Jewish:

An Israelite calls on the rabbi of a small community, and tells him that he is the victim of a general conflagration in which his house was razed. He is now collecting funds to rehabilitate himself, and he wants the rabbi's assistance. "Have you a document from your rabbi that you are a fire victim?" interrogates the leader of the community. "I had one," replies the "nisraf" dismally, "but that, too, was burnt." (Pp. xii–xiii)

The dialect story stresses greed and Jewish cunning; performed on an American vaudeville stage, it would be one more piece of evidence that Jews are unsavory characters, totally lacking in scruples and inordinately concerned about money. After all, dialect stories—whether they feature shiftless blacks, drunken Irishmen, or swindling Jews—depend on cultural stereotypes to make their respective points. At the turn of the century these were deemed necessary to speed up the process of assimilation and to make identifiably "foreign" types feel unpatriotic. In short, the vaudeville stage tells us a good deal about America's growing pains, but precious little about genuine Yiddish humor.

By contrast, the second fire story is both more subtle and more humane. The *nisraf* is, after all, certainly not greedy nor is his plight merely a fabrication. His "story," if you will, becomes a way of preserving a measure of dignity in a world that forces him to be a charity case. The *schlemiel* of Yiddish literature suggested the continual shifting between ambition and defeat that characterized the experiences of East European Jewry. And in his comic struggle for a better life, ghetto Jewry found yet another "type" for their condition. For example, they would tell the story of a beggar who was caught eating caviar at an expensive restaurant only ten minutes after the town's wealthiest citizen had given him a handout:

When the rich man saw this thing, he could hardly believe his eyes. "For shame!" he cried. "You beg money on the streets and then squander it away on caviar!"

But the beggar was indignant. "And why not," he retorted. "Before I got your ruble, I *couldn't* eat caviar. Now that I have it, I *mustn't* eat caviar. At this rate, when in the world *will* I eat caviar?"

Shtetl Jewry must have asked, on more than one occasion, "When in the world will *we* eat caviar?" Their humor was a means of adjusting to the world and the "caviar" they, presumably, could never have. In the countless jokes about *schlemiels* and *schlimazls*, ghetto Jewry created a fictive release for what might have become a psychology of bitterness and despair. And in the repertoire of shrugs and quips, among the lavish self-mockery and the exaggerated foolishness, there was a sense in which these comic characters communicated to their audiences at the very deepest levels of a collective sensibility. Perhaps the best way to illustrate the depth of "communication" I have in mind is with this: "Two elderly Jewish men sat drinking glasses of tea, one glass after another, without a word being exchanged between them. After about two hours of silence, one sighed a deep, deep sigh and said, "*Oi vay!*" His friend answered, "You're telling me!"

2

"If I Were a Rich Man": Mendele and Sholom Aleichem

Tradition has it that Sholom Aleichem gave Mendele Mocher Seforim (Mendele the Bookseller) the title "Grandfather of Yiddish Literature," which, in the light of how literary fortunes vacillate, suggests just how fleeting such honors can be. Today, of course, it is Sholom Aleichem—his literary "grandson," as it were—whose work has been rediscovered by an entire generation of American readers. For good or ill, *Fiddler on the Roof* played to packed houses on Broadway, was transmogrified into a moderately successful Hollywood film, and appears headed for the immortality of "revivals" on the boards of community theatres and high school auditoriums. Paperback editions of the Tevye stories slither in and out of print. No such fates have followed Mendele's career. I hasten to add that Yiddishists have not forgotten about him—partly, I suspect, because there were only three writers of stature during that literature's "classical" period (Mendele, Sholom Aleichem, and Y. L. Peretz), but also because Mendele is worthy of attention in his own right.

The publication of Mendele's *Dos Kleine Mentshele* (in English translation, *The Parasite*) in 1864 is generally regarded as the beginning of modern Yiddish literature. This is not to suggest, however, that Mendele's work appeared in a vacuum; as a language, Yiddish had been the tongue of Ashenazic Jewry for some nine centuries. Jews may have continued to pray in Hebrew—to a God still identified with Zion and a historically Promised Land—but their common speech reflected the wanderings of the Diaspora. Gradually, Germanic words crept into the language (although the linguistic structure of the original Hebrew was preserved wherever possible), and soon Yiddish—both as language and distinctive culture—became the identifying trait of East European Jewry.

Prior to 1864, what passed as "literature" was largely confined to *tehinot* (sentimentalized liturgies written almost exclusively for women), translations of the Pentateuch or Yiddishized versions of, say, the Arthurian legends. As Sholom Aleichem suggests in his autobiography, *The Great Fair:* "The alternatives were Hebrew or Russian. But it never occurred to anyone that Sholom could someday write in Yiddish. After all, could you consider Yiddish a language? Everyone naturally *spoke* Yiddish, but who thought of *writing* it? Yiddish was referred to as 'Ivre Taytsch,' that is, a jargon good only for women." With the advent of the Hassidic movement during the latter part of the eighteenth century, Yiddish suddenly emerged as an important vehicle for religious expression. What had once been the province of women and only the most uneducated of men was now the medium of religious story literature, parable, and even prayer. As Nahman of Bratslav put it, Hassidism's founder, Yisroel Baal Shem Tov (known as the Besht), preached to the masses of the Jewish people in Yiddish, often relying on simple stories to "lift people out of their surroundings": 'The world thinks,' said Rabbi Nahman in reply to his opponents, 'that stories are useful for putting people to sleep, but I say that the people may be awakened with stories. Even the Torah itself,' he said further, 'is clothed in stories.' "[1]

The greatest impact of Hassidism was felt among those considered *prosteh* (lower class) by the more scholarly religious elite. In a culture that valued learning—and all too often, a "learning" so pure, so *scholastic*, that it lost touch with life itself—the ignorant were virtually disenfranchised. Synagogue seats nearest the Eastern wall were reserved for those with the greatest *yikhus* (status, as defined by one's abilities as a talmudic scholar or by one's wealth), while the poor and uneducated often had to stand outside the synagogue proper.

In short, the egalitarian preaching of the Baal Shem Tov revitalized a Jewry that had grown both self-absorbed and sterile. He stressed the values of the individual heart and the effectiveness of personal prayer, arguing that sincerity was more important than empty ritual and that a simple piety was more to be desired than status in the House of Study. Even more important, the Baal Shem Tov introduced Romanticism to ghetto Jewry, replacing the aridity of *pilpul* (nit-picking pedantry, especially about matters of Jewish law) with the joys to be found in song, in dance, and in communion with nature. Above all else, Hassidism was concerned with what is now called history from the "bottom up"—that is, with the spiritual needs of the *folkmentschen*, the Jewish masses.

For example, Hassidic tradition has it that once a peasant asked how he could pray when he was unable to read Hebrew. The Baal Shem Tov inquired if he happened to know the Hebrew alphabet and when the man replied that he did, the Master said: "Then pray by repeating the letters over and over again while your heart asks the prayer and God Himself will put your letters into words." Nahman of Bratslav went even further. He urged his disciples to pour out their hearts at least one hour every day and moreover to do it "in the language which we speak"—namely, Yiddish.[2]

Enter the *Maskilim*, as members of the *Haskalah* (Enlightenment) movement were known. If the Hassidim valued emotion and the mystical experience, the *Maskilim* championed the intellect, especially as it was reflected in the wider, secular world. For them, Hebrew was the language of reason and progress—and they sought to make it serve more than the narrow goals of a parochial religion. Indeed, they envisioned a Hebrew that could be spoken and that could become the instrument for the entire spectrum of modern writing: poetry, novels, nonfiction.

Although it would be hard to imagaine two groups more antagonistic than were the Hassidim and the *Maskilim*, ironically enough both were bitterly attacked by those who numbered themselves in the religious status quo—the *Maskilim* because of their secular preoccupations; the Hassidim because they danced toward a condition of no study at all. The conflicts that resulted—secularist against mystic, and traditionists against them both—set the stage for the development of Yiddish literature.

Nor do the ironies stop there. The *Haskalah* movement had pledged itself to a campaign of liberal education, one designed to introduce the Jewish masses to new ideas and the necessity of Hebrew as the medium for their expression. As part of the program, the *Maskilim* wrote anti-Hassidic pamphlets and stories that poked fun at the ignorance and superstition they felt were Hassidism's distinguishing marks. By today's standards, these attacks would not generate a good mad, much less a plausible libel suit.

But for all the antagonism the anti-Hassidic campaigns may

have generated, they were largely a case of preaching to the choir; few, if any, of the *Maskilim*'s potential converts knew how to read modern Hebrew and thus they were soon faced with a Hobson's choice: either write in Yiddish, or risk having no audience at all. Most of the early satires (e.g., Mendel Lefin's *The First Hassid* or Isaac Ber Levinshohn's *Emek Refoim*) are of limited historical interest, but the anti-Hassidic songs of the period have managed to retain a measure of popularity—not, to be sure, as attacks on the excesses of Hassidic life but, rather, as nostalgic touchstones to the world of the *shtetl*. "Un Az Der Rebbe Zingt" ("When the Master Sings . . . then sing all his Hassidim") is an excellent example of a satire turned on its head. Originally, the song meant to imply that Hassidic disciples blindly follow wherever their leader does: when he sings, they sing; when he dances, they dance; and when he drinks (which was frequently), they drink. The *Maskilim* viewed such worshipful allegiance as both demeaning and disgusting—particularly in view of those who often emerged as Hassidic Masters. But the difficulties of writing propaganda in one language in an effort to convince the folk to learn another were enormous, especially as the Hassidic rebbes increased their popularity and influence by relying on oral traditions that skirted these linguistic problems altogether.

Literary history, however, was squarely on the side of the *Maskilim*. Writers such as Israel Aksenfeld (1787-1866) and Isaac Meir Dick (1813–93) drew from a variety of models, not least of all the Russian realism of their day, to create a literature of social criticism grounded in concrete details and an earthy humanness. Slowly, a growing interest in fiction per se began to temper the hard philosophical line that the *Maskilim* had etched between the unenlightened and themselves. Indeed, their best writers were soon able to compete for a Yiddish readership by incorporating both the folktales made popular by the Hassidic rebbes and the lofty themes of Jewish history and legend that had been the sole province of Hebrew literature.

Against this backdrop of literary squabbling and internecine warfare came the first significant writer to publish his novels in Yiddish: Sholom Abramovitch (1836–1918). He was born into a Lithuanian rabbinical family and there received a traditional yeshivah education. At the age of seventeen, however, Abramovitch joined a band of wandering beggars, thereby adding an understanding of poverty and social injustice to his formal education in Talmud/Torah.

As a young adult Abramovitch joined the *Haskalah* movement and soon became widely respected as a writer of Hebrew prose. However, events in the Jewish world gradually convinced him not only that Yiddish, rather than Hebrew, was the language of the people, but that it should also be the language of its authors. In 1862, Alexander Zederbaum founded a weekly Yiddish journal called *Kol Mevasser* as a supplement to the long-established Hebrew publiciation, *ha-Melits*. A year later Sholom Abramovitch sent him the manuscript of *Dos Kleine Menshele* (*The Parasite*), his first Yiddish novel. The decision was not an easy one. To write in Yiddish was to lose considerable prestige, particularly among the intelligentsia who felt that Yiddish literature was the stuff of lightweights. The situation would be roughly analogous to a major novelist—a Bellow or a Mailer—suddenly switching to Harlequin romances and TV sit-coms. Sol Liptzin outlines the strategies that both Abramovitch and Zederbaum used to cushion the blows that a serious Yiddish novel was bound to generate:

In order not to hurt his growing reputation as a Hebrew essayist, Abramovitch asked that this Yiddish satire be published not under his real name, but under the pseudonym of Senderl Mokher Sforim, a mythical bookseller who was peddling literary and religious wares, driving with an emaciated nag and rickety wagon along the muddy road near Berditchev. Zederbaum agreed to serialize this work but feared that readers might ascribe it to the editor himself, since Senderl was an easily recognizable variant of his own first name Alex-Sender. He therefore used his editorial prerogative and changed the pseudonym from Senderl to Mendele.[3]

As fate would have it, *Kol Mevasser,* the Yiddish supplement, became more important than *ha-Melits,* its Hebrew parent. Most of Mendele's early work—including such satiric novels as *Dos Kleine Menshele, Die Takse* (*The Meat Tax* [1869]), and *Die Klatshe* (*The Dobbin* [1873])—were sensationist exposés of the *Kahal* (ghetto officials and assorted politicians) whom Mendele blamed for the impoverished condition of Russian Jewry. In these novels Mendele outlined a series of reforms, many of which were implemented in the decades that followed. As one of his translators, Gerald Stillman, puts it: "Mendele's solution was for the wealthy to give up some of their wealth to help the poor, not through the corrupt philanthropic societies which flourished in many Jewish communities and often had their funds siphoned off by the very wealthy who purported to support them, but by creating schools to teach the children of the poor how to become useful artisans, creative workers, useful citizens."[4]

However, by the time writers such as Sholom Aleichem and Y. L. Peretz burst onto the scene some twenty years later, Mendele's pioneering formula of conventional satire and equally conventional reform had played itself out. Granted, he had become an established Yiddish writer, but the renaissance of interest in folk literature made his earlier satire seem dated, obsolete, overly "literary." So, Mendele began to revise—and sometimes to totally rewrite—many of his earlier works, bringing them into line with the new *takhlis* (purpose) of Yiddish fiction. What the *folkmentsh* needed were not so much novels that would tell them how corrupt things were, but, rather, stories that might suggest how they could survive in the midst of such *tsoris* (trouble). To the growing number of Yiddish writers Isaac Kaminner offered this advice: "Give the people something warm for its cure. A bit of wine, too. With wine—imagination, poetry—and with hope it is possible to maintain the strength of a fainting heart. Beware of cold dishes—icy criticism of old Jewish customs, chilly ridicule of Jewish matters."[5] To our ears this must sound like a strange aesthetic for a satirist, especially for one in the process of rethinking his work. But Mendele's allegiance had always been with the *folkmentsh,* and therefore his movement toward folk humor was more a matter of degree than a radical shift in kind. If the 1860s ushered in a Yiddish literature worthy of first-rate minds, the 1880s crystallized patterns of Jewish survival into the mythos of fiction. Rather than frontal attacks on the meat tax or the *Kahal,* Mendele joined in a movement that talked about tragicomic adjustments on a wider scale.

Fishke the Lame is a good example of how Mendele's work gradually altered its focus. The first version of the novel appeared in 1869, the second in 1876, and the final version in 1888. There is even a Hebrew version entitled *The Beggar Book.* The most available English translation is Gerald Stillman's (based on the third version), a text that combines an earlier socioreligious concern with his growing interest in folk humor.

In a letter to his friend Menasha Margolius (to whom *Fishke* is dedicated), Mendele discusses the way in which joy and sorrow are more often blended than they are separated: "Sad is my melody in the symphony of Yiddish literature. My works express the very core of a Jew who, even when he does sing a merry tune, sounds from afar as if he were sobbing and weeping. Why, even his festive Shabbes hymns sound as if they were taken out of the Book of Lamentations. When he laughs, there are tears in his eyes. When he tries to make merry, bitter sighs escape from the depths of his heart—it's always oy-vay, woe is me, vay!"[6] Mendele the Bookseller is not only the pseudonym of Sholom Abramovitch, but also the satiric persona of the novel itself. He travels around the countryside in a broken-down wagon drawn by an even more bedraggled horse. The very mobility of Mendele's profession is, of course, important to the satiric range of the novel, but it is also essential to his role as a messenger of consolation. After all, it was the bookseller who supplied *tehinot* for women and the all-important Book of Lamentations for men.

Thus, the bookseller felt himself especially responsible for the survival of the Jewish masses, and it is this sense of mission that makes for a number of the novel's rather curious juxtapositions. In the opening lines, for example, Mendele describes what looks to be a fairly conventional proclamation to spring, the sort of *reverdi* one finds in, say, the opening lines of Chaucer's *Canterbury Tales:* "Just when the bright sun begins to shine proclaiming another summer to the land, when people feel newly born and their hearts filled with joy at the sight of God's glorious world" (p. 17).[7] But joy has a way of spawning sadness, and in the space of a few sentences we find Mendele balancing the universality of spring with culturally specific ruminations on *Tishah b'Ab:* "Just then the time for wailing and weeping arrives among Jews. This time of sorrow brings with it a host of mournful days: days of fasting, days of self-torment, days of grief and tears—starting at the end of Passover and lasting well into the damp cold deep mud of autumn" (p. 17).

Such a peculiarly Yiddish sensibility is difficult, if not impossible, to define. Joy and sorrow—as Mendele suggests—were seen as opposite sides of the same coin. Thus, the ghetto Jew could think of himself as simultaneously elevated and diminished. In the space of a quip he could move from sentimentality to skepticism. Ironic perspectives came easily, but the same thing could also be said of intimacy. As Cynthia Ozick describes the language that is older by centuries than Chaucerian English, "Yiddish is especially handy for satire, cynicism, familiarity, abuse, sentimentality, and resignation, for a sense of high irony, and for putting people in their place and events in bitter perspective: all the defensive verbal baggage an involuntary migratory nation is likely to need en route to the next temporary

refuge."[8] In short, the Yiddish language and the richly tapes-
tried humor it created became strategies of survival. Given their
powerlessness, the pragmatism we believe in made little sense.
Pogroms cut across the lines of economic success, political action, or efforts at universalism. To a drunken Cossack, all Jews
were the same: crack the victim's head and it bled.

Psychic health was, to be sure, another matter, and it is here
that Judaism and Jewish folk culture agreed: both celebrated
life, although not without ironic winks from the latter. As the
Yiddish proverb would have it, "You could live if they let you."
But, alas, *they* never do. Even more to the ironic point, to "live" is
to be involved with illusions, with the stuff that dreams are made
of. Thus, jokes measured the ironic distance between what is and
what might have been, and Yiddish culture manufactured them
with the same dazzling efficiency that Birmingham made cloth:

> Once there was a poor man, a *schlemiel*. He was so unhappy that he
> took pleasure in daydreaming. One day he uttered the following prayer:
> "Dear God—give me ten thousand dollars for the New Year. I'll tell
> you what—I'll make a deal with you. I swear to give five thousand dollars
> of this amount for charity, the other half let me keep. You say you have
> doubts about my honorable intentions?—then give me the five thousand
> and *you* give to charity yourself."

In this way Yiddish authors of the 1880s returned to the
Hassidic tradition and its dependency on anecdote at the same
time that they added twists of their own. The Hassidic tale
moved inexorably to a moral point and usually in ways that called
attention to the wonder-working rebbe at its center. For the
Hassid, no claim was too outlandish to be believed. Or put
another way, self-mockery is conspicuously absent in the tales
attributed to the Hassidic Masters. The *Maskilim* were, of course,
happy to fill that particular gap, but it was the business of more
consciously literary artists to shape a distinctive sensibility out of
the raw material of the past.

Mendele was the first Yiddish writer large enough in spirit
and scope to replace the narrow concerns of social satire with a
wide-ranging comic spirit. In *Fishke,* he assembled characters
who would become the stock types of Yiddish humor. His
portrait of the wandering bookseller came first. He is a man who
worries that he might not reach his customers in time for *Tishah
b'Ab* because "this is no laughing matter—Jews without *Books of*

Lamentations!" Then there was Fishke himself, a crippled bath-house attendant who has been forced to marry a professional beggar. Ordinarily the beggar in Yiddish humor is known as the *schnorrer*—that is, one who "begs" alms as if they belonged to him by divine right. His justification is a deep-seated belief that he is genuinely deserving, and his tactic for fleecing the rich is called *chutzpah* (unmitigated gall). The comic possibilities derive from the misrepresentations of reality that afflict nearly all the figures of Yiddish humor, from the simple *nudnik* (simpleton) to the more complicated *schlemiel*. And much of this high-styled incongruity has its roots in the jokes the *Maskilim* circulated during the early years of the nineteenth century. In one story, for example,

A Hassid meets a Litvak (a Lithuanian Jew known for skepticism) and they begin to have a conversation. Suddenly the Hassid says, "You know, my rebbe is so pious that God himself speaks to my rebbe."

Thinking that he might catch the Hassid off-guard, the Litvak immediately challenges him with the following question: "But how do you *know* that God speaks to your rebbe?"

"That's easy," the Hassid shoots back, "because my rebbe said so!"

Now the Litvak was sure that he had caught the bearded gentleman in an intellectual dilemma. He smiled to himself and asked, "But how do you know your rebbe isn't a liar?"

"Because," the Hassid replied, "would God speak to a liar?"

The same spirit persists in American Jewish humor among those who have long forgotten about Hassidim and Litvaks, but who misrepresent reality nonetheless:

One man walked up to another and said, "Walberg! What happened to you. You used to be short; now you're tall. You used to be blonde and have blue eyes; now you're dark with brown eyes!"

The man, startled, said, "What are you, nuts or something? My name's not Walberg!"

"Oy, even your name you changed!"

It is in this sense of "belief" that the *schnorrer* believed that charity was his due. Fishke's shrewish wife (yet another stock Yiddish character) gives him the following advice about "making it" as a professional beggar: "For a Jew to be a beggar, a successful beggar, he needs more than luck. There are many things he must learn. He has to know all the tricks. He has to be able to get under somebody's skin in such a way that the other fellow must give simply to get away" (p. 57). Granted, the special charm of the *schnorrer* is missing here as Mendele's tone makes a clear distinction between bumbling amateurs (like Fishke) and hardened professionals such as his wife.

Moreover, the novel's structure works to create new alignments of sensibility. The clearest literary influence seems to be eighteenth-century novels such as *Tom Jones* or *Pamela*—at least to the extent that *Fishke* is episodic, sentimental, and largely dependent on coincidence. Roughly half the novel is given over to Fishke's love for a young crippled girl, while the other half—the exploits of Mendele—serves as a framing device for the narrative. As Fishke is being initiated into mysteries of professional panhandling, Mendele tells anecdotes about more lovable *schnorrers:* "At a meal for paupers given by a wealthy man in honor of his child's marriage, a beggar who was invited arrived dragging with him another who wasn't. When they asked, 'Uncle, how is it that you brought along another mouth to feed?' he answered, 'Oh, that's my son-in-law. I give him room and board' " (p. 59). The result makes for interlocking grids of social criticism and the comic spirit—with the cards stacked to favor ostensible failures.

There are moments as well when Mendele and Reb Alter shift from considerations of personal failure to sweeping social pronouncements. But even here the satire seems more gentle, less directed toward a specific agenda of laws or programs than it is to a comic assessment of the Jewish situation in general. They will digress, for example, into an "evolutionary" view of Jewish history or construct other, equally absurd, hypotheses:

Once a Jew has broken himself of the vile passion of eating, food ceases to be a matter of importance to him, and he can spend the rest of his life requiring almost nothing. . . . there is great hope that with the passing of time—if only the kosher meat tax is retained and the activities of the charity worker and their brethren go unhampered—Jews will drift further and further from eating until among future generations there will be no trace of the digestive tract at all, except for piles.   (P. 61)

. . . .

The pages [probably of the *Talmud*] were all of different colors and also different sizes. The letters were smudged and unclear and of different types. . . . It was laid out in strips—narrow ones with small print on both sides, a broad strip with bigger type in the center, and below this, a belly of tiny type set in like poppy seeds; and between these patches of print, stretched like narrow ribbons of blank space across the page up and down, like little pathways in the forest. These are some of the qualities that a Jew in our part of the world looks for in a book.   (P. 63)

To be sure, there is still the kosher meat tax, still the pokes at the *Kahal*—but there is also a certain amount of good cheer clinging to the exaggerations. Rather than external harangue, Mendele developed the capacity to turn his mockeries inward, to laugh at himself as easily as at others.

In this sense, the luckless *schlimazl* became an important comic type in *Fishke,* and many of the jokes about this figure found their way into Mendele's fiction. At one point Reb Alter tells about a match he had tried to arrange between the newborn children of two wealthy merchants:

The two of them [the fathers] were straining at the leash. . . . My commission was as good as in my pocket. I had decided how much dowry to settle on my daughter. I was already bargaining with a ragpicker for an old satin coat for myself. Shirts were my last worry. They would wait until later. The good Lord would provide. . . . Well, to make a long story short—nothing! Just listen what happens to me! I tell you, a man with no luck is better off not being born. Just as we were ready to break pots in celebration, we happened to remember the bride and groom, and what do you think? Believe me, it hurts even to talk about it. The whole thing was a flop! No, it was ten times worse than a flop! It just blew up in my face! Listen to my misfortune and how the wrath of God descended on me: the two merchants each had—what do you think they had? They each had a son!   (P. 40)

But if Reb Alter is the *schlimazl,* the victim of accidents not of his own making, he and Mendele are also *schlemiels* who misrepresent reality so badly that they delude themsleves into thinking they can live from the "profits" of their absurd trades. As Reb Alter puts it, "Israel is one big pauper," and in the following lines one can readily see how this might be so:

women's books of supplication for *The Tales of Baba.* . . .
prayer scrolls for good luck charms. . . .
Chanukah candles for wolves-teeth talismans. . . .
Although not a single kopek passed through our hands, we were both immensely pleased with the trading process itself. After all, we had both been swapping, bartering, trafficking, giving and taking, and keeping very busy.   (P. 60)

For Mendele, the humor of poverty was a matter of juggling his belief in man's potential for moral grandeur—his ability to endure the slings and arrows of an outrageous world—and his slashing indictments of greed, provinciality, and assorted knaveries. From this curious blending came Yiddish literature's first tough-minded satire and the first movement toward an equally tough-minded folk humor. Granted, the two protagonists of Mendele's *Travels of Benjamin III* are traditional *schlemiels,* but here the satire is directed more toward personal ineptitude than toward a refusal by society at large to launch an Operation Bootstrap. As the following passage suggests, they are also archetypal *luftmenshen,* bounding from one "vocation" to another in fruitless searches to end their poverty:

Ask a Jew of Teneyadevkeh how he earns his living. His first reaction is to stand there paralyzed. The poor man is befuddled, and he doesn't know what to say. A little later, he revives and begins to explain, "Praise the Lord! I have, thank God, as you see right here and now, a gift from his Blessed Name, an instrument, a musical voice, and I also recite the supplemental prayers during the Solemn Days. Occasionally I am a *Mohel* [ritual circumciser], and before Passover I knead dough for making *matzos*—there isn't another kneader like me in the world, I tell you here and now! Sometimes, I manage to make a match, I do. Also this is between me and you, I have an interest in a tavern which can be milked a little. I have a goat which can be milked a lot."

On purely literary grounds, however, *Fishke* is the more satisfying work. While both novels find their subject material in the abject poverty of Russian Jewry, in *Fishke,* Mendele is able to filter social criticism through a variety of humorous perspectives. As much as one may laugh at the seriocomic misfortunes of Mendele the Bookseller or Reb Alter, there is a sense in which we can also learn from characters who have a feel for ironic juxtaposition in their very bones. As Mendele puts it when he speaks about his ambivalent feelings toward his wife: "It was magic. It was like—how can I explain it—like scratching one of those itching sores that I get sometimes. It was pain and pleasure, both together" (p. 118).

Sholom Aleichem had hardly learned his *aleph-bays* [the first letters of the Hebrew alphabet] when Mendele published *Dos Kleine Menshele* (1864). In fact, Sholom Rabinowitz—the man who was to become Yiddish literature's greatest folk writer—was born in 1859, a scant five years before. His earliest training was in Hebrew literature, and his first creative effort was a Hebrew version of *Robinson Crusoe*. Curt Leviant, one of Sholom Aleichem's most knowledgeable translators, points out that "through his lifetime, Sholom Aleichem never neglected Hebrew; he corresponded with his relatives in Hebrew and hoped one day to translate his own works into the sacred tongue."[9]

By now the story of his meeting with American humorist Mark Twain has become legend, part of the apocrypha handed down from teacher to student. Presumably Twain came to see Sholom Aleichem when the latter first arrived in America because, as Twain put it, people kept calling him "the American Sholom Aleichem." One assumes that if Sholom Aleichem did not, in fact, return the compliment—by insisting that *he* was always called "the Yiddish Mark Twain"—the quip is at least in character. After all, both Twain and Sholom Aleichem were national writers in the best, and rarest, senses of the term—that is, able to be read and enjoyed by the entire spectrum of their respective societies, from the scholarly professor to the average school-child.

That much said, however, let me hasten to add that it is in his *differences* from a Mark Twain that Sholom Aleichem's achievement can best be gauged. For all his apparent popularity, I suspect that Twain was more often misunderstood than properly appreciated by an enthusiastic American public. Novels such as *Pudd'nhead Wilson* or *The Mysterious Stranger* were considered atypical Twain—the products of an aging, disillusioned mind; the *real* Twain could be found along the banks of the Mississippi, in novels filled with nostalgic portraits of an unfettered boyhood.

Granted, Twain was *always* more complicated than some readers of *Adventures of Huckleberry Finn* have been willing to admit, but my point is simply that Sholom Aleichem avoided many of these problems in advance. Alienation did not dog his heels as it did Twain's. Although Sholom Aleichem's family was comparatively well off and his education far surpassed the normal ghetto fare, his allegiance to the poor was as lacking in ambivalence as it was undivided. The essentially low view that increasingly darkened Twain's vision and that turned him into "God's fool" made genuine sympathy with the *folk*—be they frontier braggarts or Boston bramin—difficult; by contrast, Sholom Aleichem's dying words—"Let me be buried among the poor, that their graves may shine on mine and mine on theirs"—strike us as heartfelt, uttered without the ironies we have come to expect in literary personalities and totally unqualified by the machinery of ambivalence.

Indeed, when Sholom Aleichem died—in the New York City of 1916—more than one hundred fifty thousand people attended his funeral, proof, should any be required, of the special relationship between a Yiddish author and his audience. When *our* best writers die, there is a terrible temptation to skip the funeral and instead to begin the business of churning out the definitive biography, the critical study, the elegiac article.

And too, there is a special sense in which Sholom Aleichem's audience shared in not only the world view of *Yiddishkeit,* but also in the peculiarly multilingual qualities of that world. A modernist poet such as T. S. Eliot may have assumed that his readers shared the best that had been thought and said in the Western tradition—Dante and Shakespeare, Baudelaire and Buddha—that they could read French, German, Italian, Latin, and Sanskrit, but the truth of the matter is that most of us spend as much time on "glosses" to *The Waste Land* as we do on the poem. That this is the case is hardly surprising, given the decline of the West that was Eliot's subject—and Eliot himself would have been surprised least of all. Sholom Aleichem's "givens" make for intriguing comparisons, for not only could he *assume* that his readers were familiar with Hebrew (the language of Torah), Aramaic (the language of Talmud), Yiddish (the language of the *shtetl*), and Russian (the language of their adopted country), they actually *were:*

> No wonder Sholom Aleichem's audiences used to roll in the aisles with laughter. The juxtaposition of a lofty phrase in Hebrew or Aramaic with a homey Yiddish phrase which is supposed to explain it but has no bearing on it whatsoever—that is the gist of Tevye's humor. . . . For example: when Tevye goes to see the priest and the priest's dog jumps on him, he says, "I gave them this quotation to chew on. "*Lo yechratz kelev l'shonah,*" which means literally, "not a dog shall bark," and comes from Exodus, Chapter II, verse 7: "But against any of the children of Israel not a dog shall bark." Tevye follows this with the Russian proverb: "*Nehai sobaka daram nie bresche,*" and interprets the whole thing to mean, "Don't let a dog bark for nothing."[10]

Although Sholom Aleichem did not devote full time to "writing" until some sixteen years prior to his death, his literary productivity is nothing short of phenomenal: some forty volumes of stories, plays, and novels. He is best known, of course, as the author of the Tevye stories, although more often than not, it is a Tevye people have seen on Broadway rather than encountered in one of Sholom Aleichem's books. This is unfortunate, because many of the efforts to popularize his work have been misleading: the highly stylized "Hassidic" dancing of Jerome Robbins and the hasty wedding of folk material and Tin Pan Alley are only a few of the problems. Even the title—*Fiddler on the Roof*—comes from a painting by Marc Chagall rather than from the writing of Sholom Aleichem. In this sense Brooks Atkinson is probably right when he suggests that Sholom Aleichem "would relish the irony of being the source of a Broadway musical that cost $475,000 to produce and that began its run with an advance ticket sale of $650,000."[11]

For Sholom Aleichem, Tevye is a tragic figure, a man caught in a rapidly changing world over which he has little, if any, control. If he tends to sentimentalize the *shtetl*'s poverty, to reject Mendele's satiric solutions for an even heavier dosage of Yiddish humor, it is because the very values of *Yiddishkeit* were crumbling beneath his feet. Tevye, of course, would hardly have thought of himself as a *symbol*, although he might have written himself down as a *schlimazl*, as a man more sinned against than sinning, as the victim of "accidents" he did not engineer. For a Tevye, life is a matter of suffering, but that notion did not foreclose either the life-affirming stance or a humor of self-mockery. To the contrary, Tevye—and presumably, Sholom Aleichem's readers— could see a connection between moral identity and tragic grandeur. Far from being the *schlemiel* who was the rightful recipient of the *shtetl*'s condescending laughter, a figure such as Tevye was as much the "hero" to his society as, say, Achilles or Aneas were to theirs. Sholom Aleichem's long-suffering protagonist champions the values of the heart, for all his chronic misquoting and compulsive misdoing. In Tevye's *tsoris*, *shtetl* Jewry saw a reflection, albeit diminished, of its own fate; and his tales seemed especially poignant when a son began to read Karl Marx or a daughter threatened to marry outside the faith—not as an etiquette book that might teach one the proper postures to strike on such occasions, but, rather, both as a source of comfort and a cause for celebrating the human condition.

Although Sholom Aleichem created a wealth of individual characters, they all shared in a poverty that was the ground zero of his humor: Mottel, the cantor's son, became the archetype of the Jewish child in literature. Full of bounce and unflagging good cheer, Mottel meets every tragedy in his life—even orphan-hood—with an unquenchable optimism. When his father dies, Mottel thinks: "I don't have to pray; I don't have to sing. I'm free of everything. It's grand to be an orphan." Menahem-Mendl, a relative of Tevye, is the archetypal *luftmentsh,* the very essence of accommodation and a will to survive. With his eye continually twinkling—due to yet another get-rich scheme or perhaps a new "occupation"—Menahem-Mendl wanders from place to place as the luckless *schlimazl.* He dabbles in stocks, in land speculation, and in various "businesses" until he finds his true calling which is (as it must be) *writing.* Under the illusion that this new profession is an easy one, Menahem-Mendl writes his long-suffering wife that their success is virtually assured:

> I asked the paper to notify me in case they liked my style. If it was any good, I'd just keep writing. And guess what? It took them only six weeks to reply. They liked my article very much and suggested that I expand it. If my stuff would be good, they would gladly publish it and pay me a kopek per line. You understand? A ruble for every hundred lines. I immediately grabbed a pen to figure out how much I could write. I calculated that during one long summer day, I could write at least one thousand lines. Which brings it up to almost three hundred rubles per month.   (P. 162)

Needless to say, the newspaper fails to answer Menahem-Mendl and his dream of easy rubles takes a spot on his growing list of schemes gone sour.

However, it is Tevye who best captures the tragicomic spirit of the Diaspora. When he says, "With God's help I starved to death—I and my wife and children—three times a day, not counting supper" (p. 127), he gives the term "tragic affirmation" a new twist. Like man, God is expected to act like a *mentsh,* and should He refuse, Tevye has every right to complain. In his attempt to characterize the mercurial Tevye, Maurice Samuel suggests that he is

> the indestructible individualist, and this is not to be misinterpreted as anarchist. He is, in a baffling way, a blend of individualist and tradi-tionalist. Yet he is also something of the revolutionist; and indeed, it is more than revolutionary to believe in God and take Him to task sensibly than not to believe in Him and denounce Him in unmeasured language.

Here, too, however, Tevye is in the tradition. The orthodox Jewry of which he is a part is not unacquainted with protests directed at the Lord of the Universe for His mismanagement of human affairs.[12]

For example, Tevye realizes full well that Menahem-Mendl is a "gadabout, a wastrel, a faker and a worthless vagabond," but he is fascinated by his stories of "high finance" nonetheless. In this sense, Tevye contributes to his own economic misfortunes by listening to a spinner of dreams until he too becomes a dreamer. As Tevye puts it, Menahem-Mendl told him "stories of Yehupetz and Odessa, of how he had been ten times over, as they say, 'on horseback and thrown off the horse.' A rich man today, a beggar tomorrow, again a rich man, and once more a pauper. He dealt in something I had never heard of in my life—crazy-sounding things—stocks, bonds, shares-shmares, Malzev, schalzev. The devil alone knew what it was. The sums he reeled off his tongue were fantastic—ten thousand, twenty thousand, thirty thousand—but he threw around money like matches" (p. 5). And yet, for all of Menahem-Mendl's wild, speculative talk about wealth, one must remember that this was a world with equally curious notions about what constituted poverty. In hard dollars, nearly all the Jews of the *shtetl* were poor, but if a man could afford to "make *shabbos*" (i.e., to set a large, festive table on Friday night and to take Saturday off), he was, in their terms, "rich." For the Jews who lived in what Maurice Samuel calls "the world of Sholom Aleichem," financial defeats could be sustained because, at the bottom line, they may not have been that important.

Even Sholom Aleichem's characterization of Menahem-Mendl suggests that there is no reality to the world of business, and that like the *luftmentsh* himself, it is all "air." On the other hand, Tevye's bank account of one hundred rubles is real, substantial, and, of course, ripe for Menahem-Mendl's picking. A *schlimazl*—especially a kindhearted one such as Tevye—cannot keep such a fortune for long. At the first opportunity he will give it to a *schlemiel* with Big Plans:

"Just what I've been trying to tell you," he [Menahem-Mendl] breaks in. "When will you have the opportunity to put in a hundred rubles and take out, with God's help, enough to marry off your daughter and to do all the other things besides?"

And he went on with his chant for the next three hours, explaining how he could make three rubles out of one and ten out of three. First you bring in one hundred rubles somewhere, and you tell them to buy ten pieces of I-forget-what-you-call-it, then you wait a few days until they do it. You send a telegram somewhere else to sell the ten pieces and buy twice as many for the money. Then you wait and they rise again. You shoot off another telegram. You keep doing this until the hundred rubles becomes two hundred, then four hundred, then eight hundred, then sixteen hundred. It's no less than a miracle from God.   (P. 7)

It is, perhaps, a far cry from Menahem-Mendl's telegrams to the IBM computers that presumably will never let you lose in Saul Bellow's *Seize the Day*, but the general idea is the same. Like Tamkin, the minor character who dupes a desperate Tommy Wilhelm out of his last two hundred dollars, Menahem-Mendl is the economic *schlemiel* whose personal misfortunes (as well as those they cause) are self-created. And although Tevye realizes that giving away his hundred rubles is foolish (he thinks at one point: "If I should lose out, if it should fall butter-side-down? Better not think of it"), he "speculates" anyhow.

Not surprisingly, the venture is a complete failure. Not only has Menahem-Mendl lost all of Tevye's money, but both a cow and a calf die as if to add insult to the mounting injuries. "When luck turns against you," Tevye declares, "you are lost." Deprived of his money, Tevye falls back on a tradition that, even as he mangles its quotations, seems able to sustain him. Thus, unlike the "luckless" characters of other literature, Tevye can accept his defeats with a shrug and a bit of talmudic wisdom:

> I don't even want to ask you where my money went. I understand only too well. My blood money went up in smoke, it sank into the grave. . . . And whose fault is it if not mine? I let myself be talked into it. I went chasing after rainbows. If you want money, my friend, you have to work and save for it; you have to wear your fingers to the bone. I deserve a good thrashing for it. But crying won't help. How is it written? "If the maiden screamed—you can shout until you burst a blood vessel." Hindsight, as they say. . . . It wasn't fated that Tevye should be a rich man. As Ivan says, "Mikita never had anything and never will." God willed it so. *The Lord giveth and the Lord taketh away*."   (P. 14)

In "Modern Children," Tevye stands with one foot rooted firmly in the past while the other searches uneasily for a solid foundation in the present. As Tevye tells Sholom Aleichem: "Modern children, did you say? Ah, you bring them into the world, sacrifice for them, you slave for them day and night—and what do you get out of it? You think that one way or another, it would work out according to your ideas or station. After all, I don't expect to marry them off to millionaires, but then I don't have to be satisfied with just anyone either. So I figured I'd have a little luck with my daughters" (P. 16). But of course, it is with his daughters that Tevye has the least luck of all. The patriarchal system—like most of the old values—is not what it used to be, and although Tevye's daughters continue to love him very much, they assert their independence (especially in matters of the heart) in ways that would have been unthinkable a generation before. Indeed, romantic love is the force that thwarts one likely "match" after another. His eldest daughter, Tzeitl, marries a religiously learned but hopelessly impoverished tailor; Tevye's other daughters set their caps for more worldly figures: Chodel, on a student revolutionary; and Chava on a non-Jewish Russian.

Tevye himself remains committed to the orthodoxy of his own fashioning, but he is also flexible enough to accommodate the whims of his daughters—all of them, that is, except Chava, who converts to Christianity. And while he may not be able to understand why "modern children" prefer to arrange their own matches (as opposed to relying on the wisdom and experience of professionals), his Yiddish heart is stronger than his objections. Granted, he cannot forgive Chava—to become an apostate was the one truly unforgivable sin—but the decision to say her premature *Kaddish* [prayer for the dead] is heartwrenchingly difficult nonetheless.

Curiously enough, when his youngest daughter, Beilke, does snag a wealthy man, Tevye is not as overjoyed as one might have imagined he would be. Love, it seems, has counted for more than Tevye would admit, or put another way, he protests too much about the poor string of sons-in-law. As things turn out, however, Beilke's husband loses his money and Tevye's long-promised trip to Israel becomes a hasty, impoverished flight to America. Yet his final words to Mr. Sholom Aleichem (in the story "Tevye Reads the Psalms") are of faith in God and in the survival of Jewry:

Today we met on the train, Mr. Sholom Aleichem. Tomorrow this same train can take us to Yehupetz. A year later it can cast us in Odessa, Warsaw, perhaps even in America. Unless of course the Almighty takes a good look around and suddenly decides: "You know what, children? I think it's high time for the Messiah." Oh how I wish he'd play a nasty trick like that on us, that ancient God of ours. Meanwhile live and be well, have a good trip, and send my best to all our fellow Jews. Tell them not to worry, for our ancient God still lives. (P. 32)

Such is the nature of what I have called Tevye's "ironic affirmation." With the world of the *shtetl* all but disintegrated and "modern children" threatening to abandon its traditions entirely, Tevye not only continues to pattern his life on the Old Ways, but he also has a perfect faith that the Old Ways will somehow prevail. On the other hand, however, Tevye has the wisdom necessary to see that the world around is, indeed, changing, and that his daughters both demand and require a different sort of "love" than had existed between himself and his wife Golde. As Julius and Francis Butwin describe Tevye, he is the "perfect *schlimazl*" and also the perfect *kasril,* the man whom nothing in life can down." And now, more than fifty years after Sholom Aleichem's death, Broadway audiences and an increasing American readership have come to see Tevye's "wisdom" as less parochial than they had imagined. They too see the point of the old Yiddish proverb: *Abi gezunt—dos lebn men zikh aleyn nemen* (Your health comes first—you can always hang yourself later).

3
The *Schlemiel* on Main Street

If the *schlemiel* of Yiddish humor was a character whose ineptness suggested a world in which you could never win, that feeling quickly disappeared when he was transplanted to the opportunistic soil of America. Suddenly, "winning" became a genuine possibility, and *schlemiels* such as Motke Habad or Menahem-Mendl took a back seat to David Levinsky and a thousand other varieties of Horatio Alger with a skull cap. Sol Liptzin argues that American Jewish literature falls into three roughly distinct periods: immigrant assimilation, acculturation, and rediscovery.[1] Abraham Cahan's *Rise of David Levinsky* (1917) is the prototype of the first. Leslie Fiedler is probably right when he calls it "a love-story, or more precisely a story of the failure of love,"[2] but in David's systematic shedding of his ("yeshivah student") sensibility and in his dogged determination to carve out his share of wealth from the garment industry's pie, he became an index of possibility for an entire generation of newly Americanized Jews.

Granted, Cahan's portrait is a scathing one. The Levinsky who turned four pennies into a million dollars is a loveless, unlovable man—uncomfortable in anything but a plain brown suit, uncomfortable in fashionable restaurants, uncomfortable in his soul. As Isaac Rosenfeld pointed out nearly forty years ago:

Levinsky is a man who cannot feel at home with his desires. Because hunger is strong in him, he must always strive to relieve it; but precisely because it is strong, it has to be preserved. It owes its strength to the fact that for so many years everything that influenced Levinsky most deeply—say, piety and mother love—was inseparable from it. For hunger, in this broader, rather metaphysical sense of the term that I have been using, is not only the state of tension out of which the desires for relief and betterment spring; precisely because the desires are formed under its sign, they become assimilated to it, and convert it into the prime source of all value, so that the man, in his pursuit of whatever he considers pleasurable and good, seeks to return to his yearning as much as he does to escape it.[3]

This quotation tells us much about Levinsky and perhaps even more about the alienated, disaffected Rosenfeld, but in either case, it speaks to that period in which American Jewish authors confronted American reality, in all its coarseness and splendor, its profound disappointment and its giddy potential, for the first time.

Some writers—Mary Antin, for example—gushed about the America they saw through lace curtains, without embarrassment, without irony, and certainly without humor. A book such as Antin's *Promised Land* (1912), an account of the life she left and the life she found, is long on patriotism (three cheers for the red, white, and blue would hardly have struck Antin as sufficient) and very short indeed on the collective memory. As Antin would have it, one can, one ought, yea, one *must* shed the old skin of the Old World in order to march off—properly in step and to the right drumbeat—into the American future. It made for uplifting stuff, as antique on one hand as Crevecoeur's speculations, in 1782, about this "new [American] man," and as fresh as the newest arrival on Ellis Island. In any event, here was "optimism" with all capital letters, and no room left for the self-deprecating quips about beating death by opening a funeral parlor:

This is my latest home, and it invites me to a glad new life. The endless ages have indeed throbbed through my blood, but a new rhythm dances in my veins. . . . The past was only my cradle, and now it cannot hold me, because I am grown too big . . . No! it is not I that belongs to the past, but the past that belongs to me. America is the youngest of the nations, and inherits all that went before in history. And I am the youngest of America's children, and into my hands is given all her priceless heritage, to the last white star espied through the telescope, to the last great thought of the philosopher. Mine is the whole majestic past, and mine is the shining future.[4]

By contrast, other writers—tougher, harder-boiled than Antin—focused on the arithmetic of poverty and pluck that made for picaresque anti-heroes such as the Meyer Hirsch of Samuel

Ornitz's *Haunch, Paunch and Jowl* (1923). As Ornitz's shocking exposé would have it, adaptability—rather than Antin's brand of idealism—is what immigrant Jewish youngsters learned best, first in the street gangs of their crowded tenement neighborhoods, and then in the labyrinthian corruption of the court system. Learning to live by one's wits meant not only survival, but also—at least in the case of Meyer Hirsch—a steady stream of promotions.

Antin and Ornitz make for interesting points of comparison, not only in the diametrically opposed visions they held as young writers, but also in the respective ways their subsequent lives unfolded. Antin graduated from Barnard College and later married the son of a Lutheran minister. Granted, she often wondered "if the conversion of the Jew to any alien belief or disbelief is ever thoroughly accomplished" (and in a certain sense, the very impulse to write *The Promised Land* is a reflection of this ambivalence); yet, it wasn't until the rise of Adolph Hitler that Antin was moved to acknowledge her kinship with the people of Israel. She died in 1949, having lived through the great wave of Russian Jewish immigration, the Holocaust, and the establishment of the state of Israel. However, her testimonial to America remained essentially the same as it was in 1912, when she first announced her "rebirth" and went on, in *The Promised Land,* to chronicle it. By contrast, Samuel Ornitz made his way to Hollywood, where a scriptwriter, if he were clever, might make a wage that eluded most novelists. In large measure, Hollywood turned out to be congenial to both Ornitz's talent and his temperament—that is, until the chilly political climate of the 1950s, with its cold war and red scares, its House Un-American Activities Committee and Senator Joseph McCarthy forced him to trade a modest reputation as a journeyman screenwriter for the martyrdom and notoriety that came with being one of the Hollywood Ten.

But that is to jump ahead of our story. During the years that the David Levinskys and the Meyer Hirsches were trying so desperately to move from greenhorn to "alrightnik," from press-er to cutter, from runner to political "aide," a group of young American writers—T. S. Eliot, Ernest Hemingway, John Dos Passos, Archibald MacLeish—made their collective way across an ocean the Jewish immigrants had recently crossed. Give or take a few years and they might well have waved to each other as they crossed the ocean—the restless and disillusioned on one side; the eager and the ambitious on the other.

By any measure, the American expatriates of the 1920s were a talented, restless bunch. Many of them were in flight from the Midwest and the middle-class values it so smugly, so unquestionably, stood for. When Ernest Hemingway reputedly described the well-heeled Oak Park, Illinois, of his childhood as a place of "wide lawns and narrow minds," he might well have been speaking for all those eager to give Main Street the Bronx cheer and the Champs Élysée a respectful *bon jour*.

However, given their situation as expatriates, as "outsiders," as members of what Gertrude Stein called "the lost generation," it is hardly surprising that their art would, in effect, turn the established order upside down by focusing on codes of behavior and significant gestures that either made somebody "one of us" or that, conversely, consigned him or her to a life beyond the pale. Robert Cohn, the Jew-as-outsider in Hemingway's *Sun Also Rises,* stands as a mean-spirited, textbook case of the phenomenon: a sloppy romantic, a whiner par excellence, and, worst of all, a man who acts badly under pressure. Cohn, in short, spoils his chances, and to the Lost Generation crowd—who knew how to slosh down a drink or appreciate a bullfight or treat a broad such as Brett Ashley—he had all of the *schlemiel's* essential parts but his warmth.

Like much that separates Hemingway from T. S. Eliot, the way they responded to Jewish characters or to a growing Jewish "influence" in the arts suggests much about their respective backgrounds. Hemingway's cultural anti-Semitism was an inheritance, something one simply acquired in those times, in those places. It was, in large measure, neither the result of experience nor the consequence of systematic thought. To be sure, immigrant energy may well have threatened the orderly world Hemingway felt so ambivalent about, but he was more interested in the inappropriate uses to which a spoiled Cohn put Princeton boxing lessons than in why he took them in the first place. By contrast, the anti-Semitic brushstrokes in Eliot's poetry (e.g., "Bleistein with a Baedeaker") and in his essays reflect a view in which the very traditions of English culture—its Christian moral values, its essential conservativism, its literary tradition—must be protected from the undue, and unsavory, influence of the Jews. For Eliot, the self-appointed Anglophile "protector," Jews were despoilers, rather than *schlemiels*. One—that is, if the one were Eliot—could easily imagine their corrupting modernity debasing *everything*.

Indeed, among the major modernists, only James Joyce was sufficiently "marginal" himself—as a Dubliner in exile from his family, his church, his state—to fully imagine a protagonist such as Leopold Bloom. For while Bloom may be many things—including the anti-heroic, modern equivalent of Odysseus, as well as the representative modern man—he is also the quintessential *schlemiel.* He is, in short, the architect of his comic misfortunes. But that said, one wants to hasten to add that he is also the man whose humanity ultimately triumphs over his *tsoris*—over the small-minded Dublin world he travels through on 16 June 1904; over the phallic power of a Blazes Boylan; over the elemental Molly Bloom.

It is easy to see, however, how a humor of failure—whether it revolves around a Tevye or a Bloom—would seem out of place to those newly arrived in the "land of opportunity." To the immigrant sensibility, stories about *schlemiels* and *schlimazls* seemed "un-American," and for those who wanted to avoid the tag of "greenhorn," this was a serious charge indeed. Moreover, as Freudian psychology began to shape the very atmosphere of twentieth-century life, it became harder and harder to believe that anybody could really be a *schlimazl*—that is, a person not really responsible for his bad luck. Among the disparate elements that the Yiddish world could incorporate were homespun versions of astrology, especially those that accounted for somebody born under a "bad star." Fate had dealt the *schlimazl* his comic hand. By contrast, modern readers quickly learned that "accidents" are not really accidents at all, and the *schlemiel* who had been the cause of his misfortune tended to merge with the *schlimazl* who had not.

In the 1930s, the proletarian novel gave a number of American Jewish authors the chance to talk about the ways a "golden dream" had turned color only a short decade or two after the engagement. Perhaps the best-known example of the genre is Michael Gold's *Jews Without Money* (1930), a loose collection of portraits/vignettes of tenement life on New York's squalid lower East Side. For many critics, it was the first important example of proletarian fiction from an American Jewish perspective. But while it is true that Gold's ideological heart belonged to the Kremlin, and that he kept the radical faith in pieces he published for the *Daily Worker* and *New Masses,* the influential Communist journal he edited, it is also true that the book is more poignant than it is doctrinaire, more inclined toward sentimentality than revolution. This is particularly true when one balances the bulk of the scenes in *Jews Without Money* against the oratory of its conclusion. Mikey, Gold's protagonist and spokesman, ends the novel by equating the revolution with "the true Messiah," but we are not likely to be convinced. Gold's editorial pronouncements may justify such emotions, but for better or worse, his novel does not. We feel an arbitrary, insistent—even perhaps ambivalent—hand at work.

Nonetheless, some things about proletarian fiction were clear indeed: the seriousness of its subject matter foreclosed the possibility of humor; the earnestness of propaganda elbowed out the ironic quips of the traditional *schlemiel;* and Jewish tradition—in both its cultural and religious senses—was seen as incompatible with the new social consciousness.

Even the novels of the period that did not look as if they were written with Marx in one hand and Engles in the other were generally unsympathetic to the assumptions of an older Yiddish literature. Henry Roth's *Call It Sleep* (1934), for example, owes far more of its lyrical texture, its aesthetic detachment, its stream-of-consciousness to James Joyce than to Sholem Aleichem. When Roth describes David Schearl, the novel's young protagonist, standing before the kitchen sink of his tenement apartment, the scene—with only minor alterations—might have taken place in the Dublin of Stephen Dedalus: "This world had been created without thought of him. He was thirsty, but the iron hip of the sink rested on legs tall almost as his own body, and by no stretch of arm, no leap, could he ever reach the distant tap. Where did the water come from that lurked so secretly in the curve of the brass? Where did it go, gurgling in the drain? What strange world must be hidden behind the walls of a house!"[5]

Since its celebrated "rediscovery" in 1964, who would quarrel with Liz Harris's claim that *Call It Sleep* is "surely the most lyrically authentic novel in American literature about a young boy's coming to consciousness, and arguably the most distinguished work of fiction ever written about immigrant life"?[6] In its day, of course, *Call It Sleep* was lumped into the large, slippery category of proletarian fiction, despite the fact that its portrait of urban squalor counted for less than its rendering of Freudian psychology, and its sense of "political awakening" was muted by the fact that its protagonist was only eight years old when he experienced the "strangest triumph, strangest acquiescence" that is the novel's final epiphany.

For our purposes, however, what may loom more importantly is the substitution of tragic formula for self-deprecating humor. Albert Schearl's deepest nightmare—and the source of his relentless paranoia—is that he may have been cuckolded, that David may not be his legitimate son. And while the novel resists a clear answer, the Oedipal tensions that result are painfully, vividly rendered. Such comic relief as there is in a novel filled with dislocation, with terror, with vaguely mystical yearnings, and with floating guilts is provided by an oversized Aunt Bertha and the candy store that, for her, represents Eden incarnate.

Curiously enough, 1934 was also the year of Nathanael West's *Cool Million,* a novel that set about dismantling myths about the American Dream by dismantling a naïve, protagonist named Lemuel Pitkin. As his first name suggests, this Lemuel is a distant cousin of Swift's gullible protagonist, one who leaves his home with thirty dollars and an unshakeable belief that "this is the land of opportunity." The result, of course, is a bitter reversal of the typical Horatio Alger scenario; rather than finding his fortune, Pitkin moves from one disaster to another: his teeth are pulled, his right eye is removed, his leg is amputated. He is scalped and finally killed—all in the name of "the right of every American boy to go out into the world and there receive fair play and a chance to make his fortune in industry and probity without being laughed at or conspired against by sophisticated aliens."

Given a Pitkin who sees no connection between his ineptitude and his resulting misfortunes, *schlemiel* seems the proper word to write West's protagonist down. But one hastens to add that here is a *schlemiel* who never had a chance, so stacked, and so bitter, were West's cards against him. Put another way: the terms of *A Cool Million*'s parody are quickly established, and one soon tires of the repetitious pratfall. There is none of the ironic humor here that characterized Tevye's claim that "with God's help I starved three times a day," none of the charm that turned classical *schlemiels* into beautiful losers.

In his more famous novels—say, *Miss Lonelyhearts* (1933) or *The Day of the Locust* (1939)—West couples accident and failure with tougher-minded assessments of the American condition. In *The Day of the Locust,* for example, Hollywood is portrayed as a land filled to overflowing with *schlemiels* of every sort. Indeed, Hollywood is the great mythical West to which people gravitate with their dreams. But sunshine and navel oranges only deepen the despair; and in that final tableau of terror—toward which the novel points from its opening page—the mobs rush you, the locusts devour the Pharaoh's land, and the Apocalypse unleashes its full, psychic fury.

Miss Lonelyhearts has much the same message, although here the grotesques of suffering come via airmail. Like Pitkin, "Miss Lonelyhearts"—the reluctant writer of a "sob sister" column for a newspaper—is a knight in a rigged cause. The more he relates to the suffering of his readers, the more he suffers "accidents" of his own: he is knocked down in taverns, mocked unmercifully by his boss (whose name, "Shrike," suggests the butcher-bird who impales his victims on thorns), and finally killed (mistakenly, ironically) by a jealous husband who misconstrues his intentions.

West died prematurely, the victim of a car accident, in 1940. At the time, he was thirty-seven years-old and had written four novels. During his lifetime West was numbered among those writers with an affection for the grotesque, for the savagely satiric—in short, for the surrealistic. However, in the decades that followed his death, West emerged as an important "influence" for many American Jewish fictionists—this, despite the fact that he took considerable pains to distance himself from Jewishness. Nonetheless, in a novel such as Edward Louis Wallant's *Pawnbroker* (1962), the affinities with *Miss Lonelyhearts* are unmistakable. What West may have lacked in terms of a relation to traditional Jewish materials or to a distinctively Jewish vision, postwar writers were quick to fill in. Perhaps West signals an end to that period of assimilation among American Jewish writers in which joining non-Jewish fraternities at Brown University loomed as more important than confronting the implications of one's identity closer to home. In any event, Jewishness must have struck West as impossibly parochial, as delimiting both the scope and the bite of the fiction he wanted to write. For him, Nathanael Wallenstein Weinstein was a name that cried out for changing, and remembering the advice of Horace Greeley, he "went West" with a vengeance.

But to talk about how critics and fellow writers went about reconsidering West during the heyday of the American Jewish renaissance is to leap ahead of the chronological story. During the 1930s, novelists such as Meyer Levin and Daniel Fuchs were still writing about their respective neighborhoods—Chicago for Levin; Williamsburg for Fuchs—and trying to figure out if one's world was Jewish, American, or a tenuous combination of the two. For example, a novel such as Levin's *The Old Bunch* (1937), allows us to follow the diverse paths that a group of some twenty boys and girls from Chicago's West Side (the "old bunch") take on their respective odysseys through American culture. By contrast, Fuchs's *Williamsburg Trilogy* (1934–1937) is largely restricted to the bustling, colorful, often eccentric life of tenement Brooklyn. Indeed, as Allen Guttmann argues, "Daniel Fuchs was the first to take apart the world of Sholom Aleichem's Kasrilevka and to reconstruct it on the sidewalks of New York."[7] There are, to be sure, *schlemiels* aplenty in *The Williamsburg Trilogy*, although the term tends to define those who dream rather than hold down "regular jobs," and especially those who specialize in harebrained inventions:

"You and your ideas!" Ruth said, her eyes glistening with tears. "You've got a million ideas and you ain't even got a job. You wanted the subways to put in radio sets so that the people they shouldn't get bored riding in the trains. You wanted to open a nation-wide chain of soft-drink stands from coast to coast, only they should sell hot chicken soup. In cups. You wanted to invent a self-sustaining parachute for people to stay up in the air as long as they felt like. Every idea you got is going to make a million dollars apiece, but you ain't got a job, you ain't got a penny, all you got is a million ideas."[8]

A purist might argue that such descriptions better fit the *luftmentch* than they do the *schlemiel*. But no matter. In America, terms of disparagement—be they *nudnik* or *luftmentch, schlemiel* or *naar*—were simply that: terms of disapproval. Dreamers belonged in the Old Country or on the Yiddish stage—indeed, anywhere but in one's living room.

After World War II, however, high seriousness—be it ideological or economic, a function of one's revolutionary consciousness or of one's assimilation—gave way to more ill-defined feelings that could best be captured by the creation of psychological *schlemiels*. Granted, economic problems had never led to the rich panoply of *schlemiels* that were such an important component of Yiddish humor, but they were usually at the forefront of American Jewish fiction. Until the thirties, novels had talked about "making it" in America in chronicles extolling the virtues of capitalism and the value of hard work. During the Great Depression, proletarian novels shifted the emphasis to social reform and more equitable ways of dividing the wealth. However, as American Jewry moved en masse to the suburbs—and in ways that *shtetl* Jewry never could have imagined, even in the wildest dreams of their *luftmentchen*—competition gradually replaced survival both as a concern and as an occasion for humor. During the 1950s, alienation declined in something like a direct proportion to one's stake in the System. The result—at least on literary fronts—was the creation of a *schlemiel* who tends to see his problem, but not much of a solution. His dilemma is, in short, psychological. If the traditional *schlemiel* adopted an ironic posture to face a world he could not beat (but also could not quit), his contemporary counterpart finds himself living on the bare edge of things, embracing darkly comic thoughts of failure at the very moment he is committed to systems of success.

The greatest differences, however, lie in the arena of action. Stories about traditional *schlemiels* were never psychologically oriented—that is, a person was a *schlemiel* by virtue of what he "did," not by what he might have *thought*. In this important sense, there are no "inner lives" in characters such as Tevye or Menahem-Mendl, but rather a sense in which the psychology of the characters is revealed through external action. In contemporary novels, however, *schlemiels* tend to be characters of attitude—people who think they are inadequate regardless of their actual condition. Moses Herzog, for example, is doing better than a good many academics, but he continually thinks of himself in the terminology of failure—not only as a bad husband and father but also as an indifferent citizen and an ineffectual scholar. His posture as the "suffering joker"—coupled with his ability to maintain a certain amount of good cheer about it—typifies the contemporary *schlemiel*. Thus, Herzog can return to his crumbling house in the Berkshires (bought with the hard-earned dollars he inherited from Papa Herzog), give it a hard, uncompromising look, let the assorted ironies of his disastrous domestic situation (including its cuckoldry) sink in, and say: "*Hineni!*" ("Here I am!"). Given all that he is, all that he has become, Herzog cannot *not* think without allusions—in this case, to the "*Hineni*" that the biblical patriarchs traditionally uttered when they heard God's call.

In the chapters that follow I will discuss versions of contemporary *schlemiel* hood in more detail, by concentrating on selected works by Isaac Bashevis Singer, Bernard Malamud, Saul Bellow, Philip Roth, and Woody Allen. No doubt other writers might have worked as well, but I happily leave the telling of their sagas to others. And as for any guilts, I leave those to jokes about the bar-mitzvah boy who wore his new red shirt rather than a new blue one, or about the Jewish mother who doesn't mind—"you shouldn't worry"—about sitting in the dark.

4
The Isolated *Schlemiels* of Isaac Bashevis Singer

> *Going from place to place, eating at strange tables, it often happens that I spin yarns— improbable things that could never have happened—about devils, magicians, windmills, and the like.*
>
> —*"Gimpel the Fool"*

"Devils, magicians, windmills, and the like"—these are the elements we have come to expect in the fiction of I. B. Singer, almost as if the flesh of the epigraph were the flesh of Gimpel, but its essential spirit is the spirit of Singer. Since 1935, he has been eating at the "strange tables" of America, with bizarre tales of *shtetl* Europe as his meal ticket. That he has so long been a fixture in American letters is as much a fact as his sixty-odd books (ranging from novels both thick and slender through memoirs and meditations on theology to collection after hard-backed collection of short stories). He is, in short, one of our most prolific writers and surely one of our most honored. His two National Book Awards and the 1978 Nobel Prize for literature head a list that, like his bibliography, runs for several pages.

American readers find this simultaneously exotic and discon-certing. It is not simply that he continues to write in Yiddish—an appropriate language, Singer quips, for ghost stories—or even that he severely restricts his tales to an immigrant's America. These facts, characteristic though they may be of Singer's fictive world, hardly begin to exhaust what makes his self-imposed isolation so darkly comic.

Not since Mark Twain has a writer made for such good newspaper copy, been so armed with the "quotable." If Singer is an anomaly, he is also a charmer. When his stories first began appearing in national magazines such as the *New Yorker* or *Playboy*, much was made of the fact that Singer was *sui generis*, that his work was translated and published without ever appearing in its original Yiddish, that he re-created an all-but-forgotten world of nineteenth-century Jewry in roughly the same way that a Hawthorne reimagined the world of New England Puritanism. Add other touches—his vegetarianism, for example, or his deep commitment to what struck most readers as an old-fashioned (that is, non-Freudian, nonmodernist) aesthetic—and the result turned Singer into that rarest of birds: a best seller the literary critics took seriously.

And yet, for all the discussion about the curious differences between Singer and his American readership, several important considerations were overlooked. Although steadfastly loyal sub-scribers to the *Jewish Forward* (where Singer continues to pub-lish—in Yiddish, and under a variety of pseudonyms) would be quick to disagree, the convulsions of history have turned him into a Yiddish writer without a Yiddish *takhlis*. For those reared in an American tradition where "artists," almost by definition, must be unappreciated before they can, later, be rediscovered (one thinks of Melville, of Poe, of countless others), the very notion of a warm, reciprocal relationship between author and audience smacks of blasphemy. Granted, there are exceptions— Americans have always held Emerson in high regard, although for widely differing reasons, and Mark Twain surely qualifies as a "national writer," one able to be appreciated across an entire spectrum of sociocultural grids—but the more normal case places a special trust between a serious (i.e., demanding) writer and his small band of ardent boosters. However, should that "trust" be broken, should our favorite find his or her way onto the best seller list and the cover of *Time* (thus, of course, becoming *everyone's* favorite), higher brows cannot help but feel a bit cheated, a little betrayed.

This problem simply did not exist for the Yiddish writer. His was an intimate relationship with the *folkmentsh,* and if the literature that resulted was not always *by* the folk, it was at least *of* and *for* them. As Joseph C. Landis puts it: "The Yiddish writer could observe all the defects of Jewish life, yet never feel himself alienated. Perhaps he perceived himself as in the larger sense a continuator of a prophetic tradition which might indeed excori-ate man's iniquities but never felt that it was either unheeded or defied with impunity. . . . The Yiddish writer, part of the mighty moral stream, never felt that he was a voice crying out in the wilderness."[1] To these sentiments, a critic more at home with an American tradition might reply—as Michael Fixler does—that

Yiddish literature is "provincial, often sentimental and appreciated almost exclusively by those for whom it was written."[2] Neither remark, however, tell us much about I. B. Singer. If the function, the *takhlis*, of writers such as Mendele or Sholom Aleichem was to give *Yiddishkeit* a fully rounded, human face, if their work was synonymous with a specific culture, a particular people, the Holocaust turned their world into an ashy smoke. Given the nightmare of twentieth-century history, to talk about the Yiddish writer's ability to sustain his audience, to lift their spirits, is to turn "sustenance" into a macabre joke.

In this regard, a typical Sholom Aleichem story such as "A Wedding Without Musicians" may be instructive. It concerns the reactions of a *shtetl* community to the threat of a pogrom. A trainload of soldiers is speeding toward their village, and rumors about the eventual onslaught are flying just as fast. At the railway yard, however, the cars are accidently uncoupled, and the whole affair turns out to be a "wedding without musicians," an engine that chugs into the *shtetl* with its "fists" left far behind. It is not hard to see why a Sholom Aleichem could envision such a story and an I. B. Singer—all too aware of how Nazi trains delivered their human cargo with deadly efficiency—cannot. In their introduction to *A Treasury of Yiddish Stories,* Irving Howe and Eliezer Greenberg put the problem this way: "The Yiddish prose writers of the past two or three decades have found it increasingly difficult to locate their subject matter. In America they find themselves trapped between two subjects: the old world that has been obliterated, the new world they do not always firmly command."[3]

In general, Yiddish fictionists have had more success looking backward. A novelist such as Chaim Grade (*The Agunah, The Yeshiva*) so reanimates that time, that place, of late nineteenth-century mittel-Europe one begins to feel what the ethical-ascetic grip of, say, the Musar movement must have been like. Nor is the renewed interest of a comfortably assimilated third generation limited to Yiddish writers. As I mentioned elsewhere, the rediscovery of *Call It Sleep,* Henry Roth's 1934 novel about New York City's lower East Side, represents an "index of accomplishment," a fashionable way of remembering what an earlier generation had been just as happy to escape, and to forget. In 1934, Roth's book pressed directly on the nerve in ways that must have made the novel a disturbing experience for American Jews trying hard to shed Yiddish accents and Old World customs.

Granted, *Call It Sleep* is still a terrifying novel, although now we tend to see the terror as having more to do with the protagonist's psyche, with his Oedipal complex, than with his social milieu. In this sense, *Fiddler on the Roof* makes the point about "Jewish roots" in less threatening, less complicated ways. Here is *mame-loshen* (the "mother tongue," or Yiddish) aplenty, with Hassidic dances directed by Jerome Robbins and songs straight from the heart of Tin Pan Alley. There is little doubt, I think, that Singer reaped the benefit of an atmosphere thick with Jewish nostalgia; it is equally true that his work strikes none of the chords so successfully exploited by those who make kitsch their business.

By contrast, Singer's *shtetl* is an emotionally charged, highly personal domain, the sort of fictive world we find in the stories of Nathaniel Hawthorne or in the novels that Faulkner spins about Yoknapatawpha County. In Singer's case, the vision he brings to his material—whether it be set in Eastern Europe or an immigrant's America, in Israel or South America—is as appealing as it is protean. Despite the very long arc of his career, Singer manages to remain simultaneously the shy *yeshivah* boy and the urbane sophisticate; he balances curiosity against skepticism, temporal obsessions against an eternity that looks, suspiciously, like faith. Above all, however, Singer's best work reminds us of that mysterious power that genuine stories always have. For all his justly deserved awards, none speaks as eloquently to his genius as the 1982 edition of *The Collected Stories of Isaac Bashevis Singer*. These short fictions—equally divided between the time-less and the time-bound, between a world tethered to faith and one surviving in anguished doubt—are our century's rhythms etched in a manageable, thoroughly human scale.

The typical Singer protagonist may wink with one eye, but the other remains wide open—exacting in its descriptive precision and its deeply human understanding. For example, in "The Captive" (included in *A Crown of Feathers*, 1973), a visit to Israel prompts this observation: "In the paper before me I read about thefts, car accidents, border shootings. One page was full of obituaries. No, the Messiah hadn't come yet. The Resurrection was not in sight. Orthopedic shoes were displayed in a shop across the way."

It is to such a world of maimed bodies and even more severely maimed psyches that Singer brings the ordering function of Art. As one character (in "The Briefcase") puts it: "What could a fiction writer add to the naked facts? Sensationalism and melodrama had become our daily diet. The unbelievable was all too believable." Granted, other contemporary writers suffer from the same dilemma (one thinks, for example, of Philip Roth bemoaning the ways in which the absurdities of Life outstrip the imaginative powers of Art or, more recently, of Tom Wolfe taking minimalists such as Raymond Carver or Ann Beattie to task for not writing bulky, realistic novels such as *The Bonfire of the Vanities*); but Singer keeps faith with his belief that the bizarre is as much a continuing surprise as it is a constant expectation. In "Lost," a character may *claim* that demons could not exist in New York ("Demons need a synagogue, a ritual bathhouse, a poorhouse, a garret with torn prayer books—all the paraphernalia you [Singer's narrator-persona] describe in your stories," but collections such as *A Crown of Feathers* are filled with evidence to the contrary. There may be a difference of "degree" between the Yiddish externals of, say, "The Lantuch" (which concerns an elfish demon in the *shtetl*) and the California ethos of "The Bishop's Robe," but there is precious little difference in *kind*. Fixed ideas—wherever they may reside—lead to the compulsive, lustful, irrationally obsessed behavior that is Singer's most congenial subject. Each collection merely added to the collective history of such characters.

There are, of course, other factors that account for Singer's isolation. If he staunchly refuses to cash in on the growing market for low-grade *mameloshen,* he is also unwilling to repeat the artistic formulae of earlier Yiddish writers. Put another way, Singer is a Yiddish writer, but one who does not fit easily within the traditions of Yiddish fiction. And to his Yiddish critics, this is blasphemy of the first water. As one of them put it: "We [i.e., Yiddishists] find Bashevis Singer enjoys a much more important place in American literature . . . than in Yiddish literature. The Yiddish reader is much less enthusiastic over Bashevis Singer's unpleasant stories than his non-Jewish readers."[4] Nor is this curious inhumanity of one Yiddishist to another limited by the boundaries of America. Yiddish scholar Elias Schulman reported, with no small satisfaction, that even in "faraway Moskow, Aaron Vergelis, editor of the monthly *Sovietish Heimland,* railed against Bashevis Singer for his sickly eroticism."[5] To be sure, this was a criticism of relatively small circulation, a case in which Yiddish writers, less successful than Singer, *kvetched* (complained) to the choir.

That changed quickly, dramatically, when Cynthia Ozick's story, "Envy, or Yiddish in America" appeared, first in the pages of *Commentary* magazine, and then in her hardcover collection, *The Pagan Rabbi and Other Stories* (1969). Ozick's thinly disguised story of Singer and his Yiddish critics brought the simmering resentments to a rapid boil. A Yiddish poet and the editor of an obscure Yiddish journal—one who writes sentimentally about love, the other who writes sentimentally about death—are joined in one thing alone: a mutual hatred of Ostrover (read, Singer), the upstart Yiddish fictionist who packs the YMHA when he gives a reading, who disarms university professors with his witticisms, who has a translator, an American publisher—in short, all the trappings of Success. The latter, of course, they never mention, but Ozick's deliciously satiric tone makes it abundantly clear that jealousy is conspicuous by its absence, and that they protest far too much about all the ways Ostrover/Singer misses the Yiddish mark:

> They hated him for the amazing thing that had happened to him— his fame—but this they never referred to. Instead they discussed his style: his Yiddish was impure, his sentences lacked grace and sweep, his paragraph transitions were amateur, vile. Or else they raged against his subject matter which was insanely sexual, pornographic, paranoid, freakish—men who embraced men, women who caressed women, sodomists of every variety, boys copulating with hens, butchers who drank blood for strength behind the knife.[6]

The issue, of course, is less whether one should regard Singer as primarily a Yiddish writer or as an American one, but, rather, whether he can treat certain themes without incurring the wrath of the rabbis and the more timid elements of the Jewish press. The "certain themes" are, not surprisingly, sexual ones, and the answer seems to be "no." Leslie Fiedler observes that "this is, of course, standard stuff, the sort of criticism continually made of Philip Roth or Allen Ginsberg; and we are surprised to find it directed against someone who writes in Yiddish."[7] In the days since Fiedler made those observations Singer has been awarded the Nobel Prize—always an occasion that encourages more Jewish pride than embarrassment—and Singer has, if anything, redoubled his efforts in the charm department. Only those who continue to follow Singer's fiction know that dark, iconoclastic beat goes on.

The bald truth of the matter is that any serious American Jewish fictionist soon becomes a veteran in the battle to free himself from an unwanted, unsought-after position in institutional Judaism's PR department, and with I. B. Singer, the Yiddish writer entered the fray, this time on American soil. In the old country, the charges were much the same, although there at least the sting of satire was confined to Jewish readers. Singer's very popularity threatened to widen the discussion in ways that made Yiddishists uncomfortable. They frankly worried about so much dirty linen appearing in the public lines of the *New Yorker* or the *New York Times*, and Jacob Glatstein speaks in a communal voice when he calls Singer "the first Yiddish writer to put his so-called heroes on the same level with the heroes in non-Jewish literature."

And so Singer finds himself plagued by requests that have nothing whatever to do with the fiction he actually writes. Yiddishists implore him to be a *mentsh,* while American academics secretly hope that he will move into the twentieth century so that his fiction will fit more easily into discussions of postmodernist theory. There is even a problem with his sympathetic readers, particularly among those who are fascinated by dybbuks and devils, and who see Singer as a prophet of the irrational and the thrillingly bizarre (i.e., tapping walls for wine and other bits of cabalistic chicanery). For them, the world of I. B. Singer has the *feel* of fourth-dimensional, hallucinatory experience—all of which leads to the chilling prospect of a generation that had deified Salinger's ersatz East now being replaced by a cult that worships Singer.

However, like Matthew Arnold, Singer might best be described as a man living between two worlds, "one dead, the other powerless to be born." Part of the problem is, of course, the problem of America. In "A Wedding in Brownsville," a character speculates about an upcoming wedding he has been asked to attend, and in the process, he levels a devastating shower of criticism against American Jewry: "Everything about such celebrations [i.e., the wedding] irritated him now; the Anglicized Yiddish, the Yiddishized English, the ear-splitting music and unruly dances. Jewish laws and customs were completely distorted; men who had no regard for Jewishness wore skullcaps and the reverend rabbis and cantors aped the Christian ministers."[8] Given the twin conditions of an authenticity forever lost and the pale carbon copy he finds in America, Singer—like Gimpel—is a man without a home, forced to go "from place to place," spinning the improbable yarns that will earn him a meal.

But that said, to understand the world that formed Singer—both in its assets and its liabilities, its creative nourishment and its severe restriction—one must take full account of the homogenizing force that Talmud/Torah exerted on the people of the *shtetl*. A mood of moderation—minutely specified and highly regulated—spread over every facet of life like a thick syrup. If Hawthorne re-created Puritan worlds where the premium was put on "faith," Singer's experience was not only a more direct, more existential encounter, but also one that placed the greatest emphasis on "deeds." What you did mattered greatly. Scholars turned their attention both to *mitsvos* (613 Divine Commandments given in the Torah) and *halakha* (legal portion of the Talmud) until the result was a manual for living that covered virtually every area of human behavior—from the proper way to tie one's shoes in the morning to the appropriate prayer said before falling asleep. There were, moreover, few (if any) viable alternatives for those unwilling to accept the yoke of law: an elaborate system of courts ruled on everything from the legality of a divorce to the *kashruth* (kosherness) of a chicken. It is this world of courts that Singer recounts in his autobiographical sketches entitled *In My Father's Court*.

However, what the book, for all its loving attention and obvious expertise, does not make clear is the deep ambivalence with which the young Singer viewed these activities. Trained in the *yeshivas* of Europe to be a rabbi, he turned instead to the emerging intellectual currents around him (in particular, Spinoza) and with the help of his older brother, the Yiddish fictionist I. J. Singer, made the fateful decision to become a writer himself. That he should, in effect, dedicate a book filled with nostalgic warmth to the memory of his father and his world of the *Beth-din* (the religious court) while he followed the literary example of his older brother (who often turns out to be a surrogate father in subsequent dedications) suggests divided loyalties at the deepest levels of consciousness.

American readers are, of course, familiar with the fictive re-creations we find in Hawthorne or Faulkner, and we recognize as well the value of reconstructed myth (Faulkner's South or Hawthorne's Puritan world) as pivotal to the tension that makes for great art. With Singer, however, the process of re-creating a *shtetl* world is complicated by the fact that Polish Jewry was virtually unchanged from the seventeenth to the twentieth centuries. What Singer experienced as a child was a world in the last terrible stages of flux, and before he could make a separate peace either with the Old or the New, the cunning of History turned Eastern European Jewry into a landscape of ghosts.

In this sense, Singer's fiction is an effort to ressurrect the Old Country he chose to leave by sketching with as fine a brush as possible the life that had existed there. It is, to be sure, a multifaceted portrait, one that surrounds realistic detail with skepticism, with doubt, and, above all else, with the nagging questions that are characteristic of great writers: Why were we born? Why do we suffer? What does Life mean? What constitutes truth?

If Mendele focuses on the Yiddish world's public aspirations and disappointments, Singer concentrates instead on the repressions and neurotic fantasies that lay just beneath its "official" sanctions. And while Singer is more comfortable with, say, the erotic mysticism of the Cabala than he is with the modernity of Freudian psychoanalysis, he hardly needed to hunt far for instances of bizarre behavior. Jewish law created its own *dybbuks*, its own brand of demons. And as Singer's first novel—*Satan in Goray* (1955)—suggests, the devil is a very busy, very operative figure, one who represents the collective unconscious of a people whose messianism could, at extreme moments, embrace that frenzy Gershom Scholem calls the "holiness of sin."

Given these historical pressures and their acceleration in the twentieth century, Singer's *schlemiels* tend to be characters duped not so much by their desires for worldly success, but rather by their faith in the world itself. What had served as a strategy of survival for Sholom Aleichem or Mendele—namely, the persistent tone of self-mockery and criticism—found itself transposed into a new, and I would argue, "modernist," key. As the *schlemiel* ish protagonist of Singer's "Gimpel the Fool" puts it: "No doubt the world is entirely an imaginary world, but it is only once removed from the true world. At the door of the hovel where I lie, there stands the plank on which the dead are taken away. . . . Another *schnorrer* is waiting to inherit my bed of straw. When the time comes I will go joyfully. Whatever may be there, it will be real, without complication, without ridicule, without deception. God be praised; there even Gimpel cannot be deceived (p. 21).[9] The echoes may suggest a loose Platonism, but the effect in Singer's canon points toward a more pervasive dichotomy between slavery and freedom, between a belief in a world that deceives and a life "without complication, without ridicule, without deception." In the Yiddish joke, the *schlemiel* is dogged by an ill luck, somehow of his own making. What the jokes celebrate—for all their pratfall and farce—are victories of common sense. Life's human comedy outstrips the illusion of man-made follies.

The Yiddish *schlemiel* was, in short, a corrective to pride and the impulse toward overreaching that have always been staple ingredients of Western literature. The very language militated against sententiousness, and was, instead, particularly good at pulling down the vanities of those who take themselves too seriously. After the Holocaust, however, it became difficult, if not impossible, to extend these techniques into the modern world, especially as the *schlemiel* became increasingly involved with life or death situations. Even Singer's stories for children reflect this change; for example, in "The First Schlemiel" (a modern version of a "Wise Men of Chelm" story), the emphasis is on an attempted suicide that is doomed, as it must be in a *schlemiel* story, to be a comic failure. Granted, "The First Schlemiel" is every bit as much responsible for his misfortune as previous *schlemiels*, but the net result is quite different. In this case, Singer's *schlemiel* plays out his comic role in a mistaken quest for death—a theme utterly foreign to the Yiddish humorist, but very much at the center of a modern drama such as Samuel Beckett's *Waiting for Godot.*

Singer, however, is drawn toward what Saul Bellow calls "the Death Question"—a matter earlier humorists had simply suspended on the grounds that their *takhlis* was to sustain the living and to celebrate "life." Even the nostalgic portraits of his life in Warsaw are filled with memories of death, with the shrouded and ghostly figures who plague his sensibility on the foreign soil of New York City. One of these sketches is called "The Suicide," and another one, "Reb Asher the Dairyman," ends on this note: "After we had left Warsaw [during the First World War], we continued to hear news of him [Reb Asher] from time to time. One son died, a daughter fell in love with a young man of low origins and Asher was deeply grieved. I do not know whether he lived to see the Nazi occupation of Warsaw. He probably died before that. But such Jews as he were dragged off to Treblinka. May these memoirs serve as a monument to him and his like, who lived in sanctity and died as martyrs."[10]

According to the *Jewish Encyclopedia*, one of the possible linguistic sources for the term *schlemiel* is the Hebrew phrase *sheluach min 'el*, generally translated as "sent away from God."[11] The phrase thus suggests exile and alienation, perhaps even scapegoatism, and it is easy to see how religious minds might connect recurrent bad luck with one who is out of God's graces. However, as the root words are used in biblical text, the more likely translation for the phrase would be "sent *from* God"—in the sense of biblical messenger. Like many expressions in modern Hebrew, the development of *sheluach min 'el* owes as much to usage as it does to formal linguistics; in any event, the ambivalence I'm suggesting has much to say about the way Singer's *schlemiels* actually work.

The most famous and certainly the most widely read of all Singer's works is still "Gimpel the Fool." Both Irving Howe (who helped to arrange its translation by Saul Bellow and its publication in *Partisan Review*) and Alfred Kazin have pointed out the similarities to Y. L. Peretz's "Bontsha the Silent," but neither critic has elaborated on the connections. For many American readers, the story of Bontsha is a heavy dose of Yiddish sentimentalism, the sort of unadulterated play to the emotions that makes for a parochial, second-rate product. As they might put it, Bontsha's signature, his leitmotif, if you will, is silent suffering: "He lived unknown, in silence, and in silence he died. He passed through our world, like a shadow. When Bontsha was born no one took a drink of wine; there was no sound of glasses clinking. When he was confirmed he made no speech of celebration. He existed like a grain of sand at the rim of a vast ocean, amid millions of other grains of sand exactly similar, and when the wind at last lifted him up and carried him across to the other shore of that ocean, no one noticed, no one at all."[12]

As a Yiddish Everyman, Bontsha thus crystallized the experiences and aspirations of a people who saw themselves reflected, all too clearly, in the mirror of his life. This is not to suggest, however, that Bontsha's readers were as isolated as he was; rather, it was Bontsha—orphaned and alone, silent and long-suffering—who became a convenient index for the *tsoris* of a people, if not of individual persons. Sholom Aleichem's humor cast an ironic yet loving eye at this world; Peretz tried to accomplish much the same result by projecting a sentimental gaze toward the next one—so it might seem to those not prone to reading the fable of Bontsha through a Yiddishist's eyes. For Bontsha's "silence," his extreme passivity, is less a cause for sentimental celebration than it is a call to action. Granted, life *is* crowded with others, and the human condition imposes sobering limitations, but Peretz's story, for all its folkloric character, remains committed to the activities, to the *words*, that would insist that "this world" can become a world more attractive. In this sense, Bontsha's life is less an emblem of suffering rewarded than it is a cautionary tale.

For contemporary writers (Saul Bellow, for example), the sheer weight of numbers—whether they are crowding into a subway train or competing for space in academic journals—is cause enough for despair. Bontsha, however, sees "others" as a necessary condition of life, one best dealt with in silence: "When Bontsha was brought to the hospital ten people were waiting for him to die and leave his narrow little cot; when he was brought from the hospital to the morgue twenty were waiting to occupy his pall; when he was taken out of the morgue forty were waiting to lie where he would lie forever. Who knows how many are now waiting to snatch from him that bit of earth?" (p. 224).

To be sure, the point of Bontsha's story is made in heaven rather than on earth. There, Bontsha's bottomless humility embarrasses even the angels when he answers their order to "Choose! Take whatever you want!" with a timid request for a hot roll and butter every morning. And like the Rabbi of Nemerov (in Peretz's famous story "If Not Higher"), the resulting tableau of Bontsha among the angels causes them to "bend their heads in shame at this "unending meekness they have created on earth." Because the story presumably endorses versions of holiness beyond even those sponsored by the official religion, it encourages its sentimental readings. But Bontsha's suffering was never meant to be equated with the symbolic sufferers one finds in the fiction of American Jewish writers such as Bernard Malamud or Edward Louis Wallant. If Bontsha is the saint-as-*mentsh*, if he is an extension of the *shtetl's* belief in the transitory nature of his life and the eternal justice of *Gan-Eyden* (literally, the Garden of Eden, and used to indicate a heavenly afterlife), he is also a study of passivity grown grotesque.

By contrast, Singer's Gimpel is simultaneously *schlemiel* and saint, the "*sheluach min 'el*"—the one "sent away from God"—and cast in the role of group joke. His "foolishness" is directly related to his naïveté, his willingness to believe even the most preposterous of *bobbemysehs* (literally, "grandmother's stories"): "They said, 'Gimpel, you know the rabbi's wife has been brought to childbed?' So I skipped school. Well, it turned out to be a lie. How was I supposed to know?" (p. 3). Unlike Bontsha, Gimpel responds to peer pressure in ways that follow the standard psychoanalytic line about sadomasochism to the letter. For his victimizers, the cruel sport is spoiled only by the fact that Gimpel makes such an easy target. On Gimpel's side, his endless rationalizations and verbal outbursts (no creature of silence he!) cannot disguise what we, and his analysts, recognize all too clearly. As Theodor Reik suggests, "Psychoanalysis would characterize a Shlemiel as a masochistic character who has the strong unconscious will to fail and spoil his chances."[13]

And yet, Gimpel also seems to be a man more sinned against than sinning where traditional elements of *schlemiel* hood are concerned. Granted, he later marries a woman whose virtue is less than doubtful, alternating between the roles of cuckold and father to her growing brood of illegitimate children. But for all this, Gimpel does not contribute to his failures in the way that more classical *schlemiels* did. Instead, Gimpel is the *schlemiel* as wise-fool, the satiric persona whose innocence becomes an indicator of the depravity that surrounds him. Critics—and particularly those well grounded in the traditional modes of Yiddish satire—have had difficulty with what they feel is an undue concentration on the grotesque and physically disgusting in Singer's stories: "His characters still seem always indecently carnal; man is caught in his animal functions of eating, drinking, lusting, displaying his body, copulating, evacuating, scratching. He is riddled with hideous and deforming diseases, most often venereal: the bone-ache, falling hair, a decayed nose, ulcerous teeth, boils, scruff . . . and any trace of the beautiful or the spiritual is always is in danger of being destroyed by the weight of this mere 'stuff.'[14] Although the passage quoted above tells us more about Gimpel's world than much of what passes as Singer criticism, it was not written about Gimpel specifically or even about Singer in general. Indeed, the quotation is taken from Alvin B. Kernan's seminal study of satiric technique, *The Cankered Muse*—the "his" refering to the fictive world of the satirist.

To be sure, Gimpel stubbornly maintains his belief in much the way that Bontsha kept his silence. As he puts it: "What's the good of *not* believing? Today it's your wife you don't believe; tomorrow it's God himself you won't take stock in." And here, despite the bleakness, the sheer *dreck*, that surrounds Gimpel, is where Singer and the traditional satirist part company. Unwilling to remain the mere butt of sadistic jokes, Gimpel turns his attention to the next world, shedding the skin of a man sent *away* from God in favor of a new role as the one sent *from* Him. Although "the schoolboys threw burrs" at his wedding and the House of Prayer "rang with laughter" at the circumcision of his illegitimate son (standard enough treatment for stereotypical *schlemiel*-cuckolds!), Gimpel remains characteristically saintlike: "I was no weakling. If I slapped someone, he'd see all the way to Cracow. But I'm really not a slugger by nature. I think to myself, let it pass. So they take advantage of me."

Whereas the traditional *schlemiel* is blissfully unaware of his comic difficulties, Gimpel prefers to leave the doors of imagination and metaphysical possibility wide open. At every turn of comic misfortune, every outlandish explanation given to justify deception, Gimpel steadfastly reaffirms that "everything is possible." When the town teases him, he counters with the notion that "a whole town can't go altogether crazy"; when he catches his wife in the very act of adultery, he refuses to shout because "he might wake the children"; and when his marriage produces six illegitimate children, he remembers the rabbi's words that "belief itself is beneficial."

But that said, if Gimpel is immune to the cruel vicissitudes of this world, he is more than impressed by the supernatural possibilities of the next one. And it is this dimension of devils and their ability to deceive that makes Singer's story more than a "Bontsha the Silent" in modern dress. For Peretz, the next world is a bastion of unbounded reward and an occasion for easy sentimentality; by contrast, Singer's vision is riddled with doubt. When the Spirit of Evil suggests that Gimpel "ought to deceive the world" by contaminating the bread of Frampol with filth, the prospect of revenge is tempting indeed.

Only the fear of judgment in the world to come stops him, and even this is systematically broken down by a devil who is infinitely better at hitting nerves than are Gimpel's earthly tormentors. Thus, when the devil finally convinces him that "there is no world to come," the notion of falsehood, of deception, takes a quarter turn, introducing new complexities at the very moment it destroys old fears: "They've sold you a bill of goods and talked you into believing you carried a cat in your belly. What nonsense!" For the Gimpel who had characterized himself as "the type that bears it and says nothing," the insight is shattering. After all, the falsehoods of this world—its pranks and perennial deceptions—are one thing, but those of the next are another matter altogether.

Thus, Gimpel's exchange with the devil resembles a negative catechism, the rude instruction that characters of initiation — one thinks of, say, Nick Adams in Hemingway's "Killers" or Ike McCaslin in Faulkner's "Bear" — receive as part of their growth into the ways of the modern world. Gimpel's learning differs only in its metaphysical directions and in the bizarre nature of his antagonist; otherwise, the scene has immediate parallels as its question/answer format moves toward insight:

"Well then," I said, "and is there a God?"
He answered, "There is no God either."
"What," I said, "is there, then?"
"A thick mire."   (P. 19)

But if the devil prompts Gimpel to vengeful action, the ghost of his dead wife urges him toward repudiation. As he waits for Frampol's urine-laden bread to rise, he is interrupted by visions of his wife Elka. At the moment of her death Gimpel had imagined that "dead as she was, she was saying, 'I deceived Gimpel. That was the meaning of my brief life.'" Now Elka returns from the world of Gehenna to trick him no longer: "You fool!" she said. "You fool. Because I was false is everything else false too? I never deceived anyone but myself."

Deception, then, is the leitmotif of Gimpel's story — from the devil's thesis ("the whole world deceives you") to its antithesis in Elka ("I never deceived anyone but myself"). However, Gimpel is less the synthesis that my Hegelian terminology might imply than he is an artist that *shtetl* life hurt into story. In this sense he functions as the *sheluach min 'el* — the *schlemiel* ostensibly "sent away from God" at the same time that his new understanding equips him for the role as the artful messenger "sent *from* God." For as Gimpel comes to discover, there "were really no lies": whatever doesn't really happen happens in the world of dreams and if not today, then tomorrow; if not tomorrow, then "a century hence if not next year." The result is a portrait of Gimpel as the wandering wiseman/storyteller, the artist-as-*Lamed Vovnik* (one of the thirty-six Righteous Men whose humble, and secret, piety sustains the world), the *schlemiel* who props up the world with fantastic stories instead of humble deeds.

The ambivalent qualities of the *sheluach min 'el* also help to explain why the protagonists of Singer's novels generally move beyond an alienation from God to a master/slave relationship.

Irving Buchen suggests that "in this arc which runs from free-dom to slavery . . . we may have a final way of reconciling his modernity and traditionalism as well as his realism and super-naturalism."[15] I suspect that Buchen is being overly optimistic about a "final reconciliation" among the disparate elements that make up Singer's fictive landscape, but I do think there is a conscious movement on his part from worlds of consensus (where they call you "fool") to worlds of the imagination (where they call you "Author!"). Wrenched from the definable context that had given birth to the traditional *schlemiel*, Singer's characters emerge as *schlemiels* of faith, created as their distance from God in-creases and altered (much like Gimpel) as it lessens. The *schlemiel* of Yiddish humor tended to blunder in socioeconomic situa-tions, mistaking his brand of reality for conditions as they actually were. In this sense he created — or at least contributed — to his own misfortune. Singer's *schlemiels*, however, tend to fail in more metaphysical arenas, confusing freedom with slavery, gen-uine faith with superficial doubt.

Yasha Mazur, the protagonist of *The Magician of Lublin*, begins as both master and slave. Ostensibly his movement has been away from the homogeneity of the ghetto and from God Himself. "Like every other magician, Yasha was held in small esteem by the community" — partly because of long-standing fears about magic per se, and partly because his profession had no *takhlis*. His ties to Orthodox Judaism are loose and, indeed, his entire relationship to the world of the *shtetl* might best be described as "marginal": "He wore no beard and went to synagogues only on Rosh Hashonah and Yom Kippur; that is, if he happened to be in Lublin at the time" (p. 1).

And yet, "it was risky to debate with him since he was no fool." Not only did he read Russian and Polish, but he was also informed about Jewish matters and "had even studied the Tal-mud as a boy." Not surprisingly, Yasha becomes an index of mystery to Lublin's more conventional citizens. To some, he was simply "a reckless man!" who "had once spent a whole night in the cemetery" to win a bet, challenging a whole structure of superstitions and the Evil Eye itself. However, the clearest po-larities about Yasha are those that crystallize deep-seated as-pects of the *shtetl* sensibility. Yasha may well have been a charac-ter who inspired ambivalent reactions on the part of Lublin residents, but to the Hassidim, for example, he was a person who "practiced black magic and owned a cap which made him

invisible, capable of squeezing through cracks in the wall"—
qualities, by the way, that betray their own belief in the mystical
and irrational. On the other hand, the Litvaks of Lublin (known
for their skepticism) said "he was merely the master of illusion."

Against this background of shifting cultural and religious
values, Yasha has a multiple identity in the best traditions of the
contemporary hero, his various guises moving outward in concentric circles. The result is a curious figure, "half Jew, half
Gentile—neither Jew nor Gentile." As Singer puts it, "It was one
of his [Yasha's] attributes to adjust to any character." And indeed, Yasha seems able to project an endless series of illusions—
to his professional audiences, to his paramours, to the townspeople of Lublin, and, not least of all, to himself.

Even Yasha's physical appearance foreshadows the Protean
character of his ambivalent personality; although he was forty
years old, he "looked ten years younger." Moreover," he was a
short man, broad-shouldered and lean-hipped; he had unruly
flaxen hair and watery blue eyes, thin lips, a narrow chin and a
short Slavic nose. His right eye was somewhat larger than his left,
and because of this he always seemed to be blinking with insolent
mockery" (p. 2). Among the many metaphorical tightropes he
walks is that thin line between youth and age, particularly when
his mind demands more than his body can perform. The novel
opens with a catalog of Yasha's physical skills: he "could flex his
body in any direction"; he "could walk on his hands, eat fire,
swallow swords, turn somersaults like a monkey"—in short, "no
one could duplicate his skill."

As a magician, then, Yasha has all the requisite credentials, but
as a man he finds himself attracted to mysteries that have no
marketable value. The cycle of nature, for example, gives rise to
a speech that reveals as much about Singer's preoccupations as it
does about Yasha's: "Every leaf and stalk had its inhabitant: a
worm, a bug, a gnat, creatures barely discernible to the naked
eye. . . . Where did they come from? How did they exist? What
did they do in the night? They died in winter, but, with summer,
the swarms came again. How did it happen?" (p. 3). The lines
strike contemporary readers as an echo of Holden Caulfield's
nagging concern about where the ducks in Central Park went,
although the thought of a Salinger-in-caftan is not usually the
sort of modernity one associates with I. B. Singer. Rather, Yasha's
reverie suggests the separation between his public role as magician and his private drift toward the transcendental. As the one

sent away from God, Yasha tends to link "concern" with sexual activity. He is more the traveling fertility god than the wandering magician, and many of his best performances are given in bed rather than on stage. But that said, Yasha is also the *sheluach min 'el* as man sent *from* God, the one who takes on the burdens of the world.

Much of his progress throughout the novel is a search for some sense of heightened emotion. As Yasha puts it: "It's all because I'm so bored," and indeed the notion of boredom is his recurrent leitmotif. If the *shtetl*—founded as it was on the official religion—embraced moderation as its dominant philosophy, Yasha yearns for extremes. He extends his dimensions of concerns-for-others like a series of concentric circles, reaching out to assume burdens well beyond the call of duty. His loyalty to Esther is a case in point, particularly when viewed from the *shtetl*'s perspective of home and hearth. Yasha may strike contemporary readers as decidedly less than a model husband, but that he continues to regard her as a wife at all is to defy the sexual codes of *shtetl* society. As Zborowsky and Herzog point out: "Like many shtetl prerogatives, divorce is available chiefly to the man. The primary ground is infertility, which is attributed to the woman. Conception is credited to him but if it fails to occur the blame is hers. If after ten years she has not borne a child he may divorce her and in fact is required to do so. There have been cases where a devoted couple were forced to part because they were childless. The social pressure was too much."[16] Like much of the sociology in *Life Is with People,* this reading both oversimplifies and overstates the case. But no matter, Singer's novel makes its own compelling, dramatic case. Esther—whose very name suggests loyalty and faithfulness—"had tried all sorts of remedies for barrenness," but to no avail. As the childless one, she has little status in Lublin society in much the same way that her husband is a virtual outcast because of his profession. Moreover, it was rumored that "God had sealed her womb"—thus providing a physical analog to Yasha's spiritual torment.

And yet, the seemingly irreligious Yasha is infinitely better for Esther than a more pious husband who might well have deserted her. Yasha's moral structure may be questionable, but he "always returned to her and always with some gift in hand." Esther captures the ambivalence of Yasha's twofold role when she thinks: "The eagerness with which he kissed and embraced her suggested that he had been living the life of a saint during his absence, but what could a mere woman know of the male appetite?" (p. 5). Yasha, of course, vacillates between the physical and the spiritual, creating his own brand of *schlemiel* hood in the process. He is both saint and sinner—committed to a profession as "magician" (the one who appears to control the natural world) at the same time he yearns to explain the ineffable. To be sure, the townspeople react to the mere results of his magicianship; Esther, however, had "witnessed the days and nights spent perfecting his paraphernalia." Even so, he was still "all sorcery" to her and "she had long since come to the conclusion that she would never be able to understand all his complexities. He possessed hidden powers; he had more secrets than the blessed Rosh Hashonah pomegranate has seeds" (p. 7).

By contrast, Yasha sees both his talent and his life as cursed by a vision that sees more than it can assimilate. Like his magic tricks that depended on "secret knowledge," Yasha feels that the world itself is governed by truths he alone understands. As he puts it, "The whole world acts out a farce because everyone is ashamed to say: I do not know." That he doesn't know either is, of course, his terrible wisdom, and Yasha finds himself secretly envying those with "unswerving faith," however misguided it might be. But if Yasha has doubts about matters metaphysical, he is on firmer footing where human psychology is concerned. When Schmul begins to doubt his magic and to accuse him of being a "master of deception," Yasha pushes the borders of "secret knowledge" to the bursting point:

"Who gives a man what you believe?" Yasha said, suddenly becoming wary. Schmul was nothing but a loudmouthed fool who could not think for himself. They see with their own eyes but don't believe, Yasha thought. As for Schmul's wife, Yentel, he knew something about her that would have driven that big blockhead insane. Well, everyone has something that he keeps to himself. Each person has his secrets. If the world had been informed of what went on inside him, he, Yasha, would long ago have been committed to a madhouse.   (P. 10)

Although he may well have the information necessary to drive Schmul to the madhouse, Yasha does not use it. And in a similar fashion, *The Magician of Lublin* often creates tensions that remain mute while always circumscribed by the limits of Yasha's sensibility. Rather than a world that, in fact, becomes an asylum (as is the case in contemporary American novels such as Ken

Kesey's *One Flew Over the Cuckoo's Nest*), Singer's vision is fastened to an inner life as it swings between the poles of absolute freedom and absolute slavery. As the one "sent away from God," Yasha is alternately repulsed and attracted by the world he sees from the vantage point of his alienation: "Married at fourteen or fifteen, they [the girls of Lublin] had become grandmothers in their thirties. Old age, prematurely invited, had puckered their faces, stolen their teeth, and left them benign and affectionate" (p. 12).

Of course Yasha's easy victory is qualified by the fact they have children when he (magician though he is) remains childless. In his description of Emilia, the Christian widow and one of his more serious paramours, Yasha creates the same sort of ambivalence: "In the darkness as he walked, Emilia's face loomed before him: olive-skinned, with black Jewish eyes, a Slavic turned-up nose, dimpled cheeks, a high forehead, the hair combed straight back, a dark fuzz shadowing the upper lip. She smiled, shy and lustful, and eyed him with an inquisitiveness both worldly and sisterly (p. 12). At least one critic was so taken with Emilia's "Jewish eyes"—carefully neglecting her "Slavic nose" and other contradictory physical equipment—that he turned her into a converted Jewess. However, Emilia represents a range of possibilities, from her upturned nose (snobbishness?) to the olive hue of her skin (passion?). At one point she "had presented Yasha with a volume on the Christian religion written by a professor of Theology, but the story of the immaculate conception and the explanation of the trinity—the Father, the Son and the Holy Ghost—seemed to Yasha even more unbelievable than the miracles which the Hassidim attributed to their rabbis. 'How can she believe this?' he asked himself?" (p. 15). Granted, "Jewish blood flowed in her veins," but her Jewishness is more nostalgic memory than tangible fact. On the other hand, her present Catholicism is both an intellectual and an emotional reality. She is, at one and the same time, "shy and lustful"; within the realm of possibility for Yasha the Magician and yet always outside of it for Yasha the Jew. Although she "was a Wolowsky on her mother's side and a great-grandchild of the famous Frankist Elisha Shur," Emilia is and always was a practicing Catholic, her name constantly suggesting a character out of Elizabethan theater. In short, their relationship is both adulterous and impossible, the very stuff that (according to Denis de Rougemont) makes for love in the Western world.

In Yasha's case, however, the adrenalin that results from such complications helps to counteract the boredom of life in Lublin. If the worldly aspects of Yasha's personality "had not been assuaged . . . through Emilia though he had tried," his more saintly characteristics must minister to her suffering and loneliness with at least an equal force. The result is to widen the dual meanings of *sheluach min 'el* until they encompass both *eros* and *agape*.

A scene from an early portion of the novel may help to explain Yasha's penchant for moral burden. Even as he thinks about returning to his adulterous affair with Emilia, the meditations of *eros* are interrupted by a more immediate situation calling for *agape:*

> Someone jostled him. It was Haskell, the water bearer, with two buckets of water on his yoke. He seemed to have sprung out of the earth. The red beard picked up glints of light from somewhere.
> "Haskell, is it you?"
> "Who else?"
> "Isn't it late to carry water?"
> "I need money for the holidays."
> Yasha rummaged in his pocket, found a twenty groshen piece. "Here, Haskell."
> Haskell bristled. "What's this? I don't take alms."
> "It's not alms, it's for your boy to buy himself a butter cookie."
> "All right, I'll take it—and thanks."
> And Haskell's dirty fingers intertwinted for a moment with Yasha's.   (P. 13)

The issue here is larger than "charity" can suggest. In the first place, the term is often confused with the Hebrew *tsedakah* (righteousness), a word that emphasizes responsibility rather than impulsive altruism. More important, the whole business of giving and taking pity at stake between Yasha and Haskell is reminiscent of the central pun in Bernard Malamud's story "Take Pity!" Not only does Yasha seek to preserve the other's dignity, but as their hands intertwine, he also takes on the burden of Haskell's suffering. Granted, the resulting tableau is a small moment, but it is symptomatic of Yasha's general behavior throughout the novel.

I ronically enough, the scene is also an index of Yasha's systematic degradation. With Haskell, Yasha could preserve both distance and involvement because the water bearer is simply another expression of the poverty that was the *shtetl's* status quo. Later in the novel, however, he meets a professional beggar, this time with traumatic results. As Yasha hobbles back from an abortive attempt to commit a robbery, he vacillates between the poles that push him away from God and those that pull him back: on one hand he had failed to crack an easily opened safe, "but what did that prove? That you were unnerved, exhausted, light-headed?"; while on the other hand, Yasha has a semi-mystical experience in a synagogue that leads him to feel that "he must be a Jew! A Jew like all the others!" Both possibilities merge as Yasha implores God to resolve the ambiguities that have become his defining mark: "He raised his eyes toward the pallid sky. If You want me to serve You, oh God, reveal Yourself, perform a miracle, let Your voice be heard, give me some sign, he said, under his breath."

But God sends neither sign nor words. Rather, Yasha is forced to confront a crippled beggar who is, in effect, his secret sharer, his surrogate brother:

Just then Yasha saw a cripple approaching. He was a small man and his beard, cocked to one side, *appeared* to be trying to tear itself loose from his neck. So also with his gnarled hands—they *seemed* about to crack from his wrists even while he was collecting alms. *Apparently* his legs had only one goal; to grow more twisted. His beard had the same contorted look and was in the act of tearing itself from his chin. Each finger was bent in a different direction, plucking, it *seemed,* an unseen fruit from an unseen tree. He moved in an unearthly jog, one foot in front of him, the other scraping and shuffling behind. A twisted tongue trailed from his twisted mouth, issuing between twisted teeth. Yasha took out a silver coin and sought to place it in the beggar's hand but found himself hampered by the odd contortions of the man. *Another magician? he thought, and felt a revulsion, an urge to flee.* He wished to throw the coin to the other as quickly as possible, but the cripple *apparently* had his own game—pushing closer, he sought to touch Yasha, like a leper determined to infect someone with his leprosy. . . . *He wanted to run but his own feet began to tremble and twitch as if imitating the cripple's.* (P. 126; italics mine)

As my italics suggest, it is illusion—apparent realities—that link Yasha to the crippled beggar. And finally it is the world itself that emerges as the greatest illusion of all. For Singer, the *schlemiel* pins his hope on the seeming realities of the world, on fantasies of a Faustian control over nature, or on his ability to manipulate magic. Yasha's movement in the novel is more than a progress from simplified concepts of freedom to equally simplified strattegies of slavery. Granted, Singer's protagonist may cover all these bases at one point or another, but his game has been carefully rigged from the beginning.

Consider, for example, the scenes that frame the novel in a complementing tableau. Yasha is often called upon to "give" in ways that transcend the financial. In a sense, he is the solitary artist consumed by problems that must be solved within the confines of his particular "craft or sullen art," but he is also an increasingly put-upon savior, a Yiddish version of Nathanael West's Miss Lonelyhearts, caught up in ever-widening spheres of responsibility. To Magda, his boyish assistant and sometime mistress, he represents the attention and security missed in her childhood. More than a mere lover, Yasha is a substitute father, the "magician" who can transform his physical defects into artistic virtues:

> She [Magda] was in her late twenties but appeared younger; audiences thought her no more than eighteen. Slight, swarthy, flat-chested, merely skin-and-bones, it was hard to believe that she was Elizabeta's child. Her eyes were grayish-green, her nose snub, her lips full and pouting as if ready to be kissed, or like those of a child about to cry. Her neck was long and thin, her hair ash-colored, the high cheekbones roseola-red. Her skin was pimply; at boarding school she had been nicknamed the Frog. She had been a surly, introspective schoolgirl with a furtive air, given to preposterous antics. Even then she had already proved unusually agile. She could scurry up a tree, master the latest dance, and, after lights out, leave the dormitory by way of the window and later return the same way. Magda still spoke of the boarding school as a hell hole. Inept at her studies, she had been taunted by her schoolmates because her father had been a smith; even her teachers had been hostile. . . . When her father died, Magda left the school without a diploma. Soon afterwards, Yasha hired her as his assistant.   (P. 23)

Even more than Yasha himself, Magda is only fully alive when she performs the complicated stunts of their circus act, and when it looks as if Yasha will leave her, she has no real alternative but suicide.

However, if Magda sees Yasha as the Good Father who can save her, her mother sees him as the wealthy Jew who can feed her. She "looked forward to Yasha's visits not only for her daughter's sake, but for her own as well. He always brought her something from Lublin: some delicatessen, liver, halvah, or store-bought pastry. But even more than the delicacies, she longed for someone with whom to converse" (p. 26). Yasha, on the other hand, enjoys the danger generated by his illicit affair, counteracting the notion of boredom with periodic shots of adrenalin. The metaphor of the tightrope—associated with his public career as well as his numerous paramours—becomes the symbolic shorthand of Yasha's *schlemiel* hood: "Funny, but he, Yasha, lived his whole life as if walking the tightrope, merely inches from disaster." But if life often suggests a "falling," Yasha's dreams are filled with fantasies of flight. As the danger of Bolek's attack (more imagined than real) magnifies itself into hysteria, Yasha "dreamt that he was flying. He rose above the ground and soared, soared. He wondered why he had not tried it before—it was so easy, so easy. He dreamt this almost every night, and each time awoke with the sensation that a distorted kind of reality had been revealed to him. . . . What a sensation it would cause throughout the world if he, Yasha, flew over the rooftops of Warsaw or better still—Rome, Paris, or London" (p. 30).

J. S. Wolkenfield points to this passage as an example of Yasha's "Faustian dreams of Power," but the emphasis seems more Messianic than Faustian.[17] The applause of "Rome, Paris, or London" is only part of Yasha's plan; ultimately even his fantasies return to the *shtetl*, to a heritage that colors his unconscious as much as its laws bind his public life in Lublin:

> Now, with a pair of artificial wings he flew over the capitals of the world. Multitudes of people ran through the streets, pointing, shouting and as he flew, he received messages by carrier pigeon—invitations from rulers, princes, cardinals. . . . He, Yasha, was no longer a magician, but a divine hypnotist who could control armies, heal the sick, flush criminals, locate buried treasures, and raise sunken ships from the depths. He, Yasha, had become the emperor of the entire world. . . . In his imagination he even let the Jews out of exile, gave them back the land of Israel, rebuilt the temple of Jerusalem. (P. 40)

But powerful as they are, Joseph-like dreams hardly exhaust Yasha's repertoire. His stock of mental tricks and tightropes is designed to shore up adrenaline against the enforced homogeneity that surrounds him. His profession—fraught as it is with danger—is a natural arena for playing out a wide assortment of fantasies, but Yasha does a convincing job of duplicating them in his private life as well. The sheer range of his women—from those who are socially acceptable to those who are not—suggest a penchant for living life at the extremes. It is precisely this sort of thinly veiled autobiography (the literary artist turned wandering storyteller or, better yet, circus magician) that provides Singer with a convenient metaphor against which he can play out his own ambivalent feelings about ghetto life. For Yasha, the women include his long-suffering wife, his boyish assistant, a high-class paramour, and an abandoned prostitute. Each provides a potential for complication, to say nothing of danger, and Yasha spends much of the novel living from such capital gains. The more illicit, threatening, or absurd the situation is, the better Yasha seems to like it. When he sleeps with Magda he thinks about her brother and his anti-Semitic threats: "One false move on his [Yasha's] part and Bolek would surely plunge a knife into her heart." When he arrives at Piask, he is drawn toward Zeftel, partly because of her pitiful condition, but mostly to heap yet another complication onto an already complicated life: "He came to her through back-alleys and gave her three ruble bills. He now carried a present for her from Warsaw—a coral necklace. It was madness. He had a wife, he had Magda, he was wildly infatuated with Emilia; what was he looking for on top of this dungheap?" (p. 33).

No doubt Yasha's obsessions are an attempt to live in the heightened imagination rather than the humdrum of life, although for Singer, one is never quite sure which realm is which. If Gimpel's progress toward transcendent knowledge makes the point that the poles ought to be reversed, perhaps Yasha's vacillation is the same theme played in a modified key.

For Yasha, the big moment (i.e., his ill-considered, and inept, foray into crime) comes when his fantasies impinge directly on his ability to act, when self-deception turns him into a *schlemiel*. Not surprisingly, his attempt to play lockpicker, rather than magician, is doomed in advance, but like the failure of all *schlemiels*, it is a self-created one. For example, Yasha imagines that "the old man lay in bed, his face completely covered in blood," although it is clear that the old man is merely sleeping. When Yasha finally realizes his mistake, he switches to yet another guilt-riddled metaphor, this time converting the entire apartment into a symbolic synagogue: "The windows faced the East." In short, Singer's magician is a bust as a confidence man: he makes a hasty exit only to hurt his leg in the fall and then manages to console himself with the thought that he "can live without a leg"—already assuming that he is suffering from gangrene. He flees from the scene of his abortive robbery, taking shelter in a synagogue—only to have the ritual fringes of his prayer shawl "lash him across the eye."

The ever-mounting "accidents" serve as concrete reminders that a change, a swing from the one sent away from God to the one sent from Him is in the air. As Yasha puts it: "Twice in one day there had been unveiled to him things which were best concealed. He had looked on the faces of death and lechery and had seen that they were the same. And even as he stood there staring, he knew that he was undergoing some sort of transformation, that he would never be the Yasha he had been" (p. 80). As it turns out, Yasha the Penitent is every bit as much a figure of isolation as the solitary magician had been. He remains, in short, a mystery to those around him—perhaps even more so than before. Instead of the lock-picking and card tricks that had so amused the Lublin riffraff, Yasha is reputed to be a *tsaddik* (a wonder-working holy man), and the crowds that had formerly come to be entertained by his "magic" now flock to be cured by his mysticism: "Yasha now received people daily from two until four in the afternoon. So as to avoid confusion, Esther wrote numbers on cardboard and distributed them, as it was done in the offices of busy physicians. . . . Before long there was talk in the city of the miracles performed by Yasha the Penitent. He only had to make a wish, it was rumored, and the sick grew well; it was said that a conscript had been pulled right out of the hands of the Russians, that a mute had regained speech, and a blind man his sight" (p. 189).

All this attention—at first unwanted, then tolerated, then accepted as part of his daily routine—has its effects on Yasha. Although his brick cell means the end to literal mobility, fantasies of flight continue undiminished: "He would think of new tricks to perform, new jokes with which to entertain audiences, new illusions and stunts with which to bewilder them. Again he danced on the tightrope, turned somersaults on the high wire, sailed over the rooftops of cities, trailed by a jubilant crowd" (p. 190).

There is a crucial difference, however, because Singer's most representative protagonists tend to move through the world of illusion until they come out on the other side. In *The Slave*, for example, Jacob moves toward a master/slave relationship with God because, paradoxically, it offers him more freedom than the illusions of freedom he had found on earth. Likewise, Gimpel lights out for even broader territories than Huck Finn when he finally realizes that his "foolishness" is simply a consensus opinion and little else. Ostensibly, Yasha has made much the same movement, but with some important caveats; he wants to have his egg cookie and eat it too. If he compulsively took on the burdens of the world as the wandering magician-savior, things have not changed greatly in his guise as a hermit-saint:" One after another they all came with their troubles. They spoke to Yasha the magician as if he were God: "My wife is sick. My son must go to the army. A competitor is outbidding me for a farm. My daughter has gone mad" (p. 191). Thus Yasha becomes a filter for the world's suffering, listening at the door of his cell to its *tsoris*. But in much the same way that he had confused theatrical effects with Messianic properties, Yasha now suffers for sins more imagined than real. And yet, with the possible exception of Magda, the various women he had "wronged" managed to survive, and even to *more* than survive: "Perhaps you remember Zeftel? She was the girl who was married to Leibush Lekach. . . . She's now a madam in Buenos Aires. Married some fellow named Herman. He left his wife for her. They own one of the biggest brothels" (p. 193). Indeed, Yasha may have had visions of deterministic justice—of a Zeftel abandoned and sick with disease—but this is simply to suggest that Yasha's illusions come in a variety of conventional packages. For Esther, Yasha is home, nevermore to roam after bigger audiences or new conquests. Moreover, in her case there is a certain amount of enviable notoriety connected with being the wife of Yasha the Penitent. She is no longer the same long-suffering, pitiable *hausfrau* she once was.

But it is Emilia who provides the sharpest, most ironic cut of them all. The novel ends with her letter to Yasha relating tales of newer "angels" and greener pastures since he has left the scene: "I could not have managed if (you recall my financial situation) an angel in human form had not come to our assistance, a friend of my dear departed husband, Professor Marjan Pydzewski. What he did for us cannot be related in one letter" (p. 200).

In important ways the double-sided nature of Singer's *sheluach min 'el* stands midway between the traditional Yiddish *schlemiel* and his rediscovery by contemporary American Jewish authors. What cannot be overemphasized, however, is the problematic condition built into Singer's aesthetic, not only because twentieth-century history raises serious questions about culture and survival, but also because Singer bristles when Yiddishists accuse him of crimes against their literary tradition. Even when he makes a conscious effort to re-create the bustling, vibrant Yiddish world that was destroyed by the Nazis—as he does in "traditional," three-decker historical romances such as *The Manor* (1967) or *The Estate* (1969)—what strikes one, again and again, is his capacity to render details vividly and particularly: the tufts of hair shooting out wildly from a character's chin, the hawk-like eyes of a *femme fatale,* and always, his utter openness to human experience in all its permutations. Unfortunately, Singer's descriptive powers have not generally fared well when translated to the silver screen. The film version of *The Magician of Lublin* is one case in point; Barbra Streisand's *Yentl* is another. However, Paul Mazursky's recent film, *Enemies, A Love Story*—based on Singer's novel of the same title—might well be the exception that proves the rule. There, the medium is not confined to period settings and costumes but, rather, to the visualization of what survivorhood and disorientation, obsession and sexual guilt, mean as they are etched into the faces and subtle gestures of its characters.

Nonetheless, I would argue that, beyond these general concerns, beyond even Singer's extraordinary talents as a storyteller, there is a desire to mediate between the world of men and the world of God. I have tried to show how the reputed fools in Singer's canon take on special qualities as they move toward an individual, and generally mystical, relationship with God. In recent years Singer has written a number of short stories in which a writer-narrator, one clearly modeled on himself, listens to characters who spill out their bizarre tales. Such a protagonist, drawn as he is to sit through sagas of sexual woes and other assorted griefs, has obvious affinities with the hapless *schlemiels* of earlier Yiddish writers. However, rather than belaboring these connections—especially since Singer is hardly a postmodernist writer given to experimentation for experimentation's sake—let me suggest, instead, that what seem either to be new directions or important refinements of older strategies are more likely to be minor variations of the *schlemiel* as *sheluach min 'el.* Like any serious writer, Singer is interested in posing the tough questions. In his case, they include not only the standard ones about why we are born, why we suffer, and why we die, but also those that speak to his special condition—namely, where can a Yiddish literature go without an audience to read it, without a *takhlis* to write it, without a living community to inspire it? Given all this, it is small wonder that Singer's work seems so obsessed with ghosts. And yet his protagonists believe—regardless of the evidence—that some adjustments can be made, that there are places where even a Gimpel cannot be deceived. Moreover, I would argue that Singer's *schlemiels,* isolated and perplexed though they may be, emerge as the best index of man's rage to justify God's ambiguous ways, and the ranges he will travel in that pursuit.

5
The *Schlemiel* as Moral Bungler: Bernard Malamud's Ironic Heroes

If a writer such as Isaac Bashevis Singer had to face the agonizing problem of re-creating a ghetto experience that had been too short-lived, Bernard Malamud and a host of other postwar American Jewish writers had to discover the boundaries of a heritage that, for them, had hardly lived at all. As J. C. Levinson suggests, "after Buchenwald and Hiroshima, fiction can hardly remain the same, and in the most interesting of our postwar novelists, it has indeed changed."[1] Nonetheless, the Holocaust remained a troubling subject for American Jewish writers: the prospect of confronting the six million Jewish dead—either in terms of literary metaphor or the gut response of socioreligious feeling—seemed so overwhelming, so intimidating, so resistant to the very enterprise of fiction-making that many preferred a numbed silence to the risks of trivializing an experience geography and good luck had spared them.

The result was yet another example of the cunning of history: American Jewish writers—traditionally caught in the private difficulty of defining both the terms of their "Americanness" and their particular brand of "Jewishness"—now found themselves called upon to hold forth on public issues at the very moment when they probably had no desire to speak at all. For a writer such as Bernard Malamud, the Jew became a natural symbol for the postwar sensibility, the index of an age questing belief on one hand, but wrenched out of religious contexts on the other. Thus, the Jews in his fiction emerged as "a type of metaphor . . . both for the tragic dimension of anyone's life and for a code of personal morality."[2]

Subsequent literary history made a case for the validity of such observations, but they always suggested that something akin to a

77

literary plot had been abrew: the Malamuds and Bellows of the world somehow hatching up the whole thing in a lower East Side delicatessen. Writing in *Commentary* magazine, critic Robert Alter sounded a cautionary note, one designed to have us focus on the aesthetic shortfall that can result "when a writer assigns a set of abstract moral values to the representatives of a particular group, the connection thus insisted on may strike the reader as arbitrary, an artistic confusion of actualities and ideals."[3] Granted, Alter's point is provocative enough on its terms, but even more so when one remembers that it was magazines such as *Commentary* that, in effect, created the general atmosphere in which talk about an "American Jewish renaissance" flourished. Alter's charge could, of course, be brought to bear against more writers than Bernard Malamud, but it is Malamud we tend to think of first. His Jews always appear from an offstage "nowhere," so filled with suffering that one imagines they have just changed clothes after a four-thousand-year trek across the desert. Moreover, we are asked to accept—yea, to *believe*—that this is an a priori state of being, part of the author's *donnée* beyond our questioning. The result was a significant shift in the way American Jewish writing was perceived—a thirties' concern with the "human" condition slowly evolved into a fifties' fascination with a "Jewish" one.

Granted, Malamud's most characteristic tensions are created in this confusion between actualities and ideals. The *schlemiel* may well have been a comic figure whose self-created failures became an index of socioeconomic limitatation, but such a character is out of place in arenas of affluence and endless mobility. Marcus Klein sees the change as one from novels of alienation (i.e., works in which characters of sensibility "protect" themselves by systematically moving beyond the boundaries of a hostile society) to those that evidence what he calls "accommodation."[4] Rather than, say, a Stephen Dedalus symbolically flapping his wings in the last lines of Joyce's *Portrait of the Artist as a Young Man* and dreaming about a bohemian life in Paris, the contemporary American writer found himself commuting from the suburbs, squarely within the System and only vaguely unhappy about the situation.

However, at the same time that writers were learning to accommodate, to preserve a measure of individuality beneath the folds of their gray flannel suiting, there was a growing concern about the larger moral issues attendant to the time. In some respects, the French Underground had it easier; their existential nausea was the result of a particular time, a particular place, and, most of all, a particularly charged condition. By contrast, American writers were anxious about their anxieties, partly because theirs were delayed until after the war, and partly because affluence simultaneously mutes and complicates the existentially troubled soul. For American Jewish writers, the figure of the *schlemiel* became a way of dealing with the more troubling aspects of this condition, a way of talking about moral transcendence rather than economic advancement.

In Malamud's case, the *schlemiel* tends to be a moral bungler, a character whose estimate of the situation, coupled with his overriding desire for "commitment," gives rise to a series of comic defeats. Indeed, Malamud's canon is filled with such *schlemiels,* from the early stories of *The Magic Barrel* (1958) and *Idiots First* (1963) to his *Pictures of Fidelman* (1969), *The Tenants* (1971), and *Rembrandt's Hat* (1973); from novels of comic suffering such as *The Assistant* (1957) or *A New Life* (1961) to *Dubin's Lives* (1979), *God's Grace* (1982) or the recently published, posthumous novel-in-progress, *The People* (1989).

Let me begin with "The Magic Barrel," a story that has long been regarded as quintessential Malamud—in form, in content, and most of all, in vision. Considered as a whole, "The Magic Barrel" is an initiation story, although the exact dimensions of its "initiation" are hard to pin down. It opens innocently enough— "Not long ago there lived in uptown New York, in a small, almost meager room, though crowded with books, Leo Finkle, a rabbinical student in the Yeshiva University"—as if to answer the objections of critics who continually demand that American Jewish literature be more Jewish and less like "literature." But for all its lower East Side touches—the Yiddishized diction and realistic local detail—Jewishness is as much a literary illusion in "The Magic Barrel" as Negro dialects are in *Adventures of Huckleberry Finn*. Like most of Malamud's protagonists, Leo Finkle's problem is an inability to love, a failure to link his isolation with the isolation of others. As a consequence, Finkle is initiated into "suffering" almost by accident. He "had been advised by an acquaintance that he might find it easier to win himself a congregation if he were married," so Finkle opens himself to eros, to *shadchens* (marriage brokers), and to his fate as a *schlemiel*. Initially, the rabbinical student is radically different from the mercurial matchmaker—Finkle represents the force of Law

while Salzman stands for the power of Flesh. And yet, Salzman—
for all his vulgarisms—betrays a "depth of sadness" that Finkle
uses as a convenient mirror for his own.

The progress of the moral *schlemiel* nearly always involves
identification with suffering and some strategy for taking on the
burdens of others. In Malamud's most earnestly serious novels,
similar movements are chronicled both with a straighter face
and a tongue more prone to lashing out at social injustice than
lodging ironically in its cheek. In this sense the *schlemiels* of
Malamud's canon bear a striking resemblance to the classical
folk figure; both desire to change the essential conditions of
their lives, but each is inadequate to the task. Comic misfortune
dogs their collective heels. In Finkle's case, sympathy is as much
his leitmotif as Salzman's is fish. Each of the "much-handled"
cards in Salzman's magic barrel represents a person whose
aloneness is a counterpart of his own.

Granted, Salzman is more pimp than "commercial cupid"—
regardless of Finkle's elaborate rationalizations about the honor-
able tradition of the *schadchen*. In fact, what Finkle really imagines is a world in which hundreds of cards—each one longing for
marriage—are churned about and finally brought together by
the indefatigable matchmaker's machinations. Finkle's *schlemiel*
hood is a function of his willingness to believe in such highly
romantic visions, and moreover, to replace them with new combi-
nations as quickly as old ones turn sour.

That Salzman plays the con man to such a willing dupe is
hardly surprising. After all, Finkle has the words "live one"
written all over his face. At a used-car lot he'd be looking
anxiously for an automobile; at a marriage broker's, he's desperately seeking a wife. So far as Salzman's sales pitches are concerned, the two commodities are virtually the same: "Sophie P.
Twenty-four years. Widow one year. No children. Educated high
school and two years college. Father promises eight thousand
dollars. Has wonderful wholesale business. Also real estate. On
the mother's side comes teachers, also one actor. Well known on
Second Avenue" (p. 196).[5] In this way, the juxtapositions of
Finkle's hesitation about "buying" and Salzman's aggressive brand
of "selling" create what might have been a purely comic situation. However, Finkle gradually begins to see Salzman's portfolio
as a microcosm of the world's suffering and his shoulders as the
proper place on which it might rest. What breaks down, of
course, are the very pillars of Finkle's world—the justifications of

Tradition, the pragmatic need for a wife, the commonsensical arguments for using a matchmaker in the first place.

Moreover, if the "much-handled cards" of Salzman's portfolio make it clear that others suffer the loneliness and indignation of being damaged, passed-over goods, Finkle's traumatic meeting with Lily Hirschorn forces him to realize, for the first time, "the true nature of his relationship to God, and from that it had come to him, with shocking force, that apart from his parents, he had never loved anyone" (p. 205). "The Magic Barrel" is a love story, one that operates simultaneously on the levels of eros and agape. That Finkle's "learning" leads him to admit his essentially love-less condition, his particular death of the heart, is a necessary precondition for the *schlemiel* hood that will follow. But Lily Hirschorn, important though she might be as a catalyst, is simply another frantic figure yoo-hooing after a life that had already passed her by. There are dozens of similar stories in Salzman's "magic barrel." Moreover, if Finkle had been conned by Salzman, so had Lily. After all, she expected to meet a biblical prophet, a man "enamored with God," and instead she found herself walking with a man incapable of passion either in the physical or the spiritual senses of the term. In the Finkle-Salzman-Hirschorn triangle, then, the end result is initiation; Finkle finds out how and what he is, and in the context of the story this information provides the tension, the essential ground condition, that moral bunglers are made of.

Stella, of course, provides the occasion. Unlike the typical Salzman portrait, Stella's dime-store photo suggested that she "had *lived,* or wanted to—more than just wanted, perhaps re-gretted how she had lived—had somehow deeply suffered" (p. 209). In a world where "suffering" is the standard for one-upmanship, she is the hands-down winner. A Lily Hirschorn may have wanted to live, Finkle himself has the urge to try, but it is Stella who has actually been there. And it is through the figure of Stella (her name suggesting the ironic star that guides Finkle's destiny) that the prospective rabbi hopes to "convert her to goodness, himself to God."

Thus, a new triangle is created: Finkle represents a tortured attempt to achieve spiritual resurrection; Salzman (variously characterized as Pan, Cupid, or other fertility figures) emerges as a Yiddish version of Creon; while Stella vacillates between the scarlet of her prostitution and the whiteness of her purity.

Indeed, it is Finkle's highly stylized movement toward Stella that turns him into a *schlemiel,* at least in the sense that his goal of spiritual regeneration is incommensurate with his activity. The result is a moral counterpart of more traditional stories in which the *schlemiel* aspires to financial success only to sow the seeds of his own destruction.

The concluding tableau crystallizes the matter of Finkle's "salvation" and/or "destruction" without providing the luxury of a clear reading direction. On one hand, Finkle runs toward Stella, seeking "in her, his own redemption" in ways that make this now passionate rabbi akin to the biblical Hosea. On the other hand, however, Salzman remains just "around the corner . . . chanting prayers for the dead." Is this *kaddish* for Finkle? For Stella? Or, perhaps, for Salzman himself? In much of Malamud's early fiction, ironic affirmations become an essential part of his aesthetic—as if movements toward moral change were not enough, but total regeneration is not possible. In Malamud's greatest stories—"The Angel Levine," "Take Pity!," "The Jew Bird"— moral allegories slip easily from the gritty surfaces of realistic detail to surrealistic fancy, and back again. At their most achieved they have the feel of Marc Chagall paintings.

The Assistant is cut from the same bolt of cloth (marked "Judaic suffering") that gave us the moral qualms of a Leo Finkle. In this case, however, Morris Bober's circumstances strike us as grounded in the quotidian detail of his failing grocery store rather than in the luxury of Finkle's self-consciousness. Unlike Finkle, Bober is neither the protagonist nor the moral filter of his tale. Rather, his suffering merely *is,* and it is the task of Frankie Alpine, his assistant, to learn what such suffering means and how it might apply to his own situation.

Granted, Frankie has what can only be called some curious notions about Judaism, but then again, Bober—for all his heartfelt sighs—may not be the best instructor. For example, at one point in the novel Bober claims that he suffers "for the Law," although it is hard to see precisely how Law—in the sense of the Torah's 613 Divine Commandments—operates in Morris's life. Rather, Bober is portrayed as a secular *tsaddick,* a righteous man who once "ran two blocks in the snow to give back five cents a customer forgot." His cachet is good deeds: the roll he provides to the sour, gray-haired, vaguely anti-Semitic Polish woman who wakes him up each morning; the endless credit he extends to the "drunk women"; and his insistence that he shovel his sidewalks on Sunday mornings because the snow "don't look so nice for the goyim that go to church."

And yet, the bulk of Bober's suffering is not circumscribed by economics or even by the harsh reality that "in a store you were entombed." Rather, it is the unspoken, often elusive failures of fatherhood that torment Bober's soul. In Malamud's world, people always seem out of breath from carrying too many bundles, both psychical and psychological; when they finally *do* rest for a glass of tea, we tend to believe in their long, soulful sighs, and to feel that the suffering is both earned and appropriate:

> Breitbart, the bulb peddler, laid down his two enormous cartons of light bulbs and diffidently entered the back. "Go in," Morris urged. He boiled up some tea and served it in a thick glass, with a slice of lemon. The peddler eased himself into a chair, derby hat and coat on, and gulped the hot tea, his Adam's apple bobbing.
> "So how goes now?" asked the grocer.
> "Slow," shrugged Brietbart.
> Morris sighed. "How is the boy?"
> Breitbart nodded absently, then picked up the Jewish paper and read. After ten minutes he got up, scratched all over, lifted across his thin shoulders the two large cartons tied together with clothesline and left.
> Morris watched him go.
> The world suffers. He felt every *schmerz*.
> At lunchtime Ida came down. He had cleaned the whole store.
> Morris was standing before the faded couch, looking out of the rear window at the backyards. He had been thinking of Ephraim.   (Pp. 6–7)

Jonathan Baumbach characterizes the novel as the intertwining biographies of surrogate fathers and surrogate sons. As he puts it, "*The Assistant* has two central biographies: the life and death of Morris Bober, unwitting saint, and the guilt and retribution of Frank Alpine, saint-elect, the first life creating the pattern and possibility of the second. At the end, as if by metamorphosis, the young Italian thief replaces the old Jewish storekeeper, the reborn son replacing the father."[6] In important ways, Bober's situation echoes that of *Ulysses'* Leopold Bloom although Ephraim is not Rudy, nor is Frankie Alpine Stephen Dedalus. What strikes us as similar, however, is the manner in which the respective "adoptions" take place.

Bober's suffering, of course, remains constant; it is a condition of his life and the necessary result of Ephraim's death. Frankie, on the other hand, vacillates between visions of absolute goodness and the reality of compulsive evil. What he needs are standards for moral behavior, of which the life of St. Francis is one and the life of Morris Bober is another. About St. Francis he says: "For instance he gave everything away that he owned, every cent, all his clothes off his back. He enjoyed to be poor. He said poverty was a queen and he loved her like a beautiful woman" (p. 31). He might well have been speaking about Bober, and indeed, as he grows into his role as "assistant," the distinction between the two figures gradually blurs. However, what Frankie really identifies with is a style of suffering, confusing his own masochism with the martyrs from his Catholic childhood and the Jewishness of his grocer boss. In this way he too becomes a moral *schlemiel,* the man whose estimate of the situation is as wrong-headed as his strategies for attaining moral perfection. What he desires is nothing short of sainthood, and in this respect, his movement toward Bober's brand of Jewishness parallels Finkle's attraction to Stella. Once again, the dovetailing of salvation and destruction becomes the index of Malamud's ironic affirmation, the comic result of *schlemiel* ish behavior.

But that said, let me hasten to add that Frankie does not immediately resemble the *schlemiels* one remembers from Yiddish jokes nor does Bober's "suffering" seem totally ironic. There is a sense in *The Assistant* that at least a part of Malamud is playing it straight, believing both in Bober's essential goodness and in Frankie's ability to learn from it. Things crystallize in the funeral scene, at the point where tensions begin to shift from the father/owner to his assistant/son. The Rabbi—unfamiliar with Bober and called in for the occasion—delivers the following eulogy at his graveside:

My dear friends, I never had the pleasure to meet the good grocery man that he now lays in his coffin. He lived in a neighborhood where I didn't come in. Still and all I talked this morning to people that knew him and I am now sorry that I didn't know him also. . . . All told me the same, that Morris Bober, who passed away so untimely—he caught double pneumonia from shoveling snow in front of his place of business so people could pass by on the sidewalk—was a man who couldn't be more honest. . . . Helen, his dear daughter, remembers from when she was a small girl that her father ran two blocks in the snow to give back to a poor Italian lady a nickel she forgot on the counter. Who runs in wintertime blocks in the snow without rubbers to protect his feet, two blocks in the snow to give back five cents that a customer forgot? . . . He was also a very hard worker, a man that never stopped working. How many mornings he got up in the dark and dressed himself in the cold, I can't count. . . . So besides being honest he was a good provider.

When a Jew dies, who asks if he is a Jew? He is a Jew, we don't ask. There are many ways to be a Jew. So if somebody comes to me and says, "Rabbi, shall we call such a man Jewish who lived and worked among gentiles and sold them pig meat, trayfe, that we don't eat, and not once in twenty years comes inside a synagogue, is such a man a Jew, rabbi?" To him I will say, "Yes, Morris Bober was to me a true Jew because he lived in the Jewish experience, which he remembered and with the Jewish heart." (Pp. 229–30)

I suspect that Bober might well be considered a prize *schlemiel* by those prone to give the passage a hard-boiled, ironic reading. After all, when the Rabbi asks, "Who runs in wintertime without a hat or coat?" the answer that springs to such minds is "a *schlemiel*, that's who!" Those more inclined to let the text formulate their responses will point out that while Bober might care about his customers, the fact is that they continually desert him for fancier food and lower prices. Indeed, at nearly every point in the rabbi's makeshift remarks the truth of the matter undercuts his well-meaning sentiments. For example, it is easier to number Bober among the Lamed Vov than it is to think of him as a "good provider." His daughter reads *Don Quixote* and dreams of worlds beyond the confines of the grocery store, at the same time blaming Bober for spoiling her chances. His wife simply complains—about business, about Helen's boyfriends, and finally about Bober himself.

Moreover, there is the sticky matter of Bober's "Jewishness." The rabbi's words of consolation may have cheered a good many American Jewish hearts who share much the same definition, but it hardly answers the question in a novel where "who" or "what" is a Jew looms as centrally important. For Bober, Jewishness is inextricably bound up with suffering, with a common humanity, of which Jews—bound by the Law—carry an inordinately large share. As I mentioned earlier, whatever Bober might mean by the Law, it is clearly not *Halakha* that he has in mind. As he puts it, "Nobody will tell me that I am not Jewish because I put in my mouth once in a while, when my tongue is dry, a piece of ham." The issue, he insists, boils down to who has the "Jewish heart," and when Frankie asks why Jews "suffer so damned much," Bober can only reply:

"They suffer because they are Jews."

"That's what I mean [Frankie counters], they suffer more than they have to.")

"If you live, you suffer. Some people suffer more, but not because they want. But I think if a Jew don't suffer for the Law, he will suffer for nothing."

"What do you suffer for, Morris?" Frank said.

"I suffer for you," Morris said calmly.   (P. 125)

Part of Bober's "mystery"—particularly to a disciple like Frankie—is the ambivalent quality of his instruction. All men suffer, but some Jews suffer in ways that are special and that smack of redemption. Moreover, the champion sufferers—those Frankie once described as having the ability to hold the pain in their gut the longest—apparently also come equipped with Jewish hearts. Granted, neither Frankie nor Morris is schooled in the theological niceties, but their ruminations raise certain questions nonetheless: Do Jews alone possess Jewish hearts? If not, can a non-Jew acquire one? And if so, how?

For Frankie, the answer seems clear enough: Morris "suffered," and to be like him, one must suffer in the same manner. "All men," Malamud is reputed to have once exclaimed, "are Jews," and one could offer up *The Assistant* as Exhibit A. However, for all his seeming folly, for all the personal goodness wasted and the unnecessary sufferings endured, Bober's life seems more a tragic commentary on the American Dream than an ironic joke about self-destruction. No matter how wrongheaded he might have been about his customers, his family, or his friends, Bober's life contained an essential dignity, a certain bittersweetness that justified his sighs and convinced us that they were significant.

The fate of his assistant is, however, quite another matter. In Frankie's first outing after Bober's death he makes a *schlemiel* out of himself—literally, tragi-comically, irrevocably: "Then the diggers began to push in the loose earth around the grave and as it fell on the coffin the mourners wept aloud. Helen tossed in a rose. Frank, standing close to the edge of the grave, leaned forward to see where the flower fell. He lost his balance, and though flailing his arms, landed feet first on the coffin" (p. 231).

Spectacular though it might be, Frankie's pratfall at the gravesite is merely one incident in a long series of self-created accidents. And one fears that his efforts to create a new, Bober-like life for himself will simply be more of the same. For example, his decision to become a convert—a striking reversal of the usual direction in American Jewish fiction—is riddled with ambiguity and undercutting ironies. That it is a Judaism he does not understand and that cannot possibly sustain him is only part of the problem. In effect, Frankie's situation is akin to Ike Mc-Caslin's in Faulkner's "Bear." Like Bober, Sam Fathers has an intuitive wisdom about the woods that Ike patiently tries to discover. But with Sam Fathers dead and the woods slowly disappearing, the "wisdom" no longer works. Frankie's case is complicated because the novel raises real questions as to whether or not he ever understood Bober, much less his "Jewishness" or the value of his suffering.

For Frankie, conversion points to plot developments that exist beyond the novel's final page. We accept the tableau frozen in the concluding paragraph of "The Magic Barrel" as part and parcel of the short story, but it is harder to know what to do with Frankie. Are we to presume that he will emulate Bober by taking over the grocery store? Will he now be the one to supply the gray-haired Polish woman with her six o'clock roll and the "drunken women" with endless credit? And, of course, will he marry Helen and turn her slowly into an Ida? What we *do* know is that a newly circumcised Frankie drags himself around "with a pain between his legs," one that both "enraged and inspired him"—and we might add, a pain that attracted as much as it repulsed.

At least part of the appeal must be chalked up to Frankie's long-standing masochism. The old guilts must be punished, and what better, more ritualistic way than by circumcision? Implicit in the act are the complicated strands of sexual punishment (for his attempted rape of Helen), castration anxiety (for Bober as Oedipal father), and religious conversion (for a Covenant he does not understand). In this disparate quest for moral perfection, Frankie Alpine emerges as more *schlemiel* than authentic Jew, more as victim of his desire for sainthood than as "saint." At the end, he sees himself transmogrified into a surrealistic version of St. Francis, reaching into a garbage can to give Helen a wooden rose: "He [i.e., St. Francis] tossed it into the air and it turned into a real flower that he caught in his hand. With a bow he gave it to Helen, who had just come out of the house. 'Little sister, here is your little sister the rose.' From him she took it, although it was with the love and best wishes of Frank Alpine" (pp. 245–46). Finkle, too, had clutched flowers to his anxious breast and raced toward his disastrous/redemptive meeting with

Stella. In a similar fashion, Frank Alpine speeds toward an equally ambivalent destiny, duping himself with the belief that he is no longer an "assistant," and that Bober's humanity will soon be his.

The progress of the moral *schlemiel* continued with *A New Life*, but this time Malamud added large doses of the slapstick humor traditionally associated with the figure. However much Bober and Alpine merit inclusion among Malamud's moral bunglers, it is hard to think of *The Assistant* as a comic novel; in Malamud's world, a mom-and-pop grocery store not only severely restricts economic possibilities, but also sharply curtails what we might think of as bounce, as good cheer: "In a store you were entombed." Indeed, in a whole series of works from the early Malamud stories reprinted in *The People* to *The Fixer* (1966), metaphorical prisons abound, whether they be cast as grocery stores or Czarist prisons.

S. Levin, "formerly a drunkard," hails from the same *zeitgeist*, one Philip Roth once described as a "timeless depression and placeless lower East Side." In *A New Life*, however, Malamud transports his luckless protagonist to the American West and the groves of Academia. That Levin should be a *schlemiel* is as much an a priori assumption as is Bober's "suffering." After all, the traditions of academic satire—like those that clustered around academic treatments of the West as "virgin land"—were established conventions long before S. Levin headed across the Hudson.

Still, one could argue that one might move a Malamud protagonist out of the city, but not move the city out of the character. In this sense, *A New Life* shares the same concerns, the same tensions, that energized Malamud's earlier fiction, although, this time, Levin's role as moral *schlemiel* includes generous doses of the *schlemiel* as capital-*B* Bungler. During the first few chapters much is made of the fact that Levin is the *schlemiel* out West and newly arrived in academia—the economic scheming of his ghetto ancestors now turned toward the business of departmental tenure and perhaps even an eventual Ph.D. "Bearded, lonely," and looking around for a sign of welcome, Levin is a perfect candidate for the assorted "accidents" that will befall him. He is, in short, the rabbinical student of "The Magic Barrel" turned upside down, the flip side of Finkle's brand of poignant aloneness. Met by Gerald Gilley, Director of Freshmen Composition, Levin spends his first evening at Cascadia College in a series of outrageous "goat who came to dinner" jokes—alternating, as the standard definition of the *schlemiel* would have it, between the one who "spills the soup" and the one who "gets spilt upon."

Indeed, Levin wastes little time establishing his credential as that innocent victim of bad luck, the *schlimazl:* "They sat down at the round table, for which he felt a surprising immediate affection. Pauline had forgotten the salad bowl and went in to get it. When she returned she served the casserole, standing. A child called from the kitchen. Distracted, she missed Levin's plate and dropped a hot gob of tuna fish and potato into his lap" (pp. 9–10). But that said, poor Levin is denied even the luxury of classical *schlimazl*hood. In a post-Freudian world there *are* no accidents, or at least nothing that is allowed to remain an innocent "accident" for long. And so Malamud begins what turns into a series of pants jokes. Levin's trousers are, of course, ruined and all the elements of a minor "scene" are present. Pauline then suggests that Levin change into her husband's trousers (a foreshadowing that will hardly escape sharp-eyed Freudians), and after much argument, the matter seems to resolve itself after Levin "changed into Gilley's trousers in the bathroom."

With the fresh duds, however, comes new *tsoris*. Coaxed into telling the Gilley's youngest son a story, "Levin, scratching a hot right ear, began: 'There was once a fox with a long white beard—' Erik chuckled. In a minute he was laughing—to Levin's amazement—in shrieking peals. Levin snickered at his easy success, and as he did, felt something hot on his thigh. He rose in haste, holding the still wildly laughing child at arm's length, as a jet of water shot out of the little penis that had slipped through his pajama fly" (p. 13). Unfortunately, the total effect suffers from those aesthetic laws governing diminishing returns and suggests that what might work in, say, a Laurel and Hardy film or on the vaudeville stage may not be equally effective on the printed page. On this point, Robert Alter distinguishes between the rhythms of a short story and those of a sustained novel: "The *schlemiel*, it should be said, lends himself much more readily to revelation in a short story than to development in a novel, perhaps because his comic victimhood invites the suddenness and externality of slapstick; when that technique is merely multiplied in being transformed to a novel—where we expect more subtlety and innerness, a more discursive and analytic treatment of character—the comedy becomes a little tedious."

Alter makes a telling observation, although I would hasten to add that *A New Life* claims our attention on grounds other than comic victimhood. Ultimately, Levin's moral bungling matters more than his pratfalls. But that said, let us return to Levin's bedraggled trousers and the ways that Malamud simultaneously uses, and transposes, the running gag into new keys. Part of the progress of the *schlemiel* has to do with "great expectations" that are either perpetually unfulfilled or systematically undermined. For roughly the first hundred pages, the prevailing temper of *A New Life* is one of ironic reversal, with comic episodes drawn from Levin's career as a novice teacher or his misadventures as a would-be lover—and always ending, as they must, with *tsoris* for Levin's pants.

His night on the northwestern town with Sadek, a graduate student as "foreign" to the terrain as Levin, is an excellent case in point. In a very real sense, these two rather bizarre characters complement themselves: Levin, the former drunkard and ex-high school teacher from the impersonal East, and Sadek, a Syrian graduate student whom Levin describes as a "fanatic about hygiene. The fumes of Lysol stank up the bathroom for a half hour after he had been in it; he [Sadek] rubbed everything he touched—before, not after—with his personal bottle. He was majoring in sanitary bacteriology and taking courses in rat control and the bacteriology of sewage" (p. 73). Sadek's concern for the physical parallels Levin's attention to the moral. Granted, we are meant to see Sadek as excessive, indeed, as obsessed, and it is this comic dimension that qualifies him as a bit player in the continuing farce of S. Levin's life. When they vie for the hand of the fair Laverne at a local watering hole—Sadek divides his time between seduction and frequent trips to the men's room, while Levin sips his beers and dreams of love—ill luck makes sure it visits both of them. Sadek is apprehended for indecent exposure ("the toilet facilities of the tavern horrified him and he prefered not to do a major Lysol job there"), leaving the barmaid to Levin by default.

Soon the would-be lovers are alone in a barn, each captivated by the uniqueness of their respective situations—Levin, the irrepressible romantic, observing that this was "my first barn," while the more experienced Laverne reflects that she had "never done it with a guy with a beard." For Laverne, the whole business is, more or less, standard operating procedure, an effective contrast to the ways in which Levin waxes poetic at the possibilities of love, the West, and of course, a new life: "In front of the cows, he thought. Now I belong to the ages" (p. 80).

And in a sense, Levin does "belong to the ages," although not the ones he had in mind. He is the "sensitive" young man out of an earlier tradition in American literature, the sort of boy who takes sexual initiation seriously because he knows (unconsciously of course) that this is the stuff out of which great literature comes. By contrast, Malamud seems more interested in incongruity than in resurrecting yet another version of "pastoral." The result, then, is less the stuff of a conventional *Bildungsroman* than a chronicle in which the country bumpkin seduces the city slicker:

LAVERNE. Why don't you take your pants off?

LEVIN. It's cold here. Have you got a blanket to cover us?

LAVERNE. No, just the one to lay on.

LEVIN. In that case I'll keep my jacket on.

LAVERNE. But take your pants off or they'll get crinkled . . .

LEVIN. Your breasts . . . smell like hay.

LAVERNE. I always wash well . . .

LEVIN. I meant it as a compliment.   (P. 81)

To be sure, Levin's *tsoris* extends well beyond the rhetorical. If the traditional *schlemiel* is often portrayed as a cuckold, Levin may well be a modern variant—the victim of comic *coitus interruptus.* Just at the moment when "Levin rose to his knees and was about to be in her," Sadek reappears, stealing their clothing and leaving the hapless Levin victimized in the very heart of the Pacific Northwest. The incident may well be the result of ill luck or bad timing—certainly of factors beyond the hapless Levin's control, but for Laverne, the fault is clearly his: "You sure are some fine flop," she said acidly. "It's what I get for picking you instead of waiting for the one with guts." Even when Levin gallantly surrenders his trousers to Laverne—this time in a gesture of agape rather than eros—the gesture is lost in a welter of comic complications. Laverne is hit by an empty beer can when they try to hitch a ride, and when they finally arrive at her porch, she "kicked his pants off the porch. 'No, you bastard, don't ever let me see you again in your whole goddam life. Don't think those whiskers on your face hide the fact that you ain't a man'" (p. 85).

Nor are the comic misfortunes associated with his trousers limited to Levin's social life; they also play a prominent role in the tangled network of his academic difficulties. For example, during his first, nervous class at Cascadia College, he "had carefully followed the mimeographed instruction sheet"—only to discover to his amazement that academic hours are longer than he had thought. With the fifteen "official" items already covered, Levin "vaguely considered dismissing the class" when he happened to notice the boldface type at the bottom of the page: "N.B. DO NOT DISMISS YOUR CLASS BEFORE THE END OF THE HOUR. G.G., DIR. COMP." (p. 89).

The "bold-face type"—its message as unmistakable as it is threatening—is quite enough to keep Levin glued inside the classroom. After all, Cascadia is his last academic chance, one that can't be put at risk by breaking one of Gilley's rules—and on the very first day to boot. No doubt a piece of conventional satire might feature a protagonist too ignorant to entertain such thoughts, one whose wide-eyed account of "how things are" serves to expose follies in the manner of a Lemuel Gulliver or a Huckleberry Finn. Academic satire generally alters this formula. Indeed, in its best practitioners, naïveté is complicated by a curious tension between a protagonist's conviction that the college or university in question is run by incompetents and an equal desire for tenure and promotions within that very system. In short, it is the difference between a novel such as *Lucky Jim* and, say, *Up the Down Staircase*—in the former you are concerned with making faces at the college while you work for tenure by publishing scholarly articles, and in the latter you emerge as the system's darling with hardly any struggle at all.

Levin combines a penchant for accident that makes him an American counterpart of the bumbling Jim Dixon with the hard-core idealism of Bel Kaufman's heroine. We see indicators of this as Levin's first class winds toward its comic conclusion: his ever-present, ever-doomed trousers, his high hopes for teaching, his twinges of paranoia, and, most of all, his inveterate *schlemiel* ism all combine to brand him as the loser he is fated to become. Surprised, yet heartened, by the rapt attention of his new students, Levin—following Gilley's instructors to the bold-face letter—launches into the no-nonsense business of sentence diagraming until only twelve minutes of the first academic hour remain. Then, he "finally dropped grammar to say what was still on his mind":

Namely, welcome to Cascadia College. He was himself a stranger in the West but that didn't matter. By some miracle of movement and change, standing before them as their English instructor by virtue of appointment, Levin welcomed them from wherever they came: the Northwest states, California, and a few from beyond the Rockies, a thrilling representation to a man who had in all his life never been west of Jersey City. If they worked conscientiously in college, he said, they would come in time to a better understanding of who they were and what their lives might yield, education being revelation. At this they laughed, though he was not sure why. Still if they could be so good-humored early in the morning it was all right with him. . . . In his heart he thanked them, sensing he had created their welcome of him. They represented the America he had so often heard of, the fabulous friendly West. . . . "This is the life for me," he admitted, and they broke into cheers, whistles, loud laughter. The bell rang and the class moved noisily into the hall, some nearly convulsed. As if inspired, Levin glanced down at his fly and it was, as it must be, all the way open.　(Pp. 89–90)

I have quoted the scene at length so that Levin's comic victimhood could speak eloquently for itself. There are, of course, other instances where Levin plays the slapstick *schlemiel*. In his mock seduction of Avis Fliss, a fellow teacher at Cascadia, Levin finds new ways to reenact his abortive evening with Laverne as the scene shifts from pastoral barns to the desks in academic offices. And here, too, the comedy revolves around *coitus interruptus*, although this time it is none other than the dreaded Gilley who adds a dash of paranoia to the proceedings. In the same spirit, Levin's accident-plagued ride to meet Nadalee at a motel suggests the self-created failures that are the legacy of the traditional *schlemiel*.

However, Levin's car troubles—like his pants problems—are the stuff of vaudeville, as I mentioned earlier, rather than a sustained novel, especially when Levin's pattern of comic difficulties is established within the first hundred pages. Whereas a novel such as Joseph Heller's *Catch-22* works on a theory of reoccurring absurdity (e.g., Milo Minderbinder's mushrooming empire), the focus of *A New Life* keeps shifting uneasily between academic pratfall and acadmic protest. The result not only raises questions about the novel's singleness of purpose, but also forces us to see his protagonist as split, even distorted, between his roles as perennial bungler and moral idealist.

Levin's notebook gives perhaps the best clues to the tensions that will ultimately consume the novel: "One section of the notebook was for 'insights,' and a few pages in the middle detailed 'plans.' . . . Among Levin's 'insights' were 'the new life hangs on an old soul,' and 'I am one who creates his own peril.' Also, 'the danger of the times is the betrayal of man' " (p. 58).

We have come to expect that Levin's vision of a "new life" based on geographical change is destined to fail. As Mark Goldman points out, Levin is the "tenderfoot Easterner . . . (always invoking nature like a tenement Rousseau). 'Now he took in miles of countryside, a marvelous invention.' "[7] But whatever the "new life" might be or how ironic such slogans ultimately turn out, it hangs, as it must, on Levin's "old soul." Moreover, if Levin's notebook is a repository of private understanding, it is often at odds with the facts of his public behavior.

In a similar fashion, the novel's academic satire has been misunderstood by a number of critics who were quick to point out that they were equally indignant about schools such as Cascadia and teachers such as Gilley. After all, "The danger of the times *is* the betrayal of man," and it is not hard to see how this statement was interpreted as having something to do with the preservation of the liberal arts, with the humanities in general, and with English departments in particular. Ruth Mandel, for example, sees Cascadia College in these terms: "Here is a stereotyped, mediocre, service-oriented English department. The instructors are organization men of the worst kind, men who should know better, men educated in the humanities. The school is a Cascadian Madison Avenue, a school where the emphasis is on practical learning, prestige, school-board approval, and the well-rounded, shallow man who must be an athlete if he wishes to be accepted. The attack is devastating. Malamud's intentions are clear."[8] But are they? If Levin is to function as the traditional satiric persona, his credentials are hardly in order. After all, S. Levin does not come "from a world of pastoral innocence," nor is he "the prophet come down from the hills to the cities of the plain; the gawky farmboy, shepherd or plowman come to the big city."[9] Rather, Levin ("formerly a drunkard") arrives in this untainted (?) West from New York City, the very seat of Eastern corruption. He is, in this sense, a reverse Nick Carraway, one who follows his dream of a liberal arts college westward—only to find, instead, the drudgery of required freshman composition and the treachery of departmental politics.

But that said, Levin often seems more akin to the Kurtz of Conrad's "Heart of Darkness" than he does an ironic variant of the Carraway from Fitzgerald's *Great Gatsby*. Far from being the innocent one simultaneously attracted to and repulsed by corruption (Nick), Levin, like Kurtz, enters the heart of Cascadia College's darkness with high hopes of humanizing the system. Granted, he is as surrounded by absurdities as was Kurtz: one colleague continually revises his *Elements of Composition,* 13th edition, the required text for Levin's courses; another colleague labors fitfully on a Laurence Sterne dissertation that nobody will publish; still another cuts out pictures from old *Life* magazines for a proposed "picture book" of American literature. But Levin, as it turns out, is neither appalled nor paralyzed by the curious directions that publish-or-perish takes at Cascadia; after all, he had some plans of his own:

> He could begin to collect material for a critical study of Melville's whale: "White Whale as Burden of Dark World," "Moby Dick as Closet Drama." . . . Levin began to read and make notes but gave up the whale when he discovered it in too many critical hats. He wrote down other possible titles for a short critical essay: "The Forest as Battleground of the Spirit in Some American Novels." "The Stranger as Fallen Angel in Western Fiction." "The American Ideal as Self-Created Tradition." Levin wrote, "The idea of America will always create freedom"; but it was impossible to prove faith. After considering "The Guilt-ridden Revolutionary of the Visionary American Ideal," he settled on "American Self-Criticism in Several Novels." Limiting himself, to start, to six books, Levin read and re-read them, making profuse notes.　(P. 267)

The proposed articles—one has the sinking feeling that one has encountered them before, either in print or around the table of a graduate seminar—serve a number of functions. First, they suggest the ironic dimensions of Levin's purity, a matter not nearly as important in the groves of academia as it will be in the regeneration of his moral fiber. It is, after all, the "others" who have sold out, turning their talents from humanity to commercialism—not Levin. *His* projected articles are awash with speculations about American guilt and Edenic innocence—all in the best traditions of Cotton Mather, Henry Adams, and the Modern

Language Association (MLA). Levin might differ from these august presences in degree, but certainly not in kind.

Malamud surely means this hatful of titles to be ironic, although I also suspect that more than a few readers secretly thought that "The Stranger as Fallen Angel in Western Fiction" had the makings of a publishable piece. My point, however, is simply this: Levin's overriding concern is for moral preservation, both in the collective sense of America and in the individual sense of Self. If his academic fantasies are those of a *luftmentsch*, they must be seen in the larger context of Levin's moral structure. In this sense the pettiness of Cascadia College is only a backdrop for Levin's more pressing concerns: his inability to love, his lack of commitment, his perennial death of the spirit.

With his last "insight"—namely, that "I am the one who creates his own peril"—Levin unconsciously hints at the ties that bind him to traditional *schlemiels* from Ibn Ezra onward. It is, after all, the *schlemiel* who "creates his own peril," who is the architect of his own destruction, and Levin's insight is an accurate appraisal of his behavior in the novel thus far. Neither a "new life" in terms of geographical moves to a mythical West nor his romantic notions about the groves of academia can save Levin from himself.

In short, whatever comic spirit derives from the incongruity of a Levin plunged knee-deep into Nature, learning how to drive a car, or being initiated into the internecine political warfare of Cascadia College fizzles out almost completely when he moves toward Pauline and the larger complications she will suggest. For a time it looks as if Levin will revivify the legend and the legacy of Leo Duffy. After all, Levin arrives with a Duffy-like beard, begins his career in Duffy's abandoned office, and ends the novel as Pauline's lover-husband.

That said, however, Malamud has more in mind for S. Levin than one more tale of academic martyrdom. Whereas a Duffy commits suicide (the final "protest" and one that is certain to have "meaning"), Levin gradually switches roles from academic complainer and/or critic to moral bungler. At one point in the novel, Levin tells Pauline about his first "awakening," his initial encounter with the new life:

> For two years I lived in self-hatred, willing to part with life. I won't tell you what I had come to. But one morning in somebody's filthy cellar, I awoke under burlap bags and saw my rotting shoes on a broken chair.

They were lit in dim sunlight from a shaft or window. I stared at the chair, it looked like a painting, a thing with a value of its own. I squeezed what was left of my brain to understand why this should move me so deeply, why I was crying. Then I thought, Levin, if you were dead there would be no light on your shoes in this cellar. I came to believe what I had often wanted to, that life is holy. I then became a man of principle.   (P. 204)

And it is from this mushrooming sense of "principle" that Levin's link to other characters in the Malamud canon is established. Granted, his concerns take in the vast range of contemporary problems (unlike the more isolated, more claustrophobic ones of, say, Frankie Alpine), but the mechanisms are virtually identical. For Malamud, the important thing may not be that a Gilley or a Fabrikant are exposed, but rather that a Levin finally acts. However, moral action is almost always a qualified commodity in Malamud's world, more an occasion for ironic failures than for spiritual successes. Moreover, if Levin's academic fantasies had a ring of moral urgency about them, consider the following slice of Levin's wishful thinking:

He must *on principle* not be afraid. "The little you do may encourage the next man to do more. It doesn't take a violent revolution to change a policy or institution. All it takes is a good idea and a man with guts. Someone who knows that America's historically successful ideas have been liberal and radical, continuing revolt in the cause of freedom. 'Disaster occurs if a country finally abandons its radical creative past' — R. Chase. Don't be afraid of the mean-spirited. Remember that a man who scorns the idealist scorns the secret image of himself. (Levin's notebook: 'Insights.') Don't be afraid of names. Your purpose as self-improved man is to help the human lot, notwithstanding universal peril, anxiety, continued betrayal of freedom and oppression of man. He would, as a teacher, do everything he could to help bring forth those gifted few who would do more than their teachers had taught, in the name of democracy and humanity." (Whistles, cheers, prolonged applause.) The instructor took a bow at the urinal.   (P. 230)

Meditations of this sort occur often in the john, as any disciple of Norman O. Brown or Martin Luther would attest. In addition, however, Levin's fantasies have an elastic quality about them; they stretch until the savior of the Humanities in general and of Cascadia College's English Department in particular becomes the Christ-like savior of the entire planet: "He [Levin] healed the

sick, crippled, blind, especially children. . . . He lived everywhere. Every country he came to was his own, a matter of
understanding history. In Africa he grafted hands on the hand-
less and gave bread and knowledge to the poor. In India he
touched the untouchables. In America he opened the granaries
and freed the slaves" (p. 273). For Malamud, the giving of bread
is a particularly telling symbolic act. As I suggested earlier, it
encompasses such moments as Bober giving an early morning
roll to the Polish woman or Yakov Bok (in *The Fixer*) giving *matzoh*
to a wounded Hassid. During a symposium held at the University of Connecticut, Malamud kept stressing the connection,
placing a strong emphasis on Levin's dream of giving bread and
knowledge to the world's poor as evidence both of the novel's
moral growth and its positive ending.

Malamud was, of course, not the only one who had thoughts
about how the bread motif worked in his fiction. Much has
already been written about the Protean character of Levin's
name—from the overly formal S. Levin to the more relaxed
"Sam." Mark Goldman sees the line "Sam, they used to call me
home" as especially important because these "concluding words
end the search for Levin, happily surrendering S. for Seymour,
Sy for sigh, even Pauline's Lev for love, simply to identify with the
real past." Evidently part of the contemporary critic's equipment
is the ability to play name games with ingenuity and patience.
And while the shifting quality of "S. Levin" may not be as
challenging, as fraught with meaning, as, say, the possibilities
built into Moses Elkannah Herzog or nearly any character from
a John Barth novel, I suspect the crucial pun is centered on the
protagonist's last name rather than on the varieties of his first.
As the "leaven" of *A New Life*, he makes "bread"—that is to say,
life itself—possible.

To be sure, most reviewers saw *A New Life* as an extended
exercise in irony, one far less life-affirming than either Malamud's protestations or my wordplay on Levin/leaven would
suggest. They were, for example, annoyed that the novel ended
with Levin forced to give up a college teaching career that had
barely begun, and his grandiose fantasies about doing even an
greater good outside the profession did not help. For them, the
crux of the matter was freedom: in his imaginary articles, Levin
muses that the "idea of America will always create freedom"; in
his reveries on the john, he suggests that the betrayal of freedom
is the very thing a self-improved man (i.e., himself) must com-

bat; and perhaps most significant of all, in his final showdown with Gilley, he insists that Pauline is a "free agent." But the novel per se makes the dramatic point that what Levin calls "freedom" others would label "entrapment." As Robert Alter puts it: "Levin suffers the *schlemiel'* s fate—ousted from the profession of his choice, burdened with a family he didn't bargain for and a woman he loves only as a matter of principle, rolling westward in his overheated jalopy toward a horizon full of pitfalls" (p. 72). Perhaps this reluctance to see Levin leave the profession (as opposed to just Cascadia College) has something to do with the complicated reasons Oregon State—the ostensible model for Cascadia—kept asking Malamud back to lecture. Granted, a part of the impulse is purely pragmatic. When Malamud's fictionalized account of academic life in Corvalis was first published, it must have been painful reading indeed, and no doubt there were those who unfurled the banners marked "unfair!" or "unrepresentative!" But, in time, even bad press has a marketable value—after all, *A New Life* put the school "on the map"— and Oregon State (which has hosted its share of Malamud conferences and had a hand in making sure that the proceedings were published) can take a certain amount of pride in the fact that he once taught there.

Moreover, the mechanics of Levin's last, fateful decisions also work on the most personal of levels. As a hard-boiled Jake Barnes might sneer through his clenched teeth, it is "pretty to think" that academic life might be better at some other, more enlightened school, and indeed, Malamud's subsequent career at Bennington College suggests that perhaps it can. But I would hasten to add that this tells us more about Levin's critics than about Levin himself. He accepts Gilley's absurd condition that he never teach on the college level again because his ambitions are more oriented toward becoming a "savior" than a mere professor.

Nonetheless, Levin rushes toward a salvation that strikes more objective observers as hellish. At one point, Gilley gives Levin a dose of what Saul Bellow calls "reality instruction": "An older woman than yourself and not dependable, plus two adopted kids, no choice of yours, no job or promise of one and assorted headaches. Why take that load on yourself?" (p. 360). With only slight changes, the lines might have dropped from Pinye Salzman's lips and the world of "The Magic Barrel." Like Salzman, Gilley has a talent for persuasion and his arguments are so commonsensical that Levin is reduced to gestures that combine *schlemiel* hood with moral revolt. "Because I can, you son of a bitch" simultaneously answers Gilley's final question and seals Levin's fate. Like Finkle, it is Levin's zeal to affect a moral change, to create "a new life" that has unwittingly willed his destruction. And like the final scene of "The Magic Barrel," the last lines of *A New Life* are packed with ambiguity: "Two tin-hatted workmen with chain saws were in the maple tree in front of Humanties Hall, cutting it down limb by leafy limb, to make room for a heat tunnel. On the Student Union side of the street, Gilley was aiming a camera at the operation. When he saw Levin's Hudson approach he swung the camera around and snapped. As they drove by he tore a rectangle of paper from the back of the camera and waved it aloft. 'Got your picture!' " (pp. 366–67).

On one hand, there is the terrifying "picture" of Levin's departure—the battered Hudson on the verge of breaking down and the human relationships inside very likely to follow suit—while on the other hand, there is the "limb by leafy limb" destruction both of Nature and Humanity. Gilley might have gotten one picture but it is doubtful if he "got" the other. After all, "pictures," rather than words, are the stuff Gilley's sensibility is made of; one thinks immediately of the photographic "evidence" he collected against poor Duffy and of the stacks of old *Life* magazines that comprise the raw materials of his scholarly research. No doubt this concentration of the visual pleased McCluhanites in their day and semioticians in our own, but in the context of the novel Gilley's camera and his pictures suggest an unwillingness to demonstrate either human emotion (Duffy) or moral concern (Levin). His projected *Picture Book of American Literature* will be as much a failure as the sordid pictures of his personal life. Malamud once remarked that Gilley's last "picture" will leave a permanent impression on his mind, but I have an easier time imagining him plotting to replace the *Elements* with his own "pictorial history"—a situation that should not be too difficult at Cascadia.

From the stories of *The Magic Barrel* collection to *A New Life*, Malamud creates one ironic triangle after another, all by way of suggesting that moral bungling is at least as likely a possibility as moral regeneration. With a novel such as *The Fixer*, however, Malamud alters the formula in a number of significant ways. Rather than drawing from personal experience (i.e., *A New Life* as a fictionalized account of his unhappy days teaching freshman composition at Oregon State) or spinning yet another moral fable about a metaphorical lower East Side, Malamud turned to the mythic potential of the Mendele Beiliss case. In a strange, probably inexplicable turn of literary events, Maurice Samuel's *Blood Accusation,* a highly readable, thoroughly researched account of the same event, appeared during the same year. Malamud may or may not have counted this as good luck, but the coincidence does suggest that the moral overtones of this most famous of all "blood libel" trials was very much a part of the contemporary sensibility. And too, the sales both of Malamud's "fiction" and Samuel's "fact" hint that these concerns were shared by those in the markeplace as well as by those who write for it.

That said, let me hasten to point out that *The Fixer* is only loosely based on the Beiliss case. As Robert Alter suggests: "One feels in *The Fixer* that for Malamud 1911 is 1943 in small compass and sharp focus, and 1966 writ very large. The Beiliss case gives him, to begin with, a way of approaching the European holocaust on a scale that is imaginable, susceptible of fictional representation" (p. 74). There are really two issues here: the first involves Malamud's choice of subject matter. Although aspects of moral growth had always been part of his fictional landscape, never before had response and occasion been so intimately joined in ways that intimated the Holocaust. The second issue is that of employing the *schlemiel* as a character who would be harmonious both with the theme and the plot of a novel.

Yakov Bok is a *schlemiel* in the classical sense of the term. Cuckolded and then deserted by his wife, he seems to have come from a long line of those who were the innocent victims of absurd accident: "His own father had been killed in an incident not more than a year after Yakov's birth—something less than a pogrom and less than useless: two drunken soldiers shot the first three Jews in their path, his father had been the second" (p. 4). Yet, neither the death of his father nor the impoverished condition of his own life are enough to make a handwringer out of Yakov. As the name "Bok" suggests, Yakov remains obstinate, the Yiddish translation meaning either a goat or an unbendable piece of iron, while the English "balk" characterizes his reluctance to move forward. For the more ingenious, it is only a short distance (linguistically at least) from "Bok" to "Bog," the Russian word for Christ. Yakov may begin the novel as the would-be cynic who drank his tea unsweetened ("It tasted bitter and he blamed existence"), but his speeches are filled with hints of the knowing sighs that will come later:

In my dreams I ate and I ate my dreams. Torah I had little of, Talmud less, though I learned Hebrew because I've got an ear for language. Anyway, I knew the Psalms. They taught me a trade and apprenticed me five minutes after age ten—not that I regret it. So I work. . . . I fix what's broken—except in the heart. In this shtetl everything is falling apart— who bothers with leaks in his roof if he's peeking through the cracks to spy on God? And who can pay to have it fixed let's say he wants it, which he doesn't. If he does, half the time I work for nothing. If I'm lucky, a dish of noodles. Opportunity here is born dead.   (Pp. 6–7)

Opportunity may be born dead in the *shtetl*, but perhaps things will go better in Kiev. Unfortunately, Yakov finds himself beleaguered by the accidents that befall him along the way— none of which (ironically enough) he is able to "fix." Moreover, it is his penchant for doing good deeds that contributes to his misfortune and that seals his kinship with other moral bunglers in the Malamud canon. For example, spotting a peasant woman "wearing a man's shoes and carrying a knapsack, a thick shawl wrapped around her head," he

drew over to the side to pass her but as he did Yakov called out, "A ride, granny?"

"May Jesus bless you." She had three gray teeth.

Jesus he did not need. . . . Then as the road turned, the right wheel struck a rock and broke with a crunch. . . . But with hatchet, saw, plane, tinsmith's shears, tri-square, putty, wire, pointed knife and two awls, the fixer couldn't fix what was broken.   (P. 22)

The scene is a foreshadowing of more *tsoris* to come. When he finally arrives at Kiev—ostensibly only a stopover on his way to Amsterdam—Yakov "went looking for luck," but finds a drunken member of the anti-Semitic Black Hundreds instead. What follows is an ironic parody of the Joseph story. In this case, Yakov, or "Jacob," functions as a version of the biblical Joseph who finds himself in a foreign land and soon rises to the position of overseer. Of course, Yakov's station is not nearly so grand. He is, in truth, merely the supervisor of a brick factory owned by the drunken man he once rescued from the snow. For a brief moment it looks as if the fixer has beaten the odds, has opportunity aplenty. He moves into a non-Jewish neighborhood and, like Joseph, goes about the business of assimilation.

However, if the drunken Aaron Latke is the mock-Potiphar of the piece, his daughter, Zinaida Nikolaevna, plays the role of temptress, her frustration at Yakov's "morality" aiding his final imprisonment. At this point, Yakov makes much of the fact that he is "not a political person. . . . The world's full of it but it's not for me. Politics is not my nature." But a scant twenty pages later Yakov will find himself arrested for the ritual murder of a Russian boy and on trial for his very life. And, again, his moral bungling contributes to his troubles. In a scene that closely parallels the rescue of his anti-Semitic boss, Yakov saves a Hassid from the torments of an angry mob and even offers him a piece of bread. Ironically enough, Yakov—ever the *schlemiel*—makes his offer during Passover, a religious holiday in which the eating of leavened bread is strictly prohibited. The Hassid will eat only matzo: "Pouring a little [water] over his fingers over a bowl, he then withdrew a small packet from his caftan pocket, some matzo pieces wrapped in a handkerchief. He said the blessing for matzos, and sighing, munched a piece. It came as a surprise to the fixer that it was Passover" (p. 65). The matzos are, of course, the basis of the ritual murder charge that has been brought against Yakov. The State claims that Yakov killed a Russian boy and drained his blood to make the ritual cakes. At first Yakov, who is hardly an observant Jew and who, in fact, did not even realize that it was the Passover season until his encounter with the Hassid, refuses to take the questions of his Russian captors seriously. In short, the accusation is not only false, but also absurd:

"Are you certain you did not yourself bake this matzo? A half bag of flour was found in your habitat."
"With respect, your honor, it's the wrong flour. Also I'm not a baker. I once tried to bake bread to save a kopek or two but it didn't rise and came out like a rock. The flour was wasted. Baking isn't one of my skills. I work as a carpenter or painter most of the time—I hope nothing has happened to my tools, they're all I've got in the world—but generally I'm a fixer, never a matzo baker."   (P. 102)

However, it takes Yakov only a short time to realize that "I'm a fixer but all my life I've broken more than I fix." As the time he spends in prison begins to monopolize the novel, Yakov becomes more conscious of his own role in his calamity: "If there's a mistake to make, I'll make it." The long and agonizing prison scenes (which have caused at least one reviewer to complain about needless repetition) make Yakov's sufferings realistic as opposed to merely metaphorical. Whatever else a Yakov may be, his chains and the inhuman treatment he receives are real. Unlike a Morris Bober who suffered "for the Law" or even an S. Levin who had "suffering" built into his psyche, there are no a priori assumptions here for readers to suspend their disbeliefs about.

Furthermore, Yakov earns his rights as an Everyman. Caught in a web of bureaucratic absurdity, he suggests that "somebody has made a serious mistake," only to find that the case against him is growing stronger every day. If a novel such as Kafka's *Trial* makes the point that K's crime is merely "living"—and that message had a certain appeal for hand-wringing existentialists who saw most of life as an absurd waste of time anyhow— Malamud's protagonist takes a significantly different tack: "He feared the prison would go badly for him and it went badly at once. It's my luck, he thought bitterly. What do they say—'If I dealt in candles the sun wouldn't set.' Instead, I'm Yakov the Fixer and it sets each hour on the stroke. I'm the kind of man who finds it perilous to be alive. One thing I must learn is to say less—much less, or I'll ruin myself. As it is I'm ruined already" (p. 143).

Yakov's learning involves an understanding of his group iden- tity, the Jewishness that he unsuccessfully tries to abandon and his own responsibility in the design of his fate. There is much talk of "luck" in *The Fixer,* but as Yakov's speech suggests, there is a connection between Fate and individual posture. Yakov's stance is that of the classical *schlemiel,* and he half-remembers lines that are significant in this figure's history. The allusion ("What do they say?—'If I dealt in candles . . .' ") is, of course, to the epigrams of Ibn Ezra. Theodor Reik's study, *Jewish Wit,* provides the following commentary:

The great Hebrew-Spanish poet Ibn Ezra (1092-1167) was exposed to the slings and arrows of a fortune as outrageous as that of any Schlemiel. Driven from place to place by poverty and restlessness, he wrote the self- destructive epigram: "If I should undertake to sell candles, the sun would never set; if I should deal in shrouds, no one would ever die." From these lines of a poet in the twelfth century, a direct line leads us to the humorous and pathetic figures that Charlie Chaplin created and who have their home in the Jewish East End of London.[10]

To be sure, the self-destructive posture that Reik mentions has become the standard fare of contemporary stand-up comics who trade on the fact that they are losers, that they "get no respect,"—and that this has been the case since early childhood. However, this alone does not credential their *schlemiel* hood. Equally important is comic recognition, that sigh of pathetic insight that sees the moment as both terribly important and ultimately inconsequential.

Yakov's learning comes slowly, interspersed by scenes in which momentary bits of self-deprecation are offset by the systematic torture of his captors. One by one his friends betray him—victims of bribery for the most part—until Yakov is left totally alone. Even his one Russian ally, Bibikov (a Russian version of Eugene Debs who spouts lines such as "if the law doesn't protect you, it will not, in the end, protect me"), is murdered or, what seems more likely, is forced to commit suicide. Yakov, on the other hand, wears his prayer shawl under his suit ("to keep warm"), employing strategies of pragmatism to stay alive.

Indeed, the result of Yakov's suffering is an understanding that goes well beyond the postures of classical *schlemiel* hood. If the first stage in Yakov's development is a period in which he sees himself as the unlucky victim of external accident (the material things that break and somehow cannot be "fixed"), his second stage involves an internalized self-knowledge. Rather than in the frenzied movement normally associated with pratfall, it is in complete stasis (represented both realistically and symbolically by his chains) that he begins to understand. The third stage turns this self-knowledge into transcendental wisdom. For example, Yakov now realizes that he "was the accidental choice for the sacrifice. He would be tried because the accusation had been made, there didn't have to be any other reason. Being born a Jew meant being vulnerable to history, including its worst errors" (p. 143).

And too, in the matter of his cuckoldry, Yakov seals his fate as classical *schlemiel* at the same moment he rises above it. In their tireless efforts to extract his confession, the authorities finally allow Yakov's wife a short visit. At first Yakov is annoyed ("to betray me again"), but he soon learns that Raisl is more interested in the fate of her illegitimate child than in complying with the Russians: she had returned to their *shtetl* when the child was a year and a half old, only to find out that "they blame me for your fate. I tried to take up my little dairy business but I might as well be selling pork. The rabbi calls me to my face, pariah. The child will think his name is bastard" (p. 289). And so Yakov is forced to make a "confession" of a very different sort than the one Raisl had proposed originally. Like the *schlemiel* of the medieval story, Yakov acknowledges the illegitimate child as his own: "On the envelope, pausing between words to remember the letters for the next, he wrote in Yiddish, 'I declare myself to be the father of Chaim, the infant son of my wife Raisl Bok. He was conceived before she left me. Please help the mother and child, for this, amid my troubles, I'll be grateful.' Yakov Bok" (p. 292).

In the medieval story, the *schlemiel* is first cuckolded and then duped into believing that he is, in fact, the father of an illegitimate child. His lot was to live among neighbors who knew better and to be the butt of their thinly veiled jokes about his questionable manhood. Yakov, by contrast, knows full well what he is doing; the child may not be his, but he alone can give Chaim (the name, significantly enough, meaning "life" in Hebrew) a life within the *shtetl* community. Normally, the progress of a *schlemiel* ends with an ironic sigh, a realization that his "great expectations" have been systematically unfulfilled. In *The Fixer*, however, Malamud moves beyond the postures and significances of a single life, suggesting that Yakov's learning can have an effect on future generations.

After many years Mendele Beiliss was finally released, the charges of "blood libel" brought against him dropped. He immigrated to New York's lower East Side, where he sold his story to the Yiddish newspapers but otherwise lived his final years in an increasing obscurity. The Dreyfus case far overshadowed his. In Malamud's fictional account, however, Yakov ends the novel driven through a teeming crowd on the way, at long last, to his "trial" and an almost certain death. There are overtones here of Camus' *Stranger*, but with some important differences. Gone are the artful ambiguities that had characterized Malamud's earlier work. Yakov Bok may be moving toward a literal death, but one does not feel the invisible hand of irony at work. His last moments share little with those of Leo Finkle or S. Levin. Rather, we see Bok as a character who began his life as accident-prone and morally neutral, the bitter and obstinate "Bok," but who exists with tragic dignity and a speech designed to warm the most political heart in Malamud's audience: "One thing I've learned, he thought, there's no such thing as an unpolitical man, especially a Jew. You can't be one without the other, that's clear enough. You can't sit still and see yourself destroyed" (p. 335). To be sure, Malamud had intimations of the American civil rights movement in mind as he crafted the terms, and the rhythms, of Yakov's final speech. In *The Fixer*, childhood memories of hearing about the Mendele Beiliss case from his father mixed with contemporary headlines. The result is a moral fable with a political coating.

At the end of his career Malamud would return to a variant of this form, but with considerably less success. *God's Grace* sacrifices the dramatically convincing to the didactically insistent. In a word, this is a case in which the "allegorical" overwhelms. On the other hand, in collections such as *Pictures of Fidelman* and *Dubin's Lives*, versions of the *schlemiel* stood Malamud in good stead. The six episodes that comprise the former are, in a sense, a requiem—often zany, occasionally steeped in the formality of a high mass—for Arthur Fidelman, anti-hero, would-be artist, and inveterate *schlemiel*. What he must learn, through a series of painful lessons administered by an unrelenting Susskind, is that taking full stock of one's failure is simultaneously the first step toward becoming fully human, toward becoming a *mentsh*. As Ruth Wisse observes,

No matter how intimate his knowledge of life or how edifying his many adventures of body and soul, his art never improves. He works among compromises, with dictated subjects, tools, circumstances. This is a generalized portrait of the artist as schlemiel, a man drawn on the same scale as other men, small and silly, but involved in a recognizably human enterprise. . . . To live within the comedy of human limitations, while striving to create the aesthetic verities in some eternal form—that is the artistic equivalent to the *schlemiel*' s suspension between despair and hope.[11]

By contrast, the William Dubin of *Dubin's Lives* is a disciplined, even earnestly dogged, biographer and not, inconsequently, a very productive one. As the novel opens he has a handful of successful biographies behind him and one—on D. H. Lawrence—in the works. Jogging, he meditates (or perhaps vice versa) about what it means to be William Dubin, "formerly of Newark, New Jersey," a fifty-six-year-old man who gives pattern and significance to dead men's lives. In a word, something essential is missing in the Dubin who jogs through the Vermont countryside, who moves through Nature itself, like a stranger:

In sum, William Dubin, visitor to nature, had introduced himself along
the way but did not intrude. He gazed from the road, kept his distance
even when nature halloowed. Unlikely biographer of Henry David
Thoreau—I more or less dared. Even in thought nature is moving.
Hunger for Thoreau's experience asserted itself. . . . Thoreau gave an
otherwise hidden passion and drew from woods and water the love
affair with earth and sky he's recorded in his journals. "All nature is my
bride." His biographer-to-be had been knocked off his feet on first
serious encounter with nature, a trip to the Adirondacks with a school
friend when they were sixteen. . . . [It] had turned him on in the
manner of the Wordsworthian youth in "Tintern Abbey": "The sound-
ing cataract haunted like a passion." Dubin, haunted, had been roused
to awareness of self extended in nature, highest pitch of consciousness.
He felt what made the self richer: who observes beauty contains it. . . .
He wanted nature to teach him—not sure what—perhaps to bring forth
the self he sought—defined self, best self?   (Pp. 9–10)

Sensibility, rather than "suffering," makes Dubin's character
memorable. As Malamud's novel would have it, biographers
become the lives they write about. Dubin is the condition writ
large and comic.

But that said, let me hasten to add that *some* things about
Dubin's *Lives* look very familiar indeed: A protracted winter
follows Dubin's infatuation with the twenty-two-year-old Fanny
Bick like the Shakespearian night the day. In such a world the
heart swoons and the snowflakes fly; Dubin's book, *The Passion of
D. H. Lawrence: A Life*, is symmetrically balanced with Dubin's
personal life in ways that smack of formalism's last hurrah; and
yet again, moral impulses lead, ironically, to botched results.

By the usual measures, of course, Dubin, the biographer, has
made it. He is by now a permanent, successful fixture of Center
Campobello life, a "biographer" rather than, say, an impoverished grocer or itinerant matchmaker. Which is to say, Dubin
would find little company in the constricted world of Malamud's
most representative short stories. Nonetheless, shadows of the
Great Depression still fall across his life. In short, he is a typical
Malamud character under the skin, however untypical his situation might be. It is hard for men like Dubin to feel entirely
comfortable in the world.

Malamud, of course, used to think of this as a peculiarly
"Jewish" condition. Now it seems more a function of male
menopause or middle-aged crisis or whatever fashionable term

for this low-level, gnawing *angst* one prefers. Here, for example, is the cerebral Dubin alternately musing and panting about the nubile Fanny:

It annoyed him a bit that he had felt her sexuality so keenly. It rose from her bare feet. She thus projects herself?—the feminine body—beautifully formed hefty hips, full bosom, nipples visible—can one see less with two eyes? Or simply his personal view of her?—male chauvinism: reacting reductively? What also ran through his mind was whether he had responded to her as usual self, or as one presently steeped in Lawrence's sexual theories, odd as they were. He had thought much on the subject as he read the man's work.   (P. 23)

Fortunately, *Dubin's Lives* is more complex, more interesting, and certainly more indebted to the comic spirit than most contemporary versions of the December-May syndrome tend to be. Part of the credit goes to Dubin's wife, Kitty. Her "crime," as it were, is that after twenty-five years of marriage, raw sexuality no longer steams upwards from her bare toes. My hunch is that this will matter less to mature readers than it obviously does to the comically rendered Dubin. Moreover, those willing to pull Dubin up short, to hector him about the dangers of becoming an ersatz Lawrence are hardly in short supply. Add Malamud's own flair for undercutting irony and the result takes the edge off Dubin's extensive, and allusion-filled, rationalizations.

In fact, Malamud remains far better on comic failure than he is on amorous success. Dubin's assignation with Fanny in romantic Venice is filled with comic interruptions and the assorted pratfalls of which *schlemiel* hood is made. Not since *A New Life* has Malamud been so funny about a would-be lover's parched forehead and cloying tongue. But contemporary novels demand more than a Dubin who trips over his feet while chasing Fanny Bick. He must, eventually, slip her between the sheets or, in this case, tangle her among the (Lawrentian?) flowers. Alas, on this score neither Malamud nor Dubin is D. H. Lawrence. They are not even John Updike.

To be sure, Dubin wriggles out of the dilemma by being as much "father" as lover and more biographer than either. And too, his liaison with Fanny becomes more serious as (1) she grows as a person, and (2) she becomes more wife than mistress. In short, Dubin finds himself doubly married. It is a neat irony, one that suggests Life is more telling than Art, and that writing about Lawrence is, finally, less at the heart of the matter than living with Kitty/Fanny. Thus, we watch Dubin as comic complications turn him into the "subject" of a biography masquerading as a novel, or perhaps of a novel masquerading as a biography. In any event, Dubin becomes the *schlemiel*-as-biographer, the man whose life reduplicates in miniature what he had once writ large. That the patterns—mythic, seasonal, inextricably tied to the "lives" he had formerly written about—suggest a partial return to Malamud's first novel—*The Natural* (1952)—is true enough, but the final notes struck in *Dublin's Lives*—like the somewhat darker ones in *Pictures of Fidelman*—speak to love, to commitment, to a man's responsibility. As Shimon Susskind puts it to Fidelman: "Tell the truth. Don't cheat. If it's easy it don't mean it's good. Be kind, specially to those that they got less than you." In the lonely prisons of their respective *schlemiel* hoods, Malamud's protagonists discover both the truth and the terrible cost of Susskind's instruction. Such quests may turn a character into moral bungler, but I would add, they can also turn him into a *mentsh*.

6
Saul Bellow's Lovesick
Schlemiels

Time for you and time for me,
And time yet for a hundred indecisions,
And for a hundred visions and revisions,
Before the taking of a toast and tea.

—*J. Alfred Prufrock*

If Bernard Malamud's relationship to Jewish material has been primarily fabulist/fantastic (e.g., *The Magic Barrel*), symbolic (e.g., *The Assistant*), or the stuff of moral allegory (e.g., *The Fixer*), the Jewish "matter" in Saul Bellow's fiction has always seemed more personal and immediate. As he puts it in his widely reprinted introduction to the Dell paperback collection entitled *Great Jewish Stories* (New York, 1965): "For the last generation of East European Jews, daily life without stories would have been inconceivable. My father would say, whenever I asked him to explain any matter, 'The thing is like this. There was a man who lived. . . .' 'There was once a scholar. . . .' "There was a widow with one son. . . .' 'A teamster was driving on a lonely road. . . ' " (p. 11). In many respects Bellow's progress has been a matter of integrating such material into the fabric of American literature, of blending the feel for Yiddish prose rhythms that resulted in his dazzling translation of I. B. Singer's "Gimpel the Fool" with an ear for literary parody that made *Henderson the Rain King* a comic version of Conrad's "Heart of Darkness."

Maxwell Geismar suggests that "just as J. D. Salinger, by the middle fifties, was the spokesman of the college undergraduates, Saul Bellow was the favorite novelist of the American intellectuals."[1] But if the last decades have proven anything, it is that we are awash with spokespersons—from those who raced into print to tell us that "print" was obsolete to those who now argue that our most interesting fictionists are not imaginative writers at all, but literary theoreticians. In Bellow's case, the

111

difference between himself and other novelists who attracted fashionable attention is often the difference between innovator and popularizer, between synthesizing the time or merely being part of it, between a conscious role as novelist and a person who has written a novel. Certainly one of the tests of the contemporary writer is how "contemporary" he or she can be—not in terms of dotting a text with snatches from pop songs or Whitmanian catalogs of what one might find at a K-Mart, but, rather, in the honesty and force with which tough issues are raised and tough assessments made. The novelists who strike us as culturally important are the ones who ask, "Where are we now?" and who answer their own question in significant ways.

When *Seize the Day* was first published in 1956, Leslie Fiedler talked about the "ritual indignities" of new writers and the nearly mythic patterns of Bellow's publication: "His first novel a little over-admired and read by scarcely anyone; his second novel was once more critically acclaimed, though without quite the thrill of discovery and still almost ignored by the larger public; his third novel, thick, popular, reprinted in the paperbacks and somewhat resented by the first discoverers, who hate seeing what was exclusively theirs pass into the public domain; and now a fourth book; a collection of stories, most of which have appeared earlier, a new play and a new novella."[2] However, unlike our best living poets—who find themselves patronized as "young" until they are card-carrying members of the AARP—our best novelists endure the rites of literary initiation, and in the case of Saul Bellow, one could argue that he has even prevailed. Like Malamud, he has twice won the National Book Award (for the *Adventures of Augie March* in 1953 and for *Herzog* in 1964); a Pulitzer Prize for *Humboldt's Gift* (a 1975 novel that, ironically enough, included cracks about "poulitzers"); and of course, the Nobel Prize in 1976. What began as a groundswell—in the days when Maxwell Geismar could call Bellow "the Herman Wouk of the academic quarterlies"[3]—has become a thriving, seemingly inexhaustible academic industry. There are more book-length studies about Saul Bellow than about both Roths (Henry and Philip), I. B. Singer, and Bernard Malamud combined.

We turn to Bellow, I think, because as Fiedler once put it, he is "not merely a writer with whom it is possible to come to terms, but one with whom it is *necessary* to come to terms."[4] Although much has been made of the special qualities of postwar fiction—

Jonathan Baumbach, for example, claims that "since 1945, the serious American novel has moved away from naturalism and the social scene to explore the underside of consciousness"[5]—the sad fact is that all too many of our serious writers have been paralyzed by the great experiments of the twenties, or conversely, they have been so mesmerized by the giddy playfulness of metafiction that they no longer believe that fiction *matters*—that is, matters centrally to the cultural rhythms of a nation—as it once did. It is this dual sense of "waiting for the end"—either that final burial of the Great American Novel we have been expecting on a daily basis for decades, or the novel grown so inward, so convoluted, that it "deconstructs" altogether—that prompted Fiedler (in another critical country as it were) to begin a book about contemporary literature with this bit of hand-wringing, downbeat news:

> It is with a sense of terror that the practicing novelist in the United States confronts his situation today; for the Old Men are gone [Faulkner and Hemingway], the two great presences who made possible both homage and blasphemy, both imitation and resistance. It is a little like the death of a pair of fathers or a pair of gods; like, perhaps, the removal of the sky, an atmosphere we were no longer aware we breathed, a firmament we had forgotten sheltered us. The sky we can pretend, at least, is heaven; the space behind the sky we cannot help suspecting is a vacuum.[6]

But even Faulkner and Hemingway, mighty though they were, are not the alpha and omega of the contemporary writer's heritage. When we sadly remember that "there were giants in those days," we tend to think first of Proust or Mann, of Joyce or Eliot. Ours is a generation of writers who gaze at the urban labyrinths of *Ulysses* or the magisterial slopes of *The Magic Mountain* and say with Prufrock: "How should I then presume?/ And how should I begin?"

And yet for all the scope and intensity of modernist classics, their authors were not only confident that they were "right" about the wastelands and the assorted betrayals of modern life, but also that there was plenty of time in which to "tell you all." Indexes of time—that is, the amounts writers imagine they have and how they imagine they can use it—became a central factor for twentieth-century authors. In the heyday of modernist experimentation the heady business of "proving" that an inner life existed (meticulously documented in, say, Leopold Bloom's lyrical day in Dublin) or that the general culture was in decline (e.g., Eliot's *Waste Land*) required heroic efforts, even if—or more correctly, precisely because—the worlds they wrote about were so anti-heroic.

After all, Eliot's *Waste Land* (1922) runs more than four hundred lines, which is an incredible amount of space to devote to the proposition that London's bridges are falling down. To be sure, Eliot felt compelled—such being the nature of a Harvard education—to expand upon his initial observation about April as the cruelest month by dragging in as much supporting evidence from the Western traditon as he possibly could. My point, however, is that there was also a giddy joy connected with plotting the wasteland's longitude and latitude, of demonstrating—brilliantly, definitively—just how rotten modern life really was.

Not surprisingly, the characteristic stance of the wasteland's best geographers was one of premature age, a situation that is always easier to accept in its metaphorical, rather than its literal, forms. The publication of Darwin's *Origin of Species* in 1859 destroyed the certainties of the Victorian world, catching a poet such as Tennyson unprepared and in his fifties. Eliot, by contrast, was only twenty-seven when "The Love Song of J. Alfred Prufrock" was published, but it is clear that old age had already set in on an entire generation of literary minds. My point is simply that Eliot—like Prufrock, like the speaker of "Gerontian"—*felt* old, more than a little world-weary, and perhaps that is enough.

But people soon grew tired of waiting for Godots who might, or might not, arrive; instead, there was a growing interest in qualified problem-solving and in strategies that might lead to limited success. With Bellow particularly, there has been a willingness to confront the urban world for what it is—with all its dehumanizing potential—but not much belief in wastelands per se. As Marcus Klein puts it: "In the 1950's the sensible hero journeyed from a position of alienation to one of accommodation. Accommodation to the happy middling community of those years, to the suburbs, to the new wealth and the corporate conscience, to the fat gods. But the accommodation was aware of itself and for the spirit's sake, it saved a tic of nonconformity."[7]

With the possible exception of Augie March, Bellow's protagonists solve their respective problems within the context of fairly restricted societies, delicately balancing an inner life with increasing commitments to an outer world. It may have been fashionable for the Harvard undergraduate of Eliot's day to sail for England—thereby renouncing the America Ezra Pound thought of as a "half-savage country"—but that solution seems both dated and altogether self-conscious by now. In fact, the easy gesture of drawing thumb to nose is complicated endlessly in Bellow's novels by reservations that would never have occurred to a Stephen Dedalus or a Hugh Selwyn Mauberly. Herzog, for example, dangles between the two poles Klein describes as alienation and accommodation: he is a lover of highbrow literature and a sucker for *mameloshen;* a student of Heidegger as well as a product of *der heim;* a synthesizer of Big Ideas and a regular *mentsh.*

But that said, the movement from a J. Alfred Prufrock to a Moses Herzog takes more than *Yiddishkeit,* important though that concept may be in the formation of Herzog's character. Nor is it enough to say that nowadays the Robert Cohns *teach* at Princeton, in an age where "acceptance" has something to do with journals and editorial judgment but very little to do with people such as Jake Barnes and Bill Gorton.

For Bellow, the transition I've been alluding to begins with a novel designed to take the edge off the neurosis created by World War II. In this sense, *Dangling Man* became the novel Bellow had to write if he were to clear the air sufficiently to continue. Although the cramped, interior saga of Joseph, the dangling man, suffered from a variety of artistic ills—the heavy debts to Dostoyevsky's *Notes from Underground,* the general sense of "weariness" not relieved by catching all the allusions to Goethe, and most of all, the pretentiousness (half a matter of proving oneself; half a function of showing off) that often crops up in first novels—*Dangling Man* opened to generally good press. As Richard Chase put it, "the story was told with so much reticence as to give a thin, claustral quality to the whole."[8]

Jonathan Baumbauch mentions that Joseph, "isolated from his brethren like his biblical counterpart, has no real world." And yet, the biblical Joseph experienced literal pits from which he could rise to pinnacles. In fact, the biblical Joseph seems always to move in a world of enormous extremes—whether they be coats of outlandish color, prisons, or positions of high honor. While the biblical Joseph may be a character of isolation, there is never any doubt about his definition. By contrast, Bellow's Joseph lives

in an ill-defined middle: he has been classified 1-A, but has not
yet been drafted; he is unemployed, but unable to use his leisure
time productively; he is, ironically enough, free from responsibility, but denied a context in which the term might be meaning-
ful. And so, he dangles—opposing both the traditional involve-
ment/disillusionment syndrome of the standard World War I
novel and the hard-boiled Hemingway response that was its
enduring legacy. That *Dangling Man* is written in the form of a
diary—the first entry on December 15, 1942; the last on April 9,
1943—suggests not only its parallels to *Notes from Underground,*
but also the interior nature of Joseph's problems. Shut up in an
urban apartment, there are no convenient rivers into which
Joseph can plunge, thus effecting his "separate peace" from the
war. Indeed, if *A Farewell to Arms* sounded the death knell to
abstract words such as courage and honor and bravery, *Dangling
Man* shifts the ground until the possibilities of the inner life—
complicated now, to be sure, by the social institutions that
inevitably cluster about it—seemed a more appropriate response
to the condition of the fifties. Rejecting the Hemingway stance of
instant "hard-boiled-dom," Joseph becomes, for one critic at
least, a "sensitive and intelligent Robert Cohn who did not go to
Princeton."[9] And indeed, Joseph's first entry seems to insist that
this will be a modern novel stripped of the masculine hysterics
usually associated with the cult of the tough and tight-lipped:

> Today, the code of the athlete, of the tough boy—an American
> inheritance, I believe, from the English gentleman—that curious blend-
> ing of striving asceticism, and rigor, the origins of which some trace
> back to Alexander the Great—is stronger than ever. Do you have
> feelings? There are correct and incorrect ways of indicating them. Do
> you have an inner life? It is nobody's business but your own. Do you have
> emotions? Strangle them. To a degree, everyone obeys this code. . . . But
> in the truest candor, it has an inhibitory effect. Most serious matters are
> closed to the hard-boiled. They are unpractised in introspection, and
> therefore badly equipped to deal with opponents whom they cannot
> shoot like big game or outdo in daring.   (P. 9)[10]

Adherents of the code may be unpracticed in introspection, but
Joseph seems to "practice" it all too much. Instead of the grand
compensations available to the hard-boiled ("They fly planes or
fight bull or catch tarpon"), the dangling man is circumscribed
by his narrow room and the "minor crises of the day"—namely,

the "maid's knock, the appearance of the postman, programs on the radio, and the sure, cyclical distress of certain thoughts."

Added together, this is the stuff from which psychological *schlemiels* are made. Joseph suffers from failures of the spirit rather than from those of the marketplace. If his neighbor, Vanaker, "coughs"—his only method of making his presence known—Joseph prefers even quieter modes of isolation. His diary becomes an attempt to create significant gestures against the dehumanization, the regimentation, of a wartime atmosphere.

However, like other Bellow protagonists to follow, Joseph is impatient, eager to get things moving. He is, finally, neither Dostoyevsky nor is he Goethe. For all his pretenses about the sedentary, scholarly life, Joseph finds it difficult to enjoy as a "dangling man" those things that will be simply impossible in the army: "About a year ago, I ambitiously began several essays, mainly biographical, on the philosophers of the Enlightenment. I was in the midst of one on Diderot when I stopped. But it was vaguely understood, when I began to dangle, that I was to continue with them" (pp. 11-12). Given his circumstances, we are hardly surprised when Joseph's good intentions lack sticking power, and he soon discovers himself "unable to read." Books no longer either hold his interest or seem relevant to his new "dangling" condition: "After two or three pages or, as it sometimes happens, paragraphs, I simply cannot go on" (p. 10).

The result is a deep-seated hostility that seeks outlets for repressed anger at the same time it continues to profess philosophies of accommodation. In this sense Joseph is a preview of such coming attractions as Asa Leventhal, Tommy Wilhelm, and Moses Herzog. James Hall shrewdly points out that Bellow's characters tend to be compulsive "leaners," seeking support and confirmation wherever they can find it, but there is also a sense in which they also tend to push things over, to confuse angry sentiment with the pieces of china that inevitably get broken in Bellow's novels.[11] Thus, Joseph's dress becomes his "answer to those whose defiant principle it is to dress drably, to whom a crumpled suit is a badge of freedom" (p. 27). *His* suits are dark and conservative, although "counterbalanced" by shoes that are "pointed and dandyish." The result, I suppose, is to create a facade that is both alienating and accommodating—or to put the matter another way, to suggest how difficult firm stands on principle have become: "In short, the less noteworthy the better, for his purposes. . . . All the same, he manages to stand out" (p. 28).

Although much of *Dangling Man* charts its course on Joseph's inner consciousness, Bellow, like Sartre, works on the general notion that at least certain kinds of hell are other people. Joseph might fancy himself as "a sworn upholder of *tout comprendre c'est tout pardonner*" (p. 29), but his fits of temper suggest that he finds it hard to pardon anything.

In a crucial scene, for example, Joseph is having lunch with a friend when he becomes aware that an old acquaintance has been snubbing him. Granted, their original relationship was strictly political (both were Communist party members, attached to the same "cell"), but Joseph sees the moment as fraught with implications that go well beyond party loyalty, political censure, or even simple discretion. What follows is a swatch of what will become standard dialogue for the Bellow protagonist—the desperate search for consensus played against an audience that prefers endless complication to polite agreement. In any event, the more Joseph speculates about what may well be an imaginary affront, the angrier he becomes:

> "I said hello to him, and he acted as if I simply wasn't there."
> "What of it?" said Myron.
> "Does that seem natural? I was once a close friend."
> "Well?" said Myron.
> "Stop saying that, will you!" I said in exasperation.
> "I mean, do you want him to throw his arms around you?" asked Myron.
> "You don't get the point. I despise him."   (Pp. 32–33)

Eventually Joseph *does* manage to force the moment to its crisis—which in this case means creating a public scene. Working from the notion that he has "the right to be spoken to" and that the enforced lack of communication (here seen as a matter of party discipline) is "to abolish freedom," Joseph accosts his former comrade with a combination of hostility and righteous indignation:

> "I said hello to you before, didn't you notice?"
> He made no reply.
> "Don't you know me? It seems to me that I know you very well. Answer me don't you know who I am?"
> "Yes, I know you," Burns said in a low voice.
> "That's what I wanted to hear," I said. "I just wanted to be sure. I'm coming, Myron." I pulled my arm from him and we strode out.   (P. 34)

Granted, it is Joseph's very identity—rather than the conflict between party loyalty and personal friendship—that is at stake here. What Joseph demands is recognition, a sense that he matters. But like most of the outbursts that crop up in Bellow's fiction, there are always consequences. Joseph puts it this way: "I did not, and still do not, know where this outbreak came from" (p. 36).

As a result, Joseph is plagued by vague guilts and second thoughts; perhaps he should have kept his anger under control. But that much said, Joseph has a remarkable ability to recover in the way that nearly all of Bellow's irritated protagonists do. For an Augie March, bounce is the mechanism of essential energy required to move him from one picaresque adventure to the next—with "retrospective vision" defined as that which skims the best strategies from the milk of experience. Granted, Joseph moves more cautiously, balancing one rationalization against another until you make your way—slowly but surely—around the playing board. He feels, for example, that he "may be expecting too much from Myron" where the restaurant incident is concerned. After all, Myron had learned "like so many others, to praise convenience. He had learned to be accommodating. That is not a private vice; it has ramified consequences—terrible ones" (p. 38). So much for Myron. But the situation is contagious, as are Joseph's evaluations of them. Other friends also "fail" him.

And yet, even a casual glance at Joseph's diary suggests that while social events such as the Servatius party may be painful, being alone is even more so. His entry for, say, January 31, provides a good index of the problem: "Slight letup in the cold. The fury of cleanliness. One of my shirts came back from the laundry without a single button. I must complain" (p. 126). Only the prospect of resisting, of demanding his rights, of asserting his freedom—in a word, of being angry—keeps his day from degenerating systematically into total insignificance. Living as he does in what Bellow calls "those craters of the spirit" (p. 154), the anger caused by the ill-defined character of his dangling existence creates a drift toward psychological ineptness. Again, the failure of traditional *schlemiels* tended to be tangible and overt, a matter of exterior accident or pratfall that ended with victim and victimizer as the same person. By contrast, Joseph wills his destruction in more interior ways; he becomes, as it were, the victim of his inner life.

At the Servatius party, for example, Joseph is particularly annoyed when his wife begins to spend too much of her time at the punch bowl: " 'I wish you wouldn't drink tonight. It's a strong punch,' I said. My tone was unmistakable. I did not mean to be disobeyed. Yet a little later I saw her at the bowl and frowned at the quick motion with which she raised her arm and drank. I was irritated enough to consider, for a moment, striding up and snatching the glass away" (p. 44). The party and its multiple social disasters continue to prey on Joseph's mind, but this time the kicks are restrained, the slaps held back. He is, as he mentions later, only a "poor devil," if indeed he is a devil at all.

Joseph can, however, become absolutely unglued by his niece. During one of his infrequent visits to his brother's house, he hears a discussion about the sad lot of "poor civilians"—that is, people who will have to "get along on four pairs" of shoes per year, worry about a possible "run on clothes" and generally suffer the deprivations and inconveniences of wartime rationing. By contrast, Joseph refuses to become an officer because he feels that "the whole war's a misfortune. I don't want to raise myself through it" (p. 64).

Joseph's brother, crass though he may be, doesn't bother him nearly as much as his daughter Etta. For one thing, Amos is twelve years older than Joseph, and the history of the relationship might charitably be described as "strained." With Etta, on the other hand, Joseph is struck by "the resemblance she bears to me. It goes beyond the obvious similarities pointed out by the family, Our eyes are exactly alike, and so are our mouths and even the shape of our ears, small and sharp—Dolly's are altogether different. And there are other similarities, less easily definable, which she cannot help recognizing and which—our enmity being what it is—must be painful to her" (p. 62). This strong psychic identification, one that borders on secret sharing, leads directly to Joseph's ill-fated attempts to influence, as if French lessons and classical music might have a salutary effect. But Etta—naturally, even predictably—is more interested in Xavier Cugat than in Haydn. And in one of the novel's most evocative scenes, they quarrel about whose turn it is to play the phonograph. Joseph eventually loses control in what Maxwell Geismar calls "a rare act of aggression":

> "You can listen to the conga, or whatever it is, when I leave. Now, will you go and sit down and let me play this to the end?"
>
> "Why should I? You can listen to this. Beggars can't be choosers!" she uttered with such triumph that I could see she had prepared it long in advance.

"You're a little animal," I said, "as rotten and spoiled as they come. What you need is a whipping."

I caught her wrist and wrenched her toward me. . . . Seizing her by her hair fiercely, I snapped her head back. . . .

I hurried to my task, determined that she should be punished in spite of everything, in spite of the consequences; no, more severely because of the consequences.   (P. 70)

One wonders, though: is such aggression really so rare in *Dangling Man* ? When Joseph's former landlord turned off the heat and later the electricity, a fight—as opposed to a mere spanking—resulted. As Joseph puts it, revealing more about himself than he may realize: "We are a people of tantrums, nevertheless; a word exchanged in a movie or in some other crowd and we are ready to fly at each other" (p. 147). Still, the Etta incident has a character and a quality all its own. The very physicality of Joseph's action reminds us of the "force" William Carlos Williams had in mind in his short story, "The Use of Force." And too, rather than the countless, ill-defined aggressions that dot his diary, this moment strips the issue to its barest essentials. As Jonathan Baumbach observes: "That she so strongly resembles Joseph suggests that, in spanking her, Joseph is beating what he finds detestable in himself, or rather like Leventhal with Allbee is beating the objectification of himself. Etta succeeds in further victimizing Joseph by letting her parents infer that Joseph's attack was sexual (because of their physical resemblance, a kind of transferred onanism). Joseph, victimized further by his own free-floating sense of guilt, is unable to deny it" (p. 38).

That Joseph sees himself as "victim" rather than as victimizer is certainly true, but is it so much a matter of what he did or, rather, what he thinks he might have done? After all, nobody else seems especially aware that his niece resembles him. Moreover, Joseph has a penchant for manufacturing complications. For example, when he reads that a Jefferson Forman has crashed in the Pacific, Joseph immediately assumes that the dead soldier is an old classmate—even though a careful look at the facts suggests otherwise: "A Jefferson Forman is listed as having crashed in the Pacific. His home is given as St. Louis. The Jeff Forman I knew was from Kansas City, but his family may have moved in the last few years. . . . I heard he was in the merchant marine. Probably he had himself transferred when the war broke out" (p. 82). In a similar fashion Joseph had the direst possible thoughts about the marital future of the Farsons—only to discover later that they "have returned from Detroit, their training over. Susie dropped in to see Iva at the library. The baby had grippe, not a serious case. They have decided to send her to Farson's parents in Dakota, while they themselves go to California to work in an aircraft factory. Walter missed the child more than she did. They intend to send for her as soon as they settle down" (p. 160).

These reversals of imagined expectation created interior blunders in much the same way that more traditional *schlemiels* insured their failure by incorrect assessments of the external world. Caught in the craters of the spirit, Joseph vacillates between aggression as a strategy to preserve one's identity (his version of the Cartesian equation reads, "I hit, therefore I am!") and speculation about the relative virtures of alienation vs. accommodation. In one of the many lonely hours he spends with "The Spirit of Alternatives," Joseph rejects the solace of an easy, relatively painless alienation: "You have gone to its [the world's] schools and seen its movies, listened to its radios, read its magazines. What if you declare you are alienated, you *say* you reject the soap opera, the cheap thriller. The very denial implicates you" (p. 137). On the other hand, however, Joseph is all too aware that "alternatives, and particularly desirable alternatives, grow only on imaginary trees." Therefore, he resolves to make no protest: "When I am called I shall go. . . . Somehow I cannot regard it as a wrong against myself" (p. 84).

As Joseph's diary moves inexorably toward spring and the rhythms of ressurrection it traditionally connotes, he moves beyond an embrace of alternatives to a realization that all quests and "alternatives" are, finally, "one and the same": "All the striving is for one end. . . . It seems to me that its final end is the desire for pure freedom" (p. 115) In what Leslie Fiedler calls "the purest of ironies," Joseph leaves for camp, concluding his diary with the following entry: "Hurrah for regular hours! And for the supervision of the spirit! Long live regimentation!" (p. 191). The lines echo Stephen Dedalus's final entry in *A Portrait of the Artist as a Young Man,* but with all the terms turned upside down. Like other of Bellow's claustrophobic protagonists, Joseph strikes us as a Miniver Cheevy set down in the world of the contemporary American novel. He had dangled as he "thought and thought. And thought about it" in ways that threaten to make resolution impossible. Whatever else Bellow might be, he is not Kafka, and his novels, unlike Kafka's, have a way of suggesting that simple mechanisms (in this case, writing a letter to one's draft board) can push you out of the spirit's crater with great haste.

In *The Victim,* Bellow continues to exploit many of the same themes that had given substance to *Dangling Man.* Although one would not want to talk about Joseph's curiously introspective world as a bastion of good cheer, it does seem to me that the energy, and the health, generated by his last remarks suggest — at least in *sotto voce* — the life-affirming resiliency we warm to in *The Adventures of Augie March.* Granted, Augie's energy thrives without complication or borders; whatever else he might be, Augie is neither attuned to the claustrophobic nor given to whining. But that much said, let me hasten to add that he is more *schlimazl* than *schlemiel,* more the unwitting, and unlearning, victim of circumstances beyond his control than he is the conscious creator of his particular misfortunes. As James Hall points out:

> Though Augie may have learned a few things at the end — such as not to go hunting with strong-willed girls — he primarily *experiences.* If he had not gone hunting, he would have been stealing books in Chicago and piecing the world together in his mind. Thea's proposal is simply the most exciting — in anticipation — to turn up at a time when he is otherwise unengaged. Openness to experience plus a willingess to turn in an honest report is his value in itself. For any real person, of course, this can be only a partial approach to life. As a force rather than a full consciousness, Augie represents that energetic and adventurous part. The novel tests how much confidence can be placed in it if pessimism does not foreclose the question in advance.[11]

Victimhood is an a priori condition of nearly all the *schlemiels* in traditional Jewish literature and folklore; the more pressing question, of course, is the way in which the self wills its own destruction and what response the individual makes to such a misfortune. The *schlimazl,* on the other hand, has a relatively limited range of possibilities where fictive metaphors are concerned. In Nathanael West's *Cool Million,* Lemuel Pitkin emerges as a parodic abstraction of the Horatio Alger archetype, one with all his luck soured and the American Dream turned to nightmare, but with no fictive reality of his own. By contrast, Asa Leventhal is the "victim" in ways that force him to see failure as a problem of the psyche and responsibility as a consequence of misdirected anger.

Even more so than with Joseph, Leventhal lives in a world filled to the bursting point with "other people," most of whom seem intent on crowding into the same subway car. When Asa pushes back, however, his aggressiveness creates a rash of complications. Arriving at the home of his sister-in-law, for example, there is this tense moment with his nephew:

> "Where's your mother?"
> "She's in here. Who are you?"
> "Your uncle," said Leventhal. Coming into the hall he unavoidably pushed against the boy.   (P. 7)

Later, when Leventhal thinks about his wife (curiously missing from the novel's action and with so lame an excuse that one suspects she is AWOL), he remembers how she had been unfaithful to him during their engagement: "Then he asked if she had gone on seeing this man during the engagement. She said she had and only at that moment seemed to realize how serious the matter was. He started to leave, and when she tried to hold him back, he pushed her, and she lost her footing in the booth and fell" (p. 16).

To be sure, most of Leventhal's anxious, aggressive edge is reserved for the business of getting and spending in the great megalopolis. His persistent fears about a blacklist are complicated enough (Do such lists exist, or are they paranoid delusions?), but the situation gets even stickier when one adds the specialized nature of Leventhal's job to the equation. After all, there are only so many trade journals to go around—a sobering thought, indeed, for the Leventhal who remembers his former civil service job (tenured, abolutely secure) with mixtures of anxiety and regret. Most of all, however, Leventhal is nagged by the growing realization that he is the sort of person who allows anger and outrage to spoil his chances.

The first anxious days of his new job search are a good example. Leventhal quickly discovers a "spirit of utter hoplessness" and embraces it like an old friend: "The small trade papers simply turned him away. The larger ones gave him applications to fill out; occasionally he spent a few minutes with a personnel manager and had the opportunity to shake someone's hand. Gradually he became peculiarly aggressive and, avoiding the receptionists, he would make his way into an inner office, stop anyone who appeared to have authority, with coldness and with anger. He often grew angry with himself" (pp. 18-19).

It is, however, not so much a generalized, free-floating aggressiveness as it is a moment of genuine aggression that eventually becomes the center of Asa's dilemma. In Allbee (his very name suggesting allegorical properties), Leventhal confronts a situation remarkably similar to Joseph's angry, psychological encounter with Etta—although this time the tension it produces stretches out over the entire novel.

Too many readers, I think, have reacted to Allbee and to his systematic persecution of Leventhal in easy, predictable ways. For them, clear lines of distinction separate victim and victimizer. The result turns *The Victim* into an exposé of anti-Semitism along the lines of, say, Laura Z. Hobson's *Gentlemen's Agreement*. Bellow's novel, I would submit, is much more subtle and in its own way, much more disturbing. To begin at the beginning, the incident that triggers Allbee's anti-Semitic outburst and that forces Leventhal to confront both his Jewishness and perhaps more important, himself, is so buried in the unretrievable past that the novel's epigraph—an anecdote about the consequences of tossing date pits over one's shoulder and striking the innocent—seems more evidence of Leventhal's "guilt" than the narrative provides. In an effort to help the badly floundering Leventhal, Allbee sets up a job interview with his boss, a man named Rudiger. Unfortunately, but not surprisingly, the interview goes badly, and Leventhal makes an already unpleasant situation worse by screaming at his potential employer. Years later, Allbee—now a solid down-and-outer—returns to accuse Leventhal of deliberately insulting Rudiger, thus linking Asa's revenge with Allbee's unemployment. Leventhal, of course, denies all responsibility and promises himself that "if he follows me now I'll punch him in the jaw. I'll knock him down." He thought, "I swear I'll throw him down and smash his ribs for him!"

But the barrage of Allbee's accusations preys on Leventhal in ways that "hitting" cannot solve. For more traditonal writers such as Robert Penn Warren, the point about the past is that it *is* retrievable—moreover, that it is absolutely essential to retrieve it if one is to understand the present moment and move beyond it into the future. But that said, Asa Leventhal is not akin to the Jack Burden of *All the King's Men*, and for him, there is no way of looking at the scene in Rudiger's office either through the diligence of historical research or the miracle of instant replay. Rather, Leventhal is forced to do what Bellow's characters do best—rationalize and *lean:*

> He [Allbee] must have brooded over the affair for years, until he convinced himself that Rudiger had fired him because of that interview. Of course, it was true enough that Rudiger had a rotten temper, probably was born bad-tempered, but not even he would fire an employee, not for what the man himself had done but because of someone he had recommended. "How could he?" Leventhal asked himself. "Not a good worker; never." It was absurd. Allbee must have been fired for drunkenness. When could you get a drinking man to acknowledge that he had gotten into trouble through drinking, especially when he was far gone? And this Allbee was far gone.   (Pp. 36–37)

In Leventhal's case, however, rationalizations have a nasty habit of turning on themselves. A "good worker" never gets fired, but that is exactly what Leventhal himself is worrying about when he takes an afternoon off—complicated, of course, by the spectre of an industry-wide black list. Allbee, in effect, presses at the nerve of Asa's deepest fears and very quickly becomes the objectification of his *angst,* the secret sharer of his fate.

In this case, even "leaning" has its darker side, as Asa's friends never quite give him the support, the assurance, he had hoped for. After the Rudiger incident, Leventhal began to worry about the possible consequences of his action: *Was* there a blacklist? *Could* Rudiger ruin his career? Granted, his friend Harkavy assures him that "there isn't a thing he [Rudiger] can do to you. Whatever you do, don't get ideas like that into your head. He can't persecute you. Now be careful. You have that tendency, boy, do you know that?" (p. 46). Leventhal, of course, has precisely that sort of "tendency," but hearing about it, second-hand, as it were, is hardly what Leventhal was angling for when he unpacked his heart to Harkavy. Besides, he was not

assurred. And on afterthought he had misgivings about Harkavy's reference to persecution. Harkavy used such words whether they fitted or not. Rudiger's anger was not imaginary, and he was a man to fear. There were blacklists: that was well known. Of course he had not actually worked for Rudiger, and Rudiger could not blacklist him as a former employee. In the nature of it, it must be a secret process, passing through many conversations, private and professional. After all, Rudiger was influential, powerful. And who knew how things were done, through what channels? It was downright silly of Harkavy to speak of imaginary persecution.   (P. 47)

A mind operating this way finds itself much more drawn to an Allbee than to a Harkavy. What Asa demands is a world that singles him out for special attention—indeed, that is why he takes such a perverse pleasure in imagining Rudiger manipulating secret empires to affect his destruction—and Allbee answers this need in bold relief. Initially, Leventhal tolerates his outrageous accusations because even an enemy is better than nobody at all. Besides, Allbee, unlike Harkavy, confirms his sense of the world as a risky business where one slip can have lifelong consequences.

For the dangling man, there was a modicum of joy in "anticipating the minor crises of the day"—among which was the maid's knock. Leventhal also feels this keen sense of loneliness. In an early scene Leventhal relaxes after a particularly grueling day at the office when

there was a short ring on the bell. Eagerly he pulled open the window and shouted, "Who is it?" The flat was unbearably empty. He hoped someone had remembered that Mary was away and had come to keep him company. There was no response below. He called out again, impatiently. It was very probable that someone had pushed the wrong button, but he heard no other doors opening. Could it be a prank? This was not the season for it. Nothing moved in the stairwell, and it only added to his depression to discover how he longed for a visitor.   (P. 23)

When Allbee finally does make his presence known, Leventhal is so hungry for human contact that even "trouble" is preferable to tedium. Put another way, tensions (even those that are anxiety-producing and not a little neurotic) are surefire adrenaline producers, proof positive that one is fully alive. And as the full impact of his victim/victimizer pact with Allbee unfolds, Leventhal finds himself living on both sides of what turns out to be a very slippery coin.

Granted, Leventhal means to "clear" himself, and in this regard he goes first to Harkavy and then to his friend Williston, but what he collects only muddies the ethical waters. Leventhal ostensibly wants his friends to say the obvious—namely, that he is right and that Allbee is wrong. Instead, they shower him with versions of what Moses Herzog contemptuously calls "reality instruction"—advice that sounds as sensible as Ann Landers, but that is laced with brutal reality's harsher truths. Harkavy, for example, tells him: "You want the whole world to like you. They're bound to be some people who don't think well of you. As I do, for instance. Why isn't it enough for you that some do?" (p. 88).

The systematic movement toward Allbee is carefully documented: Allbee accepts Leventhal's money, moves into his apartment, even dons his bathrobe. And Leventhal, not to be outdone, gets drunk at Harkavy's birthday party, affecting an identification with his alcoholic antagonist. In short, their fates intertwine in what Kenneth Burke calls "symbolic overlap."

But just when it looks as if Mary will never return and that Allbee will never leave, Leventhal simply throws him out and suddenly things look very much improved: Mary, his long-absent wife, not only returns, but also soon becomes pregnant. Leventhal lands an excellent position with *Antique Horizons;* "his health was better"; and the newly reconstituted Leventhals can even afford a night out at the theater.

To be sure, the old, irritable Leventhal is never out of the picture entirely. After returning the ten dollars that Williston had given him for Allbee, he waits for a reply—already prepared to assume the worst: "But no reply came from Williston, and Leventhal was too proud to write a second letter; that would be too much like pleading. Perhaps Williston felt that he had kept the money from Allbee out of malice. . . . At first he was deeply annoyed; later he prepared some things to say to Williston if they should meet. But the opportunity never came" (pp. 286–87).

As for Allbee, Leventhal continued to hear rumor about "some journalist, from New England originally, who hit the bottle," but he preferred to believe that "he had continued to go down. By now he was in an institution, perhaps, in some hospital, or even already lying in Potter's Field" (p. 287). While such ignoble fates might be the logical conclusion of a naturalistic novel—one thinks of, say, Hurstwood's slow, agonizingly downward spiral in Dreiser's *Sister Carrie*—this is not the case in *The Victim.* In fact, Leventhal's victimhood is largely a matter of his own psychology; he is the misinterpreter of reality, the one who operates on the truths of feeling rather than on the truth of fact. Therefore, when he is angered at Williston or when he imagines Allbee's poetically justified death, the result is to once again suggest how *schlemiels* are created in a post-Freudian novel. Pratfall gives way to psychology, plot complications count for less than interior reversals—and in the case at hand, an Allbee who meets Leventhal at the theatre, not only very much alive, but also (from all appearances) doing quite well for himself, thank you. At best, Allbee is merely a catalyst for the attitudes and anxieties Leventhal already had. In this sense, then, the *schlemiel* -as-victim becomes the victim of himself, the center turns inward ("implodes," as the currently fashionable word would have it), and the psyche is seen as more important than the precipitating situation.

Granted, what I've been describing is, at best, only half of Bellow's loaf. His novels tend to alternate between studies of psychological stasis and exercises in exuberant celebration. In novels such as *Dangling Man* and *The Victim*, there is usually a claustrophobic setting (nights as hot as Bangkok, subways stuffed with other people, tiny rooms in which people scratch away at their diaries) and a pitched battle between the forces of sensibility and those of the will. Both Joseph and Asa are creatures with their fingers always poised at the pulse, ready to report at every instance exactly how they feel, but they are also men on the edge of anger. At times the bottled-up rage gives way to an action of sorts (generally, a clumsy, ineffective shove), but each is quick to speculate about the consequences. Granted, Asa strikes us as a good deal more active than Joseph; he rides to Staten Island, and hitting Allbee does bring about some measure of good health.

By contrast, in Bellow's novels of celebration, movement is not only easier but also much less complicated. Critics tend to think of, say, Augie March as a bit of the *schlimazl*, but he wins too often and too easily for such a luckless definition. Fascinated though he may be with character types, Augie adopts the best of an Einhorn or a Grandma Lausche, and moves on—often through a landscape crowded with minor characters such as Mimi, Clem, or Kayo—without much sense that one must pay for insights with suffering or that experience as such will ever run out. Henderson, too, lives in a world of seemingly infinite possibility, and in his quest to find a limiting and direct object for "I want," one sees the primary tension of an earlier writer such as F. Scott Fitzgerald extended to its logical conclusion. For Augie, then, there is youth and the assurance that not only will he be suspicious of people over thirty, but also that he will never cross over that dreaded dividing line himself. For Henderson, there is money and the endlessly exciting quests it can buy. As James Hall puts it, of his case one can say "the trip was worth taking, the results inconclusive."

With *Seize the Day*, Bellow returned to the novel of urgency as opposed to wide vistas of leisurely good cheer. In many respects Tommy Wilhelm is an Augie grown old and slightly paunchy, his chances quickly running out. Here bounce and endurance are commodities of the fathers, and in the aging world of *Seize the Day*, it is a father, rather than his son, who has the real staying power. In sheer economic terms, Tommy may well be the greatest failure in Bellow's failure-ridden canon. The Yiddish *schlemiel* also suffered from schemes that went comically awry, but unlike Tommy, he worked in considerably smaller units. One could sigh if a match between two wealthy families turned sour because nobody bothered to check about the respective sexes of the two newly born candidates or shrug one's shoulders if a horse dropped over dead for lack of oats, but such responses hardly seem appropriate to, say, the stock market crash of 1929. Indeed, the very charm of the Yiddish *schlemiel* depends on his ability to absorb defeat with equal measure of humorous acceptance and bittersweet disappointment.

Tommy, on the other hand, suffers from the same rage to be loved that afflicts other Bellow protagonists. His defeats, therefore, tend to be more emotional than financial, more of the psyche than the marketplace. Like Willy Loman, he believes that the "well-liked" never want, although the maxim works as poorly for him as it did for those caught in the tragic web of Arthur Miller's *Death of a Salesman*. Already in his mid-forties, Tommy has been a solid failure on a variety of fronts: as actor, as salesman, as father, and perhaps most galling of all, as son. Instead of the oppressive heat and Dostoyevskian apartment that closed in on Leventhal, Tommy lives out his empty days in the comparative luxury of the Hotel Gloriana. There, one's physical needs receive prompt and expensively courteous attention.

Life, however, is not all cigars, Coca Cola, and Unicaps. More than anything else, Tommy had "wanted to start out with the blessings of his family, but they were never given" (p. 23). Wilhelm remains—regardless of his age—one who could, as his father put it, "charm a bird out of a tree" (p. 6). However, Tommy's situation is not merely the reluctance of every father to see his son suddenly independent and a man. As Daniel Weiss suggests in his psychoanalytic study of the novel:

It is, I suppose, in those situations where life turns back on itself and breaks where it should begin that the tragic historical significance of the father-son relationship occurs. One thing seems fairly certain—that literature abounds more in those situations in which David destroys Absolom and Rustum, Schrab than those in which Theseus succeeds Aegeus and Prince Hal, King Henry—and more often than not defies the biological truism of youth succeeding age. It represents instead the efforts of an innately hostile father, who, by force of sheer vitality, or by the inertia of his established position, reverses the flow of progress and overshadows his son.[12]

Dr. Adler, Tommy's father, is not only capable of overshadowing his son or projecting such a standard of capital-*S* Success that Tommy is reduced to a capital-*F* Failure, but he is also so strong, so domineering, that his son has difficulty talking to him, much less Oedipally arranging for his murder. Therefore, Tommy's retreat into rationalization and the interior of the mind comes as no great surprise:

Another father might have appreciated how difficult this was—so much bad luck, weariness, weakness, and failure. Wilhelm had tried to copy the old man's tone and make himself sound gentlemanly, low-voiced, tasteful. He didn't allow his voice to tremble; he made no stupid gesture. But the doctor had no answer. He only nodded. You might have told him that Seattle was near Puget Sound or that the Giants and the Dodgers were playing a night game, so little was he moved from his expression of handsome, good-natured old age. He behaved toward his son as he had formerly done toward his patients, and soon it was a great grief to Wilhelm; was almost too great to bear.   (P. 11)

What Tommy demands, of course, is that his father be more the Hebrew patriarch (giving blessings, hands on shoulders, etc.), and less the Jewish doctor. The real issue is not so much "assistance" as it is *love;* for Tommy, as for Leventhal, feelings count in ways that others cannot—or will not—take into account:

It isn't the money [Tommy tries to explain], but only the assistance; not even the the assistance, but just the feeling. . . . Feeling got me in dutch at Rojax. I had the feeling that I belonged to the firm, and my *feelings* were hurt when they put Gerber in over me. . . . If he [Dr. Adler] was poor, I could care for him and show it. The way I *could* care, too. If I only had a chance. He'd see how much love and respect I had in me. It would make him a different man, too. He'd put his hands on me and give me his blessing.   (Pp. 56–57)

The vacuum Tommy feels is soon filled by Tamkin who dispenses stock tips instead of biblical blessings, quack psychology rather than medical advice. Tamkin is simultaneously a charlatan and a charmer, a character of exotic mystery to those who live at the Gloriana hotel and a standard fixture in subsequent Bellow novels. He is also the *schnorrer* who lets Tommy keep him company at lunch only to stick him with the tab, and the *luftmentsh* whose manipulations are more "in the air" than they are on the Stock Board.

For Tommy, however, Tamkin represents the last, desperate straw, and he stays with his speculations in rye and lard until the last dime. Tamkin's foolproof system and the various machines that never allow you to plunge into debt have failed; Tommy seized the day and found it bone dry. However, he does manage to achieve a catharsis of sorts in the novella's closing lines. Unblocked at the funeral home into which he stumbles as he chases after Tamkin, Tommy, at last, cries. His tears suggest, in Bellow's cadenced, but ambiguous prose, the "consummation of his heart's ultimate need"—presumably visible tokens of his realizations that death is the fate of every man (his dead and unmourned mother, his lost father, himself), and that an unpacked heart (one might even say, a *Jewish* heart) is the only path to Tommy's authentic Self.

Tommy's failure is not so much a matter of playing his money on the wrong commodity or even of falling in with bad company, but, rather, a disposition that makes life on the middle ground impossible. Like Bellow's other protagonists, Tommy is irritable and impatient. There is a sense in which he itches to get moving—even if it means that there are risks involved. What makes Tommy different from the Yiddish *schlemiel* is the manner in which their respective failures are willed. The Yiddish *schlemiel* is usually unaware of the impending doom his foolishness creates, and therefore his "failures" always comes as a surprise—even though his neighbors may have been laughing in anticipation for some time. Tommy, on the other hand, has been pinning his hopes on avatars of Tamkin all his life. The fact that he ends his speculative career with a Tamkin suggests, I think, a way of externalizing what have been constant, but lower keyed, anxieties. And his ability to shed tears—to unblock, as it were—must be seen as a sign of health, however much the gesture is misinterpreted by the other mourners.

With *Herzog* (1964), Bellow began to suggest some directions out of intellectual wastelands and the irritations that had afflicted his more aggressive protagonists. Indeed, during the period between *Herzog* and *Humboldt's Gift* (1975), stage-center was monopolized by the protagonist-as-historian, rather than the traditional concerns of the historical novel. As Bellow himself has suggested: "People don't realize how much they are in the grip of ideas. We live among ideas much more than we live in nature. . . . People's lives are already filled with mental design of one sort of another."[13] In this regard, *Herzog, Mr. Sammler's Planet* (1970), and *Humboldt's Gift* form a loose trilogy, one concerned with the impress of ideas on the fabric of contemporary culture, and with the comic interaction between a culture's notion of ideas and Bellow's embattled spokesmen. Unlike Tommy, these are protagonists more likely to utter ironic, urban prayers ("Lead me not into Penn Station," quips Moses Herzog) than to flood the world in tears, more prone to trade wisecracks on the street than to hide between the pages of a solipsistic journal. In an age which pays both lip service and hard cash to the special importance of intellect, such protagonists grow to expect the gingerly treatment due an endangered species. After all, there was a time in American literature when one was marked for Special Handling on quite other grounds. George Willard, the center of consciousness in Sherwood Anderson's *Winesburg, Ohio*, is filled with that sensitive stupidity which earmarks him as a good listener and which will, presumably, stand in good stead when he writes up his recollections in the "tranquility" of the big city. By contrast, Moses Herzog earns his way from grant to grant as a bonafide egghead—no small task given a literary tradition that prefers to outshoot its antagonists and to restrict its reading to the labels of whiskey bottles.

Granted, life as the Academy's darling is a decidedly mixed blessing. People respond to Herzog with nearly equal doses of admiration and thinly veiled condescension. As the Unwashed would have it, old saws like "if you're smart, why ain't you rich?" become the unspoken: "And if you were really so smart, how come your wife kicked you out?" This is bad enough, but those who appoint themselves as Herzog's instructors into the nature of the Real are even worse. They elbow into his life with teeth bared and a stomach for the worst brutalities quotidian life can offer.

Herzog is peculiarly unequipped to deal with the hard edges of a reality seemingly cut off from time and wrenched from better, more humanistic continuities. What we need, he half-playfully insists, is a "good five-cent synthesis," one that would provide "a new angle on the modern condition, showing how life could be lived by renewing universal connections; overturning the last of the Romantic errors about the uniqueness of the Self; revising the old Western Faustian ideology; investigating the social meaning of Nothingness" (p. 23). It is a grand, wonderfully nutty dream, the stuff that makes protagonists such as Artur Sammler, Charlie Citrine, and the Benn Crader of *More Die of Heartbreak* tick. Bellow's urban comedians are more likely to be men of moral vision than accountants of hard fact. Their respective sagas are chapters in what Citrine calls "the intellectual Comedy of the modern mind." In Herzog's case, everything militates against him making good on his early promise as a scholar: the sleazy cultural moment, Reality Instructors, Potato Lovers, nearly *any* woman, and of course, Herzog himself.

One shorthand way of putting this might be to say that victimhood finally meets its comic match. More than any Bellow character thus far, Herzog is a *schlemiel* with solid credentials: he is both cuckold and "suffering joker," the architect of his misfortune, as well as a man perfectly capable of turning irony inward. What he refuses to be, however, is a *victim*. Indeed, the sweep of *Herzog* works—often laboriously—toward justification: "Late in Spring, Herzog had been overcome by the need to explain, to have it out, to justify, to put in perspective, to clarify, to make amends." For a Milton, *Paradise Lost* is an epic attempt to justify the ways of God to man, and in certain respects, *Herzog* is its equivalent in our time—albeit, with human interactions getting the major focus and Herzog's mental letters providing a ready soapbox both for the novel's protagonist and its author.

But that said, let me hasten to add that the letters form not only the core of Herzog's—and often, Bellow's—wide-ranging ideas but also the novel's sense of urgency, of having it out once and for all with cultural nay-sayers. Such an epistolary novel may have its historical roots in eighteenth-century novels such as *Pamela* and *Humphrey Clinker*, but Herzog's letters—with their divided streams of elegant argument and psychological breakdown—suggest a distinctively modern variant.

Moreover, if the letters per se are the stuff of monologue, Herzog's truncated responses to them—as the world pulls him back into its quotidian grip—often suggest the flavor of an interior dialogue. That, of course, is the element providing the clearest index of difference between the badly shaken Herzog and the protagonists of earlier Bellow novels. There are, to be sure, moments of comic spirit in *Dangling Man* or *The Victim* when an interior smoldering has been misdirected or is wildly out of proportion to its cause, but one feels certain that a Joseph or a Leventhal will never see themselves in the same ironic light as their readers do. By contrast, Herzog (p. 3) takes both refuge and a measure of strength from self-mockery and a delicious taste for Jewish wit:

> Answer a fool according to his folly, lest he be wise in his own conceit. Answer not a fool according to his folly, lest thou be like unto him. Choose one.

I began this chapter by suggesting that Eliot enjoyed all the advantages of an automatic posture and the leisure time in which to "tell you all" that is simply not available in Bellow's world. With *Herzog,* even the general assurance that one is "right" gives way to qualification and lingering doubts. Indeed, for those who have long enjoyed sniping at Bellow for writing a "literature of ideas" (something, of course, that Bellow denies, even as he mounts up one "idea" after another in his defense), perhaps his most recent denial—included as part of his fore-word to Alan Bloom's *Closing of the American Mind*—is worth quoting in full:

> There are times when I enjoy making fun of the educated American. *Herzog,* for instance, was meant to be a comic novel: a Ph.D. from a good American university falls apart when his wife leaves him for another man. He is taken by an epistolary fit and writes grieving, biting, ironic and rambunctious letters not only to his friends and acquaintances, but also to the great men, the giants of thought, who formed his mind. What is he to do in this moment of crisis, pull Aristotle from the shelf and storm through the pages looking for consolation and advice? . . . Cer-tain readers of *Herzog* complained the book was difficult. Much as they might have sympathized with the unhappy and comical history pro-fessor, they were occasionally put off by his long and erudite letters. Some felt that they were being asked to sit for a difficult exam in a survey

course in intellectual history and thought it mean of me to mingle sympathy and wit with obscurity and pedantry.

But I was making fun of pedantry! . . . I meant the novel to show how little strength "higher education" has to offer a troubled man.[14]

Eliot, too, meant for J. Alfred Prufrock to make a comic point, one about how spontaneity dies a quick, ignominious death among the clutter of tea and cakes and ices—and, of course, brittle, overly self-conscious talk. Indeed, there are times when the parallels between Prufrock and Herzog are as striking as their final adjustments are different. For example, Herzog, like Prufrock, "was losing his hair." But rather than worrying—and free-associating—endlessly about whether or not he should "part it behind" (as Prufrock does), Herzog "read the ads of the Thomas Scalp Specialists with the exaggerated skepticism of a man whose craving to believe was deep, desperate. Scalp experts! So . . . he was a formerly handsome man" (p. 3). Both Herzog and Prufrock are products of—indeed, are formed by— the Great Tradition of Western Ideas, but the uses to which they put their allusive power differ markedly. Prufrock uses the past as an index of how far we—and he—have fallen; Herzog keeps insisting that Herzogean innocence and the Herzog heart may yet carry the day. To be sure, both commodities are under heavy attack. The recurrent nursery rhyme "I love little pussy"— implying that "if you don't hurt her, she'll do you no harm"—is continually undercut by a Madeleine who hurts him anyway.

In addition, Herzog (unlike Prufrock) can bring a rich past to bear on his messy present. And very often it is this abiding sense of life at its richest—i.e., the warmth of Napolean Street covering him like a blanket—that Herzog remembers when he frames his own "overwhelming questions": "Dear Doktor Professor Heidigger, I should like to know what you mean by the expression 'the fall into the quotidian.' When did this fall occur? Where were we standing when it happened?" (p. 49).

Granted, such questions reflect a comic spirit more directly than Prufrock's hyper-serious balancing of "Do I dare disturb the universe?" with "Do I dare to eat a peach?" Prufrock, of course, is afraid to take any action at all—fearful that he might be misunderstood ("That is not what I meant at all!"); fearful that he may be inadequate ("I am no Prince Hamlet, nor was meant to be"); fearful that the mermaids are singing to somebody else. By contrast, Herzog's personal life has been filled with commitments, but they are rapidly falling apart. When he speaks about his cuckoldry, Herzog's letters reflect the age-old suspicion that *schlemiels* create their own misfortunes. For the talmudic rabbis, seductions came when one was swaying over a thick volume at the House of Study; for Herzog, they occur when men like Gersbach throw around ideas as casually as they toss off their clothing: "I'm sure you know the views of Buber. It is wrong to turn a man (a subject) into a thing (an object). By means of a spiritual dialogue, the I-It relationship becomes an I-Thou relationship. God comes and goes in men's souls. And men come and go in each other's souls. Sometimes they come and go in each other's bed, too. You have a dialogue with a man. You have intercourse with his wife" (p. 64).

Even more important, however, Herzog has dared to step beyond the clichés of modernist alienation and its standard line about the impossibility of communication. Part of the irony in Prufrock's "love song" is that it is entirely interior—not a love song in the ordinary sense at all. At best, Prufrock may be saying something vital to his readers, but what he is saying, it seems to me, is that all of us live in a rather unfortunate time. Marvell has enough energy to "seize the day"; Hamlet had a tragic stature, but all poor Prufrock has is a balding head and worries about how he looks at parties. Herzog has more than his fair share of troubles, but they have a value of their own; there is no need to dress them up with elaborate citations to the library stacks. "He was in no mood," he writes the pedantic Shapiro, "for Joachim de Floris and the hidden destiny of Man. Nothing seemed especially hidden—it was all painfully clear" (p. 74).

When Prufrock finds himself so disenchanted with modern man—the disappointing product of biological evolution and social progress—he dreams of reversing the process until he becomes "a pair of ragged claws, scuttling across the floors of silent seas." By contrast, even after the horrors of Auschwitz, Herzog can still ask if "all the traditions [have been] used up, the beliefs done for, the consciousness of the masses not yet ready for the next development? Is this the full crisis of dissolution? Has the filthy moment come when all moral feeling dies, conscience disintegrates, and respect for liberty, law, public decency, all the rest, collapses in cowardice, decadence, blood?" (p. 74). These questions, I would submit, are the shivery, overwhelming ones for our time, and beginning with *Herzog*, Bellow's protagonists are united in announcing their respective "No's, in thunder!"

Granted, the elderly Artur Sammler of *Mr. Sammler's Planet* is spared both sexual grief and comic suffering; Charles Citrine (*Humboldt's Gift*) spends his time speculating about the tragic *schlemiel* hood of Humboldt von Fleisher; Albert Corde, the dean of *The Dean's December* (1982) meditates away on his nonfiction article about Chicago; and most recently, the eggheads of *More Die of Heartbreak* (1988)—this time a world-renowned scientist and his secret-sharing nephew—add their names to the roll of those who also find themselves stumped by Freud's (in)famous question, *Was will das Weib?* ("What does woman want?").

In short, the beat that Herzog began goes on, albeit without Herzog's charm, without his Jewish wit, without his brand of *schlemiel* hood. Which is to say, Bellow's latest protagonists—like Bellow himself—do not suffer fools gladly, nor do they expect to encounter them as they shave. Rather, they insist that we pay attention as they pontificate. To be sure, Herzog also drags us along as he works out the fine points of his "grand synthesis," but if we are impressed by the occasional flashes of brilliance, we are equally convinced they will never make their way between hard covers. Herzog's life is too messy, and the man too distracted.

Nonetheless, Herzog manages to shore up what may have been ruined to preserve what may still be left. The fall from innocence—both as comment on the nation's past and as synopsis of his own history—suggests the ways in which his question to Heidigger, his nursery rhyme to Madeleine, and his historical study, *Romanticism and Christianity*, are all related. Modernism molded such materials into gloomy portraits and even grimmer prognoses. By contrast, Herzog rejects "the canned sauerkraut of Spengler's 'Prussian Socialism,' the commonplaces of the Wasteland outlook, the cheap mental stimulants of Alienation, the cant and rant of pipsqueaks about Authenticity and Forlornness. I can't accept this foolish dreariness" (pp. 74–75). When he writes to his colleague Professor Mermelstein (the man who has been systematically scooping his best ideas), he again reaffirms his faith that "we must get it out of our heads that this is a doomed time, that we are waiting for the end, and the rest of it, mere junk from fashionable magazines" (pp. 316–17).

Both Prufrock and Herzog emerge as intellectual indices of their respective decades. But that said, Prufrock's elegantly rendered pathos strikes us now as less the stuff of "confession" than as a posture of comfortable inadequacy, while Herzog—after much resistance—abandons the field of self-definition altogether. As he imagines writing to Mermelstein, "I am even willing to leave the more or less [of what Herzog "is"] in your hands. You may decide about me. You have a taste for metaphors" (p, 317)."

His solution is the Herzog heart. It is an extension of his name (the German *hertz* meaning "heart"), but more important, it is the result of a distinctively Jewish vision. As a certified academic, Herzog may have thought his way out of the wasteland, but on more emotional levels, he simply refuses to indulge in orgies of despair. Indeed, he is more likely to wave his hands to illustrate a joke than to wring them to demonstrate how bad things are. As Himmelstein puts it: "You're not one of those university phonies. You're a *mensch.*" And in this case, Himmelstein is probably more correct than he imagines.

But the lower-brow case for Herzog does not end there. For all his trenchant criticism of sentimentality's darker sides, Herzog cannot obliterate the part of him that is an inveterate "potato lover." Despite his embattled situation and his understandable bitterness, versions of potato love ooze out—for his brothers, for his children, and finally, for life itself. Herzog is, in short, the lovable bumbler, the academic *schlemiel* who had "once tucked [his] jacket into the back of [his] trousers, coming from the gentlemen's room and walked into class." His is the ironic, self-deprecating vision that cannot *not* see: absorbed in reading Kierkegaard's *Sickness Unto Death,* only a Herzog—waist-high in *tsoris*—could note that this was "nice reading for a depressive!" and only a Herzog could answer an overly enthusiastic admirer's comment that "art is for Jews!" by quipping back: "It used to be usury!"

Although he is "sick with abstraction" (Madeleine's diagnosis of Herzog's problem), he can still turn his attention to "this planet in its galaxy of stars and worlds [going] from void to void, infinitesimal, aching with its unrelated significance" and then reverse field—with "one of his Jewish shrugs"—and whisper: "*Nu, maile.* . . . Be that as it may." He is, finally, the American Jew: fully assimilated into its experiences and sharing its aspirations, teaching in its universities and flying off to its conferences, but able, nevertheless, to bring a special heritage of endurance to bear on its modern situations. To the knowledge of a Prufrock, Bellow adds an aching Herzog heart and a ready Herzog quip.

Herzog's progess in the novel is, admittedly, a tiring one—both for Herzog and its readers. By contrast, *Mr. Sammler's Planet* begins at a point well beyond Herzog's rage for a synthesizing book or even the exhaustion that stretches Moses across his pastoral hammock. Artur Sammler casts his "one good eye" on the junk of contemporary culture from a vantage point well beyond sensuality. In this sense Sammler is less an extension of the Romantic Herzog than he is a variation of the themes in Yeats's "Sailing to Byzantium." Caught in a city that has added genital-bullying to our century's "mackeral-crowded" landscape, he also concluded that "that is no country for old men." It is also not the time nor the place for further "explanations": "You had to be a crank to insist on being right. Being right was largely a matter of explanations. Intellectual man had become an explaining creature. Fathers to children, wives to husbands, lecturers to listeners, experts to laymen, colleagues to colleagues, doctors to patients, man to his own soul, explained" (p. 3). Nonetheless, *Mr. Sammler's Planet* is a book composed of exactly these sorts of "explanations." If the subways were hot and overcrowded in *The Victim*, things have worsened steadily since. Sammler walks cautiously through "invariably dog-fouled" streets, no longer surprised that the counter-culture's young look "autochtonous" or that one must search like Diogenes for a functioning telephone booth.

In *Mr. Sammler's Planet* the rage for a "charmed and *interesting* life" turns minor characters into menagerie grotesques and the city itself into a Theatre of Decadence. That much about Bellow's fiction has remained constant—in *More Die of Heartbreak* (where Fishl Vilitzer, the local representative of a West Coast maharishi, cons potential investors into playing the market "from a spiritual base"), in those who surround Clara Velde, the protagonist of *A Theft* (1989), and most recently, in the machinations that give rise to the Mnemosyne Institute in *The Bellarosa Connection* (1989). Sammler hectors nearly everyone as if he were an East European Gibbon and this was the decline and fall of New York City.

Bellow's earlier fiction was careful to keep such rancor at least half-hidden behind comic masks, but with Sammler, as well as those who follow in his increasingly neoconservative footsteps (e.g., Dean Albert Corde, Kenneth Trachtenberg, Teddy Regler, and the unnamed narrator of *The Bellarosa Connection*), enough sociopolitical *narishkeit* (foolishness) is apparently enough. Besides, Sammler *enjoys* his role as a self-styled Jeremiah among the unclean who care as little for authority as they do for Old World "culture." Not since the days of T. S. Eliot has there been such an eloquent, and extended, appeal on behalf of reestablishing that necessary relationship between tradition and the individual talent: "Antiquity accepted models, the Middle Ages—I don't want to turn into a history book before your eyes—but modern man, perhaps because of collectivization, has a fever of originality."

Mr. Sammler's Planet is, in effect, a three-tiered world: on the naturalistic level, sexuality asserts a chaotic power, one expressed in bold relief by the elegant, black pickpocket; Lal (whose manuscript is an Eastern version of Norman Mailer's *Fire on the Moon*) projects an overhanging lunar metaphor; Sammler himself directs our attention to those depths wherein each of us can rediscover the terms of our human contract. Ironically enough, of the three possibilities, it is the first that garners the largest amount of sheer space. *Mr. Sammler's Planet* is as filled with urban oddballs as it is with realistic detail. It is, in short, a world that begins to look more and more like Shula-Slawa's shopping bags—crammed to the bursting point with all manner of eccentric goods. The book's minor characters tend to irritate the priggish Sammler, but their lapsability is an index of his own strength. *He* can explain the mental designs that lie just behind the city's veneer of hustle and tough talk.

In similar ways, *Humboldt's Gift* is at once a prolonged, often painful, meditation on the responsibilities of the living to the dead and a comic paean to Chicago, full of zany romps through its streets and buildings. The result is God's plenty, both of heady thought and urban savvy. The story of Charles Citrine is divided into two separate, but unequal, parts—backward glances at what he calls his "significant dead" and the forward motions of a life growing increasingly cluttered. Von Humboldt Fleisher epitomizes the lyric poet *extraordinaire*. During the thirties his *Harlequin Ballads* was "an immediate hit," the stuff of which litrary fame—and literary power—is fashioned. But an appetite such as Humboldt's depends upon a calculated restlessness, a fight to the finish between life as it is and what his poetry might make it become. If Goethe had insisted, at the end, on "more light!" poor Humboldt required an even wider range of excesses: more enemies, more influences, more sex, more money, more. . . . As Citrine puts it: "Humboldt wanted to drape the world in radiance, but he didn't have enough cloth."

Humboldt haunts the novel both as an abiding presence and a fearful reminder. Had I. B. Singer written the novel, Humboldt would surely have been an invading *dybbuk;* Bellow seems willing to settle for the dead poet as one of Citrine's more troublesome ghosts of the heart. Humboldt had spent his life "pondering what to do between *then* and *now,* between birth and death to satisfy certain great questions," and now Citrine must face the awful possibility that the costs had outstripped their accomplishments. For one thing, the centers of power had shifted, reducing Humbolt to an object America can "love," but need not take seriously, much less *fear.*

Humboldt is, of course, not the only casualty of America's unflinching toughness. Citrine's elegiac tone reveals as much about himself as it does about his poetic master. Humboldt's epical list of "sacred words" (Alienation, Waste Land, the Unconscious, etc.) is a poignant reminder of those days when, as Lionel Abel once put it, New York was a very Russian city, a "metropolis yearning to belong to another country." Which is to say, Von Humboldt Fleisher was the American Jewish renaissance in powerful miniature. By contrast, Citrine had been "too haughty to bother with Marxism, Freudianism, the avant-garde, or any of these things that Humboldt, as a culture Jew, took so much stock in." Like Bellow himself, Citrine operates on the gut feeling that if ten New York intellectuals embrace an idea, it could not possibly have much lasting value. Both author and character prefer the naturalistic turf of Chicago (where one is forced, in Citrine's words, to become "a connoisseur of the near-nothing") to the assorted isms that Humboldt's crowd generates. And yet, Citrine finds himself uncomfortably famous as the graph of his success rises in something like a direct proportion to Humboldt's decline.

To be sure, Citrine bears more than a little resemblance to Moses Herzog. He too has a grand book more in mind than on paper, and he too suffers all the pangs of a life "in great disorder." But the Humboldt/Citrine relationship is also a version of the psychological sharing Bellow had explored in *The Victim.* Humboldt's accusations, however loony and/or unfounded, cannot be dismissed out of hand. Citrine's meditations are filled with the suspicion that Humboldt may have been right after all. Has the intellectually competitive life turned him (however unintentionally, however unconsciously) into an "operator," an enemy of true Art?

Penance requires nothing less than an "inspired levitation" toward the truth, a project big enough to prevent the "leprosy of souls." It is a tall order, as tiring as it is impossible. And not surprisingly, carrying the weight of Western thought on his shoulders takes a comic toll. In short, Citrine becomes yet another architect of his own misfortune, a *schlemiel* whose moral reclamation projects are as large as his failures. In his case, the result is a Charles Citrine ("Pulitzer Prize, Legion of Honor, father of Lish and Mary, husband of A, lover of B, a serious person and a card") who tries valiantly to square the mystical pronouncements of Rudolph Steiner (*Knowledge of the Higher Worlds and Its Attainment*) with the concrete surfaces of Chicago.

Citrine gives the effort his all, but he ends in what his analyst calls "melancholia . . . interrupted by fits of humor." Even the much-harried Artur Sammler had better luck plowing his way through Meister Eckhart. Citrine begins a Steinerian meditation only to find himself interrupted by angry knocks from the outside. In this case, the "knocks" include those by Reality Instructors who hector him about his dreaminess; lovable con men with schemes for projected books or an African mine; racketeers who run the gamut from those who dress like gentlemen and play paddle ball to those who batter expensive automobiles with baseball bats; quack spiritualists; sensuous women; and those ultimate heavies in Bellow's universe—lawyers representing an estranged wife. Citrine suffers them all—and himself—with comic grace.

After all, Citrine has long recognized that "in business Chicago, it was a true sign of love when people wanted to take you into money-making schemes." But there are other, more *literary* reasons as well. Characters such as Citrine require a thickly textured counterbalancing if the novel is to avoid spinning off into those "high worlds" Steiner writes about. Thus, the city provides Bellow with a necessary comic grounding, a way of keeping *schlemiels* like Citrine under pressure and in what he calls his "Chicago state": "I infinitely lack something, my heart swells, I feel a tearing eagerness. The sentient part of the soul wants to express itself. There are some of the symptoms of an overdose of caffeine. At the same time I have a sense of being the instrument of external powers. They are using me either as an example of human error or as the mere shadow of desirable things to come" (p. 66). I suspect that comes as close to a description of Bellow's own creative process as we are likely to get. In *More Die of Heartbreak,* Kenneth Trachtenberg, the narrative voice out simultaneously to protect and justify his dreamy, distracted uncle, puts it this way

My work was cut out for me: I was to help my dear uncle to defend himself. I didn't suppose that the Layamons meant him great harm; only they weren't likely to respect his magics or to have the notion of preserving him for the sake of his gifts. There was quite a lot at stake here. I can't continually be spelling it out [although, unfortunately, Kenneth does precisely that for long stretches of the novel]. As: the curse of human impoverishment as revealed to Admiral Byrd in Antarctica; the sleep of love in human beings as referred to by Larkin; the search for excitements as the universal nostrum; the making of one's soul as the only project genuinely worthy of undertaking.   (P. 155)

Trachtenberg's last phrase is especially important because, as we learn earlier in the novel: "The city is the expression of the human experience it embodies and this includes all personal history." The result is that if a Benn Crader, an Albert Corde, a Clara Velde, or the unnamed protagonist of *The Bellarosa Connection* are to make their respective souls, the smithy on which they will be forged is the city.

All of which brings my discussion of Bellow's sense of urban comedy full-circle, back to his lovesick, meditative *schlemiels* and their efforts to bring a humane order to the chaos of contemporary culture. Not surprisingly, the anger, the argumentation, the "mental letters," and the stump speeches generally end in silent acceptance, in a feeling that the values of the heart will, yea, *must*, prevail. At one point in *Herzog* Moses remembers how, when he was a small boy, his mother had taught him a lesson that far outweighs any truth that armies of subsequent "reality instructors" have tried to pound into him. She had rubbed her palm until a small ball of dirt appeared—empirical proof that man was made of dust and is destined to return to it. As an adult, Herzog is no longer able to believe the story as a child believes, but in many respects, *Herzog* is a novel that blends what Mama Herzog had known from a Jewish tradition with what her educated son had "learned" from an American one. In the last lines of the novel Herzog is at peace, just on the edge of telling his housekeeper, Mrs. Tuttle, not to make so much dust. And in a way, the novel itself has been out to dampen down some of the "dust" that Bellow's more irritable protagonists tend to stir up. *Herzog* ends with the letters stopped and a version of health virtually indistinguishable from sheer exhaustion. Thus, Moses Herzog leads himself, and us, out of the wasteland and into a country where if it doesn't hurt enough to cry, at least it doesn't ache too much to laugh.

7
Philip Roth: The *Schlemiel* as Fictional Autobiographer

One of the dominant voices of American Jewish literature during the past three decades, Philip Roth has had an ambivalent, even troubled, response to the Jewishness of his congenial material. He was born in Newark, New Jersey (19 March 1933), and shares that birthplace with such luminaries of contemporary letters as Allen Ginsberg, Leslie Fiedler, and Imamu Amiri Baraka (LeRoi Jones). At best, only traces of Newark still cling to the others: Allen Ginsberg bangs his prayer wheel, squeezes his harmonium, and gives every impression of being a bodhisattva; LeRoi Jones has metamorphosed himself into a true son of Africa; and Leslie Fiedler headed west, literally, to Montana and figuratively to that place in his imagination where black men and American Indians are really "Jewish" under the skin. Only Philip Roth has remained faithful, in his fashion, to what it meant to grow up Jewish in lower-middle-class Newark.

Goodbye, Columbus and Five Short Stories was published in 1959, at a moment conveniently wedged between the innocence that had characterized the 1950s and the permissiveness that was to dominate the next two decades. For better or worse, Philip Roth became a remarkably accurate barometer of the radical shift occurring in our national sensibility, not only in terms of how American Jews tended to look at themselves, but also in terms of the permutations that sexual candor could take. To be sure, the benefit of hindsight turns such judgments into easy commonplaces; in 1959 *Goodbye, Columbus* looked very odd indeed. On one hand, it was F. Scott Fitzgerald's *This Side of Paradise* in an American Jewish idiom; on the other, it was satire à la Evelyn Waugh, but without the saving graces of his urbane civility.

Even more important, however, here was an author with a

distinctive voice, one whose idiom and cadences seemed so natural, so altogether *right,* that they hardly sounded "literary" at all. But, of course, Roth's unflinching tales of suburban American Jewish life *were* literature, and literature of an impressive sort. The work not only won its twenty-six-year-old author a National Book Award, but more important, it also changed the very groundrules for American Jewish writing. If a moral fabulist such as Bernard Malamud was destined to be forever associated with his remark, apocryphal or actual, that "all men are Jews!" Roth made it clear from the beginning that all Jews were also men.

But that said, let me hasten to add that *Goodbye, Columbus* is out to show just how vulgar, how materialistic, how yucky, these Jewish men can be. And this, of course, requires the services of a cocky Neil Klugman, rather than those of a hapless *schlemiel.* In the beginning, then, there was the narrative Word, the voice that arranged, say, the fateful meeting between Neil Klugman and Brenda Patamkin or the psychological warfare between Sergeant Marx and the goldbricking Grossbart. That voice packed a *tone,* and a wallop—especially for those readers who preferred to see American Jews paraded through the public print with more dignity, more decorum. "Outrage" would be a charitable way of describing their collective response, although as the old vaudevillians like to put it, they hadn't seen nuthin' yet. A decade later Roth would raise bashing the Jews to a level of comic complaint that American literature—and certainly American Jewish literature—had not heard before.

Parts of a new novel had appeared in *New American Review,* in *Partisan Review,* in *Esquire.* Publicity about it had appeared everywhere: on talk shows, in newspapers, and, of course, among the indignant congregants of synagogues. The advance sales were staggering; rumors about what Hollywood was willing to pay for the screen rights dazzled serious writers and critics alike. It was 1969, and Roth's newest assault was a sure bet to end the decade with a literary bang. The novel was, of course, *Portnoy's Complaint.*

Such a novel is, by definition, hard to pin down. Indeed, its very *title* works on at least three levels: as a "complaint"—in the legalistic sense of an indictment—handed down against those cultural forces that have so crippled, so un-manned Alexander Portnoy; as a "complaint" in the old-fashioned sense of illness, one that Dr. Speilvogel comically describes in clinical language

as "a distortion in which strongly-felt ethical and altruistic impulses are perpetually warring with extreme sexual longings,
often of a perverse nature"; and finally, as a "complaint" in its
common usage as an expression of pain, dissatisfaction, or
resentment.

Alexander Portnoy, a thirty-three-year-old mamma's boy and
New York City's assistant commissioner of human opportunity,
has come to the end of his psychological tether as the novel
opens. That his age is the same as Christ when crucified, that he
protects the sacredness of every human oportunity (except, of
course, his own), and that he rails against injustice, against
bigotry, and the body's fears make for intriguing mythopoeic
possibilities, but that, it seems to me, is precisely the critical
point: *Portnoy's Complaint* is as filled with "possibilities" as it is
riddled with interior "contradictions." No doubt Portnoy would
insist that, like the speaker of Walt Whitman's "Song of Myself,"
he is large enough to contain multitudes. The difference, of
course, is that Whitman's epical poem has aspirations that go
well beyond his hairy-chested celebration of a cosmic, largely
imagined selfhood; by contrast, Portnoy's systematic contradictions have the look, the *feel,* of a case study, however much he
insists that they are part of a larger cultural condition.

After all, it is Portnoy's voice—alternately boasting and pleading, kvetching and self-justifying—that we hear from cover to
cover. He retains a relentless grip on the novel's point of view. For
him, the analyst's couch functions in roughly the same way that
center stage did for the Barrymores—excess comes with the
territory. Other characters are reduced to bit players, relegated
to walk-ons in the fractured chronology of Portnoy's shifting
memories.

But that said, one begins to suspect that Portnoy complaineth
a bit *too* much, that there is another side to his psychologically
crippled coin. I raise this caveat to those who were quick to
identify with Portnoy, and to shout "Portnoy c'est moi!" while
they gleefully compared the indignities of *their* childhood with
those of Portnoy's, as well as to those who pointed out, correctly
enough, that the whole Jewish mamma–Jewish son business was
neither ethnically indigenous nor particularly unique, that Italian mothers or Irish mothers or whatever share many of the
same characteristics.

What both the overly sympathetic and the overly offended
tend to miss, of course, is the novel's humor. As Portnoy puts it:

What was it with these Jewish parents—because I am not in this boat alone, oh no, I am on the biggest troop ship afloat . . . only look in through the portholes and see us there, stacked to the bulkheads in our bunks, moaning and groaning with such pity for ourselves, the sad and watery-eyed sons of Jewish parents, sick to the gills from rolling through these heavy seas of guilt—so I sometimes envision us, me and my fellow wailers, melancholics, and wise guys, still in steerage, like our forebears—and oh sick, sick as dogs, we cry out intermittently, one of us or another, "Poppa, how could you?" "Momma, why did you?" and the stories we tell, as the big ship pitches and rolls, the vying we do—who had the most castrating mother, who the most benighted father, I can match you, you bastard, humiliation for humiliation, shame for shame. (Pp. 117-18)[1]

In a very real sense, *Portnoy's Complaint* is a collection of the "stories we tell," an account of a castrating mother and a be-nighted father, and the humiliations and shames they caused. But it is also a prolonged boast—not, to be sure, in the tradition of ring-tailed roarers such as Nimrod Wildfire or Davey Crockett (who took enormous pride in the fact they could outrun, outshoot, and outfight anybody in ol' Kentuck), but, rather, in the anti-heroic tradition of a Leopold Bloom. Portnoy's tall tales, taken together, make it clear that he is more anxious, more guilt-ridden, in a word, more screwed up than anybody in Newark.

To be sure, Portnoy contributes mightily to the *tsoris* and the *tumel*. If his life is a series of comic accidents, many of them are of his own making. Take, for example, masturbation. The adolescent Portnoy, for all the vivid memories about how much he practiced and about the powerful gratifications that "wacking off" provided, had as little luck with his phallus as Chaplin's Little Tramp had with machines:

Then came adolescence—half my waking life spent locked behind the bathroom door, firing my wad down the toilet bowl, or into the soiled clothes in the laundry hamper, or *splat,* up against the medicine-chest mirror, before which I stood in my dropped drawers so I could see how it looked coming out. Or else I was doubled over my flying fist, eyes pressed closed but mouth wide open to take that sticky sauce of buttermilk and Clorox on my own tongue and teeth—though not infrequently, in my blindness and ecstasy, I got it all in the pompadour, like a blast of Wildroot Cream Oil.   (P. 16)

But for all the elaborate ways and means of his frenetic, compulsive masturbation, Portnoy is a bust at being bad. Indeed, that's the real struggle in *Portnoy's Complaint:* "to be bad—and to enjoy it! . . . But what my conscience, so-called, has done to my sexuality, my spontaneity, my courage! Never mind some of the things I try so hard to get away with—because the fact remains, *I don't*. I am marked like a road map from head to toe with my repressions."

Others, apparently, have an easier time with sin. Smolka, Portnoy's free-wheeling boyhood chum, "lives on Hostess cupcakes and his own wits"—ingesting the junk food of our junk culture without undue worries either about civilization or its discontents. By contrast, Portnoy hoards his guilty memories like a miser: in his days as an adolescent Onanist, he had spilled his seed into empty Mounds bar wrappers, into empty milk bottles, into cored apples and once, into a piece of liver that was later served up at the Portnoy family dinner table.

What he remembers most, however, about these masturbatory binges are his darkly comic failures. In this regard, none is more spectacular than his disastrous episode with Bubbles Girardi. She has "agreed"—if that is the proper word for her listless, half-hearted resignation—to jerk off one of Smolka's buddies. But there are strict conditions: the lucky stiff must keep his pants on, and *she* will count the strokes: fifty, and not a single one more. As fate would have it, Portnoy (who is a quick study when it comes to fantasy, but something of a flop in "real-life" situations) wins, and the result is comic *schlemiel* hood of the first water:

At long last, not a cored apple, not an empty milk bottle greased with vaseline, but a girl in a slip, with two tits and a cunt—and a mustache, but who am I to be picky? . . . I will forget that the fist tearing away at me belongs to Bubbles—I'll pretend it's my own! So, fixedly I stare at the dark ceiling, and instead of making believe that I am getting laid, as I ordinarily do while jerking off, I make believe that I am jerking off.

And it begins instantly to take effect. Unfortunately, however, I get just about where I want to be when Bubbles' workday comes to an end.

"Okay, that's it," she says, "fifty," *and stops!*

"No!" I cry. "More!"

"Look, I already ironed two hours, you know, before you guys even got here—"

"JUST ONE MORE! I BEG OF YOU! TWO MORE! PLEASE!"

" N-O!"

Whereupon, unable (as always) to stand the frustration—the deprivation and disappointment—I reach down and grab it, and POW!

Only right in my eye. With a single whiplike stroke of the master's hand, the lather comes rising out of me. I ask you, who jerks me off as well as I do it myself? Only, reclining as I am, the jet leaves my joint on the horizontal, rides back the length of my torso, and lands with a thick wet burning splash right in my own eye.   (Pp. 178-179)

In short, Portnoy's sexual antics are the stuff of which Borscht Belt stand-up is made, but as he keeps insisting, this is no Jewish joke, no *shpritz* (machine gun spray of comic material) about lime jello being heavy *goyish* and pumpernickle being *echt* Jewish, but rather, his *life*, where the "hoit," the pain, and the humiliation are all too real. That Portnoy can talk so glibly about masturbation, about perversions (both real and imagined), suggests the difference between this book and those of modernist masters such as Lawrence or Joyce. What they took with high seriousness, Roth reduces to the axiously flip. The cunning of history is partly to blame here; when Portnoy shouts "LET'S PUT THE ID BACK IN YID!" the effect dovetails a domesticated Freudianism into the jazzy stuff of popular culture. In this sense, what *Portnoy's Complaint* provides is an encyclopedia of moments drawn from an American Jewish ethos in its cultural death throes. And as such, one axiom is worth recalling—namely, that at the very moment when a tradition begins to question itself, to mount elaborate campaigns on behalf of retrenchment, that tradition—whether it calls itself Puritanism or Transcendentalism or American *Yiddishkeit*—is in the long arc of its decline. Exercises in nostalgia are certain to follow, as are increasingly self-conscious efforts by way of denial. What Roth saw, of course, was the possibility of liberating himself from the tribal fears that were his immigrant Jewish legacy. As he explains in *Reading Myself and Others* (1975), his book of self-conscious "explanation": "I was strongly influenced by a sit-down comic named Franz Kafka and a very funny bit he does called 'The Metamorphosis.' . . . Not until I had got hold of guilt, you see, as a comic idea, did I begin to feel myself lifting free and clear of my last book and my old concerns" (p. 21).What Roth *doesn't* tell us—indeed, what he could not have realized at the time—is just how long, how protracted, and finally how impossible this struggle was likely to be. Whatever else *Portnoy's Complaint* may be in terms of an effort—at once desperate and heroic, foolhardy and comic—to *enjoy* being bad, the novel itself is all prolegomenon. The proudest boast of Whitman's persona is that he chants his "barbaric yawp" over the rooftops of the world — *untranslatable,* utterly unique and forever unavailable to those who prefer their poetry polite and neatly captured on the page. Touch *these* "leaves," he insists, and you've touched a man! By contrast, Alexander Portnoy is the crown prince of whiners, a man with enough *tsoris* to beat all comers in a misery contest. Roth, I would argue, never quite recovered from the "surprises" (as he called them) that the extraordinary success of *Portnoy's Complaint* brought. Granted, he had *never* set himself up as a patient Griselda, and even in the "old days" — that is, the days before a Jacqueline Susann could crack up the "Tonight Show" crowd by telling Johnny Carson that she thought Roth was a good writer, but that she preferred not to shake hands with him — he tried to silence his critics by writing essays full of explanatory sound and justifying fury. However, from *My Life as a Man* (1974) onward, Roth's novels began to glance uneasily over their shoulders at who, or what, might be gaining on them; and perhaps more important, they became increasingly self-conscious about the very act of writing fiction, and about fictionality itself. Roth himself seemed divided between contradictory images of the author — one, as the *schlemiel* who has caused his own misfortunes; the other as the nice, hardworking Jewish boy who should not be confused with his *meshuganah* (crazy) protagonists.

In *Portnoy's Complaint,* Alexander *kvetches,* and then *kvetches* some more — all with the hope that "*kvetching* for me [might be] a form of truth." With *My Life as a Man,* Peter Tarnopol tells his story, and tells it, and *tells* it — all in the desperate hope that he will one day see the figure in his carpet, that the disparate pieces of his abortive marriage will fall, magically, into an aesthetic whole and at last make sense. To that end, he creates Nathan Zuckerman, a countervoice who provides the distancing that art requires. Of Zuckerman we will hear much — indeed, sometimes more than we would prefer — but Tarnopol disappears, apparently forever, with *My Life as a Man*'s final page.

The effect, of course, is the familiar modernist device of stories-within-stories, of a reflexivity that turns the house of fiction into a hall of mirrors. But that said, Roth adds a deconstructive note to the proceedings, one that may have been sounded before, but never, I would submit, so stridently or so systematically. For example, there is a moment in Joyce's *A Portrait of the Artist as a Young Man* in which the young Stephen Dedalus imagines his villanelle being "read out at breakfast amid the tapping of eggshells"; such is the callous treatment that serious writers can expect when their work falls into the hands of philistines. By contrast, Tarnopol's "useful fictions" collect enough in-depth analysis to qualify for a Norton Critical Edition. His sister Joan suggests—rightly, I think—that he "can't make pleasure credible," while his brother Morris, a specialist in blunt, no-nonsense talk, puts it this way:

> What is it with you Jewish writers? Madeleine Herzog, Deborah Rojak, the cutesie-pie castrator in *After the Fall,* and isn't the desirable shiksa of *A New Life* a kvetch and titless in the bargain? And now, for the further delight of the rabbis and the reading public, Lydia Zuckerman, that Gentile tomato. Chicken soup in every pot, and a Greshenka in every garage. With all the Dark Ladies to choose from, you luftmenschen can really pick 'em. Peppy, why are you still wasting your talent on that Dead End Kid? Leave her to heaven, okay?　(P. 107)

Indeed, the list of those with a fix on Tarnopol's stories, and on Tarnopol himself, reads like an index to the novel itself. And while it is relatively easy to dismiss, say, Dr. Speilvogel's reductively Freudian theory about the "phallic threatening mother figure" in his analysand's carpet, what is one to say of the undergraduate paper written by Karen Oakes, crackerjack close reader and ex-lover:

> In order to dilute the self-pity that (as I understand it) has poisoned his imagination in numerous attempts to fictionalize his unhappy marriage, Professor Tarnopol establishes at the outset here a tone of covert (and, to some small degree, self-congratulatory) self-mockery; this calculated attitude of comic detachment he maintains right on down to the last paragraph, where abruptly the shield of lightheartedness is all at once pierced by the author's pronouncement that in his estimation the true story really isn't funny at all. All of which would appear to suggest that if Professor Tarnopol has managed in "Salad Days" to make an artful narrative of his misery, he has done so largely by refusing directly to confront it.　(Pp. 226–27)

Such insights earn Ms. Oakes a well-deserved A+, but she is hardly alone in isolating the terms of Tarnopol's "problem," and in offering up an Rx that would cure it; the rub, of course, is that Tarnopol needs his *tsoris* and his rage if he is to keep faith with the kind of writer he is. *The Facts* confirmed what many of Roth's critics had long suspected—namely, that of all his books, *My Life as a Man* was closest to the bone:

Probably nothing else in my work more precisely duplicates the autobiographical facts. Those scenes [in which a naïve Tarnopol is duped into a disastrous marriage] represent one of the few occasions when I haven't spontaneously set out to improve on actuality in the interest of being more interesting. I couldn't have been more interesting—I couldn't have been *as* interesting. What Josie came up with, altogether on her own, was a little gem of treacherous invention, economically lurid, obvious, degrading, deluded, almost comically simple, and best of all, magically effective. . . . Without doubt she was my worst enemy ever, but, alas, she was also nothing less than the greatest creative-writing teacher of them all, specialist par excellence in the aesthetics of extremist fiction.

Reader, I married her.   (Pp. 107, 112)

To ask that a Tarnopol quit harping about his psychopathic Muse is rather like asking Roth to provide us with more "representative"—i.e., admirable—women rather than versions of the unbalanced, destructive creature he married.

As Amy Bellette puts it in *The Ghost Writer,* the master—E. I. Lonoff—is "counter-suggestable"; one manipulates him via reverse psychology in much the same manner that, say, Poe's cerebral detectives match their wits against master criminals. The "games" that result are both subtle and stylistically dazzling. To be sure, Nathan Zuckerman *dreams* many of the complications—for example, that Amy Bellette is *the* Anne Frank, an Anne Frank who survived, who "got away"; and that her extraordinary book exacts a silence, an ostensible death, in short, the shadowy life as a "ghost writer," if it is to retain its raw emotional power—but this countertext, if you will, is also an extended exercise in defending, in justifying, and I would add, in deconstructing the knotty question of an artist's responsibility.

For Doc Zuckerman, the consequences of art are as clear, as undeniable, as the Jewish nose on Nathan's face: "From a lifetime of experience I happen to know what ordinary people will think when they read something like this story ["Higher Education"]. And you don't. You can't. . . . But I will tell you. They don't think about how it's a great work of art. They don't know about art. . . . But that's my point. People don't read art—they read about *people.* And they judge them as such. And how do you think they will judge the people in your story, what conclusions do you think they will reach? Have you thought about that?" (pp. 91–92). The young Nathan Zuckerman, surprised by his father's surprise, hurt by his father's hurt, thinks about loftier matters: the shape and ring of individual sentences, the rise and resolution of dramatic tensions, in short, about aesthetic considerations far removed from those messy interferences that now travel under the banner of "reader response," but that, in Doc Zuckerman's Newark, boil down to the existential business of what is, or is not, good for the Jews. Read *this* way, Nathan's story strikes his father as an accident waiting to happen; it confirms, from one of their own no less and in public print to boot, what anti-Semites have long suspected—namely, that Jews squabble over money; that they are, in a word, kikes.

Small wonder, then, that Nathan seeks the "sponsorship," the surrogate fatherhood, of E. I. Lonoff. As a consummate Jewish American fictionist, *he* will be able to extend the welcoming hand that Nathan's own father has refused. What Nathan discovers, however, is a man so committed to "fantasy" that the slightest hint of Life has been rigorously, systematically, crowded out. "I turn sentences around," Lonoff declares, "That's my life. I write a sentence and then I turn it around. Then I look at it and I turn it around again. Then I have lunch." Although Lonoff tells his writing students that "there is no life without patience," he has little patience with the "deep thinkers" who are attracted to his work, and no doubt he would have even less patience with a deconstructive reading of his working habits.

By contrast, Zuckerman's aesthetic feeds on turbulence, on mounting tensions, on a world where sentences are shouted across a kitchen table and end in exclamation points. "You are not somebody who writes this kind of story," Doc Zuckerman insists, "and then pretends it's the truth" (p. 95). But Nathan *did* write such a story; moreover, he *is* precisely "the kind of person who writes this kind of story!" For Lonoff, such truths are as much a part of the artistic landscape as the regimen of daily reading and obsessive scribbling. Zuckerman may be a nice polite boy when invited into somebody's home, but he is not likely to be so politic when he writes up the report of his visit. With a pen in his hand, Nathan becomes a different person, and if Lonoff's "blessing" is anywhere in the text, it is in his understanding, accepting, wish that Nathan continue to be this "different" person when he sets about composing the novel we know as *The Ghost Writer.*

For those who would brand him as self-hating, as an enemy of his people, nothing short of marrying Anne Frank will suffice.

And indeed, Zuckerman imagines exactly this triumph as a logical consequence of his imaginative rescue. Not only would he who had been misunderstood now be forgiven, but his father would utter the very words Nathan most wants to hear: "Anne, says my father—the Anne? Oh, how I have misunderstood my son. How mistaken we have been!" (p. 159).

To be sure, the Anne Frank Nathan resurrects—the impassioned little sister of Kafka who lived out in Amsterdam the indictments, the hidden attics, the camouflaged doors he had dreamed about in Prague—is a psychological ringer for Nathan himself: both exact their rebellions against family, synagogue, and state in the pages of their respective works; both suffer the loss of fathers for their art; and interestesting enough, *neither* could answer Judge Wapter's questions (number 3, for example, asks: "Do you practice Judaism? If so, how? If not, what credentials qualify you for writing about Jewish life for national magazines?" [p. 103]) in ways that he would find satisfactory.

The Ghost Writer is, of course, a version of the modernist *Bildungsroman* as reflected through the lens of a Nathan Zuckerman some twenty years old and presumably light years sadder and wiser about the "madness of art" and the human costs that come with landscaping a fictional territory. For better or worse, Nathan's congenial turf turns out to be the Jews. Unfortunately, what he discovers—after publishing a scandalously successful exposé entitled *Carnovsky*—is that no analogs to his modernist precursors will wash. Try as he might, the mantle of exile that slipped so easily, so convincingly, around James Joyce's shoulders will not quite fit. Granted, there are no end of attacks, no end of those who would add Zuckerman to the list of Haman and Hitler—names that deserve being blotted out, but the Zuckerman of *Zuckerman Unbound* craves approval rather than martyrdom. Down deep, he really can't believe that his antagonists are as angry as they claim, or that they would stay mad if he just had a chance to explain himself:

Not everybody was delighted by this book that was making Zuckerman a fortune. Plenty of people had already written to tell him off. "For depicting Jews in a peep-show atmosphere of total perversion, for depicting Jews in acts of adultery, exhibitionism, masturbation, sodomy, fetishism, and whoremongery," somebody with letterhead stationery as impressive as the President's had even suggested that he "ought to be shot." And in the spring of 1969 this was no longer just an expression. . . . Oh, Madam, if only you knew the real me! Don't shoot! I am a serious writer as well as one of the boys!   (Pp. 7–8)

Zuckerman goes on to argue that his readers "had mistaken impersonation for confession," but mostly he protests too much— about the assorted difficulties that come with being rich and famous, about his misunderstood highmindedness, about his essential goodness, and perhaps most of all, about his bad luck. After all, other writers—the modernist giants, for example— had it easier: "What would Joseph Conrad do? Leo Tolstoy? Anton Chekhov? When first starting out as a young writer in college he was always putting things to himself that way" (pp. 109-10). The rub, of course, is that none of these writers grew up Jewish in Newark, had a Jewish mother pestered by reporters in Miami ("I am very proud of my son and that's all I have to say. Thank you so much and goodby" [p. 63]), and a dying father who kept faith with the conviction that "Tzena, Tzena" is going to "win more hearts to the Jewish cause than anything before in the history of the world" (p. 116).

Granted, there is much about Zuckerman's *tsoris* that has a familiar ring—not only in terms of Roth's canon (those who tsk-tsk about his candor; the shaky marriage sacrificed to the house of fiction; grotesques such as Alvin Pepler, the Jewish marine who won a bundle on a quiz show, only to be betrayed and then disgraced), but also in terms of the longer tradition of Jewish American letters. Zuckerman is guilt-ridden about the money that crashes in as copies of *Carnovsky* roll off the presses. Side-walk superintendents shower him with free advice: "You should buy a helicopter. That's how I'd do it. Rent the landing rights up on apartment buildings and fly straight over the dog-poop" (p. 4). After all, true is true: "Gone were the days when Zuckerman had only to worry about making money; henceforth he would have to "worry about his money making money." In Abraham Cahan's scathing portrait of the Alrightnik—*The Rise of David Levinsky* (1917)—success is synonymous with an ashy taste. Some sixty years later Roth gives the garment district scenario a literary twist; now High Art, rather than the spring line, can make one wealthy and estranged.

Zuckerman Unbound is, by consensus, the weakest link in the chain of books that stretches from *My Life as a Man* to *The Facts*. No doubt part of the reason is that it is also the most conventional in terms of narrative structure. Alvin Pepler, the wacky know-it-all who can match Zuckerman paranoia for paranoia, self-righteousness for self-righteousness, even manages to get in a few good licks about Zuckerman's fictional treatment of autobiographical events: "Fiction is not autobiography [Pepler's unfinished review of *Carnovsky* contends], yet all fiction, I am convinced, is in some sense rooted in autobiography, although the connection to actual events may be tenuous indeed, even nonexistent. . . . Yet there are dangers in writing so closely to the heels of one's own immediate experience: a lack of toughness, perhaps; a tendency to indulgence; an urge to justify the author's ways to men" (p. 150). One might suggest the same things about *Zuckerman Unbound*, adding a few grace notes about the ways in which self-laceration has been altered since the days when *schlemiels* shrugged their shoulders when they spilled the soup. But Pepler's point, however savvy, lacks sufficient context, enough sheer *force*, to be the counterweight that *Zuckerman Unbound* badly needs.

By contrast, *The Anatomy Lesson* gives Zuckerman's temper tantrums the postmodernist spin they deserve. "When he is sick," the novel's opening line declares, "every man wants his mother; if she's not around, other women must do" (p. 3). Zuckerman—ever the overachiever, the man of excess—is currently "making do" with four. More than two hundred pages later, Zuckerman, broken-down, hospitalized, and in the grip of sicknesses both mental and physical, will write on a clean notebook page: "WHEN HE IS SICK EVERY MAN NEEDS A MOTHER" (p. 270). But interior echoes are not the only reflexive touches that Roth introduces into this saga of Zuckerman's dark night of the soul. For example, once upon a time, Judge Wapter handed down ten indicting questions from his chambers in Newark; now Zuckerman faces the seemingly innocent queries concocted by the editors of a school newspaper: "The editors wanted to interview him about the future of his kind of fiction in the post-modernist era of John Barth and Thomas Pynchon. . . . would he please answer, at whatever length he chose, the ten questions of the sheet attached. . . . 1. Why do you continue to write? 2. What purpose does your work serve? 3. Do you feel yourself part of a rearguard action in the service of a declining traditon? 4. Has your sense of vocation altered significantly because of the events of the last decade?" (p. 280). For a Stephen Dedalus, griefs come in triads—family, church, and state. But since Stephen also fancies himself as a "priest of the eternal imagination," so do solutions: silence, exile, and cunning. In both cases, however, the world is neatly divided into trinities that remind us of his Irish Catholic upbringing and its abiding presence. By contrast, Zuckerman is plagued by Decalogues— and by their characteristic formulas of "thou shalt not's!"—without quite knowing how to respond in kind. Roth's agitated protagonists can, of course, call upon the great modernist tradition, upon ghost writers from Henry James to Franz Kafka, but something vital is lost in the translation. *Their* world is, finally, not James's (one feels confident that *he* never had to eat his childhood dinners at the end of a knifeblade), nor is it Kafka's, despite the odd metamorphosis that turns Professor Kepish into a breast. Those smart enough to catch Roth's allusions are also smart enough to know a pale copy when they see one; and those more *au courant* with Judaica than Mr. Roth would have no hesitation using the word *l'havdal* (separation) to describe the phenomenon.

Nonetheless, Zuckerman continues to see himself as a beleaguered soul, rather like the corpse being dissected in Rembrandt's painting, "The Anatomy Lesson." In Zuckerman's case, however, the fellow wielding the sharpest knife is Milton Appel, the moral critic who savaged him in an issue of *Inquiry*. Once again, those in the know knew that Roth had been tonguing a sore tooth ever since Irving Howe published an article entitled "Reconsidering Philip Roth" in a 1973 issue of *Commentary* magazine. Granted, Roth had folded criticism-as-counterweight into earlier novels, but this was bashing of a decidedly higher order. *This* attack, as Zuckerman puts it bitterly, "made Macduff's assault upon Macbeth look almost lackadaisical":

The Jews represented in *Higher Education* had been twisted out of human recognition by a willful vulgar imagination largely indifferent to social accuracy and the tenets of realistic fiction. Except for a single readable story, that first collection was tendentious junk, the by-product of a pervasive and unfocused hostility. The three books that followed had nothing to redeem them at all—mean, joyless, patronizing little novels, contemptuously dismissive of the complex depths. No Jews like Zuckerman's had ever existed other than as caricature, as literature that could interest grown people. None of the books could be said to exist at all, but were contrived as a species of sub-literature for the newly "liberated" middle-class, for an "audience," as distinguished from serious readers. Zuckerman was certainly no friend of Jews: *Carnovsky's* ugly animus proved that.   (P. 69)

Appel, in short, is no lightweight, and rail though Zuckerman might, his accusations sting. Even Appel's parentheticals—from a piece of private correspondence—find their way into Zuckerman's craw: "(and yes, I know that there's a difference between characters and authors; but I also know that grown-ups should not pretend that it's quite the difference they tell their students it is)" (p. 85).

Wounded, weakened, sick nearly unto death, what is Zuckerman to do? Not since Bloom plumbed the depths of Nighttown (in Joyce's *Ulysses*) has there been such unrelenting abasement, and such comic *schlemiel* hood. He can, of course, rant and rail; he can name-call (e.g., Appel as the "Charles Atlas of Goodness"); he can amuse himself with parlor games that satirize Appel's titles and his methodology ("The Irrefutable Rethinkings of Milton Appel"; "Right and Rigid in Every Decade: The Polemical Spasms of a Hanging Judge" [p. 92]). But best of all, he can *become* Appel by transmogrifying him, *deconstructing* him, if you will, into a Milton Appel of a very different color—namely, the Al Goldstein look-alike who publishes a sleazy pornographic magazine called *Lickedy Split*. The result is a radical impersonation, one no longer fixed on the comic exaggerations and liberations by which Roth unleashes his Zuckerman, but rather on the grotesque playfulness that turns Appel into his Other.

Nor is this the only "victory" in a novel out to shore up fragments against Zuckerman's ruin. If he had played with the prospect of marrying Anne Frank in *The Ghost Writer*, in *The Anatomy Lesson,* he toys with the idea of chucking fiction writing altogether and becoming a doctor. No more subjectivity, no more inner life, no more burrowing back, no more "chewing on everything, seeking connections"—nobody criticizes the baby an obstetrician delivers; everyone welcomes the relief from pain that an anesthesiologist promises. *This*—rather than Art—is the life that Zuckerman in middle age hankers for. Besides, what better way to appease one's parents, to give them the ultimate *nachas* (joy), than by becoming, at long last, their son, the Jewish doctor?

Granted, this counterlife is not destined to succeed, as the novel's circular first sentence suggests, and as Zuckerman/Roth's continuing output makes all too clear. Indeed, what we have in

The Counterlife is a version of Lonoff's aesthetic, but this time one that turns whole lives, rather than individual sentences, around. The result is akin to a kaleidoscope: characters become bits of colored glass that shift positions and perspectives (dead in one chapter, they spring back to life in the next) as Roth rotates his fictional cylinder in 180-degree twists. For Roth, "counter" has become an abiding, multipurpose prefix, the flashy way he slips the jabs of his opponents, and then justifies the *flash*. However, the culmulative effect of all this postmodernist carbonation can exasperate those readers who prefer their fictions "straight." As Cynthia Ozick points out in *Metaphor and Memory*, her recent collection of essays: "The characters in Philip Roth's *Counterlife* are so wilily infiltrated by Postmodernist inconstancy that they keep revising their speeches and their fates: you can't trust them even to stay dead. It goes without saying that we are forbidden to speculate whether the writer who imagined them is as anxiously protean, as cleft by doubt, as they."[2]

But, of course, Ozick has her hunches, and given the sheer number of anxious speeches in *The Counterlife* about the imagination's deconstructive powers, why shouldn't she? It is, after all, not Zuckerman alone who talks compulsively about counter-texts, who insists that "we are all the invention of each other, everybody a conjuration conjuring up everyone else," but Roth himself who marches to a similar drum in *The Facts*. As the postmodernist version of *schlemiel* hood would have it, we are not only the architects of our own troubles, but also the architects of other people's comically troubled stories. Rehearsing, yet again, the "facts" that had duped him into a marriage he fictionally chronicled in *My Life as a Man,* Roth talks about his life as if it were so much narratology: "I was telling her who I thought I was and what I believe had formed me, but I was also engaged by a compelling form of narrative responsory. I was a countervoice, an antitheme, providing a naive challenge to the lurid view of human nature that emerged from her tales of victimized inno-cence." (p. 93). Unfortunately, the Roth who sets out to introduce *The Facts* worries about presenting himself "in prose like this, undisguised." Until now he had always "used the past as the basis for transformation, for, among other things, a kind of intricate explanation to myself of my world"—and until now, the marve-lous, transformed voice that resulted had largely belonged to Nathan Zuckerman. The question, then, is a simply, but crucially important one—namely, "Is the book any good?" Only a Roth would think to ask it of a protagonist. And only Roth would append some thirty or more pages of Zuckerman's detailed, hard-hitting criticism to the bulk of "Roth's" autobiography.

Not surprisingly, Zuckerman is as unimpressed as he is discouraging. As he points out, the difference between the fictional character (namely, himself) who has obsessed Roth for the last decade and the autobiographical Philip Roth (who takes such pains to tell us about his loving mother, his understanding father, and, most of all, his life as a nice Jewish son) is precisely the difference between the dazzling excitements—and the deeper truths—of fiction and the flatter prose that results when Roth sticks too closely to the "facts": "As for characterization, you, Roth, are the least completely rendered of all your protagonists. Your gift is not to personalize your experience but to personify it, embody it in the representation of a person who is *not* yourself. You are not an autobiographer, you're a personificator" (p. 162).

Indeed, Zuckerman makes a compelling case that *The Facts* is so "steeped in the nice-guy side" that it lacks struggle, lacks hubris, lacks madness—in short, that it comes up short in every category that gives Roth's fiction a distinctive thumbprint. "With this book," Zuckerman argues, "you've tied your hands behind your back and tried to write it with your toes" (p. 169).

Granted, Zuckerman is hardly a disinterested observer. Should Roth continue to pound away at the keyboard about the "real" exploits of Philip Roth rather than about the imagined, highly exaggerated ones of Nathan Zuckerman, where would *that* put the protagonist of the Zuckerman chronicles? Theirs has become a symbiotic relationship, a case of secret sharing so deep, so abiding, that even the word *need* hardly defines its character. As Zuckerman puts it: "I'd say you're still as much in need of me as I of you—and that I need you is indisputable. For me to speak of 'my' anything would be ridiculous, however much there has been established in me the illusions of an independent existence. I owe everything to you, while you, however, owe me nothing less than the freedom to write freely. I am your permission, your indiscretion, the key to disclosure" (pp. 161–62).

In short, *The Facts* seems to be cut from the same counter-cloth that patterned his earlier books, but with an important difference. This time Roth is out to justify his life (perhaps even to *save* it) by dropping the pretenses of fiction altogether. At long last, the persona behind the mask stands up, pushes the typewriter away, and tells his own story, in his own words and with his own voice: "Like you, Zuckerman who are reborn in *The Counterlife* through your English wife, like your brother, Henry, who seeks rebirth in Israel with his West Bank fundamentalists, just as both of you in the same book miraculously manage to be revived from death, I too was ripe for another chance. If while writing I couldn't see exactly what I was up to, I do now: this manuscript embodies my counterlife, the antidote and answer to all those fictions that culminated in the fiction of you" (p. 6).

Apparently, a life crisis, if not a breakdown of considerable proportion, looms behind the autobiographical effort to smash through Roth's exhaustion with "masks, disguises, distortions, and lies." But those of us who have followed the long trail of tears, special pleading, and tantrums know enough to be on our guard. What is one to make, for example, of Roth's claim that he did *not* write *The Facts* to prove, once and for all, that "there is a significant gap between the autobiographical writer that I am thought to be and the autobiographical writer that I am"? As Maria Freshfield Zuckerman points out, there is a Latin term for such assertions—*occupatio:* "It's one of those Latin rhetorical figures. 'Let us not speak of the wealth of the Roman Empire. Let us not speak of the majesty of the invading troops, et. cetera,' and by not speaking about it you're speaking about it. A rhetorical device whereby you mention something by saying you're not going to mention it." (p. 190). Nathan, not surprisingly, talks about autobiography in terms of its inevitable "countertext"— that is, the material the conscious, manipulative self edits out:

You talk about what you were up against, what you wanted, what was happening to you, but you rarely say what you were like. You can't or won't talk about yourself as yourself, other than in this decorus way. . . . But obviously it's just as impossible to be proper and modest and well behaved and be a revealing autobiographer as it is to be all that and a good novelist. . . . This isn't unusual, really. With autobiography there's always another text, a countertext, if you will, to the one presented. (Pp. 171–72)

One could, of course, say much the same thing about Roth's *fictions,* where the alternating rhythms of construction and deconstruction, of text and countertext, of satiric attack and abject confession, have been going on for some time, and where a nice Jewish boy's preoccupation with running wild gives every indication of continuing.

8
Woody Allen's Lovably Anxious *Schlemiels*

Woody Allen's anxious, bespectacled *punin* (face) has become something of a national icon: he is the "beautiful loser" *par excellance,* the man whose urban, end-of-the-century anxieties mirror—albeit, in exaggeration—our own. To be sure, his persona is hardly as *sui generis* as many of his more adoring fans suppose; scholars need not break a sweat to establish Allen's lineage to the Little Man of Robert Benchley, to the Little Tramp of Charlie Chaplin, indeed, to a host of precursors from the pages of the *New Yorker* magazine. Modern humor depends on trouble, and Allen not only suffers all the indignities that come with a weakling's ninety-eight-pound body, but also those he conjures up in his doom-riddled mind.

No doubt a part of the Allen persona we meet on the silver screen was formed in the noisy, yoo-hooing world of his Brooklyn childhood. His memories—even if one gives comic exaggeration their due—are filled with people who shouted rather than talked, who ended their sentences with exclamation points, and who could do neither without waving their hands. Such a world—by degrees combative and warm, ebullient and anxious—tends to divide itself between those who reach over others for a ketchup bottle and those who end up getting knocked off their luncheonette stools. Allen, of course, counts himself among the latter. He is a distant cousin of the classical *schlimazl* who attracted "accidents" as if he were a lightning rod: the sword meant for somebody else; the soup that *schlemiels* traditionally spill; the bread that always falls butter-side down.

But that much said, Allen's persona adds up to something more than the usual formulation of yet another modern humorist with trouble dripping from his sleeve; for one thing, his *tsoris* has a metaphysical dimension Allen insists upon (even at times, belabors), and that we recognize like a thumbprint. At one point a philosophical Allen argues that "the universe is merely a fleeting idea in God's mind—a pretty uncomfortable thought, particularly if you've just made a down payment on a house"; at another he wonders if we "can actually 'know' the universe? My God, it's hard enough finding your way around Chinatown." Allen, in short, characteristically muses in juxtapositions. The result is a prose style in which airy ideas and gritty urban details are forced to share floor space in the same paragraph, and often on opposing sides of a semicolon.

Mark Shechner argues that Allen's persona has always been awash in "high-school existentialism"—that is, longer on posture and predictable subjects (as Shechner enumerates them, "God is dead; life has no meaning; man is a lonely speck in a vast, impersonal void") than on hard, sustained thought. Perhaps so, but there is, I would suggest, a difference between taking Allen's comedy *seriously* and taking it solemnly. Shechner, to his credit, recognizes the essential difference between the persona a comic both creates and needs, and the biographical self who may have given it impetus:

> Every comic needs some such theatrical self [in Allen's case, the *schlemiel* as sexual loser-cum-narcissist] to be not only his trademark, but his muse, the inventor of the jokes he tells. The comedian plays host to his other self which lives off him as much as he lives off it, and unless he collapses into his persona entirely, he is by profession a case of split personality. Allen the comic, we are led to understand, is by no means the same man as Allen the clarinetist; and such a self-division, it appears, is something of a professional standard. It is not only for purposes of ethnic whitewashing that nearly all Jewish comedians perform under stage names. So dependent is the comic on his other self that he comes to seek shelter under it, and asking any comedian to step out from behind the mask is a little like asking Harpo Marx to speak.[1]

By contrast, Allan Bloom, author of *The Closing of the American Mind,* not only fails to see any distinctions between Allen the persona and Allen the personality, but he also insists that *both* of them measure up to his own high intellectual standards. Bloom, of course, has made something of a specialty of the jeremiad, and it is hardly surprising he should see dangers to seriousness everywhere: in our lack of critical standards, in our worship of a mushy-headed relativism, in our vulgarized notions of nihilism. Indeed, if Bloom is even *half* right, our national fiber hasn't been in such bad shape since the days when Jonathan Edwards conjured up the image of us as "Sinners in the Hands of an Angry God." One sees sure signs of our national decay, Bloom argues, in the sheer number of colleges and universities racing to establish "Women's Studies" programs, in the rock music that teenagers blast through their Walkmen, and in such unlikely places as the films of Woody Allen.

Allan Bloom means to bash them all, but it is his attack on the Allen known as Woody that speaks most directly to our culture's mixed feelings about comedy, at least as they are articulated by its "intellectuals." According to Bloom, "Woody Allen's comedy [i.e., *Zelig*] is nothing but a set of variations on the theme of the man who does not have a real 'self' or 'identity,' and who feels superior to the inauthentically self-satisfied people because he is conscious of his situation and at the same time inferior to them because they are "adjusted."[2] In short, Allen makes us feel comfortable with our nihilism, and for this sin Bloom can offer "book lists" but no forgiveness: "Woody Allen really has nothing to tell us about inner-directedness. Nor does David Reisman nor, going further back, does Erik Fromm. One has to get to Heidegger to learn something serious about the grim facts of what inner-directedness might really mean."

Reading such testy, strident judgments, one begins to suspect that the Allan with the problem is Bloom rather than Woody. What *The Closing of the American Mind* demonstrates when it blathers on about a film like *Zelig* is precisely what H. L. Mencken once defined as the Puritan temper — namely, a deep suspicion that somebody, somewhere is having a good time.[3] It has been with us, in one form or another, from the days when Thomas Morton established his Maypole at Merry Mount in 1628 (only to have Governor John Endicott transmogrify it, in Hawthorne's verison of the tale, into a "whipping-post") to *Animal House* and the latest round of efforts to exile fraternities from college campuses.

Unfortunately, Bloom is not the only one who thinks of Allen as a philosopher rather than as an "entertainer." In *Annie Hall,* the boorish young professor of film studies (now it would be known as semiotics) holds forth on Marshall McLuhan while Allen's protagonist does a slow burn. Such show-offs know everything about the medium of cinema except what makes people love it. Unable to contain his indignation any longer, he calls the scholar's bluff, only to have McLuhan himself appear from behind a cardboard cutout and wholeheartedly agree. There may not be many such victories for the Alvy Singer who wins and then loses Annie Hall, who has worried, and continues to worry, about life's assorted troubles, but this is surely one of them.

Indeed, Allen has been "getting even" with brainy, professorial types since the days when he published his *New Yorker* sketches collected as *Getting Even* (1971). Sometimes the cracks take the form of memorable quips, like the one in *Manhattan* (1979) about the possibility of *Commentary* and *Dissent* merging into a new journal for New York intellectuals to be called *Dysentery*. And of course, there is *Stardust Memories* (1980)—a sustained exercise in biting the hands that have fed him, whether they belong to Allen's overly adoring fans, his reviewers, or those who subject his work to intense scholarly-critical scrutiny.

Not long ago I was struck by the painstaking rigor a scholar has brought to bear on Mark Twain's reading habits. Apparently, this professor has assembled enough evidence to prove what every serious reader of Twain already knew—namely, that Twain owned, and read, and, yes, *underlined*, large numbers of books, and that he perpetrated the mythos of the rustic, homespun spinner of tall tales and dispenser of lowfalutin' wisdom so as not to put off any segment of the population with the ready cash to buy one of his books or to crowd into one of his lectures. My hunch is that this scholar could demonstrate quite the opposite point about Woody Allen—namely, that he reads dust jackets and reviews, rather than "real books," and that he perpetrates the mythos of a sensitive New York egghead so he will remain the darling of those who also make it a point to keep up with our culture by reading the *New York Review of Books*.

But this much said, let me hasten to add that while I don't count Allen among our philosophers or significant social critics, I do think that his genius for parody and the systematic care-and-feeding he has given to his *schlemiel*ish persona are important additions to our cultural scene. Most humorists begin as counterpunchers—that is, as those who keep their eyes and ears fixed on the elements of the mainstream most susceptible to comic exaggeration. Parody, in short, allows one to prop his or her work against what is already known, what is already there. Franklin, Twain, Benchley—each started as a parodist, which is to say, as a ventriloquist with a difference. So, too, did the Allen Stewart Konigsberg who had mailed his jokes to newspaper columnists, had worked for ad agencies, and paid his first show biz dues writing material for other comics.

The difference, of course, is that when Konigsberg transmogrified himself into a *New Yorker* humorist named Woody Allen he labored under the long shadows cast by predecessors such as Benchley, Thurber, and S. J. Perelman. Consider, for example, this paragraph from "A Look at Organized Crime": "In 1921, Thomas (The Butcher) Covello and Ciro (The Tailor) Santucci attempted to organize disparate ethnic groups of the underworld and thus take over Chicago. This was foiled when Albert (The Logical Positivist) Corillo assassinated Kid Lipsky by locking him in a closet and sucking all the air out through a straw."[4] On its most important, most recognizable level, Allen is having some fun at the expense of what had been a popular television show—*The Untouchables*—and the spate of books about the Mob it inspired; on other fronts, he cannot quite resist the impulse to juxtapose nicknames we expect with ones we don't.

But there is also the Allen who knows the traditions of American humor as intimately as he knows the trendy stuff of popular culture. In this case, the story of Kid Lipsky's comic rub-out is lifted from the *New Yorker*'s pages rather than from the television screen, and those who knew Allen from his days as a Greenwich Village comic may well have missed the allusion as well as part of Allen's humorous point. By way of illustration, I offer the following: "Then there was Aunt Sarah Shoaf, who never went to bed at night without the fear that a burglar was going to get in and blow chloroform under her door through a tube. To avert this calamity—for she was in greater dread of anesthetics than of losing her household goods—she always piled her money, silverware, and other valuables in a neat stack just outside her bedroom, with a note reading: 'This is all I have. Please take it and do not use your chloroform, as this is all I have.' "[5] Aunt Sarah Shoaf is, of course, one of the lovable eccentrics who made James Thurber's childhood in Columbus, Ohio, so ripe for the *New Yorker*'s picking. Granted, Allen dusts off Thurber's material, gives it an appropriately urbane—which is to say, "hip"—twist, but the essential archetype had been around for a long, long time. As Thurber himself once put it, for the person beating his or her brains out trying to write a two-thousand word comic sketch, there was always "the suspicion that a piece he has been working on for two long days was done much better and probably more quickly by Robert Benchley in 1924."[6]

Like Benchley, like Thurber, like Perleman, Allen cannot recount his complicated griefs without making them seem comic. But that said, Allen also has certain advantages that they lacked. He plays, in short, to a hipper house, one that Allen himself defined as belonging to those "born after Nietzsche's edict that 'God is dead,' but before the [Beatles'] hit recording 'I Wanna Hold Your Hand.'" Moreover, Allen broke in his version of the sad-sack-as-*schlemiel* at a cultural moment when ethnicity was becoming a box-office "plus" rather than the marginal minus it had always been considered. If radio tended to obliterate regional dialects, homogenizing our speech until the diction of CBS announcers became the American equivalent of the Queen's English, then movies (and later, television) turned a country of small towns into a nation of urban states.

Granted, the process I'm alluding to happened so slowly, so subtly, that it defies precise dating. Nor is the greater receptiveness and more hospitable climate that resulted limited to Woody Allen. If one thinks of, say, Henry Roth, what cluster of events occasioned the 1964 revival, and the subsequent popularity, of *Call It Sleep* (1934), his lyrical novel about growing up amid the squalor and the terrors of New York's immigrant lower East Side? One would *like* to give the obvious answer—namely, that it's a first-rate book that had been unfairly ignored—but accounting for popular taste is more complicated. Often, timing counts for at least as much as talent. Without a different literary context that now included the work of Saul Bellow, Bernard Malamud, and another Roth named Philip; without a cultural moment in which you didn't have to be Jewish to enjoy Levy's rye bread or to know a few Yiddish words; without, in short, the sixties as they were, Henry Roth's novel might have continued its long, uninterrupted sleep. Similarly, after Benchely and even after Chaplin's comedies, films as aggressively ethnic as *Annie Hall* (1977), *Manhattan* (1979), or *Broadway Danny Rose* (1984) would have been impossible in the 1930s.

Roughly the same cultural changes affected what a stand-up comic could, or could not, do behind a mike. Lenny Bruce is usually mentioned in this connection. His daring—some would say, sacrifical—campaign on behalf of liberating language from the unspoken taboos that made four-letter words a night-club no-no, and of addressing formerly "forbidden subjects" (not only sex, but also race and religion) is, of course, part of the 1960s story. But so too is Woody Allen. His public therapy sessions (conducted, for the most part, in Greenwich Village nightclubs) cast Allen as the analysand and the audience as his "analyst." The result—as the comedy albums he recorded during the early sixties attest—was very funny stuff indeed, and Allen mined the best gags for subsequent *New Yorker* sketches and films.

As the Allen persona would proudly "boast," he was weaker, more troubled, and infinitely more sensitive than anybody in the house. Given the age and its anxieties, if Woody Allen hadn't bumbled along with his brand of urban Jewish neurosis, his thick eyeglasses, his sad face, somebody else would surely have invented him. The era of the Borscht Belt gag (e.g., "I spent a thousand dollars to have my nose fixed, and now my brain won't work"—*Bup Bup Bup*) was over. That world—which Allen resurrects as the "chorus" of older comics who hang around the Carnegie Deli swapping stories about characters like Broadway Danny Rose—may have cracked up Aunt Sadie, but not her nephews. By contrast, Allen's characteristic shrugs and quivers, his obsessive worries and pervasive guilts, his hesitant pauses and equally tentative voice, were just right for the *Playboy* crowd. To them Allen could confess, "I don't believe in an afterlife, although I plan to bring a change of underwear." Or he would offer his remembrances of neuroses past: "When we played softball, I'd steal second, then feel guilty and go back." As one critic of the Village scene during those days recalls it: "The futzing around Allen did onstage was the gestalt of a comedic antihero. . . . true neurotica."[7]

Very soon, however, Allen's onstage "futzing" became the trademark of his on-screen persona. He projected aspects of himself as weakling, as *klutz*, and most often, as *schlemiel*. Consider, for example, *Take the Money and Run* (1969) in which the story of Virgil Starkwell contains all three. As a parody both of the documentary (with its efforts to "explain," via sociopsychology, how a criminal like Starkwell comes into being) and the prison film—with its tough cons and daring, stylized escapes—Allen proves himself a resourceful enough counterpuncher to last through the film's eighty-five minutes.

But gags alone—even very good ones—will not a feature film make. What gives *Take the Money and Run* its durability are certain moments of what can only be called comic genius. It is, after all, one thing to hear the documentary's "narrator" (Jackson Beck) tell us in sonorous voice-over that Virgil Starkwell grew up in bad circumstances, bullied by older, stronger toughs, and then see a pint-sized version of the bespectacled Allen watch, helpless, as they break his glasses and smash the remains into bits; and quite another to hear the testimony of Virgil's first cello teacher—the low-keyed but exasperated Mr. Turgson. As he tells his reminiscences to the camera, we learn that Virgil loved the cello, indeed, that he stole money to pay for lessons, but we also find out that, in Mr. Turgson's words, he "had no conception of the instrument. He *blew* into it."

However (the voice-over informs us), if Virgil did not become a great cello player, he at least became proficient enough to join a local band. At this point, Allen moves beyond mere futzing to a piece of brilliant screen business: a marching band makes its way down the street with everything in apple pie order—drum major, assorted brass, the whole Sousa entourage—when suddenly we see Allen sawing away on his cello and frantically trying to keep pace with other members of the band by moving a chair and then sitting down to crank out a few bars. Like Chaplin before him, Allen knows how to translate a funny premise into physical humor. Granted, parodic energy accounts for some of the success (e.g., the dry, slightly "off" narrative tone that sets the scene), but what makes the scene really work is Virgil's capacity to build in his own defeats. Here, in short, is the *schlemiel* in one of his most traditional incarnations—namely, as the man who unwittingly sets comic disasters into motion.

In other sections of *Take the Money and Run*, Allen is content to play Virgil as the *klutz*—for example, as a would-be pool hustler who (predictably enough) ruins the felt, misses his shots, and ends up shelling out money; or as a would-be sneak thief who gets his hand caught in the gum ball machine. Virgil, in short, has all the earmarks of the typical Allen "loser"; he is too frail, too isolated, too "alienated," and, of course, too sensitive to make it here. Even the army rejects him when he identifies an ink blot as "two elephants making love to a men's glee club."

Not surprisingly, Virgil is equally inept as a criminal, but less because he is *klutzy* than because he is an inveterate *schlemiel*. Those who remember Willie Sutton (the man who once explained that he robbed banks because "that's where the money was" and who once escaped from prison by fashioning a gun out of a soap bar) take a special pleasure in the scene in which Virgil reduplicates Sutton's bust-out. There is Virgil in his cell, patiently carving a gun from a bar of soap and then applying black shoe polish for the finishing, realistic touch. It can't miss—and indeed, for a while it doesn't. Virgil takes several guards hostage and makes his way into the Big Yard—only to be caught in a sudden shower that reduces his "pistol" to a handful of soap bubbles. Build in possibilities for disaster, and disaster will surely overtake you—this is the essential message of tragedy, and also of Allen's most representative comedy. As Shechner points out, Allen has been "a closet tragedian all along," and

the air of cosmic befuddlement that now colors his thought was there from the first. He has taken to telling interviewers, "My real obsessions are religious," and "Death is the big obsession behind all I've done," and "The metaphor for life is a concentration camp, I do believe that." This last, he told *Time* magazine after *Manhattan* was released, was a line he had cut from that film but intended to use in his next. And despite efforts on Allen's part to keep *Manhattan* from drowning, as *Interiors* did, in too metaphysical a view of the modern condition, the void sneaks inexorably in. So, when Isaac Davis (Allen) and Mary (Diane Keaton) take refuge from a storm in Hayden Planetarium and conduct a flirtatious tete-a-tete amid lunar and nebular skyscapes, Allen, as director, is not just having fun with his sets, he's also reminding us that "we're lost out there in the stars." (Pp. 236–37)

Given the concerted movement *away* from metaphysical angst in *Hannah and Her Sisters* (1986)—a film that finally insists that the comic beauties of a Marx Brothers film like *Duck Soup* have a right to be, without introspection, without brooding, without metaphysical whining—Shechner might want to amend his original assessment, but I think that his general sense of Allen is on target. Even the scene from *Take the Money and Run*, where Virgil botches a bank robbery because of poor penmanship (the teller has difficulty reading his note, insisting that it says "I have a *gub*," rather than a "gun") has a downside that is both tragic and, if you will, metaphysical. To be sure, that Virgil creates so much trouble for himself ("*act* natural" comes out looking like "*abt* natural") is the stuff that *schlemiels* are made of. But poor Virgil is also caught in a world—as are we all—in which one of the vice presidents must countersign a holdup note before tellers are authorized to give out cash, and where discussions, and decisions, are increasingly made by committee. As Allen escalates the scene's pacing, Virgil finds himself awash in what literary theoreticians call "reader response"—each with an opinion and each with something like a vote. Moreover, bureaucracy exerts a power—at least over the timid—that far outstrips that of the criminal. His gun reduced to a "gub," Allen's protagonist watches helplessly as he is gradually reduced to the state of childhood (where neatness counts and teachers know how to deal with the sloppy) and the police at last arrive.

One could argue that Virgil is in the wrong business, that he simply doesn't have either sufficient talent or "calling" to be a thief. The same thing, interestingly enough, could be said of Broadway Danny Rose's equally fatal attraction to marginal entertainers. As an agent Danny Rose has collected a veritable menagerie of bizarre acts: a one-armed juggler, a one-legged tapdancer, a women who belts out eerie tunes by waving her hands over glasses filled with water. Nonetheless, Broadway Danny Rose believes in his clients, cares for them in ways that go well beyond the call of duty, and, of course, "pitches" them whenever and wherever he can. This despite the fact that those who *do* make it abandon him without so much as a by-your-leave, despite the fact that he is a marginal man in what can only be described as a marginal business.

As the *kibbutzers* in the Carnegie Deli (including such actual veterans of the Borscht Belt circuit such as Jackie Gayle, Corbett Monica, and Will Jordon) conjure up both Broadway Danny Rose and the bygone age of show biz he represents, the focus narrows to what happened when Lou Canova (Nick Apollo Forte), a saloon-singer in the Sinatra mold, began his comeback, fueled by the re-release of his one authentic 1950s hit, the nostalgia craze, and Broadway Danny Rose's willing, but ineffectual, direction.

In *Broadway Danny Rose*, Canova gives us one version that "All For Love" can take in the contemporary world (Canova pursues the wonderfully tawdry Tina Vitale [played to comic perfection by Mia Farrow] as Broadway Danny Rose chases after him, tsk-tsking all the way), but in most of Allen's films the role of erstwhile lover is reserved for Allen himself. Generally speaking, the earlier films are manned by sexual bumblers, by little boys in grownups' clothing, by those who strike us as longer on "boast" than on performance. Virgil Starkwell is a typical case. He may insist (as Allen himself did during his days as a stand-up) that the proper answer to the question, "Is sex dirty?" can only be: "It is . . . if you're doing it right," but the gap between quip and condition is so great that even the word "incongruity" doesn't quite do it justice.

Much the same thing is true of, say, the Fielding Mellish (Woody Allen) of *Bananas* (1971) although, this time, the making of the Allen *schlemiel* is more developed, more sustained. Mellish is more than a timid products tester mauled by an exercising contraption for busy executives called "Excusizer" (shades of Chaplin's losing battle with machines in *Modern Times*); he is also a portrait of Brooklyn intellectual as sexual-political loser, the man whose fortunes rise and fall in volatile San Marcos (a banana republic that produces more revolutionaries than tropical fruit) and whose wedding night is covered—by none other than Howard Cosell himself—on "Wide World of Sports." If the plotline of *Bananas* is, shall we say, loose, it allows plenty of room for Allen's spontaneous energy.

By contrast, when his films moved beyond the limitations of mere parody (e.g., *Sleeper* [the sci-fi flick]; *Love and Death* [the Russian novel]; *Everything You Always Wanted to Know About Sex, But Were Afraid to Ask* [the Dr. David Reuben best seller]), Allen's filmmaking became increasingly reflexive, that is, focused as much on the medium as on the "message." Granted, the Allen persona remained in occupancy, still nervous, still a loser, still every bit the *schlemiel,* but there were also subtle wrinkles added to his by-now recognizable features. For example, one traditional synonym for the *schlemiel* was cuckold, but in a film like *Play It Again Sam* (largely concerned with how a film buff and inveterate sad sack is finally able to transfer *Casablanca's* images into action), it is Allan Felix (Woody Allen) who cuckolds the worldy Dick Christie (Tony Roberts). And in *Annie Hall,* the tale's bittersweet unfolding depends as much upon Alvy Singer's "lovability" as upon his loserhood. As Irving Howe points out, the humor of *schlemiel* hood can take savage turns (as it does in the routines of Lenny Bruce) or tender ones. Not surprisingly, Howe numbers Allen among the latter: "Woody Allen was a reincarnated Menashe Skulnik, quintessential *schlemiel* of the Yiddish theatre, but now a college graduate acquainted with the thought of Freud and recent numbers of *Commentary.* . . . [He] exploited the parochial helplessness of Jewish sons, their feelings of sexual feebleness and worldly incapacity; but he did this with an undertone of wistfulness and affection that marked him off from most other Jewish comedians of his moment. "[8]

No doubt there are those who would point out that Allen, tender-hearted though his personae might be, is hardly above dragging in bearded Hassidic Jews whenever he wants an easy laugh (indeed, earlocks and broad black hats have been paraded through Allen's films since the days of *Take the Money and Run,* and always for their value as a quick visual gag); and others who might argue that *Stardust Memories*—its parody on Fellini films notwithstanding—is, at bottom, a mean-spirited affair. Fortunately, the sour note one often finds creeping through the humorist's mask (see Dorothy Parker, Ring Lardner, Don Marquis, James Thurber, but especially Mark Twain) has not produced a string of sequels in Allen's oeuvre.

Nonetheless, given the Allen who continues to plug away at "serious," Bergman-like efforts such as *Interiors* or, more recently, *September,* one cannot entirely discount the possibility of yet another Allen film justifying his decision *not* to remake his earlier comedies *ad infinitum.* As those before Allen discovered, humorists live so long under the lesser shadows of writing "light verse" or of providing "comic relief"—in short, of not being considered *serious*—that they learn more about the ambivalent nature of contempt than is probably good for them. In John Irving's *The World According to Garp,* his protagonist explains the situation this way: "Why did people insist that if you were 'comic' you couldn't also be 'serious'? Garp felt most people confused being profound with being sober, being earnest with being deep. Apparently, if you *sounded* serious, you were. Presumably, other animals could not laugh at themselves, and Garp believed that laughter was related to sympathy, which we were always needing more of. He had been, after all, a humorless child—and never religious—so perhaps he now took comedy more seriously than others."[9]

However, I hasten to point out that Garp's arguments (most of which Woody Allen would second) do not convince the Mrs. Poole who had written an anti-fan letter accusing him, among other things, of laughing "at people who can't have orgasms, and people who aren't blessed with happy marriages, and people whose wives and husbands are unfaithful." The comic exchange ends, as it must, with Garp's final letter (in what turns out to be a pointless, frustrating exchange on both sides), and with this particular argument's bottom line: "Fuck you."

Stardust Memories has something of the same message for those, including God, who keep urging Sandy Bates (Woody Allen) to make funnier films, to tell funnier jokes, to re-play it all again, Sandy. Small wonder that Bates turns testy and self-conscious. As he would have it, aggravation is everybody else.

They get in the way, complicate things, misunderstand, what-ever—but you can't make films without them.

And *that,* of course, is the point about *Stardust Memories.* It is about the making of itself. Rather than a film that holds a mirror up the cosmos, to a universe that riddles us with deaths that come too soon and loves that do not come at all, this time Woody Allen points his lookingglass at the silver screen itself. In its concluding moments the entire cast assembles in the rickety auditorium that has been the locale for the weekend's Sandy Bates retrospective, and they watch the film we have ourselves just watched. They file out full of wonderment and praise. Bates is a comic genius, they exclaim in unison, but we know better than to trust people on the payroll. After all, the film has bashed into senselessness those who might raise any objections. Besides, this film is *not* akin to the early Bates; rather, it points toward similarly reflexive moments in films such as *The Purple Rose of Cairo* or *Hannah and Her Sisters.*

In the final frame of *Stardust Memories,* Sandy Bates's quizzical face is fixed on the blank screen and the empty auditorium. Two unformed questions spread across his face: Was the film any good? Does it matter, one way or the other? Perhaps those are *always* the essential questions, but artists cannot over-worry them and still remain artists. In Allen's case, working conditions unmatched in the American film industry have allowed him plenty of elbow room to play his hunches. He cannot say of Sandy Bates what Flaubert said of Madame Bovery: "C'est moi!" Rath-er, Woody Allen is a case of Blakean persistence rewarded, of a person pursuing his neuroses until they become the very stuff of Art—an art, by the way, that includes not only the Manhattan haunts that have become Allen's equivalent of Faulkner's "post-age stamp of native soil" or the gallery of introspective, nervous *schlemiels* he had added to our stock of mental images but also the generous doses of humanity that infuse his work with love as well as lovability. As to Sandy Bates's questions, it is fair to say that the jury is no longer out about Woody Allen, despite the fact that he is still very much in "mid-career" and shows no signs either of slowing down or of standing still: nonetheless, his films *are* good and they *do* matter.

9
Conclusion

Back in 1968, when I was laboring over the manuscript of *The Schlemiel as Metaphor,* I found myself following the disastrous fortunes of the New York Mets with more than a casual interest. And I took heart from the obvious fact that I was hardly alone. America had fastened those bumbling, lovable losers to its collective heart—and often in ways that seemed to support the very thesis I was trying to convert from the doldrums of a dissertation to the sprightliness of a scholarly book. No doubt I exaggerated both the dull, plodding side of my dissertation and the possible "sprightliness" of its new incarnation as an academic study, but I was probably right about the Mets. They struck me, then and now, as good evidence of a wider cultural condition, one that values—yea, *worships*—competition in the marketplace at the same time that it seeks out cultural heroes who are inept, bumbling, in a word, *schlemiels.*

Twenty years later the fortunes of the Mets have much improved, but good ol' Charlie Brown is still with us, etched with the same deep worry lines and penchant for causing others to look at the mess he's made of his life and exclaim: "Good grief, Charlie Brown!" Stand-up comics come and go, but trouble remains a constant: Rodney Dangerfield (who tried a number of comic personae before hitting on the Little Man who "gets no respect"); Gary Shandling (who shares his bad luck with Fox TV audiences in much the same way that Woody Allen once unpacked his neurotic heart at the Village Gate); the "revenges"— II, III, *ad infinitum*— of the "nerds." All these, and dozens more, testify to the popularity—and the adaptability—of the *schlemiel.*

Indeed, the problem that I faced two decades ago—namely, such a giddy proliferation of cultural evidence that the term's very center threatened to no longer hold—has grown even worse. There was a time, for example, when black humorists such as Bruce Jay Friedman and Joseph Heller created protagonists whose affinities for failure bore more than a few resemblances to the classical *schlemiel*. For example, in Bruce Jay Friedman's *Stern* (1962)—a novel that no longer commands either the readership or the attention it once did—an anxious, newly transplanted suburbanite worries about everything: the high cost of landscaping, the neighborhood anti-Semite, free-floating guilts, and of course, fears that he is being cuckolded. *Schlemiel* -watchers like myself paid especial attention to the last item because Stern's overheated psyche—rather than a wayward wife—created the problem, and because he seemed such a resourceful architect of his other *tsoris*. In this sense, Stern struck me as rather like Bob Slocum, the nervous monologist of Joseph Heller's *Something Happened* (1974). Granted, it is the Death Question, rather than cuckoldry, that haunts Heller's protagonists (see *Catch-22*, et al.), but Slocum is so chillingly, so delightfully, expansive about his fears, and the novel itself is so darkly comic about the twin worlds of corporate bureaucracy and domesticity that Slocum earns our attention as one of contemporary literature's more interesting studies in the schlemiel -as-failure.

However, one could argue that the laurels for the darkest, the "sickest," the funniest, and, not least of all, the most stylistically accomplished of our current crop of black humorists should go to Stanley Elkin. As the author of collections such as *Criers and Kibitzers* (1966) and *Searches and Seizures* (1973), as well as of novels like *A Bad Man* (1967) and *The Dick Gibson Radio Show* (1971), Elkin has been a steady worker in the vineyards of the grotesque and comically outrageous. Dis-ease, both as a psychological condition and (spelled as "disease") as an index of human fraility, characterizes his work. No other writer, I would submit, could either imagine the central premise of *The Magic Kingdom*—in which a group of terminally ill children, each sporting a disease more exotic than the last one, are sent to Disneyland—or wrest so much comic material from the possibilities. But it is Elkin's most recent novel—*The Rabbi of Lud* (1987)—that puts a certifiable *schlemiel* in the driver's seat. Elkin's rabbi brings a long history of flop-ism (he had, for example, been trained at a suspicious seminary in the Carribean and has, at best, only a rudimentary knowledge of Hebrew) to his job as the rabbi of

Lud, New Jersey. As it turns out, the pulpit is a cemetery and the rabbi's only job is to officiate at funerals, because Lud is, in effect, a one-industry town, and its industry is death. Those who, for one reason or another, cannot be buried in "regular" synagogue plots are shoveled into the fields of Lud: victims of Mafia hit men (including, possibly, James Hoffa), the religiously disenfranchised, the wayward, the losers. In short, Lud, New Jersey, is the perfect place for a rabbi-*schlemiel* of Elkin's persuasion.

In fact, even as I was writing these concluding paragraphs I kept thinking of Rhoda Lerman's recent novel, *God's Ear* (1989) and the ways that her protagonist—a reluctant Hassidic rebbe whose comic misadventures take him west—would add weight to my arguments about the resilience of the *schlemiel* as a comic type. After all, if Gene Wilder could turn the adventures of a misplaced, and *schlemiel*ish Polish rabbi, into a comic Western (*The Frisco Kid*), Lerman does much the same thing in a contemporary idiom. The trouble, of course, is that if *every* comic character turns out to be a *schlemiel* under the skin, then the character, and my characterization of him, is meaningless. As my father used to say: "*Genug* (enough) already!"

Still, I worried then, and I worry now. No doubt I have omitted *somebody's* favorite (what about Inspector Clouseau? what about Roger Rabbit? I can hear reviewers asking), and no doubt I will hear—from the deconstructionists—that I did not deconstruct the *schlemiel* with sufficient theoretical energy, or—from the semioticians—that *The Name of the Rose* is *the* quintessential text about *schlemiel* hood.

On other fronts, who would argue with the thesis, recently advanced by Stephen J. Whitfield, that Richard Nixon is a "comic figure," a *schlemiel* of the first water? And what about the person who advised me to do my research in the pages of the *Congressional Record* rather than in the section of the library devoted to the humanities? The plain truth is that nobody can write, nor could others pick up (much less pay for) the book that others imagine. Indeed, all I can say to my assorted "comforters" is what I said the first time—namely, that when people in my graduate program wondered how I could write a dissertation on the *schlemiel*, I would tell them the following story:

The employees of a large company decided to have a weekly lottery, just to liven up their lives. The man who picked the lucky number won the jackpot.

For three weeks running Hymie had the lucky number. His compatriots couldn't figure out how Hymie did it. Was it just plain luck, or did he have a method of figuring it out?

At lunch one of the boys said, "Hymie, how come you're the lucky one three weeks in a row?"

Another said, "Do you have some kind of system?"

"It's simple," said Hymie. "I dream. The other night I saw eight sevens dancing before my eyes. Eight sevens are forty-eight, so I figured forty-eight had to be the lucky number; so I picked it!"

"But Hymie, eight sevens are fifty-six, not forty-eight!"

"*Nu !*" answered Hymie, "So *you* be the mathematician!"

I repeated the story when the dissertation became a book and when senior colleagues posed the same question—and I see no reason to change my story now that *The Schlemiel as Metaphor* has become, of all things, a revision. The way I figure it, Hymie was right all along.

Notes
Index

Notes

1. The *Schlemiel*'s Family Tree

1. Ruth Wisse, *The Schlemiel as Modern Hero* (Chicago: University of Chicago Press, 1971), 5.

2. Saul Bellow, introduction to *Great Jewish Stories* (New York: Dell, 1965), vii.

3. *Universal Jewish Encyclopedia* (New York: Ktav, 1943), 9, 115. Entry by Herschel Revel.

4. The specific talmudic reference may be found in Sefer Nezihim, vol. 6, Sanhedrin II, Folio 82–b. For a fuller discussion of how one might reason the connection between the biblical Shelumiel and the figure of the *schlemiel*, see Max Zeldner's "A Note on 'Schlemiel,'" *German Quarterly* 26 (March 1953): 115–17.

5. Nathan Ausubel, ed., *A Treasury of Jewish Folklore* (New York: Crown, 1948), 343. Subsequent references to Ausubel are to this volume.

6. Richard Rubenstein, *The Religious Imagination* (New York: Bobbs-Merrill, 1968), 73. Subsequent references to Rubenstein are to this volume.

7. Rubenstein, *The Religious Imagination*, 73.

8. Theodor Reik, *Jewish Wit* (New York: Gamut Press, 1962), 39.

9. Willy Pogany, forward to *Peter Schlemihl* by Adelbert von Chamisso (Philadelphia: David McKay, 1929), 3–4. Subsequent references to *Peter Schlemihl* are to this edition.

10. *The Poetry and Prose of Heinrich Heine* (New York: Citadel Press, 1948).

11. Jacob Richman, ed., *Laughs from Jewish Lore* (New York: Hebrew Publishing, 1954), xv. Subsequent references to Richman are to this edition.

12. Sigmund Freud, *Jokes and Their Relation to the Unconscious* (New York: Norton, 1960), 111.

13. Lewis Browne, *The Wisdom of Israel* (New York: Random House, 1954), 625.

14. Cited in Irving Howe and Eliezer Greenberg, eds., *A Treasury of Yiddish Stories* (New York: Viking, 1953), 26.

15. Cited in Irving Howe, *World of Our Fathers* (New York: Harcourt Brace Jovanovich, 1976), 516.

2. "If I Were a Rich Man": Mendele and Sholom Aleichem

1. Samuel Niger, "Yiddish Literature in the Past Two Hundred Years," included in *The Jewish People: Past and Present*, 3 (New York: Jewish Encyclopedia Handbooks, 1952), 168. Subsequent references to Niger are to this article.

2. Niger, "Yiddish Literature," 169.

3. Sol Liptzin, *The Flowering of Yiddish Literature* (New York: Bloch, 1963), 125.

4. Gerald Stillman, Introduction to *Fishke the Lame* (New York: Yoseloff, 1960), 6.

5. Kaminner's remarks are cited by Niger, 184-85.

6. Mendele Mocher Seforim's letter to Menasha Margolius, *Fishke the Lame*, 5.

7. All page references to quotations from the works of Mendele and Sholom Aleichem are included in the text. I have used the following editions: *Fishke the Lame*, trans. Gerald Stillman (New York: Yoseloff, 1960); *The Tevye Stories*, trans. Julius and Francis Butwin (New York: Pocket Books, 1960); "Tevye Reads the Psalms," in *Old Country Tales*, trans. Curt Leviant (New York: Putnam Sons, 1960).

8. Cynthia Ozick, "Sholom Aleichem's Revolution," *New Yorker* (28 March 1988): 99.

9. Curt Leviant, Introduction to *Old Country Tales*, 12.

10. Julius and Francis Butwin, introduction to *The Tevye Stories*, xxviii.

11. Brooks Atkinson, "The Humor of Sholom Aleichem," *Jewish Heritage* 7 (Winter 1964–65): 29.

12. Maurice Samuel, *The World of Sholom Aleichem* (New York: Schocken, 1945), 15.

3. The *Schlemiel* on Main Street

1. For a fuller discussion of the development of American Jewish literature from the immigrant experience to the present, see Sol Liptzin, *The Jew in American Literature* (New York: Bloch, 1966).

2. Leslie Fiedler, *The Jew in the American Novel* (New York: Herzl Institute Pamphlet, 1959), 17.

3. Isaac Rosenfeld, "Review of David Levinsky," in Mark Shechner, ed., *Preserving the Hunger* (Detroit: Wayne State University Press, 1987), 37.

4. Mary Antin, *The Promised Land* (Boston: Houghton Mifflin, 1969), 364.

5. Henry Roth, *Call It Sleep* (New York: Avon, 1964), 17.

6. Liz Harris, "In the Shadow of the Golden Mountain," *New Yorker* (27 June 1988), 84.

7. Allen Guttmann, *The Jewish Writer in America* (New York: Oxford University Press, 1971), 45.

8. Daniel Fuchs, *Homage to Blenholt,* in *The Williamsburg Trilogy* (New York: Avon, 1972), 30.

4. The Isolated *Schlemiels* of Isaac Bashevis Singer

1. Joseph Landis, "Who Needs Yiddish?" *Judaism* 13 (Fall 1964): 257–58.

2. Michael Fixler, "The Redeemer: Themes in the Fiction of Isaac Bashevis Singer," *Kenyon Review* 26 (Spring 1964): 371.

3. Irving Howe and Eliezer Greenberg, eds., introduction to *A Treasury of Yiddish Stories* (New York: Viking, 1953), 70.

4. Jacob Glatstein, as quoted in Leslie Fiedler's "The Circumcised Philistine and the Unsynagogued Jew," *American Judaism* 16 (Fall 1966): 33. Subsequent references to Glatstein are to this article.

5. Elias Schulman, "Notes on Anglo-Jewish Writers," *Chicago Jewish Forum* (Summer 1960): 278.

6. Cynthia Ozick, *The Pagan Rabbi and Other Stories* (New York: Knopf, 1969), 124.

7. Fiedler, "The Circumcised Philistine," 33.

8. "A Wedding in Brownsville," in *Short Friday,* trans. Isaac Bashevis Singer and Cecil Henley (New York: Farrar, Straus & Giroux, 1965), 179.

9. All pages references to quotations from Singer's works are included in the text. I have used the the following editions: *Gimpel the Fool and Other Stories,* trans. Saul Bellow (New York: Noonday Press, 1957); *The Magician of Lublin,* trans. Elaine Gottlieb and Joseph Singer (New York: Noonday Press, 1957); *The Slave,* trans. Isaac Bashevis Singer and Cecil Hemley (New York: Farrar, Straus & Cudahy, 1961); *In My Father's Court,* trans. Channah Kleinerman-Goldstein, Elaine Gottlieb, and Joseph Singer (New York: Farrar, Straus & Giroux, 1967).

10. "Reb Asher the Dairyman," in Irving Howe and Eliezer Greenberg, eds., *Yiddish Stories Old and New,* (New York: Holiday House, 1974), 168.

11. *Universal Jewish Encyclopedia* (New York: Ktav, 1943), 9, 115. Entry written by Hirschel Revel. Although the phrase "sheluach min 'el" does not appear in biblical text nor is the Hebrew "biblical" in character, when

variants of "sheluach" do appear, they are translated as "messenger." For example, a "meshulach" is defined as "one sent" while the verbal form "shaluach" means "to send."

12. "Bontsha the Silent," in Irving Howe and Eliezer Greenberg, eds,. *A Treasury of Yiddish Stories* (New York: Viking, 1954), 223.

13. Theodor Reik, *Jewish Wit* (New York: Gamut Press, 1962), 41.

14. Alvin Kernan, *The Cankered Muse* (New Haven: Yale University Press, 1959), 11.

15. Irving Buchen, "Isaac Bashevis Singer and the Eternal Past," *Critique* 8 (Summer 1966): 6–7.

16. Mark Zborowski and Elizabeth Herzog, *Life Is with People* (New York: Schocken 1952), 288.

17. J. S. Wolkenfield, "Isaac Bashevis Singer: The Faith of His Devils and Magicians," *Criticism* 4 (Fall 1963): 356.

5. The *Schlemiel* as Moral Bungler: Bernard Malamud's Ironic Heroes

1. J. C. Levinson, "Bellow's Dangling Men," *Critique* 3 (Summer 1960): 3.

2. Theodore Solotaroff, "Bernard Malamud's Fiction: The Old Life and the New," *Commentary* 33 (March 1962): 198.

3. Robert Alter, "Malamud as Jewish Writer," *Commentary* 42 (September 1966): 71. Subsequent references to Alter are to this article.

4. Marcus Klein, *After Alienation* (New York: Books For Libraries Press, 1964): 15–17.

5. All page references to quotations from Malamud's works are included in the text. I have used the following editions: *The Assistant* (New York: Farrar, Straus & Cudahy, 1957); *The Magic Barrel* (New York: Farrar, Straus & Cadahy, 1958); *A New Life* (New York: Farrar, Straus & Cudahy, 1961); *The Fixer* (New York: Farrar, Straus & Giroux, 1966); *Pictures of Fidelman: An Exhibition* (New York: Farrar, Straus & Giroux, 1969); *The Tenants* (New York: Farrar, Straus & Giroux, 1971); *Rembrandt's Hat* (New York: Farrar, Straus & Giroux, 1973); *Dubin's Lives* (New York: Farrar, Straus & Giroux, 1979); *God's Grace* (New York: Farrar, Straus & Giroux, 1982); and *The People* (New York: Farrar, Straus & Giroux, 1990).

6. Jonathan Baumbach, *The Landscape of Nightmare* (New York: New York University Press, 1965), 111.

7. Mark Goldman, "Bernard Malamud's Comic Vision and the Theme of Identity," *Critique* 7 (Winter 1964–65): 105. Subsequent references to Goldman are to this article.

8. Ruth Mandel, "Bernard Malamud's *The Assistant* and *A New Life*: Ironic Affirmation," *Critique* 7 (Winter 1964–65): 117-18.

9. Alvin Kernan, *The Cankered Muse* (New Haven: Yale University Press, 1959), 18.

10. Theodor Reik, *Jewish Wit* (New York: Gamut Press, 1962), 39–40. For a fuller discussion of Ibn Ezra and his contribution to the history of the *schlemiel*, see chap. 2.

11. Ruth Wisse, *The Schlemiel as Modern Hero* (Chicago: University of Chicago Press, 1971), 114-17.

6. Saul Bellow's Lovesick *Schlemiels*

1. Maxwell Geismar, *American Moderns* (New York: Hill &Wang, 1958), 210.

2. Leslie Fiedler, "Saul Bellow," *Prairie Schooner* 31 (Summer 1957): 103.

3. Irving Malin, ed., *Saul Bellow and the Critics* (New York: New York University Press, 1967), vii.

4. Fiedler, "Saul Bellow," 103.

5. Jonathan Baumbach, *The Landscape of Nightmare* (New York: New York University Press, 1965), 3. Subsequent references to Baumbach are to the chapter of this book entitled "All Men Are Jews."

6. Leslie Fiedler, *Waiting for the End* (New York: Stein & Day, 1964): 29.

7. Marcus Klein, *After Alienation* (New York: Books For Libraries Press, 1962), 29.

8. Richard Chase, "The Adventures of Saul Bellow: The Progress of a Novelist," *Commentary* 27 (April 1959): 29.

9. Baumbach, *Landscape*, 39.

10. All page references to quotations from Bellow's works are included in the text. I have used the following editions: *Dangling Man* (New York: Vanguard, 1944); *The Victim* (New York: Vanguard, 1947); *Seize the Day* (New York: Viking, 1956); *Herzog* (New York: Viking, 1964); *Mr. Sammler's Planet* (New York: Viking, 1970); *Humboldt's Gift* (New York: Viking, 1975); and *More Die of Heartbreak* (New York: William Morrow, 1988)

11. James Hall, *The Lunatic Giant in the Drawing Room* (Bloomington: University of Indiana Press, 1968), 166. Subsequent references to Hall are to the chapter of this book entitled "Portrait of the Aritst as a Self-Creating, Self-Vindicating, High Energy Man: Saul Bellow."

12. Daniel Weiss, "Caliban on Prospero: A Psychoanalytic Study of the Novel, *Seize the Day*, by Saul Bellow," *American Imago* 19 (Fall 1962): 115.

13. Sanford Pinsker, *Conversations with Contemporary American Writers* (Amsterdam: Rodopi NV, 1985), 14.

14. Saul Bellow, Foreword to *The Closing of the American Mind*, by Allan Bloom (New York: Simon & Schuster, 1987), 15–16.

7. Philip Roth: The *Schlemiel* as Fictional Autobiographer

1. All page references to quotations from Roth's works are included in the text. I have used the following editions: *Portnoy's Complaint* (New York: Random House, 1969); *My Life as a Man* (New York: Holt, Rinehart & Winston, 1974); *Reading Myself and Others* (New York: Farrar, Straus & Giroux, 1975); *The Ghost Writer* (New York: Farrar, Straus & Giroux, 1979); *Zuckerman Unbound* (New York: Farrar, Straus & Giroux, 1981); *The Anatomy Lesson* (New York: Farrar, Straus & Giroux, 1983); *The Counterlife* (New York: Farrar, Straus & Giroux, 1987); and *The Facts* (New York: Farrar, Straus & Giroux, 1988).

2. Cynthia Ozick, *Metaphor and Memory* (New York: Alfred A. Knopf, 1989), 20.

8. Woody Allen's Lovably Anxious *Schlemiels*

1. Mark Shechner, "Woody Allen: The Failure of the Therapeutic," in Sarah Blacher Cohen, ed., *From Hester Street to Hollywood* (Bloomington, University of Indiana Press, 1983), 232. Subsequent references to Shechner are to this seminally important article.

2. Allan Bloom, *The Closing of the American Mind* (New York: Simon & Schuster, 1987), 146.

3. Bloom is quick to point out that Bruno Bettleheim's cameo appearence as one of *Zelig*'s "witnesses" is further evidence of the Germanic strain in Allen's thought. What Bloom quite misses, however, are the marvelous self-parodies that intellectuals such as Irving Howe, Susan Sontag, and, ironically enough, Saul Bellow (Bloom's colleague and friend at the University of Chicago) contribute to Allen's pseudo-documentary.

4. Woody Allen, "A Look at Organized Crime," in *Getting Even* (New York: Random House, 1971), 14.

5. James Thurber, "The Night the Bed Fell," in *The Thurber Carnival* (New York: Harper & Row, 1945), 175.

6. Thurber, "The Night the Bed Fell," 175.

7. Phil Berger, *The Last Laugh* (New York: William Morrow, 1985), 114.

8. Irving Howe, *World of Our Fathers* (New York: Harcourt Brace Jovanovich 1976), 571.

9. John Irving, *The World According to Garp* (New York: E. P. Dutton, 1978), 166.

Index

Abramovitch, Sholom. *See* Mendele

Adventures of Augie March, The (Bellow), 112, 114, 123

Agada: definition of, 4

Aksenfeld, Israel, 20

Aleichem, Sholom, 22, 50; background of, 28–29; compared to Mendele, 17; compared to Twain, 29; contribution of, 14, 28, 30–31; *Fiddler on the Roof,* 17, 31, 51; *The Great Fair,* 18; and Hebrew, 29; irony in, 36, 58; "Modern Children," 34–35; *shtetl* and, 31; "A Wedding Without Musicians," 50. *See also* Tevye

Allen, Woody, 163–75; *Annie Hall,* 165, 166, 173; *Broadway Danny Rose,* 168, 172; childhood memories of, 163; compared to Benchley, 163, 166, 167, 168; compared to Lenny Bruce, 168, 173; compared to Chaplin, 163, 168, 170; compared to Perleman, 167–68; compared to H. Roth, 168; compared to Thurber, 168, 174; compared to Twain, 166, 174; as cuckold, 173; *Everything You Always Wanted to Know About Sex, But Were Afraid to Ask,* 173; *Getting Even,* 166; *Hannah and Her Sisters,* 171, 175; *Interiors,* 171, 174; as loser, 164, 173; *Love and Death,* 173; *Manhattan,* 166; on-screen persona of, 163–64, 169, 173; as philosopher, 164–66: *Play It Again Sam,* 173; *The Purple Rose of Cairo,* 175; as *schlemiel,* 163, 164, 168, 174; as *schlimazl,* 163, 166, 169, 170, 173; *September,* 174; *Sleeper,* 173; on Aunt Sarah Shoaf, 167; *Stardust Memories,* 166, 174–75; *Take the Money and Run,* 169–72; *Zelig,* 165

Alpine, Frank: compared to Stephen Dedalus, 83; compared to Leo Finkle, 82; compared to S. Levin, 97; compared to Ike McCaslin, 87; as *schlemiel,* 86–87; on *schlemiels,* 99

Alter, Robert: on *The Fixer,* 101; on Jew as metaphor, 78; on *A New Life,* 89, 99

American Jewish literature, 37, 77, 78, 79, 87; and Bellow, 111; and Malamud, 111; and P. Roth, 145–46

Anatomy Lesson, The (P. Roth), 157, 159
Annie Hall (Allen), 165, 168, 173
Antin, Mary: *Promised Land*, 38–39
Appel, Milton, 158–59
Assistant, The (Malamud), 79, 82–88, 111
Atkinson, Brooks: on Sholom Aleichem, 31
Ausubel, Nathan, 3, 6, 10

Bad Man, A (Elkin), 177
Bananas (Allen), 173
Barth, John, 98, 157
Baumbach, Jonathan: on *The Assistant*, 83; on *Dangling Man*, 115, 121; on post–World War II fiction, 113
"Bear, The" (Faulkner), 62; compared to *The Assistant*, 87
Beggar Book, The: translation of *Fishke the Lame*, 22
Bellarosa Connection, The (Bellow), 140, 144
Bellow, Saul, 2, 5, 21, 111–44; *The Adventures of Augie March*, 112, 114, 123; awards received by, 112; *The Bellarosa Connection*, 140, 144; compared to Aleichem, 34; compared to Eliot, 113, 114, 115; compared to Fitzgerald, 129; compared to Hemingway, 116; compared to Kafka, 123; compared to Malamud, 111, 112; compared to Peretz, 59; compared to Salinger, 111; compared to Sartre, 118; compared to I. B. Singer, 112; *Dangling Man*, 115–22; *The Dean's December*, 138; *Henderson the Rain King*, 111; *Herzog*, 5, 133–40, 144; Herzog's cuckoldry, 137; *Humboldt's Gift*, 112, 133, 138, 141, 142, 143; *More Die of Heartbreak*, 134, 138, 140, 143–44;

Mr. Sammler's Planet, 133, 139, 140, 141; "reality instruction" of, 99; *Seize the Day*, 34, 112, 130–33; *A Theft*, 140; *The Victim*, 2, 123, 125; World War II and, 115
Benchley, Robert, 163, 168
Ber Levinsohn. *See* Levinshohn, Issac Ber
Besht, the: Baal Shem Tov, 18–19
"Bishop's Robe, The" (I. B. Singer), 52
Blood Accusation (Samuel), 101
Bloom, Allan: *The Closing of the American Mind*, 135, 164, 165; on Woody Allen, 164–65
Bloom, Leopold, 83, 114, 148, 159
Bober, Morris: compared to Leopold Bloom, 83; compared to Sam Fathers, 87; compared to St. Francis, 83–84; Jewishness of, 84–86; as Oedipal father, 87; as *schlemiel*, 83–85; as secular *tsaddik*, 82; suffering of, 83, 85–86
Bok, Yakov: compared to biblical Joseph, 102; compared to Leo Finkle, 106; compared to S. Levin, 106; as cuckold, 106; meaning of name, 101; as *schlemiel*, 101, 103, 105; as tragic figure, 106
"Bontsha the Silent" (Peretz), 58–59, 60, 61
Bratslav, Nahman, 19; hassidic stories of, 18
"Briefcase, The" (I. B. Singer), 51
Broadway Danny Rose (Allen), 168, 172
Buchen, Irving: on I. B. Singer, 63
Burke, Kenneth, 128
Butwin, Francis and Julius, 36

Cahan, Abraham: *The Rise of David Levinsky*, 37, 156

Call It Sleep (H. Roth), 42–43, 50, 51, 168
Camus, Albert: compared to Malamud, 106; *The Stranger,* 106
Cankered Muse, The (Kernan), 60
"Captive, The" (Singer), 51
Catch-22 (Heller), 93, 177
Chagall, Marc, 31, 82
Chamisso, Adelbert von: *Peter Schlemihl,* 7
Chaplin, Charlie, 163
Chase, Richard, 115
Chelm, 2, 10
Chutzpah: definition of, 25
Closing of the American Mind, The (Bloom), 135, 164, 165
Collected Stories of Isaac Bashevis Singer, The (I. B. Singer), 51
Commentary magazine, 53, 78, 158, 173
Conrad, Joseph, 156; "Heart of Darkness," 95, 111
Cool Million, A (West), 43, 123
Counterlife, The (P. Roth), 159–60, 161
Criers and Kibitzers (Elkin), 177
Crown of Feathers, A (I. B. Singer), 51, 52
Cuckoldry: in the Bible, 4; in *The Fixer,* 105; in folklore, 5; in "Gimpel the Fool," 5, 61; in *Herzog,* 5

Dangling Man (Bellow): accommodation in, 117; aggression in, 117, 120, 121; alienation in, 115; background of, 115; compared to Goethe, 115; compared to *A Portrait of the Artist as a Young Man,* 122; irony in, 122; as psychological study, 117, 119
Darwin, Charles: *The Origin of Species,* 114
Day of the Locust, (West): *schlemiel* in, 43
Dean's December, The (Bellow), 138
Death of a Salesman (Miller), 130
Diaspora, the: influence of, 9, 17, 32
Dick Gibson Radio Show, The (Elkin), 177
Die Klatshe (Mendele), 21
Die Takse (Mendele), 21
Dos Kleine Menshele (Mendele), 17, 21, 28
Dostoyevsky, Feodor: *Notes from Underground,* 115, 116
Dubin's Lives (Malamud), 79, 107–10

Eliot, T. S., 113, 140; "The Love Song of J. Alfred Prufrock," 114; *The Waste Land,* 114
Elkin, Stanley: *A Bad Man,* 177; *Criers and Kibitzers,* 177; *The Dick Gibson Radio Show,* 177; *The Magic Kingdom,* 177; *The Rabbi of Lud,* 177–78
Emek Refoim (Levinshohn), 20
Enemies, A Love Story (Mazursky), 75
Estate, The (I. B. Singer), 75
Everything You Alwasy Wanted to Know About Sex, But Were Afraid to Ask (Allen), 173
Ezra, Ibn, 7; as *schlemiel,* 104

Facts, The (P. Roth), 156, 160–62
Faulkner, William, 51, 55, 113; "Bear, The," 62, 87
Faust, 7, 12
Fiddler on the Roof (Aleichem), 17, 31, 51
Fiedler, Leslie: on Bellow, 112; compared to P. Roth, 145; on *Dangling Man,* 122; on *The Rise of David Levinsky,* 37; on I. B. Singer, 53;
Finkle, Leo, compared to Frank Alpine, 87; compared to S. Levin, 88; and inability to love,

79, 81; isolation of, 79; link to folk *schlemiel*, 80; as *schlemiel*, 79
Fire on the Moon (Mailer): compared to *Mr. Sammler's Planet*, 141
"First Schlemiel, The" (I. B. Singer), 1, 57
Fishke. *See Fishke the Lame*
Fishke the Lame (Mendele): as beggar, 25; changes in, 22; characteristics of, 24–25, 25; compared to *Canterbury Tales*, 23; compared to eighteenth-century novel, 26; folk humor of, 22–23; irony in, 28; *schlemiels* in, 27–28; *schlimazls* in, 27; wife of, 25–26
Fitzgerald, F. Scott, 129; *The Great Gatsby*, 95; *This Side of Paradise*, 145
Fixer, The (Malamud), 88, 98, 100–107; background of, 100–102; Beiliss case and, 101, 106, 107; civil rights movement and, 107; compared to *The Magic Barrel*, 100; compared to *A New Life*, 100–101; foreshadowing in, 102; irony in, 102; *schlemiel* in, 101–2, 103, 104, 105–6
Fixler, Michael, 49
Folkmentschen, 19
Freud, Sigmund, 3, 10; Jewish psyche and, 13; on Jewish self-criticism, 10; *Jokes and Their Relation to the Unconscious*, 10
Freudian psychology, 7, 13, 41, 42; in Woody Allen, 169, 173; in *Call It Sleep*, 42, 51; in Malamud, 89; in I. B. Singer, 56
Friedman, Bruce Jay: *Stern*, 177
Frisco Kid, The (Wilder), 178
Fuchs, Daniel, 44–45; *The Williamsburg Trilogy*, 45

Geismar, Maxwell: on Bellow, 111, 112; on *Dangling Man*, 120

Gentlemen's Agreement (Hobson): compared to *The Victim*, 125
Getting Even (Allen), 166
Ghost Writer, The (P. Roth), 153–55, 159
Gimpel: compared to Bontsha, 59, 60; compared to Jacob, 73; as cuckold, 61; on God's existence, 60; as *schlemiel*, 56, 60, 62
"Gimpel the Fool" (I. B. Singer), 11; cuckoldry in, 5, 61; reputation of, 58; *schlemiel* in, 56, 59. *See also* Gimpel
Ginsberg, Allen, 53, 145
Glatstein, Jacob, 54
God's Ear (Lerman), 178
God's Grace (Malamud), 79, 107
Gold, Michael, 41–42
Goldman, Mark: on Malamud, 98; on *A New Life*, 94
Goodbye, Columbus (P. Roth), 145–46
Grade, Chaim, 50
Great Fair, The (Aleichem), 18
Great Gatsby, The (Fitzgerald), 95
Great Jewish Stories, 111
Greenberg, Clement, 13
Greenberg, Eliezer, 50
Guttmann, Allen, 45

Habad, Motke, 11–12, 37
Halakha: in *The Assistant*, 85; definition of, 4, 55
Hall, James: on Augie March, 123; on Bellow, 117, 130
Ha-Melits, 21
Hannah and Her Sisters (Allen), 171, 175
Harris, Liz, 42
Haskalah movement, 19, 21
Hassidism, 25; campaign against, 19–20; class structure and, 18–19; founding of, 18; in I. B. Singer, 67; Yiddish literature and, 14, 18, 24
Haunch, Paunch, and Jowl (Ornitz), 38–39

Hawthorne, Nathaniel, 165
"Heart of Darkness" (Conrad),
    95; compared to *Henderson the
    Rain King*, 111
Hebrew: conflict with Yiddish,
    18, 19, 20
Hebrew Melodies (Heine), 7–8
Heine, Heinrich: *schlemiel* in
    Hebrew Melodies, 7–8; and view
    of Jewishness, 8–9
Heller, Joseph: *Catch-22*, 93, 177;
    Something Happened, 177
Hemingway, Ernest, 39–40, 113;
    anti-Semitism of, 40; com-
    pared to I. B. Singer, 62
Henderson the Rain King (Bellow):
    compared to "Heart of Dark-
    ness," 111
Herzog, Moses: assimilation of,
    139; compared to Asa Leven-
    thal, 128; compared to J. Al-
    fred Prufrock, 136, 137, 138;
    as cuckold, 134, 137; letters of,
    135, 137; as *mensch*, 139; as
    schlemiel, 46, 134, 138; and self-
    mockery, 135; significance of
    name, 139; as victim, 134
Herzog (Bellow), 5, 133–40, 144;
    awards received for, 112; com-
    pared to *Dangling Man*, 135;
    compared to *Paradise Lost*, 134;
    cuckoldry in, 5, 134, 137; as
    epistolary novel, 134; irony in,
    135; meaning of name, 98; tra-
    ditional *schlemiel* in, 134
Hobson, Laura Z.: *Gentlemen's
    Agreement*, 125
Howe, Irving, 50, 58, 158, 173
Humboldt's Gift (Bellow), 112, 133,
    138, 141; compared to *The Vic-
    tim*, 142; *schlemiel* in, 143

Idiots First (Malamud), 79
"If Not Higher" (Peretz), 59
In My Father's Court (I. B. Singer),
    55

Interiors (Allen), 171, 174
Irving, John: *The World According
    to Garp*, 174

Jewish humor: the Diaspora and,
    9, 13; as method of survival,
    10; as method to overcome
    fear, 2; national exile and, 9;
    poverty and greed in, 15, 28,
    33, 83; self-deprecating, 43;
    self-hating, 10; source of, 9, 13,
    14
Jewish wife, 25, 105, 119–20, 124
Jews Without Money (Gold), 41
Joseph *(Dangling Man)*: com-
    pared to biblical Joseph, 115;
    compared to Robert Cohn,
    116; compared to Augie
    March, 119; compared to *The
    Victim*, 125, 129; guilt of, 119,
    121; inner consciousness of,
    118; isolation of, 115–16; as
    preview to later characters,
    117; as *schlemiel*, 119; as vic-
    tim/victimizer, 121
*Jokes and Their Relation to the Un-
    conscious* (Freud), 10
Joyce, James, 41, 42, 78, 113, 150,
    159; *A Portrait of the Artist as a
    Young Man*, 151
Joys of Yiddish, The (Rosten), 2

Kafka, Franz: compared to Mal-
    amud, 104
Kaminner, Isaac, 22
Kaufman, Bel: *Up the Down Stair-
    case*, 92
Kazin, Alfred, 58
Kernan, Alvin: *The Cankered
    Muse*, 60
Kesey, Ken: compared to I. B.
    Singer, 67; *One Flew Over the
    Cuckoo's Nest*, 66
Klein, Marcus: on Bellow, 114; on
    Malamud, 78

Kol Mevasser, 21
Konigsberg, Stewart Allen, 166.
 See also Allen, Woody

Landis, Joseph C., 49
"Lantuch, The" (I. B. Singer), 52
Lawrence, D. H., 108–10
Lefin, Mendel, 20
Lerman, Rhoda: *God's Ear,* 178
Leventhal, Asa: aggressiveness
 of, 124; compared to Joseph
 (Dangling Man), 121, 125; compared to Tommy Wilhelm, 130;
 paranoia of, 125–26; "reality
 instruction" of, 128; as *schlemiel,* 129; as victim/victimizer,
 123, 127
Leviant, Curt, 29
Levin, Meyer: *The Old Bunch,* 44–
 45
Levin, S.: bread giving and, 98;
 compared to Frank Alpine, 97;
 compared to Jake Barnes, 99;
 compared to Nick Carraway,
 94; compared to Leo Finkle,
 88, 100; as cuckold, 91; fantasies of, 97–98; and inability to
 love, 96; moral concerns of 95–
 96, 100; "reality instruction"
 of, 99; as satiric persona, 94;
 as *schlemiel,* 88–89, 93, 100; as
 schlimazl, 89; significance of
 name, 98; as victim, 93
Levinshohn, Issac Ber: *Emek Refoim,* 20
Liptzin, Sol, 21, 37
Love and Death (Allen), 173
"Love Song of J. Alfred Prufrock, The" (Eliot), 114
Luftmentsh: definition of, 13;
 Menahem-Mendl as, 32–33; as
 schlemiel, 45, 46; Tamkin as, 132

McLuhan, Marshall, 165–66
Magic Barrel, The (Malamud), 110,
 111

"Magic Barrel, The" (Malamud),
 79–82; compared to *A New
 Life,* 99; as initiation story, 79
Magician of Lublin, The (Singer),
 63–75
Magic Kingdom, The (Elkin), 177
Mailer, Norman, 21; *Fire on the
 Moon,* 141
Malamud, Bernard, 46, 146, 168;
 on academia, 94; *The Assistant,*
 82–88, 111; compared to Bellow, 111, 112; *Dubin's Lives,* 79,
 107–10; *The Fixer,* 88, 100–107;
 bread giving in, 98; *God's
 Grace,* 79; *Idiots First,* 79; irony
 in, 82, 96, 98, 100, 109; Jews
 of, 78; "The Magic Barrel,"
 79–82, 99; morality in, 97, 98;
 The Natural, 110; *A New Life,*
 88; *The People,* 79; *Pictures of
 Fidelman,* 79; *Rembrandt's Hat,*
 79; P. Roth on, 88; *schlemiels,*
 79, 80; *The Tenants,* 79
Mamme-loshen, 51, 52, 115
Mandel, Ruth, 94
Manhattan (Allen), 166, 168, 171
Mann, Thomas, 113
Manor, The (I. B. Singer), 75
March, Augie, 123, 129
Margolius, Menasha, 22
Maskilim, 20, 25; definition of, 19
Mazur, Yasha: alienation of, 65;
 compared to Faust, 71; com-
 pared to Gimpel, 72; as
 dreamer, 72; as master, 63;
 mysteriousness of, 63, 69;
 physical appearance of, 64; as
 schlemiel, 66, 71, 72; sexuality
 of, 65; as *sheluach min 'el,* 65,
 68; as *tsaddik,* 73
Mazursky, Paul: *Enemies, A Love
 Story,* 75
Mendele: background of, 20–21;
 compared to I. B. Singer, 56;
 contribution of, 14, 28; *Die
 Takse,* 21; *Dos Kleine Menshele,*

17, 21, 28; early works, 21;
Fishke the Lame, 22–27, 28; as
pseudonym, 23; rise of, 21–22;
as satirist, 22, 28; *Travels of
Benjamin III*, 28; use of Yid-
dish, 21
Metaphor in Memory (Ozick), 160
Miller, Arthur: *Death of a Sales-
man*, 130
Miss Lonelyhearts (West), 43–44;
compared to *The Magician of
Lublin*, 70; compared to *The
Pawnbroker*, 44; suffering in, 44
Mitzvos: definition of, 55
"Modern Children" (Aleichem),
34–35
More Die of Heartbreak (Bellow),
134, 138, 140, 143–44
Mr. Sammler's Planet (Bellow),
133, 139; compared to *The Vic-
tim*, 140; irony in, 141
My Life as a Man (P. Roth), 151,
152–53, 160

Natural, The (Malamud), 110
New Life, A (Malamud), 79, 88–
100; as academic satire, 88, 94;
background of, 88–92; bread
giving in, 98; compared to
Catch-22, 93; compared to *The
Great Gatsby*, 95; compared to
"Heart of Darkness," 95; compared to *Lucky Jim*, 92; compared to "The Magic Barrel,"
88, 100; compared to *Up the
Down Staircase*, 92; irony in, 98
Nordau, Max, 13
Notes from Underground (Dostoyevsky): compared to *Dangling Man*, 115, 116

Old Bunch, The (M. Levin), 44–45
One Flew Over the Cuckoo's Nest
(Kesey), 66
Origin of Species, The (Darwin), 114
Ornitz, Samuel: *Haunch, Paunch,*

and Jowl, 38–39
Ozick, Cynthia, 23, 52, 160; *The
Pagan Rabbi and Other Stories*,
53

Pagan Rabbi and Other Stories, The
(Ozick), 53
Pawnbroker, The (Wallant), 44
People, The (Malamud), 79
Peretz, Y. L.: "Bontsha the Si-
lent," 58–59, 60, 61; compared
to Aleichem, 58; compared to
Malamud, 59; compared to
I. B. Singer, 58, 61; contribu-
tion of, 14, 17; "If Not Higher," 59
Peter Schlemihl (von Chamisso), 7
Phinehas, 3, 4, 8
Pictures of Fidelman (Malamud),
79, 107, 110
Pilpul, 5, 18–19
Pogany, Willy, 7
Portnoy, Alexander, 146–51; cas-
trating mother of, 148; com-
pared to Chaplin's Little
Tramp, 148; compared to
Christ, 147; kvetching of, 151;
as mamma's boy, 147; as *schle-
miel*, 149
Portnoy's Complaint (P. Roth), 146–
51; masturbation in, 148–50;
Portnoy as *schlemiel* in, 149;
role of Jewish mamma in, 147
*Portrait of the Artist as a Young
Man, A* (Joyce), 78, 151
Promised Land (Antin), 38–39
Prufrock, J. Alfred, 115, 136–38;
quoted, 111
Purple Rose of Cairo, The (Allen),
175
Pynchon, Thomas, 157

Rabbi of Lud, The (Elkin), 177–78
Rabinowitz, Sholom. *See*
Aleichem, Sholom
Reading Myself and Others (P.
Roth), 150

"Reb Asher the Dairyman" (Singer), 57

Reik, Theodor: analysis of Ibn Ezra, 104; on *schlemiel* as psychological phenomenon, 4–5, 13, 60; on *schlemiel* in Jewish folklore, 5 *Rembrandt's Hat* (Malamud), 79

Richmond, Jacob, 9, 14

Rise of David Levinsky, The (Cahan), 37, 156

Rosenfeld, Isaac, 37

Rosten, Leo: *The Joys of Yiddish*, 2

Roth, Henry: *Call It Sleep*, 42–43, 50, 51, 168

Roth, Philip, 46, 52, 145–62; *The Anatomy Lesson*, 157, 159; awards received by, 146; background of, 145, 156; compared to Joyce, 150; compared to Kafka, 150, 155, 158; compared to Lawrence, 150; compared to I. B. Singer, 53; compared to Whitman, 147, 150; *The Counterlife*, 159–60, 161; *The Facts*, 156, 160–62; *The Ghost Writer*, 153–55, 159; *Goodbye, Columbus*, 145–46; Jewishness of, 145, 158; *My Life as a Man*, 151, 152–53, 160; *Portnoy's Complaint*, 146–51; *Reading Myself and Others*, 150; sexual anxieties of, 145, 150; *Zuckerman Unbound*, 155–57

Rubenstein, Richard, 3–4

Salinger, J. D., 64

Salzman, Pinye: as con man, 80; as persuader, 99; as "pimp," 80

Samuel, Maurice: *Blood Accuasation*, 101

Satan in Goray (I. B. Singer), 56

Schlemiel, 163; as academician, 139; adaptability of, 176; and alienation, 41, 58; Frank Alpine as, 86–87; Robert Alter

on, 89; in American literature, 37, 42; and anti-Semitism, 10, 40–41, 125; in *The Assistant*, 83–87; biblical references to, 3, 5; Leopold Bloom as, 41; Yakov Bok as, 101–7; Robert Cohn as, 40; compared with *schlimazl*, 2, 6, 14, 123; as cuckold, 5, 12, 43, 61, 91, 101, 106; definition of, 1, 6, 41, 57, 105, 123; Dubin as, 107–9; Ibn Ezra's impact on, 5–6; as failure, 12, 13, 15, 41, 43, 93, 103, 130, 171, 172, 176; Arthur Fidelman as, 107; Leo Finkle as, 79; Fishke as, 27; in folklore, 3, 6, 9; Freudian link with, 3, 7, 41, 43, 129; in "Gimpel the Fool," 56; Motke Habad as, 11–12, 37; as henpecked, 12; Moses Herzog as, 5, 46, 133–40; as inept, 37, 93, 119; Jewishness of, 7, 173; Joseph *(Dangling Man)* as, 119–23; S. Levin as 88–100; linguistic origins, 6; as *luftmensh*, 13, 45, 46; in *The Magician of Lublin*, 63–76; in Malamud, 78; as masochist, 5, 13, 60, 83; Yasha Mazur as, 70–72; in *A New Life*, 88–99; origins of, 1, 2, 57–58; in *The Rise of David Levinsky*, 37; self-mockery of, 5, 16; and sexuality, 164, 172; in I. B. Singer, 57, 60, 63, 75; Tevye as, 31–36; traditional, 96; in *Travels of Benjamin III*, 28; as victim, 7, 93, 101, 123; after World War II, 45, 57, 78–79

Schlimazl, 129, 163; Woody Allen as, 163; in American literature, 41; Augie March as, 123; biblical sources of, 9; compared to *schlemiel*, 2, 6, 14, 163; definition of, 2, 6, 123; Fishke as, 27; Freudian psychology and, 41;

S. Levin as, 89–100; linguistic sources of, 6; Menahem-Mendl as, 32, 33; Lemuel Pitkin as, 123; Tevye as, 31–36
Schnorrer, 26, 56, 132; definition of, 25
Scholem, Gershom, 56
Schulman, Elias, 52
Searches and Seizures (Elkin), 177
Seforim, Mendele Mokher. *See* Abramovitch, Sholom
Seize the Day (Bellow), 34, 112, 130–133
September (Allen), 174
Shechner, Mark: on Woody Allen, 164, 171
Sheluach min 'el, 58, 59, 62, 68, 74, 75
Shelumiel ben Zurishaddai, 2–3, 8, 10
Shtetl, 11, 12, 15, 20, 31, 33, 36, 46, 48, 52, 102, 105; importance of, 13, 55, 106; in Peretz, 59; sensibility, 63; in Singer, 50, 51, 63, 65, 68, 71
Singer, Isaac Bashevis, 48–76; alienation of, 49, 55, 58, 62; as anomaly, 48; background of, 55; "The Bishop's Robe," 52; "The Briefcase," 51; "The Captive," 51; *The Collected Stories of Isaac Bashevis Singer*, 51; compared to Aleichem, 56; compared to Arnold, 54; compared to Bellow, 57; compared to Faulkner, 51, 55; compared to Hawthorne, 49, 51, 55; compared to Mendele, 56; compared to Peretz, 58, 58–59, 61; compared to P. Roth, 53; compared to Salinger, 64; compared to Twain, 48, 49; *A Crown of Feathers*, 51, 52; eroticism in, 52, 56; *The Estate*, 75; Fiedler on, 53; "The First Schlemiel," 1, 57; Freudian

psychology in, 56; "Gimpel the Fool," 5, 56, 59–60, 61, 159; influence of, 53–55; *In My Father's Court*, 55; irrationality in, 52; "The Lantuch," 52; *Lost*, 52; *The Magician of Lublin*, 63–77; *mamme-loshen* in, 51, 52; *The Manor*, 75; Ozick on, 52–53; "Reb Asher the Dairy Man," 57; *Satan in Goray*, 56; *schlemiels* in, 56, 59, 63, 71; self-mockery and, 56; sexual themes in, 53; *shtetl* heritage in the work of, 48, 51, 52, 55, 71; *The Slave*, 73; "The Suicide," 57; "A Wedding in Brownsville," 54; as Yiddish writer, 48–49, 52–54
Singer, Israel Joshua, 55
Slave, The (I. B. Singer), 73
Something Happened (Heller), 177
Stardust Memories (Allen), 166, 174, 174–75
Stern (Friedman), 177
Stillman, Gerald, 21, 22
Stranger, The (Camus), 106
"Suicide, The" (I. B. Singer), 57
Susskind, Shimon, 110

Take the Money and Run (Allen), 169–72, 174
Tarnopol, Peter, 151, 152, 153
Tehinot, 18, 23
Tenants, The (Malamud), 79
Tevye: the Diaspora and, 32; economic failures of, 33–34; as "hero," 31; humor of, 30, 43; "ironic affirmation" of, 36; in "Modern Children," 34; as patriarch, 35; as *schlemiel*, 33; as *schlimazl*, 31, 36; stories, 31–36; in "Tevye Reads the Psalms," 35; "tragic affirmation" of, 32; as tragic figure, 31
"Tevye Reads the Psalms," (Aleichem), 35

Theft, A (Bellow), 140
This Side of Paradise (Fitzgerald): compared to *Goodbye, Columbus,* 145
Thurber, James, 167, 168
Tishah b'Ab, 23, 24
Trachtenberg, Kenneth: in *More Die of Heartbreak,* 143–44
Travels of Benjamin III (Mendele), 28
Treasury of Jewish Folklore, 3
Treasury of Yiddish Stories, 50
Trial, The (Kafka), 104
Tsaddick, 82
Tsedakah: definition of, 68
Twain, Mark: alienation in, 29; compared to I. B. Singer, 48

Untouchables, The, 167
Up the Down Staircase (Kaufman), 92

Vergelis, Aaron, 52
Victim, The (Bellow), 2, 123, 125

Wallant, Edward Louis: mentioned, 59; *Pawnbroker,* 44
Warren, Robert Penn, 125
Waste Land, The (Eliot), 114
"Wedding in Brownsville, A" (I. B. Singer), 54
"Wedding Without Musicians, A" (Aleichem), 50
Weinreich, Max, 13
Weiss, Daniel, 130
West, Nathanael: compared to Singer, 70; *A Cool Million,* 43, 123; *The Day of the Locust,* 43; influence of, 43; *Miss Lonelyhearts,* 43–44
Whitfield, Stephen, 178
Wilder, Gene: *The Frisco Kid,* 178
Wilhelm, Tommy, 34, 130, 131, 132
Williamsburg Trilogy, The (Fuchs), 45
Wisse, Ruth, 1–2, 107
Wolkenfield, J. S., 71
World According to Garp, The (Irving), 174

Yiddish humor, 53; in Woody Allen, 173; compared to American Jewish humor, 24; Hassidic tradition in, 18–20; importance of, 13; ironic aspects of, 23; satire in, 20, 22, 28; *schlemiel* in, 57
Yiddish language, 17–18, 20; humor and, 19–20; and Mendele, 21; Ozick on, 23; I. B. Singer's use of, 48–49
Yiddish literature, 52; and Abramovitch, 20–21; and lack of prestige, 21; and "purpose," 22; and I. B. Singer, 52
Yikhus: definition of, 18

Zederbaum, Alexander, 21
Zelig (Allen), 165
Zimri, 3, 8
Zuckerman, Nathan, 151, 153, 154, 155–57
Zuckerman Unbound (P. Roth), 155–57

Sanford Pinsker is Shadek Professor of Humanities at Franklin and Marshall College. He is a prolific book reviewer, literary essayist, critic, and poet, publishing his work in such magazines as *Georgia Review, Virginia Quarterly Review, Salamundi,* and many others. His books include studies on Joseph Conrad, Philip Roth, Joseph Heller, the American novel in the 1960s, the poets of the Pacific Northwest, as well as four collections of his own verse.